"Miss Merril's choices are excellent!"
—Chicago Daily News

Judith Merril, a writer herself, selects the greatest science fiction and fantasy each year for inclusion in her famous Annual. S-F, more and more, is merging with the mainstream of literature, and her anthologies brilliantly illustrate this trend.

"From the Florida Everglades to the Red Earth of Mars, there are stories to prick the imagination and superstition and bring envious sighs from Mr. Hitchcock . . . this is a book voted most likely to succeed."
—Daily Independent

"Judith Merril's annual collection is always the high point of any science fiction year."
—Rocky Mountain News

10th Annual Edition

THE YEAR'S BEST S-F

Edited by
JUDITH MERRIL

A DELL BOOK

Published by
DELL PUBLISHING CO., INC.
750 Third Avenue
New York, N.Y. 10017
Copyright © 1965 by Judith Merril
Dell ® TM 681510, Dell Publishing Co., Inc.
All rights reserved
Reprinted by arrangement with
Delacorte Press, New York, N.Y.
First Dell Printing—December, 1966
Printed in U.S.A.

ACKNOWLEDGMENTS

"Automatic Tiger" by Kit Reed, copyright © 1964, by Mercury Press, Inc. By permission of the author, and of Doubleday and Co., Inc.

"The Carson Effect" by Richard Wilson, copyright © 1964 by Galaxy Publishing Corporation. By permission of the author.

"The Shining Ones" by Arthur C. Clarke, copyright © 1964, by HMH Publishing Co., Inc. By permission of the author, and his agents, Scott Meredith Literary Agency, Inc.

"Pacifist" by Mack Reynolds, copyright © 1964 by Mercury Press, Inc. By permission of the author, and his agents, Scott Meredith Literary Agency, Inc.

"The New Encyclopaedist" by Stephen Becker, copyright © 1964 by Mercury Press, Inc. By permission of the author and his agent, Robert P. Mills.

"The Legend of Joe Lee" by John D. MacDonald, copyright © 1964 by The Hearst Corporation. By permission of the author and his agents, Littauer and Wilkinson.

"Gas Mask" by James D. Houston, copyright © 1964 by James D. Houston. By permission of the author and his agents, McIntosh and Otis, Inc.

"A Sinister Metamorphosis" by Russell Baker, copyright © 1965, by The New York Times Company. By permission of *The New York Times*.

"Sonny" by Rick Raphael, copyright © 1963 by The Condé Nast Publications, Inc. By permission of the author and his agents, Scott Meredith Literary Agency, Inc.

"The Last Secret Weapon of the Third Reich" by Josef Nesvadba, copyright © 1964 by Josef Nesvadba; English translation copyright © 1964 by Iris Urwin. By permission of the author and translator and the Czechoslovak Theatrical and Literary Agency, Prague.

"Descending" by Thomas M. Disch, copyright © 1964 by Mercury Press, Inc. By permission of the author and his agents, Scott Meredith Literary Agency, Inc.

"Decadence" by Romain Gary, copyright © 1964 by Romain Gary. By permission of the author and his agent, Robert Lantz, and of Harper & Row, Publishers, and Michael Joseph, Ltd., London.

"Be of Good Cheer" by Fritz Leiber, copyright © 1964 by Galaxy Publishing Corporation. By permission of the author and his agent, Robert P. Mills.

"It Could Be You" by Frank Roberts, copyright © 1964 by Universal Printers, Ltd., Canada; originally published in *Coast to Coast*, Sydney, Australia. By permission of the author and *Short Story International*.

"A Benefactor of Humanity" by James T. Farrell, copyright © 1958 by James T. Farrell; originally published in *The Socialist Call*. By permission of the author.

"Synchromocracy" by Hap Cawood, copyright © 1964 by the Division of Higher Education of the Methodist Church. By permission of the author.

"The Search" by Bruce Simonds, copyright © 1964 by Mercury Press, Inc. By permission of the author.

"The Pirokin Effect" by Larry Eisenberg, copyright © 1964 by Ziff-Davis Publishing Company. By permission of the author.

"The Twerlik" by Jack Sharkey, copyright © 1964 by Galaxy Publishing Corporation. By permission of the author and his agent, Theron Raines.

"A Rose for Ecclesiastes'" by Roger Zelazny, copyright © 1963 by Mercury Press, Inc. By permission of the author, and Doubleday and Co., Inc.

"The Terminal Beach" by J. G. Ballard, copyright © 1964 by *New World SF*, England. By permission of the author.

"Problem Child" by Arthur Porges, copyright © 1964 by The Condé Nast Publications, Inc. By permission of the author and his agents, Scott Meredith Literary Agency, Inc.

"The Wonderful Dog Suit" by Donald Hall, copyright © 1964 by Donald Hall; originally published in *The Carleton Miscellany*. By permission of the author.

"The Mathenauts" by Norman Kagan, copyright © 1964 by Galaxy Publishing Corporation. By permission of the author.

"Family Portrait" by Morgan Kent (ps. for R. J. Griffin), copyright © 1964 by Ziff-Davis Publishing Company. By permission of the author.

"The Red Egg" by José María Gironella, copyright © 1964 by Sheed and Ward. By permission of Sheed and Ward, publishers.

"The Power of Positive Thinking" by M. E. White, copyright © 1964 by New Directions. By permission of the author and New Directions.

"A Living Doll" by Robert Wallace, copyright © 1963 by Robert Wallace; originally published in *Harper's*. By permission of the author and his agents, Harold Ober Associates.

"Training Talk" by David R. Bunch, copyright © 1964 by Ziff-Davis Publishing Company. By permission of the author.

"A Miracle Too Many" by Philip H. Smith and Alan E. Nourse, copyright © 1964 by Mercury Press, Inc. By permission of the authors.

"The Last Lonely Man" by John Brunner, copyright © 1964 by *New Worlds SF*, England. By permission of the author and his agents, Scott Meredith Literary Agency, Inc.

"The Man Who Found Proteus" by Robert Rohrer, copyright ©

1964 by Ziff-Davis Publishing Company. By permission of the author.

"Yachid and Yechida" by Isaac Bashevis Singer, copyright © 1964 by Isaac Bashevis Singer. By permission of the author and Farrar, Straus and Giroux, Inc.

When first published, "The Carson Effect," "The Search," "The Mathenauts" and "Be of Good Cheer" appeared in slightly different form.

CONTENTS

AUTOMATIC TIGER
Kit Reed

from *Fantasy and Science Fiction*

He got the toy for his second cousin, Randolph, a knobby-kneed boy so rich he was still in short trousers at thirteen. Born poor, Benedict had no hope of inheriting his Uncle James's money, but he spent too much for the toy anyway. He had shriveled under his uncle's watery diamond eyes on two other weekend visits, shrinking in oppressive, dark-paneled rooms, and he wasn't going back to Syosset unarmed. The expensive gift for Randolph, the old man's grandson, should assure him at least some measure of respect. But there was more to it than that. He had felt a strange, almost feted feeling growing in him from the moment he first spotted the box, solitary and proud, in the dim window of a toy store not far from the river.

It came in a medium-sized box with an orange-and-black illustration and the words "ROYAL BENGAL TIGER" in orange lettering across the top. According to the description on the package, it responded to commands which the child barked into a small microphone. Benedict had seen robots and monsters something like it on television that year. "Own It With Pride," the box commanded. Edward Benedict, removed from toys more by income than by inclination, had no idea that the tiger cost ten times as much as any of its mechanical counterparts. Had he known, he probably wouldn't have cared. It would impress the boy, and something about the baleful eyes on the box attracted him. It cost him a month's salary and seemed cheap at the price. After all, he told himself, it had real fur.

He wanted more than anything to open the box and touch the fur but the clerk was watching him icily so he fell back and let the man attack it with brown paper and twine. The clerk pushed the box into his arms before he could ask to have it delivered and he took it without question, because he hated scenes. He thought about the tiger all the way home on the bus. Like any man with a toy, he knew he wouldn't be able to resist opening it to try it out.

His hands were trembling as he set it in a corner of his living room.

"Just to see if it works," he muttered. "Then I'll wrap it for Randolph." He removed the brown paper and turned the box so the picture of the tiger was on top. Not wanting to rush things, he fixed his dinner and ate it facing the box. After he had cleared the table he sat at a distance, studying the tiger. As shadows gathered in the room something about the drawing seemed to compel him, to draw him to the verge of something important and hold him there, suspended, and he couldn't help feeling that he and this tiger were something more than man and toy, gift and giver, and as the picture tiger regarded him, its look grew more and more imperative, so that he got up finally and went over to the box and cut the string.

As the sides fell away he dropped his hands, disappointed at first by the empty-looking heap of fur. The fur had a ruggy look, and for a minute he wondered if the packers at the factory had made a mistake. Then, as he poked it with his toe he heard a click and the steel frame inside the fur sprang into place and he fell back, breathless, as the creature took shape.

It was a full-sized tiger, made from a real tiger-skin skillfully fitted to a superstructure of tempered metal so carefully made that the beast looked no less real than the steely-limbed animals Benedict had seen at the city zoo. Its eyes were of amber, ingeniously lit from behind by small electric bulbs, and Benedict noted hysterically that its whiskers were made of stiff nylon filament. It stood motionless in an aura of jungle-bottom and power, waiting for him to find the microphone and issue a command. An independent mechanism inside it lashed the long, gold-and-black striped tail. It filled half the room.

Awed, Benedict retreated to his couch and sat watching the tiger. Shadows deepened and soon the only light in the room came from the creature's fierce amber eyes. It stood rooted in the corner of the room, tail lashing, looking at him yellowly. As he watched it his hands worked on the couch, flexing and relaxing, and he thought of himself on the couch, the microphone that would conduct his orders, the tiger in the corner waiting, the leashed potential that charged the room. He moved ever so slightly and his foot collided with something on the floor. He picked it up and inspected it. It was the microphone. Still he sat, watching the gorgeous beast in the light cast by its own golden eyes. At last, in the dead stillness of late night or early morning, strangely happy, he brought the microphone to his lips and breathed into it tremulously.

The tiger stirred.

Slowly, Edward Benedict got to his feet. Then, calling on all his resources, he brought his voice into his throat.

"Heel," he said.

And hugely, magnificently, the tiger moved into place.

"Sit," he said, leaning shakily against the door, not quite ready to believe.

The tiger sat. Even sitting it was as tall as he, and even now, in repose, with glossy fur lying smooth and soft against the body, every line spoke of the coiled steel within.

He breathed into the microphone again, marveling as the tiger lifted one paw. It held the paw to its chest, looking at him, and it was so immense, so strong, so responsive that Benedict, in a burst of confidence, said, "Let's go for a walk" and opened the door. Avoiding the elevator he opened the fire door at the end of the corridor and started down the stairs, exulting as the tiger followed him silently, flowing like water over the dingy steps.

"Shhhhhh." Benedict paused at the door to the street and behind him the tiger stopped. He peered out. The street was so still, so unreal that he knew it must be three or four in the morning. "Follow me," he whispered to the tiger, and stepped out into the darkness. They walked the dark sides of the streets, with the tiger ranging behind Benedict, disappearing into the shadows when it looked as if a car might pass too close. Finally they came to the park, and once they had traveled a few yards down one of the asphalt paths, the tiger began to stretch its legs like a horse in slow motion, moving restlessly at Benedict's heels. He looked at it and in a rush of sorrow realized that a part of it still belonged to the jungle, that it had been in its box too long and it wanted to run.

"Go ahead," he said congestedly, half-convinced he would never see it again.

With a bound the cat was off, running so fast that it came upon the park's small artificial lake before it realized it, spanned the water in a tremendous leap and disappeared into the bushes at the far side.

Alone, Benedict slumped on a bench, fingering the flat metal microphone. It was useless now, he was sure. He thought about the coming weekend, when he would have to appear at his uncle's door empty-handed ("I had a toy for Randolph, Uncle James, but it got away. . . ."), about the money he had wasted (then, reflecting on the tiger, the moments they had spent together in his apartment, the vitality that had surged in the room just once for a change, he knew the money hadn't been wasted). The tiger . . . Already burning to see it again, he picked up the microphone. Why should it come back when it was free again, and it had the whole park, the whole world to roam? Even now, despairing, he couldn't keep himself from whispering the command.

"Come back," he said fervently. "Come back." And then, "Please."

For a few seconds, there was nothing. Benedict strained at the darkness, trying to catch some rustle, some faint sound, but there was nothing until the great shadow was almost upon him, clearing the bench across the way in a low, flat leap and stopping, huge and silent, at his feet.

Benedict's voice shook. "You came back," he said, touched.

And the Royal Bengal Tiger, eyes glowing amber, white ruff gleaming in the pale light, put one paw on his knee.

"You came," Benedict said, and after a long pause he put a tentative hand on the tiger's head. "I guess we'd better go home," he muttered, noticing now that it was beginning to get light. "Come on—" he caught his breath at the familiarity "—Ben."

And he started for his rooms, almost running, rejoicing as the tiger sprang behind him in long, silken leaps.

"We must sleep now," he said to the tiger when they reached the apartment. Then, when he had Ben settled properly, curled nose to tail in a corner, he dialled his office and called in sick. Exhilarated, exhausted, he flung himself on the couch, not caring for once that his shoes were on the furniture, and slept.

When he woke, it was almost time to leave for Syosset. In the corner, the tiger lay as he had left him, inert now, but still mysteriously alive, eyes glowing, tail lashing from time to time.

"Hi," Benedict said softly. "Hi, Ben," he said, and then grinned as the tiger raised his head and looked at him. He had been thinking about how to get the tiger packed and ready to go, but as the great head lifted and the amber eyes glowed at him Benedict knew he would have to get something else for Randolph. This was his tiger. Moving proudly in the amber light, he began getting ready for his trip, throwing clean shirts and drawers into a suitcase, wrapping his toothbrush and razor in toilet paper and slipping them into the shoe pockets.

"I have to go away, Ben," he said when he was finished. "Wait, and I'll be back Sunday night."

The tiger watched him intently, face framed by a silvery ruff. Benedict imagined he had hurt Ben's feelings. "Tell you what, Ben," he said to make him feel better, "I'll take the microphone, and if I need you I'll give you a call. Here's what you do. First you go to Manhattan and take the Triboro Bridge . . ."

The microphone fit flatly against his breast, and for reasons Benedict could not understand it changed his whole aspect.

"Who needs a toy for Randolph?" He was already rehearsing several brave speeches he would make to Uncle James. "I have a tiger at home."

On the train, he beat out several people for a seat next to the window. Later, instead of taking a bus or cab to his uncle's place, he found himself calling and asking that someone be sent to pick him up at the station.

In his uncle's dark-paneled study, he shook hands so briskly that he startled the old man. Randolph, knees roughened and burning pinkly, stood belligerently at one elbow.

"I suppose you didn't bring me anything," he said, chin out.

For a split second, Benedict faltered. Then the extra weight of the microphone in his pocket reminded him. "I have a *tiger* at home," he murmured.

"Huh? Wuzzat?" Randolph jabbed him in the ribs. "Come on, let's have it."

With a subvocal growl, Benedict cuffed him on the ear.

Randolph was the picture of respect from then on. It had been simple enough—Benedict just hadn't thought of it before.

Just before he left that Sunday night, his Uncle James

pressed a sheaf of debentures into his hand.

"You're a fine young man, Edward," the old man said, shaking his head as if he still couldn't believe it. "Fine young man."

Benedict grinned broadly. "Goodbye, Uncle James." I have a *tiger* at home.

Almost before his apartment door closed behind him he had taken out the microphone. He called the tiger to his feet and embraced the massive head. Then he stepped back. The tiger seemed bigger, glossier somehow, and every hair vibrated with a life of its own. Ben's ruff was like snow. Benedict had begun to change too, and he spent a long, reflective moment in front of the mirror, studying hair that seemed to crackle with life, a jaw that jutted ever so slightly now.

Later, when it was safe to go out, they went to the park. Benedict sat on a bench and watched his tiger run, delighting in the creature's springy grace. Ben's forays were shorter this time, and he kept returning to the bench to rest his chin on Benedict's knee.

In the first glimmer of the morning, Ben raced away once more, taking the ground in flat, racing bounds. He veered suddenly and headed for the lake in full knowledge that it was there, a shadowed streak, clearing the water in a leap that made Benedict come to his feet with a shout of joy.

"Ben!"

The tiger made a second splendid leap and came back to him. When Ben touched his master's knee this time Benedict threw away his coat, yelling, and wheeled and ran with him. Benedict sprinted beside the tiger, careering down flat walks, drinking in the night. They were coursing down the last straight walk to the gate when a slight, feminine figure appeared suddenly in the path in front of them, hands outflung in fear, and as they slowed she turned to run and threw something all in the same motion, mouth open in a scream that couldn't find voice. Something squashy hit Ben on the nose, and he shook his head and backed off. Benedict picked it up. It was a pocketbook.

"Hey, you forgot your . . ." He started after her, but as he remembered he'd have to explain the tiger, his voice trailed off and he stopped, shoulders drooping helplessly, until Ben nudged him. "Hey, Ben," he said, wondering. "We *scared* her."

He straightened his shoulders, grinning. "How about that." Then, with a new bravado he opened the purse, counted out several bills. "We'll make it look like a robbery. Then the cops'll never believe her story about a tiger." He placed the purse out in the open, where she would see it, and then absently pocketed the bills, making a mental note to pay the woman back some day. "Come Ben," he said softly, "Let's go home."

Spent, Benedict slept the morning through, head resting on the tiger's silken shoulder. Ben kept watch, amber eyes unblinking, the whipping of his tail the only motion in the silent room.

He woke well after noon, alarmed at first because he was four hours late for work. Then he caught the tiger's eye and laughed. *I have a tiger.* He stretched luxuriously, yawning, and ate a slow breakfast and took his time about getting dressed. He found the debentures his uncle had given him on the dresser, figured them up and found they would realize a sizable sum.

For some days he was content to be lazy, spending afternoons in movies and evenings in restaurants and bars, and twice he even went to the track. The rest of the time he sat and watched the tiger. As the days passed he went to better and better restaurants, surprised to find that head-waiters bowed deferentially and fashionable women watched him with interest—all, he was sure, because he had a tiger at home. There came a day when he was tired of commanding waiters alone, restless in his new assurance, compelled to find out how far it would take him. He had spent the last of the proceeds from the debentures and (with a guilty twinge) the money he'd taken from the woman in the park. He began reading the business section of *The Times* with purpose, and one day he copied down an address and picked up the microphone.

"Wish me luck, Ben," he whispered, and went out.

He was back an hour later, still shaking his head, bemused. "Ben, you should have seen me. He'd never even heard of me—but he begged me to take the job—I had him cornered—I was a tiger—" he flushed modestly "—meet the second vice-president of the Pettigrew Works."

The tiger's eyes flickered and grew bright.

That Friday, Benedict brought home his first paycheck, and early the next morning it was Benedict who led the way to the park. He ran with the tiger until his eyes were swimming from the wind, and he ran with the tiger the next morning and every morning after that, and as they ran he grew in assurance. "I have a *tiger* at home," he would tell himself in time of crisis, and then he would forge on to the next thing. He carried the microphone like a talisman, secure in the knowledge that he could whisper in it at any time, and call the tiger to his side. He was named a first vice-president in a matter of days.

Even as his career progressed and he became a busy, important man, he never forgot the morning run. There were times when he would excuse himself from a party in a crowded nightclub to take his tiger ranging in the park, sprinting beside him in his tuxedo ,boiled shirt-front gleaming in the dark. Even as he became bolder, more powerful, he remained faithful.

Until the day he made his biggest deal. His employer had sent him to lunch with Quincy, their biggest customer, with instructions to sell him sixteen gross.

"Quincy," Benedict said, "You need twenty gross." They were sitting against a tiger-striped banquette in an expensive restaurant. Quincy, a huge, choleric man, would have terrified him a month before.

"You've got your nerve," Quincy blustered. "What makes you think I want twenty gross?"

". . ." For a second Benedict retreated. Then the tiger striping touched a chord in him and he snapped forward. "Of course, you don't *want* twenty gross," he rumbled. "You need them."

Quincy bought thirty gross. Benedict was promoted to general manager.

New title resting lightly on his shoulders, he gave himself the rest of the afternoon off. He was springing toward the door on cat feet when he was interrupted in midflight by an unexpected silky sound. "Well, Madeline," he said.

The secretary, dark, silk-skinned, unapproachable until now, had come up beside him. She seemed to be trying to tell him something—something inviting.

On impulse, he said, "You're coming to dinner with me tonight, Madeline."

Her voice was like velvet. "I have a date, Eddy—my rich uncle from Cambridge is in town."

He snorted. "The—uh—uncle who gave you that mink?

I've seen him. He's too fat," and he added in a growl that dissolved her, "I'll be at your place at eight."

"Why, Eddy . . . All right." She looked up through furred lashes. "But I should warn you—I am not an inexpensive girl."

"You'll cook dinner of course—then we may do the town." He patted his wallet pocket, and then nipped her ear. "Have steak."

As he rummaged in his sock drawer that night, his hand hit something hard, and he pulled it out with a crawly, sinking feeling. The microphone—somehow he'd forgotten it this morning. It must have fallen in among his socks while he was dressing, and he'd been without it all day. All day. He picked it up, shaky with relief, and started to slip it into his tuxedo. Then he paused, thinking. Carefully he set it back in the drawer and shut it. He didn't need it any more. He was the tiger now.

That night, still rosy with drink and the heady sounds of music and Madeline's breath coming and going in his ear, he went to bed without undressing and slept until it got light. When he woke and padded into the living room in his socks he saw Ben in the corner, diminished somehow, watching him. He had forgotten their run.

"Sorry, old fellow," he said as he left for work, giving the tiger a regretful pat.

And "Got to hustle," the next day, with a cursory caress. "I'm taking Madeline shopping."

As the days went by and Benedict saw more and more of the girl, he forgot to apologize. And the tiger remained motionless in the corner as he came and went, reproaching him.

Benedict bought Madeline an Oleg Cassini.

In the corner of the living room, a fine dust began to settle on Ben's fur.

Benedict bought Madeline a diamond bracelet.

In the corner, a colony of moths found its way into the heavy fur on Ben's breast.

Benedict and Madeline went to Nassau for a week. They stopped at an auto dealer's on their way back and Benedict bought Madeline a Jaguar.

The composition at the roots of Ben's alert nylon whiskers had begun to give. They sagged, and one or two fell.

It was in the cab, on his way home from Madeline's apartment, that Benedict examined his checkbook carefully for the first time. The trip and the down payment on the car had brought his accounts to zero. And there was a payment due on the bracelet the next day. But what did it matter? He shrugged. He was a man of power. At the door to his apartment he wrote the cabbie a check, grandly adding an extra five dollars as tip. Then he went upstairs, pausing briefly to examine his tan in a mirror, and went to bed.

He woke at three o'clock in the morning, prey to the shadows and the time of day, uneasy for the first time, and in the cold light of his bed lamp, went through his accounts again. There was less money than he'd realized—he had to go to the bank to cover the check for the cabbie, or the down payment on the Jag would bounce. But he'd written a check for the last installment on the bracelet, and that would be coming in, and the rent was overdue. . . .

He had to have money now. He sat in bed, knees drawn up, musing, and as he thought he remembered the woman he and Ben had frightened that first day, and the money in her purse, and it came to him that he would get the money in the park. He remembered rushing down on the woman, her scream, and in memory that first accidental escapade with the tiger became a daring daylight robbery —hadn't he spent the money? And as he thought back on it he decided to try it again, beginning to forget that the tiger had been with him and in fact, forgetting as he slipped into a striped sweatshirt and tied a kerchief at his throat that he was not the tiger, so that he went out without even seeing Ben in the corner, running in low, long strides, hurrying to the park.

It was still dark in the park and he paced the walks, light-footed as a cat, expanding in a sense of power as he stalked. A dark figure came through the gates—his prey— and he growled a little, chuckling as he recognized her— the same sad woman—frightened of a tiger—and he growled again, running toward her, thinking, as he bore down on her, *I will frighten her again*.

"Hey!" she yelled, as he rushed at her and he broke stride because she hadn't shrunk from him in terror; she was standing her ground, feet a little wide, swinging her handbag.

Eyeing the pocketbook, he circled her and made another rush.

"Hand it over," he snarled.

"I beg your pardon," she said coldly, and when he rushed at her with another growl, "What's the *matter* with you?"

"The pocketbook," he said menacingly, hair bristling.

"Oh, the *pocketbook*." Abruptly she lifted the purse and hit him on the head.

Startled, he staggered back, and before he could collect himself for another lunge, she had turned with an indignant snort and started out of the park.

It was too light now to look for another victim. He peeled off the sweatshirt and went out of the park in his shirtsleeves, walking slowly, puzzling over the aborted robbery. He was still brooding as he went into a nearby coffee shop for breakfast, and he worried over it as he ate his Texas steak. The snarl hadn't been quite right, he decided finally, and he straightened his tie and went too early to work.

"The Jaguar company called me," Madeline said when she came in an hour later. "Your check bounced."

"Oh?" Something in her eyes kept him from making anything of it. "Oh," he said mildly. "I'll take care of it."

"You'd better," she said. Her eyes were cold.

Ordinarily he would take this opportunity—before anyone else came in—to bite her on the neck, but this morning she seemed so distant (probably because he hadn't shaved, he decided) and he went back to his office instead, scowling over several columns of figures on a lined pad.

"It looks bad," he murmured. "I need a raise."

His employer's name was John Gilfoyle—Mr. Gilfoyle, or Sir, to most of his employees. Benedict had learned early that the use of the initials rattled him, and he used them to put himself at an advantage.

Perhaps because he was off his feed that morning, perhaps because Benedict had forgotten his coat, Gilfoyle didn't even blink. "I've no time for that today," he snapped.

"You don't seem to understand." Benedict filled his

chest and paced the rug in front of the conference desk softly, noting uneasily that his shoes were muddy from the fiasco in the park, but still the tiger. "I want more money."

"Not today, Benedict."

"I could get twice as much elsewhere," Benedict said. He bored in as he always did, but there seemed to be a flaw in his attitude—perhaps he was a bit hoarse from running in the early-morning air—because Gilfoyle, instead of rising with an offer, as he always did, said, "You don't look very snappy this morning, Benedict. Not like a company man."

". . . The Welchel Works offered me . . ." Benedict was saying.

"Then why don't you *go* to the Welchel Works." Gilfoyle slapped his desk, annoyed.

"You *need* me," Benedict said. He stuck out his jaw as always, but the failure in the park had left him more shaken than he realized, and he must have said it in the wrong way.

"I don't need you," Gilfoyle barked. "Get out of here or I may decide I don't even want you."

"You . . ." Benedict began.

"Get out!"

"Y—yessir." Completely unnerved, he backed out of the office.

In the corridor, he bumped into Madeline.

"About that down payment . . ." she said.

"I—I'll tend to it. If I can just come over . . ."

"Not tonight," she sniffed. She seemed to sense a change in him. "I'm going to be a little busy."

He was too shattered to protest.

Back at his desk, he mulled over and over the figures in his notebook. At lunch he stayed in his chair, absently stroking his paperweight—a tiger-striped lump he had bought in palmier days, and as he stroked it he thought of Ben. For the first time in several weeks he dwelled on the tiger, unexpectedly, overwhelmingly homesick for him. He sat out the rest of the afternoon in misery, too unsure of himself now to leave the office before the clock told him it was time. As soon as he could he left, taking a cab with a five-spot he had found in a lower drawer, thinking all the time that at least the tiger would never desert him, that it would be good to take Ben out again, comforting to run with his old friend in the park.

Forgetting the elevator, he raced up the stairs and into his living room, stopping only to switch on a small lamp by the door. "Ben," he said, and threw his arms around the tiger's neck. Then he went into his bedroom and hunted up the microphone. He found it in his closet, under a pile of dirty drawers.

"Ben," he said softly into the microphone.

It took the tiger a long time to get to his feet. His right eye was so dim now that Benedict could hardly see him. The light behind the left eye had gone out. When his master called him to the door, he moved slowly, and as he came into the lamplight, Benedict saw why.

Ben's tail was lashing only feebly, and his eyes were dimmed with dust. His coat had lost its luster, and the mechanism that moved his response to Benedict's commands had stiffened with disuse. The proud silver ruff was yellow, spotted here and there where the moths had eaten it too close. Moving rustily, the tiger pressed his head against Benedict.

"Hey, fella," Benedict said with a lump in his throat. "Hey. Tell you what," he said, stroking the thinning fur, "soon as it gets late enough, we'll go out to the park. A little fresh air—" he said, voice breaking, "fresh air'll put the spring back in you." With an empty feeling that belied his words, he settled himself on the couch to wait. As the tiger drew near, he took one of his silver-backed brushes and began brushing the tiger's lifeless coat. The fur came out in patches, adhering to the soft bristles and Benedict saddened, put the brush aside. "It'll be OK, fella," he said, stroking the tiger's head to reassure himself. For a moment Ben's eyes picked up the glow from the lamp, and Benedict tried to tell himself they had already begun to grow brighter.

"It's time," Benedict said. "C'mon, Ben." He started out the door and down the hall, going slowly. The tiger followed him creakily, and they began the painful trip to the park.

Several minutes later the park gates loomed reassuringly, and Benedict pushed on, sure, somehow, that once the tiger was within their shelter his strength would begin to return. And it seemed true, at first, because the darkness braced the tiger in some gentle way, and he started off springily when Benedict turned to him and said, "Let's go."

Benedict ran a few long, mad steps, telling himself the tiger was right behind him and then slowed, pacing the tiger, because he realized now that if he ran at full strength Ben would never be able to keep up with him. He went at a respectable lope for some distance, and the tiger managed to keep up with him, but then he found himself going slower and slower as the tiger, trying gallantly, moved his soft feet in the travesty of a run.

Finally Benedict went to a bench and called him back, head lowered so the tiger wouldn't see that he was almost crying.

"Ben," he said, "forgive me."

The big head nudged him and as Benedict turned, the faint light from the one good eye illuminated his face. Ben seemed to comprehend his expression, because he touched Benedict's knee with one paw, looking at him soulfully with his brave blind eye. Then he flexed his body and drew it under him in a semblance of his old powerful grace and set off at a run, heading for the artificial lake. The tiger looked back once and made an extra little bound, as if to show Benedict that he was his old self now, that there was nothing to forgive, and launched himself in a leap across the lake. He started splendidly, but it was too late—the mechanism had been unused for too long now, and just as he was airborne it failed him and the proud body stiffened in midair and dropped, rigid, into the lake.

When he could see well enough to make his way to the lake, Benedict went forward, still grinding tears from his eyes with heavy knuckles. Dust—a few hairs—floated on the water, but that was all. Ben was gone. Thoughtfully, Benedict took the microphone from his pocket and dropped it in the lake. He stood, watching the lake until the first light of morning came raggedly through the trees, struggling to reach the water. He was in no hurry because he knew, without being told, that he was finished at the office. He would probably have to sell the new wardrobe, the silver brushes, to meet his debts, but he was not particularly concerned. It seemed appropriate, now, that he should be left with nothing. ■

Newsmen are the practicing sociologists of our time. On and off the record, they observe (as the most dedicated and perceptive scholars or reformers seldom can) the bare bones of contemporary society: the economic, technological, institutional realities on which the political musculature and social skin are molded.

The combination of newsman-science-fiction-writer has a tradition that goes back to Cleve Cartmill, and includes Clifford Simak, Cyril Kornbluth, and Richard Wilson, a tradition of excellence, and also of rarity. It is not surprising that recent trends in SF have attracted more newsmen to the field—but it did startle me to realize that there are more newsmen represented in this Annual than any other single occupation.

Mrs. Reed is actually an ex-newswoman—but very recently so. She was voted "New England Newspaperwoman of the Year," twice in eight years while combining newswork with short-story writing, a private life as a faculty wife, the birth of two children, and her first two novels. (Latest: **At War as Children,** Farrar, Straus and Giroux, 1964.) A Guggenheim novel award last year finally took her out of the ranks of the working press.

Dick Wilson describes himself as "a sometime novelist (three published and one going begging), but still basically a newsman"—although his job is now on the other side of the news fence, as chief of the news bureau at Syracuse University. He served his apprenticeship in sci-fi-fan amateur publications, and "on the rim of the copy desk at Fairchild Publications." He got into newswork proper during World War II, when he was assigned (somewhere in New Guinea) to "pasting up Terry and the Pirates comic strips on the backs of old aerial photographs," because they contained more up-to-date information than the official news.

He has worked on wire-service news desks in Chicago, Washington, and New York, for Transradio Press and then Reuters. "The Carson Effect" grew out of his own experience at the New York Reuters desk, trying to write a "forward-throwing" story for London on the eve of Caryl Chessman's execution in California.

THE CARSON EFFECT
Richard Wilson
from *Worlds of Tomorrow*

               Andrew Grey sat tensely at the national news desk of *The New York Times,* remembering the last time he had been asked to write an impossible story.

He had been, then, in New York, and therefore North American, correspondent for an overseas wire service, European Press. A celebrated case at the time was that of Zeb Speed, a convicted killer who had spent a dozen years in the death house at Utah's state prison while he prepared appeal after appeal based on his careful research in the prison library. Finally Speed's resources appeared to be exhausted and the governor set the next day, a Friday, for Speed's execution.

But Speed spent Thursday addressing last-ditch appeals to the Vatican, the White House, to every senator and to each of the Supreme Court justices. There were new developments every hour. Grey was trying frantically to keep up with the story, swallowing aspirin and black coffee as he revised and re-topped, when Paris sent him a service message requesting a forward-looking story under Friday's date.

This request reached Grey at six P.M. He was in New York, covering the story from the machines of the American press services, making an occasional long-distance telephone call, and drawing on his knowledge of Utah's death house, seen a year ago when he had covered a riot at the prison.

He knew the kind of story Paris wanted: a simple, straightforward piece with "today" in the first sentence. It might read:

SALT LAKE CITY, Feb. 4 (EP)—Zeb Speed, his last appeal denied, was due to choose whether he would die today by the hangman's noose or by a squad of riflemen aiming at a tag pinned over his heart.

Speed, part-Indian convicted killer of 12 whose claim that his trial was unconstitutional, bolstered by appeals researched in the prison library . . .

That was what Euro wanted. The only trouble was that midnight, European time, being six P.M. New York time, was only four P.M. Utah time. There were still eight hours of Thursday remaining for Zeb Speed. Anything Andy Grey wrote as a Friday story before midnight Utah time (eight A.M., Paris time) would be science fiction.

Not being a writer in that genre, he sent Euro a service message which read: "Regret fast-breaking developments in Utah, where it only four P.M. make tomorrow-dated story out of question. Propose cabling spot developments, leaving rewrite desk do forward-throwing piece as feel warranted."

It was exactly this sense of caution which got Andrew Grey fired from his European Press job (Speed's last appeal was denied and he was executed on Friday, choosing the firing squad) and hired by *The New York Times*.

Now Andy Grey sat hunched over his portion of the *Times'* national news desk, trying to write, as responsibly as he could, a story far more difficult. A copy boy dropped the latest fragment of the story in front of him. He already had more facts than he needed. There were bits and pieces from all over.

When you hear the tone, it will be exactly 10:26 A.M., *Eastern Standard Time.*

Douglas Roche tried to walk casually from the door of the bank to the waist-high tables where the deposit and withdrawal slips were kept.

He'd never done anything like this before. He took a deep breath, wiped his sweating palms on the sides of his coat and picked up a pen. He printed on the back of a withdrawal slip: "Give me $10,000 in medium size bills. Don't do anything crazy, this bottle is full of nitro."

Roche was thirty-four years old, married, with three kids. He had a job that paid him $127 a week before deductions. He also had a mortgage, a second mortgage, a car, a deepfreeze, a new TV, a power lawn mower, a revolving charge account with three-figure balance, new storm windows and a bill three months overdue at the high-priced grocery store that delivered and gave credit.

He had two dollars and eighteen cents and a subway token in his pocket and his wife had just gone to the hospital to have an operation. They had let her in without payment in advance only because he promised to bring $200 at nine o'clock tomorrow morning. He didn't have hospitalization; that had been one of the things he'd economized on. He'd also heard that surgeons charged up to a thousand dollars for a laminectomy. He hadn't yet discussed fees with doctors. Oh, yes, there was the bookmaker. Roche owed him fifty bucks.

Doug Roche was no bank robber. He was just a man driven to the wall. But now he was a bank robber.

He got into the shortest line; only one person was ahead of him at the teller's window. But the person was a woman with a wad of books and papers in her hand which she handed to the teller one by one: a deposit in the checking account; a payment on the personal loan; a deposit in the savings account; a money order to be cashed; a dollar in the Christmas Club. Finally she was finished.

Doug Roche thought for the last time of walking away. But there was nowhere to walk to. He shoved the note across the counter and opened his fist to show the little bottle containing a colorless liquid. It was only water, of course.

The teller looked up from the note and Roche made a small threatening motion with the bottle. At the same time he began to regret that he had demanded so much. Two thousand dollars would have got him out of his immediate troubles. Ten thousand might get him a bullet in the back from some hidden guard.

But the teller said: "Sure. Don't worry; I won't do anything foolish." He began taking bills out of the drawer and stuffing them in a big manila envelope. Roche saw the wrappers on the wads of bills: $1,000; $5,000; $3,000; $50,000.

Almost hysterically, he said in a strangled voice: "That's enough!"

"One more," the teller said, and shoved in a thin stack whose wrapper said $100,000.

Roche tried to keep his voice steady as he said: "Okay. Don't ring the alarm till I'm out the door or I throw the bottle right at you.

"Don't worry," the teller said again. Then he said: "God bless you."

Roche, perspiring, so nervous that he nearly dropped the manila envelope, turned and walked toward the door. It took all his determination not to run. He went out into the shopping crowds, turned a corner and walked fast. He went into a department store and out the exit on the far end and took the subway out to Queens. But nobody chased him.

He got home and locked the door and pulled down the the shades. He put the manila envelope on the kitchen table and got a can of beer from the refrigerator and peeled it open. He took a big swig and lit a cigarette and counted his money.

. . . two hundred and twenty-three thousand six hundred and fifty dollars. $223,650.

By the time he had finished a second can of beer he had counted the money five times. It always came to the same amount. Just under a quarter of a million dollars. He felt numb.

After a while he took a ten-dollar bill from one of the stacks and put the rest in a paper bag, which he hid under the sink among other paper bags containing potatoes and onions.

He went out intending to buy a bottle of whiskey and get drunk. Instead he came back with a take-out order from a Chinese restaurant and ate his first full meal in days.

Later he took out the money and counted it again. Minus the ten dollars, it came to $223,640. He began to laugh and couldn't stop himself. For a long time he laughed hysterically, lying on the bed and muffling his face in the pillow.

Finally he got up, washed, shaved and put on a clean shirt. He took $200, put the rest back under the sink and went to see his wife in the hospital.

When you hear the tone, it will be exactly 2:17 P.M., Eastern Standard Time.

Freida Barring—some of the older women in the office called her Theda Bara in fun, as she was anything but a glamor girl—went hesitantly to the head bookkeeper's cubicle. She was nervous because the expense money she wanted to collect was a whole $3.65 and the man who'd authorized it had quit a month ago. He had forgotten to sign a petty-cash slip. It would be Freida's word against the company's.

What happened was that the assistant sales manager, the man who'd quit, had asked her to take a cab downtown and pick up some papers he needed right away. He'd told her to have the cab wait and it had waited what seemed to Freida a long time.

It was a complicated story to have to explain and she dreaded the ordeal she faced with the head bookkeeper of Schlarf & Son, a man notoriously reluctant to part with a nickel.

But today the head bookkeeper, a gray-haired man in his fifties, was almost jovial. "Ah, Miss Barring," he said. "What can we do for you? Sit down, sit down."

Freida sat on the edge of the chair and said: "It's about a petty-cash slip. I had to take a cab for Mr. Westfall— this was before he left—and it's $3.65. That includes a 35-cent tip and I laid it out, but if you don't think I should have tipped the driver, then it's only $3.30. I mean Mr. Westfall didn't specifically say to tip him and maybe Schlarf & Son don't authorize—"

The head bookkeeper held up a hand. "The tip is authorized, Miss Barring, of course. Here." He opened a drawer and lifted the lid of a metal box filled with bills and change. "Three dollars and sixty-five cents even. Just sign this slip."

Freida signed and took the money. She got up to go, tremendously relieved. This was wonderful. Now she could pay the electric-light bill before next payday, by which time they would have shut off the electricity.

"Don't go, Miss Barring," the head bookkeeper said. "There's another little matter we can settle as long as you're here." He smiled in a sad-kind way which filled Freida with dread. Were they going to fire her for her audacity in demanding the cab fare? Had they found out about the half dozen boxes of paper clips she'd taken home to make that stupid mobile hanging from the ceiling of her kitchenette?

But the head bookkeeper was saying: ". . . your pension plan. We find you've overpaid your share by $34 a year. And since you've been with Schlarf & Son a trifle over 12 years, we owe you $414.80. Plus interest, of course."

He began counting out the money in twenties and tens. It made quite a pile on the desk.

"I hope you don't mind taking it in cash, Miss Barring," he said. "You see, our check-writing machine has broken down."

In a daze, Freida took the money and put it in her bag.

"And now, Miss Barring, Mr. Schlarf has asked me if you'll show that you forgive him by taking the rest of the day off."

Freida stammered: "But it's only two-thirty . . ."

"To be sure. But Mr. Schlarf thought you might have some shopping to do. A new hat, maybe. You have a beautiful day for it."

When you hear the tone, it will be exactly 3:49 P.M., Eastern Standard Time.

Billy Boyce, aged six, was going shopping. He had saved up seventy-four cents to buy his mother a birthday present. His sister, aged fourteen, gave him twenty-six cents more, which made it an even dollar, and said she'd pay the sales tax.

They were on Fifth Avenue and had walked past many fascinating windows. There was a five-and-ten around the corner.

"Do I hafta go to the five-and-ten?" Billy asked. "Do I *haf*ta?"

"You've only got a dollar," his big sister said. "Where do you want to go—to Tiffany's?"

"Sure, Tiffany's," Billy said. It sounded nice.

Eunice, his sister, thought why not? She was going to be fifteen soon and in a few years she'd be eighteen and maybe by then somebody would have proposed. She'd never been to Tiffany's or anywhere like it. It would be a good idea to see what they had, just in case. She could always tell the clerk that she was just humoring her little brother.

"As a special favor to you, Billy," Eunice said, "we'll go

to Tiffany's. But don't be disappointed if you don't have
enough money. They're expensive in there."

"Okay," Billy said, "but I got a whole dollar."

Such nice things they had! Rings and necklaces and
brooches (Eunice called them broaches) and earrings and
pendants and lockets and especially rings and necklaces.

"I want that one for mommy," Billy said, pointing to a
glittering diamond necklace resting in a velvet box. There
was a discreet price tag: $6,760 plus F. T.

Eunice smiled at the clerk to show she was humoring
her little brother. The clerk smiled back. "It is nice, isn't
it?" he said. "We're having a special on that one today."

She could imagine. Even at 10% off it would be . . .
6,760 minus 676 equaled whatever it equaled, plus 10%
back on for the federal tax.

"Do you have anything a little . . . you know, not quite
so *gaudy?*" she asked, to show him that it was a question
of taste, not price.

"This is, if I may say so, not gaudy," the clerk said. "And
if the young man really wants it for his mother . . ."

"I want it," Billy said. "I got a whole dollar."

The clerk smiled and Eunice was mortified.

"That's not quite enough," the clerk said. "You see,
there's the ten percent federal tax and the four percent
sales tax. I'm afraid this necklace comes to one dollar and
fourteen cents."

"But I only got a dollar," Billy said. Eunice was glaring
at the clerk.

"Perhaps," he said, "the young man would care to have
us spread the payments over three months—say forty
cents down and forty cents a month for the next two
months? That would include the credit charge."

"Don't kid him, mister," Eunice said. "He's just a little
boy." She was *so* embarrassed. "Don't you have a nice
. . . sweater clasp or something?"

"No, miss," the clerk said, smiling. "We have nothing
like that in my section. And I am anxious to make this sale.
I'll tell you what I'll do. I'll pay the federal tax myself.
That leaves it at a dollar four. Do you have four cents you
might lend him?"

Eunice was a woman of the world, as she had often told
herself. There are times when you must seize the oppor-

tunity or call the bluff. She took a nickel out of her pocketbook and put it on the counter. "There," she said. "We'll take it, Mr. Smarty Pants. Give him your dollar, Billy."

Billy dutifully took the crumpled bill out of his pocket and put it on the counter. "Could you wrap it up nice?" he asked.

"It will be the nicest package you ever took home, Billy," the clerk said.

"My mother's birthday's tomorrow but we're giving her her presents tonight," Billy said.

"I'm glad to hear it," the clerk said. "That's really the best way."

When you hear the tone, it will be exactly 4:03 P.M., Eastern Standard Time.

Orion Newcastle, who had fought hard for his party's top nomination and then, heartbreakingly, had seen it go to a much less capable man, hurried to the office of that man, now the President of the United States.

Vice-President Newcastle, who had not attended the secret National Security Council meeting that morning, had no idea what the urgent summons to him could mean.

Orion Newcastle had missed other N.S.C. meetings, sometimes by his own choice. After all, his role there was usually limited to telling a few stories to the early-comers before the President arrived and, later, replying, "Certainly, Mr. President" whenever the other man said "Don't you agree, Orion?"

Since the convention he had always agreed. After all, there was the President's second term to be considered. Orion had no wish to be dumped, as Roosevelt had dumped Henry Wallace for Harry Truman. Orion sincerely hoped he bore no ill will toward the President. It certainly was his devout wish that the President should live to complete two full terms. But no one could read the future and man was mortal, as had been confirmed several times in Newcastle's own lifetime. Thus it was wise not to jeopardize one's position by thought or deed. And the Honorable Orion Newcastle, Vice-President of the United States, walked a little faster toward the President's office.

When he got there, he found not only the President but the Secretary of State, the Chief Justice, the Speaker of the

House, the top leadership of both parties in Congress, the diplomatic correspondents of the Washington newspapers and the chief Washington correspondents of the nation's other leading papers and of the world's press services.

Orion knew all these men by their first names. They had drunk each other's liquor and told each other bawdy stories. One or two of them, he knew, were responsible for spreading the so-called Orion Stories which had become a national fad, and which held him up to ridicule because of the Down-East accent which he had never lost. But all of them, it seemed to him, were now looking at him with new, and in some cases unprecedented, respect. He could not imagine what was in their minds.

So he said, grinning and broadening his accent slightly: "Well, Mr. President and gentlemen—Mr. President and *other* gentlemen, *I* should say—what solemn occasion is this?"

But none of them laughed at his quip. The others looked to the President, who said finally, after gazing out the window and then at each of them in turn:

"Gentlemen, in accordance with the provisions of the Constitution of the United States of America, I am resigning in favor of the Vice-President."

Although he must have hinted at this in some way before Orion came in, there was a murmur of dissent which the President stilled by holding up his hand.

"It's all been decided, gentlemen. I have drawn up the necessary papers—which I now sign." He scratched his name quickly several times. "They require only the signatures of some of you to make them official and binding. Then in your presence, Mr. Newcastle will be sworn by the Chief Justice as the next President of the United States."

"But why, sir?" the Secretary of State asked. "What possible reason can you have?"

"One of the very best," the President said with a wry smile. "The reason is simply that I have learned, gentlemen, on the highest authority, that I have only a few more hours to live."

And within the quarter-hour the shocked assemblage had signed their names and watched Orion Newcastle, whom two or three of them considered to be nothing more than an aging buffoon, be sworn in as President of the United States.

When you hear the tone, it will be exactly 7:10 P.M., Eastern Standard Time.

Andrew Grey wasn't the only newsman trying to write the impossible story, of course. Fully 15 others in the huge newsroom were assigned to various angles. But his was to be the main story, the one which would appear in the right-hand column of page one under the eight-column, three-bank headline.

The final editions of the evening papers had already had a bash at it. To them it was a straightforward, if hopeless, story to be told. Perhaps the *Post* told it more simply than its rivals, with the one-word headline: "DOOMSDAY."

Actually it was the penultimate day, the day before doom. This was what the President had been leading up to when he said shortly after four P.M. that he had only a few more hours to live. What he meant, and what he said a few minutes later, was that everybody was going to die. The end was due at midnight, Eastern Standard Time (nine P.M. Pacific Standard Time, five A.M. the next day London time, six A.M. Paris time, seven A.M. Mecca time, eight A.M. Moscow time) and so on around the poor doomed world.

The President had known for some weeks that the end was approaching. So had the State Department and, abroad, 10 Downing Street, the Quai D'Orsay, the Vatican and the Kremlin. Computers in all the capitals had been working at top speed, 24 hours a day, looking for a flaw, a way out, anything. The computers—Communist, neutral and Western—agreed there was no way out. There was nothing Earth could do to save itself.

Had it been a meteor, this extraterrestrial menace, something might have been done. Even a good-sized asteroid, having strayed out of orbit and into a collision course with Earth, could have been broken up into relatively small, harmless chunks that would burn up in the Earth's atmosphere if the world powers cooperated in firing their space-age weapons at it.

But there was no way known of dispelling a cloud of noxious gas so huge it would envelop the Earth for 37 days, poisoning every breathing thing.

The evening papers put out their final editions and their staffs went home to their loved ones, went out to get drunk, went to holy places to pray. The *Journal-American* said:

WORLD ENDING

President, Pope,
Kremlin
Confirm Holocaust

NO WAY OUT FOR EARTH
Moon Flight Couple Also Doomed

The *World-Telegram* revealed the reasons behind the President's resignation in favor of Orion Newcastle—the fact that during World War II, when both were unknown noncoms, the older man, though wounded, had dragged the younger one inch by inch through a minefield to an aid station and to the treatment there which had saved his life; and the fact that Newcastle had never again mentioned that incident, publicly or privately, in all the years since the war. A man of such courage and unselfishness, who, moreover, had been elected by the people to the second-highest office in the land, surely was entitled to be President, if at all possible, during the last several hours of his and the world's existence—even if he was an incompetent buffoon.

The *World-Telegram* also found room for half a dozen human-interest stories. There was the one about the bank president who had been told confidentially by his friend the Secretary of the Treasury about the imminent end, and who had amused himself by taking a teller's place and giving away vast sums of money, including a quarter million or so to a bank robber who had threatened to blow up the place with nitroglycerine but who obviously was an amateur with a little jar of water. There were the stories of the publisher who had given the beatnik poet a $15,000 advance on an impossible sheaf of nonverses, and of the partner in Tiffany's who, pretending to be a clerk, had sold a little boy a seven-thousand-dollar necklace for a dollar fourteen.

Only an elite few had known the truth before the

President's announcement but the truth had trickled down among the influential, moneyed group, enabling many who had never before considered playing the role to become philanthropists in various ways, either for the honest fun of it, or because of the good will this presumably would lay up for them in the next world, if any.

Oh, about that moon flight couple. They were a cosmonaut and a cosmonette, so-called, Russian. They were doomed like the rest of humanity, Tass explained unhappily, because the killer cloud would envelop the moon as well as the Earth and the space between them.

Let's get back to our man on the *Times,* Andy Grey, struggling with syntax in his attempt to write today's story from tomorrow's mythical (because nonexistent) point of view. To put it another way, he was trying to manipulate the language so his story would look back as honestly as possible, from a day that wouldn't exist, on the events of Earth's last day.

Yet his story could not be 100% positive.

The first edition appeared at ten P.M. and there was always the possibility, however slight, that something might happen between press time and midnight to change everything. Theoretically it was an impossible story to write. Actually, though, it could be done if it were sufficiently hedged, with enough loopholes left.

Andy Grey rolled another sheet of copy paper into his typewriter, lit another cigarette (at least lung cancer would never touch him now) and tried again to write a lead that would, as they say, "stand up" through all editions, both those that came out tonight and those printed, or due to be printed, tomorrow.

The world came to an end yesterday. Of course you couldn't say *that.* If it had, there'd be no one left to write such a sentence.

The Earth was due to be destroyed last night, the top international scientists agreed. Said when? Last night, presumably. But the concept of "last night" cannot exist unless there is a "today" to look back from. Thus, if the world had ended last night, there could be no today and the sentence, designed to be read by today-people, was nonsense.

There will be no today, despite the date on this news-

paper. Never in *The New York Times*—too whimsical!

It could have been done entirely with out-of-town datelines like Washington, London and Moscow—there were plenty of such stories already in type under "yesterday's" date—but the publisher and president of the paper had decided that the overall lead had to be an undated one, so-called, written from the point of view of the date of the newspaper: "today," meaning tomorrow.

Andy Grey crumpled up his umpteenth piece of copy paper and lit his next cigarette, reflecting that the problems posed by European Press in bygone days were pikers compared to his present dilemma.

A copy boy brought Andy the first editions of "tomorrow's" tabloid, the *Daily News,* which came out two hours earlier than the *Times.*

"END NIGH," the *Daily News* said in its biggest, thickest headline type. Before pursuing this to p. 3, where the story was, Grey turned to the center fold minus one, to see what the editorial said. Typically colloquial, it was headed "SO LONG, EVERYBODY," and went on:

> We hear we're wasting our time writing this editorial for a paper that won't hit the stands today (which is really tomorrow to us—that is, the man writing this), but there's an old show-business adage which, adapted to our business, applies here: the paper must come out if it's at all possible.
>
> We naturally greet the news of our impending doom, and yours, as so dramatically described by our Washington man on page 3, with mixed emotions . . .

Grey envied the *News* its easy, colloquial approach to doomsday. Inside was a sidebar under these encouraging words: "RELIGIOUS LEADERS PLEDGE HEREAFTER."

None of this was of any help to Grey.

He was well into his fourth pack when the boy came up with the *Herald Tribune,* which had obviously advanced its publication time. The *Trib,* which had been livelying itself up these many years, much to the *Times'* annoyance, had put all its columnists on the front page, as if to assuage the grief of its readership by showing them that Walter Lippmann, John Crosby, David Lawrence, Judith

Crist and Art Buchwald were going, too. Each had something wise, funny, wry or profound to say about the putative end of the world. Donald I. Rogers, the financial editor, was not on the front page but his comment was summarized there, in the Topic A column. He said, in part, "If these words are read today, I predict the biggest, best, bull-est day Wall Street has ever had!!!" (Exclamation points his.)

The *Trib*'s headline, all-encompassing in its simplicity, said: "NO TOMORROW?"

That question mark, after the word which so magnificently ignored the petty journalistic fetish of yesterday-to-day-tomorrow by transmuting itself into its metaphorical sense—meaning, loosely, the future—was the despair of every other newspaper editor in New York and, eventually, the world.

Because, of course, the world did not end.

There had been a mistake by the computers, which had been operating on old data, fed to them by old programmers, who had got their stuff from old scientists.

Had it been 1900 when the noxious cloud touched Earth, or even 1930, mankind, not to speak of animalkind, birdkind, fishkind and insectkind, would have perished instanter. But, in the years between, Earthmen had contaminated their atmosphere with radiation, automobile exhaust, DDT and other anti-insect sprays, smokestack exhaust, cigarette, cigar and pipe smoke, autumn weed smoke from the proliferating suburbs and multifarious miscellaneous contaminants. It was this unwholesome combination, called by some the "Rachel Carson effect," which saved Earth.

The whole shemozzle, as Buchwald later called it, was far more poisonous than the petty little toxic-cloud menace alleged to have been threatening the planet.

What had happened was that humanity, little by little over the decades, had built up immunities to the various poisons it was forced to live with and ingest. The cumulative immunity was a fantastically powerful one which it would have taken a real hoopdinger of a menace, as Earl Wilson was to put it, to outdo.

Thus Earth lived—as recorded in an Associated Press flash sent (by who knows what group of dedicated newsmen) at 12:01 A.M. EST. It said, simply, "FLASH—EARTH LIVES," and there were an awful lot of bells ringing on the teletype machines. UPI was only about half a minute behind with its own realization that another day had begun.

Consternation reigned, of course.

There was a bull market, as the *Trib*'s Don Rogers predicted.

There was also a lot of panic in high places as the bosses who had given it away went crazy trying to get it back.

And an awful lot of people, from President Orion Newcastle to little Billy Boyce, weren't giving up a thing. ∎

Certain qualities are essential to the good newsman: a capacity for accurate and detailed research; a feeling for the "human angle"; and just that touch of precognition (all right, call it hunch—or even extrapolation) that tells him where to turn for the next story.

Arthur Clarke, somehow, has never been a newsman: physicist, mathematician, astronomer, inventor, skin-diver, treasure-hunter, lecturer and teacher, he has been editor, author, journalist, encyclopaedist, and (most recently) scenarist. (By the time you read this, the two-way Clarke-(Strangelove) Kubrick collaboration, **2001: A Space Odyssey**, should be in print in book form, and ready for release on film.)

Clarke is a curiously free man. There is a detachment about him which seems less a traditional "British reserve" than a sort of disassociation from the gravity-ridden surface world—as if his true home were in free-fall space, or perhaps in free-floating oceanic deeps. He approaches his multiple interests with a sort of visitor-on-Earth enthusiasm: I have seen him display, with equal delight, gold coins from a treasure-hunt diving trip; a new press release on the Kubrick collaboration; a hotel-window view of New York's skyline through his new Questar telescope; and the plastic-label-maker with which he was turning out stickups for his one-man campaign: HELP STAMP OUT POP ART!

He is, generally, a vigorous man with an opinion. In an article in Playboy last year, "The Meddlers," he wrote: "A certain amount of meddling is an excellent thing. It laid the foundations of experimental science and modern technology. But the intelligent meddler must abide by a few commonsense rules, of which the most important are: (1) Do not attempt the unforseeable; (2) do not commit the irrevocable."

"Intelligent meddler" is probably as good a description of "experimental scientist" as any other. And certain qualities are necessary for the job: a capacity for detailed research; a faculty for accurate extrapolation (or hunch, or precognition); and (for intelligent meddling) a recognition of the human values involved.

In a survey conducted by the fan magazine Double : Bill, Clarke gave as his reason for writing science fiction: "Because most other literature isn't concerned with reality."

And of course it is also true that certain qualities are essential to the good science-fiction writer; the ability to project future hunches (or precognitions, or extrapolations) must rest on a capacity for detailed, accurate research; and it cannot be good fiction of any sort unless the author has a deep awareness of the human (or other) elements involved.

THE SHINING ONES
Arthur C. Clarke
from *Playboy*

When the switchboard said that the Soviet Embassy was on the line, my first reaction was: "Good—another job!" But the moment I heard Goncharov's voice, I knew there was trouble.

"Klaus? This is Mikhail. Can you come over at once? It's very urgent, and I can't talk on the phone."

I worried all through the 20-minute drive to Geneva, marshaling my defenses in case anything had gone wrong at our end. But I could think of nothing; at the moment, we had no outstanding contracts with the Russians. The last job had been completed six months before, on time, and to their entire satisfaction.

Well, they were not satisfied with it now, as I discovered quickly enough. Mikhail Goncharov, the commercial attaché, was an old friend of mine; he told me all he knew, but it was not very much.

"We've just had an urgent cable from Ceylon," he said.

"They want you out there immediately. There's serious trouble at the hydrothermal project."

"What sort of trouble?" I asked. I knew at once, of course, that it would be the deep end, for that was the only part of the installation that had concerned us. The Russians themselves had done all the work on land—but they had had to call on us to fix those grids, 3,000 feet down in the Indian Ocean. There is no other firm in the world that can live up to our motto: "ANY JOB, ANY DEPTH."

"All I know," said Goncharov, "is that the site engineers report a complete breakdown, that the Prime Minister of Ceylon is opening the plant three weeks from now and that Moscow will be very, very unhappy if it's not working then."

My mind went rapidly through the penalty clauses in our contract. The firm seemed to be covered, because the client had signed the take-over certificate, thereby admitting that the job was up to specification. However, it was not as simple as that; if negligence on our part were proved, we might be safe from legal action, but it would be very bad for business. And it would be even worse for me, personally; for I had been project supervisor in Trinco Deep.

Don't call me a diver, please; I hate the name. I'm a deep-sea engineer, and I use diving gear about as often as an airman uses a parachute. Most of my work is done with TV and remote-controlled robots; when I do have to go down myself, I'm inside a minisub with external manipulators. We call it a lobster because of its claws; the standard model works down to 5,000 feet, but there are special versions that will operate at the bottom of the Marianas Trench. I've never been there myself, but will be glad to quote terms if you're interested. At a rough estimate, it will cost you a dollar a foot plus a thousand an hour on the job itself.

I realized that the Russians meant business when Goncharov said that a jet was waiting at Zurich, and could I be at the airport within two hours?

"Look," I said. "I can't do a thing without equipment—and the gear needed even for an inspection weighs tons. Besides, it's all at Spezia."

"I know," Mikhail answered implacably. "We'll have another jet transport there. Cable from Ceylon as soon as you know what you want: it will be on the site within twelve hours. But please don't talk to *anyone* about this; we prefer to keep our problems to ourselves."

I agreed with this, for it was my problem, too. As I left the office, Mikhail pointed to the wall calendar, said "Three weeks," and ran his finger across his throat. And I knew he wasn't thinking of *his* neck.

Two hours later I was climbing over the Alps, saying goodbye to the family by radio and wondering why, like every other sensible Swiss, I hadn't become a banker or gone into the watch business. It was all the fault of the Piccards and Hannes Keller, I told myself moodily; why did they have to start this deep-sea tradition, in Switzerland of all countries? Then I settled down to sleep, knowing that I would have little enough in the days to come.

We landed at Trincomalee just after dawn, and the huge, complex harbor—whose geography I've never quite mastered—was a maze of capes, islands, interconnecting waterways and basins large enough to hold all the navies of the world. I could see the big white control building, in a somewhat flamboyant architectural style, on a headland overlooking the Indian Ocean. The siting was pure propaganda—though of course if I'd been Russian I'd have called it "public relations."

Not that I really blamed my clients; they had good reason to be proud of this, the most ambitious attempt yet made to harness the thermal energy of the sea. It was not the first attempt; there had been an unsuccessful one by the French scientist Georges Claude in the 1930's and a much bigger one at Abidjan, on the west coast of Africa, in the 1950's.

All these projects depended on the same surprising fact—that even in the tropics the sea a mile down is almost at freezing point. Where billions of tons of water are concerned, this temperature difference represents a colossal amount of energy and a fine challenge to the engineers of power-starved countries.

Claude and his successors had tried to tap this energy with low-pressure steam engines; the Russians had used a much simpler and more direct method. For over a hundred years it had been known that electric currents flow in many materials if one end is heated and the other cooled; and ever since the 1940's Russian scientists had been working to put this "thermoelectric" effect to practical use.

Their earliest devices had not been very efficient—though good enough to power thousands of radios by the heat of kerosene lamps—but in 1974 they had made a big, and still secret, breakthrough. Though I fixed the power elements at the cold end of the system, I never really saw them; they were completely hidden in anticorrosive covering. All I know is that they formed a big grid like lots of old-fashioned steam radiators bolted together.

I recognized most of the faces in the little crowd waiting on the Trinco airstrip; friends or enemies, they all seemed glad to see me—especially Chief Engineer Shapiro.

"Well, Lev," I said, as we drove off in the station wagon, "what's the trouble?"

"We don't know," he said frankly. "It's your job to find out—and to put it right."

"Well, what *happened?*"

"Everything worked perfectly up to the full-power tests," Shapiro answered. "Output was within five percent of estimate until 01.34 Tuesday morning." He grimaced; obviously that time was engraved on his heart. "Then the voltage started to fluctuate violently, so we cut the load and watched the meters. I thought that some idiot of a skipper had hooked the cables—you know the trouble we've taken to avoid *that* happening—so we switched on the searchlights and looked out to sea. There wasn't a ship in sight; anyway, who would have tried to anchor just *outside* harbor on a clear, calm night?

"There was nothing we could do except watch the instruments and keep testing. I'll show you all the graphs when we get to the office. After four minutes everything went open circuit. We can locate the break exactly, of course —and it's in the deepest part, right at the grid. It *would* be there, and not at *this* end of the system," he added gloomily, pointing out of the window.

We were just driving past the solar pond—the equivalent of the boiler in a conventional heat engine. This was an idea that the Russians had borrowed from the Israelis; it was simply a shallow lake, blackened at the bottom, holding a concentrated solution of brine. It acts as a very efficient heat trap, and the sun's rays bring the liquid up to almost 200 degrees Fahrenheit. Submerged in it were the "hot" grids of the thermoelectric system, every inch of two fathoms down. Massive cables connected them to my department, 150 degrees colder and 3,000 feet lower, in the undersea canyon that comes to the very entrance of Trinco harbor.

"I suppose you checked for earthquakes?" I asked, not very hopefully.

"Of course. There was nothing on the seismograph."

"What about whales? I warned you that they might give trouble."

More than a year before, when the main conductors were being run out to sea, I'd told the engineers about the drowned sperm whale found entangled in a telegraph cable half a mile down off South America. About a dozen similar cases are known—but ours, it seemed, was not one of them.

"That was the second thing we thought of," answered Shapiro. "We got on to the fisheries department, the navy and the air force. No whales anywhere along the coast."

It was at that point that I stopped theorizing, because I overheard something that made me a little uncomfortable. Like all Swiss, I'm good at languages, and have picked up a fair amount of Russian. There was no need to be much of a linguist, however, to recognize the word *"sabotash."*

It was spoken by Dimitri Karpukhin, the political advisor on the project. I didn't like him, nor did the engineers, who sometimes went out of their way to be rude to him. One of the old-style Communists who had never quite escaped from the shadow of Stalin, he was suspicious of everything outside the Soviet Union, and most of the things inside it. Sabotage was just the explanation that would appeal to him.

There were, of course, a great many people who would not be exactly brokenhearted if the Trinco power project failed. Politically, the prestige of the U. S. S. R. was committed; economically, billions were involved, for if hydrothermal plants proved a success, they might compete with oil, coal, water power and, especially, nuclear energy.

Yet I could not really believe in sabotage; after all, the Cold War was over. It was just possible that someone had made a clumsy attempt to grab a sample of the grid, but

even this seemed unlikely. I could count on my fingers the
number of people in the world who could tackle such a
job—and half of them were on my payroll.

The underwater TV camera arrived that same evening,
and, working all through the night, we had cameras,
monitors and two kilometers of coaxial cable loaded
aboard a launch by morning. As we pulled out of the
harbor, I thought I saw a familiar figure standing on the
jetty, but it was too far away to be certain and I had other
things on my mind. If you must know, I am not a good
sailor; I am only really happy *underneath* the sea.

We took a careful fix on the Round Island lighthouse
and stationed ourselves directly above the grid. The self-
propelled camera, looking like a midget bathyscaphe, went
over the side; as we watched the monitors, we went with it
in spirit.

The water was extremely clean and extremely empty,
but as we neared the bottom, there were a few signs of life.
A small shark came and stared at us, then a pulsating blob
of jelly went drifting by, followed by a thing like a big
spider with hundreds of hairy legs, tangling and twisting
together. At last the sloping canyon wall swam into view;
we were right on target, for there were the thick cables running down into the depths, just as I had seen them when
I made the final check of the installation six months before.

I turned on the low-powered jets and let the camera drift
down the power cables. They seemed in perfect condition,
still firmly anchored by the *pitons* we had driven into the
rock. It was not until I came to the grid itself that there
was any sign of trouble.

Have you ever seen the radiator grille of a car after it's
run into a lamppost? Well, one section of the grid looked
very much like that. Something had battered it in, as if a
gargantuan madman had gone to work on it with a sledge
hammer.

There were gasps of astonishment and anger from the
people looking over my shoulder. I heard *"sabotash"* muttered again, and for the first time began to take it seriously.
The only other explanation that made sense was a falling
boulder, but the slopes of the canyon had been carefully
checked against this very possibility.

Whatever the cause, the damaged grid had to be replaced. That could not be done until my lobster—all 20 tons of it—was flown out from the Spezia dockyard where it was kept between jobs.

"Well," said Shapiro, when I had finished my visual inspection and photographed the sorry spectacle on the screen, "how long will it take?"

I refused to commit myself. The first thing I ever learned in the underwater business is that no job turns out as you expect. Cost and time estimates can never be firm, because it's not until you're at least halfway through a contract that you know exactly what you're up against.

My private guess was three days. So I said: "If everything goes well, it shouldn't take more than a week."

Shapiro groaned. "Can't you do it quicker?"

"I won't tempt fate by making rash promises. Anyway, that still gives you two weeks before your deadline."

He had to be content with that, though he kept nagging at me all the way back into harbor. When we got there, he had something else to think about.

"Morning, Joe," I said to the man who was still waiting patiently on the jetty. "I thought I recognized you on the way out. What are *you* doing here?"

"I was going to ask you the same question."

"You'd better speak to my boss. Chief Engineer Shapiro —meet Joe Watkins, science correspondent of *Time* magazine."

Lev's response was not exactly cordial. Normally, there was nothing he liked better than talking to newsmen, who arrived at the rate of about one a week. Now, as the target date approached, they would be flying in from all directions. Including, of course, from Russia; and at the present moment Tass would be just as unwelcome as *Time*.

It was amusing to see how Karpukhin took charge of the situation. From that moment, Joe had permanently attached to him as guide, philosopher and drinking companion a smooth young public-relations type named Sergei Markov. Despite all Joe's efforts, the two were inseparable. In the middle of the afternoon, weary after a long conference in Shapiro's office, I caught up with them for a belated lunch at the government resthouse.

"What's going on here, Klaus?" Joe asked pathetically.

"I smell trouble, but no one will admit anything."

I toyed with my curry, trying to separate the bits that were safe from those that would take off the top of my head.

"You can't expect me to discuss a client's affairs," I answered.

"You were talkative enough," Joe reminded me, "when you were doing the survey for the Gibraltar Dam."

"Well, yes," I admitted. "And I appreciate the write-up you gave me. But this time there are trade secrets involved. I'm—ah—making some last-minute adjustments to improve the efficiency of the system."

And that, of course, was the truth; for I was indeed hoping to raise the efficiency of the system from its present value of exactly zero.

"Hmm," said Joe sarcastically. "Thank you very much."

"Anyway," I said, trying to head him off, "what's *your* latest crackbrained theory?"

For a highly competent science writer, Joe has an odd liking for the bizarre and the improbable. Perhaps it's a form of escapism; I happen to know that he also writes science fiction pseudonymously, though this is a secret well kept from his employers. He has a sneaking fondness for poltergeists and ESP and flying saucers, but lost continents are his real specialty.

"I *am* working on a couple of ideas," he admitted. "They cropped up when I was doing the research on this story."

"Go on," I said, not daring to look up from the analysis of my curry.

"The other day I came across a very old map—Ptolemy's, if you're interested—of Ceylon. It reminded me of another old map in my collection, and I turned it up. There was the same central mountain, the same arrangement of rivers flowing to the sea. But *this* was a map of Atlantis."

"Oh, no!" I groaned. "Last time we met, you convinced me that Atlantis was the western Mediterranean basin."

Joe gave his engaging grin.

"I could've been wrong, couldn't I? Anyway, I have a much more striking piece of evidence. What's the old national name for Ceylon—and the modern Singhalese one, for that matter?"

I thought for a second, then exclaimed: "Why, Lanka,

of course. Lanka—Atlantis." I rolled the names off my tongue.

"Precisely," said Joe. "But two clues, however striking, don't make a full-fledged theory; and that's as far as I've got at the moment."

"Too bad," I said, genuinely disappointed. "And your other project?"

"This will really make you sit up," Joe answered smugly. He reached into the battered briefcase he always carried and pulled out a bundle of papers.

"This happened only one hundred and eighty miles from here and just over a century ago. The source of my information, you'll note, is about the best there is."

He handed me a photostat, and I saw that it was a page of the London *Times* for July 4, 1874. I started to read without much enthusiasm, for Joe was always producing bits of ancient newspapers, but my apathy did not last long.

Briefly—I'd like to give the whole thing, but if you want more details your local library can dial you a facsimile in ten seconds—the clipping described how the 150-ton schooner *Pearl* left Ceylon in early May, 1874, and then fell becalmed in the Bay of Bengal. On May 10, just before nightfall, an incredibly enormous squid surfaced half a mile from the schooner, whose captain foolishly opened fire on it with his rifle.

The squid swam straight for the *Pearl*, grabbed the masts with its gigantic arms and pulled the vessel over on her side. She sank within seconds, taking two of her crew with her; the others were rescued only because the steamer *Strathowen* was in sight and had witnessed the incident herself.

"Well," said Joe, when I'd read through it for the second time, "what do you think?"

"I don't believe in sea monsters."

"The London *Times*," Joe answered, "is not prone to sensational journalism. And giant squids exist, though the biggest *we* know about are feeble, flabby beasts and don't weigh more than a ton, even when they have arms forty feet long."

"So? An animal like that couldn't capsize a one-hundred-and-fifty-ton schooner."

"True—but there's a lot of evidence that the so-called *giant* squid is merely a large squid. There may be decapods in the sea that really are giants. Why, only a year after the *Pearl* incident, a sperm whale off the coast of Brazil was seen struggling inside gigantic coils which finally dragged it down into the sea; you'll find the incident described in the *Illustrated London News* for November 20, 1875. And then, of course, there's that chapter in *Moby Dick . . .*"

"What chapter?"

"Why, the one called 'Squid.' We know that Melville was a very careful observer, but here he really lets himself go. He describes a calm day when a great white mass rose out of the sea 'like a snow-slide, new slid from the hills.' And *this* happened here in the Indian Ocean, perhaps a thousand miles south of the *Pearl* incident. Weather conditions were identical, please note.

"What the men of the *Pequod* saw floating on the water —I know this passage by heart, I've studied it so carefully —was 'a vast pulpy mass, furlongs in length and breadth, of a glancing cream color . . . innumerable long arms radiating from its center, and curling and twisting like a nest of anacondas.' "

"Just a minute," said Sergei, who had been listening to all this with rapt attention. "What's a furlong?"

Joe looked slightly embarrassed.

"Actually, it's an eighth of a mile—660 feet." He raised his hand to stop our incredulous laughter. "Oh, I'm sure Melville didn't mean that *literally*. But here was a man who met sperm whales every day, groping for a unit of length to describe something a *lot* bigger. So he automatically jumped from fathoms to furlongs. That's my theory, anyway."

I pushed away the remaining untouchable portions of my curry.

"If you think you've scared me out of my job," I said, "you've failed miserably. But I promise you this—when I do meet a giant squid, I'll snip off a tentacle and bring it back as a souvenir."

Twenty-four hours later I was out there in the lobster, sinking slowly down toward the damaged grid. There was no way in which the operation could be kept secret, and Joe was an interested spectator from a nearby launch. That was the Russians' problem, not mine; I had suggested to Shapiro that they take him into their confidence, but this, of course, was vetoed by Karpukhin's suspicious mind. One could almost see him thinking: "Just *why* should an American reporter turn up at this moment?"—and ignoring the obvious answer that Trincomalee was now big news.

There is nothing in the least exciting or glamorous about deep-water operations if they're done properly. Excitement means lack of foresight, and that means incompetence. The incompetent do not last long in my business, nor do those who crave excitement. I went about my job with all the pent-up emotion of a plumber dealing with a leaking faucet.

The grids had been designed for easy maintenance, since sooner or later they would have to be replaced. Luckily, none of the threads had been damaged and the securing nuts came off easily when gripped with the power wrench. Then I switched control to the heavy-duty claws and lifted out the damaged grid without the slightest difficulty.

It's bad tactics to hurry on an underwater operation. If you try to do too much at once, you are liable to make mistakes. And if things go smoothly and you finish in a day a job you said would take a week, the client feels he hasn't had his money's worth. Though I was sure I could replace the grid that same afternoon, I followed the damaged unit up to the surface and closed shop for the day.

The Russians hurried the thermo-element off for an autopsy, and I spent the rest of the evening hiding from Joe. Trinco is a small town, but I managed to keep out of his way by visiting the local cinema, where I sat through several hours of an interminable Tamil movie in which three successive generations suffered identical domestic crises of mistaken identity, drunkenness, desertion, insanity and death, all in Technicolor and with the sound track turned full up.

The next morning, despite a mild headache, I was over the site soon after dawn. (So was Joe, and so was Sergei, all set for a quiet day's fishing.) I waved cheerfully to them as I climbed into the lobster, and the tender's crane lowered me over the side. Over the other side, where Joe couldn't see it, went the replacement grid. A few fathoms down I lifted it out of the hoist and carried it to the bottom of Trinco Deep, where, without any trouble, it was installed by the middle of the afternoon. Before I surfaced again, the lock nuts had been secured, the conductors spot-welded, and the engineers on shore had completed their continuity tests. By the time I was back on deck, the system was under load once more, everything was back to normal, and even Karpukhin was smiling—except when he stopped to ask himself the question that no one had yet been able to answer.

I still clung to the falling-boulder theory, for want of a better one. And I hoped that the Russians would accept it, so that we could stop this silly cloak-and-dagger business with Joe.

No such luck, I realized when both Shapiro and Karpukhin came to see me with very long faces.

"Klaus," said Lev, "we want you to go down again."

"It's your money," I replied. "But what do you want me to do?"

"We've examined the damaged grid, and there's a section of the thermoelement missing. Dimitri here thinks that —someone—has deliberately broken it and carried it away."

"Then they did a damn clumsy job," I answered. "I can promise you it wasn't one of *my* men."

It was risky to make such jokes around Karpukhin, and no one was at all amused. Not even me; for by this time I was beginning to think that he might have something.

The sun was setting when I began my last dive into Trinco Deep, but the end of the day has no meaning down there. I fell for 2,000 feet with no lights, because I like to watch the luminous creatures of the sea as they flash and flicker in the darkness, sometimes exploding like rockets just outside the observation port. In this open water there was no danger of a collision; in any case, I had the panoramic sonar scan running, and that would give far better warning than could my eyes.

At 400 fathoms, I knew that something was wrong. The bottom was coming into view on the vertical sounder, but it was approaching much too slowly. My rate of descent was far too low; I could increase it easily enough by flooding another buoyancy tank, but I hesitated to do so. In my business, anything out of the ordinary needs an explanation; three times I have saved my life by waiting until I had one.

The thermometer gave me the answer. The temperature outside was five degrees higher than it should have been, and I am sorry to say that it took me several seconds to realize why.

Only a few hundred feet below me, the repaired grid was now running at full power, pouring out megawatts of heat as it tried to equalize the temperature difference between Trinco Deep and the solar pond up there on land. It wouldn't succeed, of course; but in the attempt it was generating electricity, and I was being swept upward in the geyser of warm water that was an incidental by-product.

When I finally reached the grid, it was quite difficult to keep the lobster in position against the upwelling current, and I began to sweat uncomfortably as the heat penetrated into the cabin. Being too hot on the sea bed was a novel experience; so also was the miragelike vision caused by the ascending water, which made my searchlights dance and tremble over the rock face I was exploring.

You must picture me, lights ablaze in that 500-fathom darkness, moving slowly down the slope of the canyon, which at this spot was about as steep as the roof of a house. The missing element—*if* it was still around—could not have fallen very far before coming to rest. I would find it in ten minutes or not at all.

After an hour's searching I had turned up several broken light bulbs (it's astonishing how many get thrown overboard from ships—the sea beds of the world are covered with them), an empty beer bottle (same comment) and a brand-new boot. That was the last thing I found, for then I discovered that I was no longer alone.

I never switch off the sonar scan, and even when I'm not moving I always glance at the screen about once a minute to check the general situation. The situation now was that a large object—at least the size of the lobster— was approaching from the north. When I spotted it, the range was about 500 feet and closing slowly. I switched off my lights, cut the jets I had been running at low power to hold me in the turbulent water, and drifted with the current.

Though I was tempted to call Shapiro and report that I had company, I decided to wait for more information. There were only three nations with depth ships that could operate at this level, and I was on excellent terms with all of them. It would never do to be too hasty and to get myself involved in unnecessary political complications.

Though I felt blind without the sonar, I did not wish to advertise my presence, so I reluctantly switched it off and relied on my eyes. Anyone working at this depth would have to use lights, and I'd see them coming long before they could see me. So I waited in the hot, silent little cabin, straining my eyes into the darkness, tense and alert but not particularly worried.

First there was a dim glow, at an indefinite distance. It grew bigger and brighter, yet refused to shape itself into any pattern that my mind could recognize. The diffuse glow concentrated into myriad spots, until it seemed that a constellation was sailing toward me. So might the rising star clouds of the galaxy appear from some world close to the heart of the Milky Way.

Even then I was not really frightened. I could not imagine what was approaching, but I did not believe that any creature of the sea could touch me inside six inches of good Swiss armor plate.

The thing was almost upon me, glowing with the light of its own creation, when it split into two separate clouds. Slowly they came into focus—not of my eyes, but of my understanding; and I knew that beauty and terror were rising toward me out of the abyss.

The terror came first, when I saw that the approaching beasts were squids, and all Joe's tales reverberated in my brain. Then, with a considerable sense of letdown, I realized that they were only about 20 feet long—little larger than the lobster and a mere fraction of its weight. They could do me no harm; and quite apart from that, their indescribable beauty robbed them of all menace.

This sounds ridiculous, but it is true. In my travels I have seen most of the animals of this world, but none to match the luminous apparitions floating before me now. The colored lights that pulsed and danced along their bodies made them seem clothed with jewels, never the same for two seconds at a time. There were patches that glowed a brilliant blue, like flickering mercury arcs, then changed almost instantly to burning neon red. The tentacles seemed strings of luminous beads trailing through the water—or the lamps along a superhighway, when you look down upon it from the air at night. Barely visible against this background glow were the enormous eyes, uncannily human and intelligent, each surrounded by a diadem of shining pearls.

I am sorry; that is the best I can do. Only the movie camera could do justice to these living kaleidoscopes. I do not know how long I watched them, so entranced by their luminous beauty that I had almost forgotten my mission. That those delicate, whiplash tentacles could not possibly have broken the grid was already obvious. Yet the presence of these creatures here was, to say the least, very curious. Karpukhin would have called it suspicious.

I was about to call the surface when I saw something incredible. It had been before my eyes all the time, but I had not realized it until now.

The squids were talking to each other.

Those glowing, evanescent patterns were not coming and going at random. They were as meaningful, I was suddenly sure, as the illuminated signs of Broadway or Piccadilly, not the ones that spell out words, but those that form pictures. Every few seconds there would be an image that almost made sense to me, but vanished before I could interpret it. I knew, of course, that even the common octopus shows its emotions with lightning-fast color changes—but this was something of a much higher order. It was pictorial—or pictographic—communication; here were two living electric signs flashing messages to each other.

When I saw an unmistakable picture of the lobster, my last doubts vanished. Though I am no scientist, at that moment I shared the feelings of a Newton or an Einstein at some moment of revelation.

Then the picture changed, in a most curious manner. There was the lobster again, but rather smaller. And there beside it, much smaller still, were two peculiar objects.

Each consisted of a pair of black dots surrounded by a pattern of radiating lines.

I said that we Swiss are good at languages. However, it required little intelligence to deduce that this was a formalized squid's-eye view of itself and that what I was seeing was a crude sketch of the situation. But why the absurdly small size of the squids?

I had no time to puzzle that out before there was another change. A third squid symbol appeared on the living screen—and this one was enormous, completely dwarfing the others. The message shone there in the eternal night for a few seconds; then the creature bearing it shot off at incredible speed and left me alone with its companion.

Now the meaning was all too obvious. "My God!" I said to myself. "They feel they can't handle me. One of them has gone to fetch Big Brother."

And of Big Brother's capabilities I already had better evidence than Joe Watkins, for all his research and newspaper clippings.

That was the point, you won't be surprised to hear, when I decided not to linger. But before I went, I thought I would try some talking myself.

After hanging there in darkness for so long, I had forgotten the power of my lights. They hurt my eyes and must have been agonizing to the unfortunate squid. Transfixed by that intolerable glare, its own illumination utterly quenched, it lost all its beauty, becoming no more than a pallid bag of jelly with two black buttons for eyes. For a moment it seemed paralyzed by the shock; then it darted after its companion, while I soared upward to a world that could never be the same again.

"I've found your saboteur," I told Karpukhin when they opened the hatch of the lobster. "If you want to know all about him, ask Joe Watkins."

I let Dimitri sweat over that for a few seconds while I enjoyed his expression; then I gave my slightly edited report. I implied—without actually saying so—that the squids I'd met were powerful enough to have done all the damage; and I said nothing about the conversation I'd overseen. That would only cause incredulity; besides, I wanted time to think matters over and to tidy up the loose ends—if I could.

Joe has been a great help, though he still knows no more than the Russians. He's told me what wonderfully developed nervous systems squids possess—and has explained how some of them can change their appearance in a flash through what amounts to instantaneous three-color printing, thanks to the extraordinary network of "chromophores" covering their bodies. Presumably this evolved for camouflage; but it seems natural—even inevitable—that it should have developed into a communication system.

But there's one thing that worries Joe.

"What were they *doing* around the grid?" he keeps asking me plaintively. "They're cold-blooded invertebrates. You'd expect them to dislike heat as much as they object to light."

That puzzles Joe; but it doesn't puzzle me. Indeed, I think it's the key to the whole mystery.

Those squids, I'm now certain, are in Trinco Deep for the same reason that there are men at the South Pole or on the Moon. Pure scientific curiosity has drawn them from their icy home to investigate this geyser of hot water welling from the sides of the canyon. Here is a strange and inexplicable phenomenon—possibly one that menaces their way of life. So they have summoned their giant cousin (servant? slave?) to bring them a sample for study. I cannot believe that they have a hope of understanding it; after all, no scientist on earth could have done so as late as a century ago. But they are trying, and that is what matters.

Tomorrow, we begin our countermeasures; I go back into Trinco Deep to fix the great lights which Shapiro hopes will keep the squids at bay. But how long will that ruse work if intelligence is dawning in the deep?

As I dictate this, I'm sitting here below the ancient battlements of Fort Frederick, watching the moon come up over the Indian Ocean. If everything goes well, this will serve as the opening of the book that Joe has been badgering me to write. If it doesn't—then hello, Joe, I'm talking to *you* now. Please edit this for publication in any way you think fit, and my apologies to you and Lev for not giving all the facts before; now you'll understand why.

Whatever happens, please remember this: They are beautiful, wonderful creatures; try to come to terms with them if you can.

TO: Ministry of Power, Moscow
FROM: Lev Shapiro, Chief Engineer,
Trincomalee Thermoelectric Power Project

Herewith the complete transcript of the tape recording found among Herr Klaus Muller's effects after his
last dive; we are much indebted to Mr. Joe Watkins,
of *Time* magazine, for assistance on several points.

You will recall that Herr Muller's last intelligible
message was directed to Mr. Watkins and ran as
follows: "Joe! You were right about Melville! The
thing is absolutely gigan——" ■

"I had been dreaming for nights that I could breathe water. The
dreams were so realistic that I woke up each morning thinking
that I was going to try it. And when I was out on that coral, I
was almost tempted to start breathing."

U.S.N. Lieut. Cmdr. Robert Thompson,
("Room at the Bottom of the Sea,"
Saturday Evening Post, Sept. 5, 1964.)

The far reaches of space are no more mysterious or inimical
to the surface creatures of Earth than the much closer depths
of her oceans. Alan Shepard became a national hero in 1961 by
riding a pressurized rocket capsule 116.5 miles up into the
troposphere. But when four Navy officers spent eleven days without pressure suits, at a depth of 192 feet, in and out of a
specially designed underwater craft called Sealab I, hardly a
handful of outside specialists as much as knew the project
existed.

The Navy's objective is to enable men to explore the ocean
bottoms with equipment no bulkier than Scuba gear, and the only
real problem the first experiment ran into was its own success.
The men began to find it hard to remember that the atmosphere
of the sea (even 2 feet down, let alone 200) will not support
naked human life.

Here on the surface we do not remember for different reasons.
We know more about outer space than oceanic depths simply
because there are vastly more "information offices," lobbyists,
public-relations men, and publicity agents working to sustain
interest in the economically and strategically vital aerospace
program.

For much the same reason, we tend to know more about the prospects for man in space than about the physical realities of a wartorn peninsula in Asia where, as I write, Americans are dying in the defense of a "good" political system against one we call "bad." The people who live there are, like ourselves, citizens of Earth; yet to most of us the language, customs, and physical environment of a Vietcong village would be as strange and unmanageable as those of some alien planet.

I spoke of Arthur Clarke before as an unusually free man. Certainly he is one of the very few who exercises the global freedoms guaranteed in the U.N. Declaration of the Rights of Man: no accidents or happenstances of language, geography, skin color, creed, or flag have succeeded in alienating him from his right to membership in the human race. British-born, he now makes his permanent home in Ceylon, but he lives and works, actually, all over the world.

Mack Reynolds is as different from Arthur Clarke in background, education, temperament, and personality as two good science-fictionists can be. Reynolds is a bawdy, hearty, beer-drinking, well-met-indeed man, whose most likely reason for leaving Earth would be to look into the political situation on Mars (and write home about it to Rogue magazine, as their travel editor).

"My mother's people went to California in the Gold Rush," he writes (from Spain, at the moment). "My father was twice candidate for President of the United States. . . . I was once bitten by a vampire [bat—JM] and had to be treated for rabies. . . . Once while traveling across the Sahara to Timbuctoo I was kidnapped by Tuareg. . . . I was once offered a soldier-of-fortune job for Chiang Kai-shek. . . . I was once detained by the Jordan police because I couldn't prove I was neither Jewish nor a Jehovah's Witness. . . . I once stole a perfect Etruscan vase out of an Italian tomb. . . . And I once participated . . . as an observer . . . in a demonstration against the U.S. Embassy in Moscow. . . . Although I loathe being shot at, I've been in half a dozen wars, revolutions and military revolts. . . . I once bought a Ming-dynasty vase for six dollars from a Chinese Communist. . . . I believe the world is going through an unprecedented revolution, not only in the political field but in science, sexual and other mores, medicine and socioeconomic systems. And I'm all for it. . . ."

Reynolds owns neither a Questar nor Scuba gear, to the best

of my knowledge—but he, too, is what I call a free man. And he knows beer and politics the world over.

PACIFIST
Mack Reynolds
from *Fantasy and Science Fiction*

It was another time, another space, another continuum.

Warren Casey called, "Boy! You're Fredric McGivern, aren't you?"

The lad stopped and frowned in puzzlement. "Well, yes, sir." He was a youngster of about nine. A bit plump, particularly about the face.

Warren Casey said, "Come along, son. I've been sent to pick you up."

The boy saw a man in his mid-thirties, a certain dynamic quality behind the facial weariness. He wore a uniform with which young McGivern was not familiar, but which looked reassuring.

"Me, sir?" the boy said. "You've been sent to pick me up?"

"That's right, son. Get into the car and I'll tell you all about it."

"But my father said . . ."

"Your father *sent* me, son. Senator McGivern. Now, come along or he'll be angry."

"Are you sure?" Still frowning, Fredric McGivern climbed into the helio-car. In seconds it had bounded into the second level and then the first, to speed off to the southwest.

It was more than an hour before the kidnapping was discovered.

Warren Casey swooped in, dropped two levels precipitately and brought the helio-car down in so dainty a landing that there was no perceptible touch of air cushion to garage top.

He fingered a switch with his left hand, even as he brought his right out of his jacket holding a badly burned out pipe. While the garage's elevator sunk into the recess below, he was loading the aged briar from an equally ancient pouch.

In the garage, Mary Baca was waiting nervously. She said, even though she must have been able to see the boy, "You got him?"

"That's right," Casey said. "I've given him a shot. He'll be out for another half hour or so. Take over, will you, Mary?"

The nurse looked down at the crumpled figure bitterly. "It couldn't have been his father. We have to pick on a child."

Casey flicked a quick glance at her as he lit the pipe. "It's all been worked out, Mary."

"Of course," she said. Her voice tightened. "I'll have him in the cell behind the rumpus room."

Down below he went to the room that had been assigned him and stripped from the uniform. He went into the bath and showered thoroughly, washing out a full third of the hair that had been on his head and half the color in that which remained. He emerged from the bath, little refreshed and some five years older.

He dressed in an inexpensive suit not overly well pressed and showing wear. His shirt was not clean, as though this was the second day he had worn it, and there was a food spot on his tie.

At the small desk he picked up an automatic pencil and clipped it into the suit's breast pocket and stuffed a bulky notebook into a side pocket. He stared down at the gun for a moment, then grimaced and left it. He departed the house by the front door and made his way to the metro escalator.

The nearest metro exit was about a quarter of a mile from Senator McGivern's residence and Warren Casey walked the distance. By the time he arrived, he had achieved a cynical quality in his expression of boredom. He didn't bother to look up into the face of whoever opened the door.

"Jakes," he said. "H.N.S. McGivern expects me."

"H.N.S.?" the butler said stiffly.

"Hemisphere News. Hemisphere News Service," Warren

Casey yawned. "Fer crissakes, we gonna stand here all day?
I gotta deadline."

"Well, step in here, sir. I'll check." The other turned
and led the way.

Casey stuck a finger into his back. His voice went flat.
"Don't get excited and maybe you won't get hurt. Just take
me to the Senator, see? Don't do nothing at all might make
me want to pull this trigger."

The butler's face was gray. "The Senator is in his study.
I warn you . . . sir . . . the police shall know of this immediately."

"Sure, sure, Mac. Now just let's go to the study."

"It's right in there . . . sir."

"Fine," Casey said. "And what's that, under the stairway?"

"Why, that's a broom closet. The downstairs maid's
broom . . ."

Casey brought his flat hand around in a quick clip. The
servant folded up with a lung-emptying sigh and Casey
caught him before he hit the floor, dragged him to the
broom closet, pushed and wedged him inside. He darted a
hand to a vest pocket and brought forth a syrette. "That'll
keep you out for a couple of hours," he muttered, closing
the closet door.

He went over to the heavy door which the butler had
indicated as Senator McGivern's study, and knocked on
it. In a moment it opened and a husky in his mid-twenties,
nattily attired and of obvious self-importance, frowned at
him.

"Yes?" he said.

"Steve Jakes of Hemisphere News," Warren Casey said.
"The editor sent me over . . ." As he talked, he sidestepped
the other and emerged into the room beyond.

Behind the desk was an older edition of nine-year-old
Fredric McGivern. A Fredric McGivern at the age of
perhaps fifty, with what had been boyish plump cheeks now
gone to heavy jowls.

"What's this?" he growled.

Casey stepped further into the room. "Jakes, Senator.
My editor . . ."

Senator Phil McGivern's abilities included cunning and
a high survival factor. He lumbered to his feet. "Walters!

Take him!" he snapped. "He's a fake!" He bent over to
snatch at a desk drawer.

Walters was moving, but far too slowly.

Warren Casey met him half way, reached forward with
both hands and grasped the fabric of the foppish drape
suit the secretary wore. Casey stuck out a hip, twisted
quickly, turning his back halfway to the other. He came
over and around, throwing the younger man heavily to his
back.

Casey didn't bother to look down. He stuck a hand into
a side pocket, pointed a finger at McGivern through the
cloth.

The other's normally ruddy face drained of color. He
fell back into his chair.

Warren Casey walked around the desk and brought
the gun the other had been fumbling for from the drawer.
He allowed himself a deprecating snort before dropping
it carelessly into a pocket.

Senator Phil McGivern was no coward. He glowered at
Warren Casey. "You've broken into my home—criminal,"
he said. "You've assaulted my secretary and threatened me
with a deadly weapon. You will be fortunate to be awarded
no more than twenty years."

Casey sank into an easy chair so situated that he could
watch both McGivern and his now unconscious assistant
at the same time. He said flatly, "I represent the Pacifists,
Senator. Approximately an hour ago your son was kidnapped. You're one of our top-priority persons. You
probably realize the implications."

"Fredric! You'd kill a nine-year-old boy!"

Casey's voice was flat. "I have killed many nine-year-old
boys, Senator."

"Are you a monster!"

"I was a bomber pilot, Senator."

The other, who had half-risen again, slumped back into
his chair. "But that's different."

"I do not find it so."

In his hard career, Phil McGivern had faced many
emergencies. He drew himself up now. "What do you
want—criminal? I warn you, I am not a merciful man.
You'll pay for this, Mr. . . ."

"Keep calling me Jakes, if you wish," Casey said mildly.

"I'm not important. Just one member of a widespread organization."

"What do you want?" the Senator snapped.

"How much do you know about the Pacifists, McGivern?"

"I know it to be a band of vicious criminals!"

Casey nodded, agreeably. "It's according to whose laws you go by. We have rejected yours."

"What do you want?" the Senator repeated.

"Of necessity," Casey continued, evenly, "our organization is a secret one; however, it contains some of the world's best brains, in almost every field of endeavor, even including elements in the governments of both Hemispheres."

Phil McGivern snorted his contempt.

Casey went on, an eye taking in the fact that Walters, laid out on the floor, had stirred and groaned softly. "Among our number are some capable of charting world developments. By extrapolation, they have concluded that if your policies are continued, nuclear war will break out within three years."

The other flushed in anger, finding trouble in controlling his voice. "Spies! Subversives! Make no mistake about it, Jakes, as you call yourself, we realize you're nothing more than catpaws for the Polarians."

The self-named Pacifist chuckled sourly. "You should know better, Senator. Our organization is as active on the Northern Hemisphere as it is on this one." Suddenly he came quickly to his feet and bent over Walters who had begun to stir. Casey's hand flicked out and clipped the other across the jawbone. The secretary collapsed again, without sound.

Warren Casey returned to his chair. "The point is that our experts are of the opinion that you'll have to drop out of politics, Senator McGivern. I suggest a resignation for reasons of health within the next week."

There was quick rage, then steaming silence while thought processes went on. "And Fredric?" McGivern growled finally.

Casey shrugged. "He will be freed as soon as you comply."

The other's eyes narrowed. "How do you know I'll stick

to my promise? A contract made under duress has no validity."

Casey said impatiently, "Having Fredric in our hands now is a minor matter, an immediate bargaining point to emphasize our position. Senator, we have investigated you thoroughly. You have a wife of whom you are moderately fond, and a mistress whom you love. You have three adult children by your first wife, and four grandchildren. You have two children by your second wife, Fredric and Janie. You have a living uncle and two aunts, and five first cousins. Being a politician, you have many surface friends, which we shall largely ignore, but you also know some thirty persons who mean much to you."

McGivern was beginning to adjust to this abnormal conversation. He growled, "What's all this got to do with it?"

Warren Casey looked into the other's eyes. "We shall kill them, one by one. Shot at a distance with a rifle with telescopic sights. Blown up by bomb. Machine gunned, possibly as they walk down the front steps of their homes."

"You're insane! The police. The . . ."

Casey went on, ignoring the interruption. "We are in no hurry. Some of your children, your relatives, your friends, your mistress, may take to hiding in their panic. But there is no hiding—nowhere on all this world. Our organization is in no hurry, and we are rich in resources. Perhaps in the doing some of us will be captured or dispatched. It's beside the point. We are dedicated. That's all we'll be living for, killing the people whom you love. When they are all gone, we will kill *you*. Believe me, by that time it will be as though we're motivated by compassion. All your friends, your loved ones, your near-of-kin, will be gone.

"We will kill, kill, kill—but in all it will be less than a hundred people. It will not be thousands and millions of people. It will only be *your* closest friends, *your* relatives, *your* children and finally *you*. At the end, Senator, you will have some idea of the meaning of war."

By the end of this, although it was delivered in an almost emotionless voice, Phil McGivern was pushed back in his swivel chair as though from physical attack. He repeated, hoarsely, "You're insane."

Warren Casey shook his head. "No, it is really you, you

and those like you, who are insane. Wrapped up in your
positions of power, in your greed for wealth, in the preser-
vation of your privileges, you would bring us into a con-
flagration which would destroy us all. You are the ones
who are insane."

The Pacifist agent leaned forward. "Throughout history, Senator, there have been pacifists. But never such
pacifists as we. Always, in the past, they have been laughed
at or sneered at in times of peace, and imprisoned or worse
in time of war."

"Cowards," Senator McGivern muttered in distaste.

Casey shook his head and chuckled. "Never, Senator.
Don't look for cowards among pacifists and conscientious
objectors. It takes courage to buck the current of public
opinion. A coward is often better off in the ranks and
usually safer. In modern war, at least until the advent of
nuclear conflict, only a fraction of the soldiers ever see
combat. The rest are in logistics, in a thousand branches of
behind-the-lines work. One man in twenty ever glimpses
the enemy."

McGivern snapped, "I'm not interested in your philosophy, criminal. Get to the point. I want my son back."

"This *is* the point, Senator. Today we Pacifists have become realists. We are willing to fight, to kill and to die, in
order to prevent war. We are not interested in the survival
of individuals, we are of the opinion that another war will
destroy the race, and to preserve humanity we will do
literally anything."

McGivern thumped a heavy fist on his chair arm. "You
fool! The Northern Hemisphere seeks domination of the
whole world. We must defend ourselves!"

The Pacifist was shaking his head again. "We don't care
who is right or wrong—if either side is. It finally gets to the
point where that is meaningless. Our colleagues are working among the Polarians, just as we are working here in
the Southern Hemisphere. Persons such as yourself, on the
other side, are courting death just as you are by taking
steps that will lead to war."

Warren Casey stood. "You have one week in which to
resign your office, Senator. If you fail to, you will never
see your son Fredric again. And then, one by one, you
will hear of the deaths of your relatives and friends."

The Pacifist agent came quickly around the desk and the older man, in an effort to escape, pushed his chair backward and tried to come to his feet. He was too clumsy in his bulk. Warren Casey loomed over him, slipped a syrette into the other's neck.

Senator Phil McGivern, swearing, fell to his knees and then tried to come erect. He never made it. His eyes first stared, then glazed, and he dropped back to the floor, unconscious.

Warren Casey bent momentarily over Walters, the secretary, but decided that he was safe for a time. He shot a quick look about the room. What had he touched? Had he left anything?

He strode quickly from the room, retracing his path by which the butler had brought him fifteen minutes earlier, and let himself out the front door.

His cab pulled up before the aged, but well-preserved, mansion, and he dropped coins into the vehicle's toll box and then watched it slip away into the traffic.

He walked to the door and let himself be identified at the screen. When the door opened, he strolled through.

A young woman, her face so very earnest in manner that her natural prettiness was all but destroyed, sat at a desk.

Rising, she led the way and held the door open for him and they both entered the conference room. There were three men there at the table, all of them masked.

Casey was at ease in their presence. He pulled a chair up across from them and sat down. The girl took her place at the table and prepared to take notes.

The chairman, who was flanked by the other two, said, "How did the McGivern affair go, Casey?"

"As planned. The boy proved no difficulty. He is now at the hideaway in charge of Operative Mary Baca."

"And the Senator?"

"As expected. I gave him full warning."

"The secretary, Walters. He was eliminated?"

"Well, no. I left him unconscious."

There was a silence.

One of the other masked men said, "The plan was to

eliminate the secretary to give emphasis to the Senator as to our determination."

Casey's voice remained even. "As it worked out, it seemed expedient to follow through as I did."

The chairman said, "Very well. The field operative works with considerable range of discretion. No one can foresee what will develop once an operation is underway."

Warren Casey said nothing.

The second board member sighed. "But we had hoped that the sight of a brutal killing, right before him, might have shocked Phil McGivern into submission immediately. As it is now, if our estimates of his character are correct, the best we can hope for is capitulation after several of his intimates have been dispatched."

Casey said wearily, "He will never capitulate, no matter what we do. He's one of the bad ones."

The third board member, who had not spoken to this point, said thoughtfully, "Perhaps his immediate assassination would be best."

The chairman shook his head. "No. We've thrashed this all out. We want to use McGivern as an example. In the future, when dealing with similar cases, our people will be able to threaten others with his fate. We'll see it through, as planned." He looked at Casey. "We have another assignment for you."

Warren Casey leaned back in his chair, his face expressionless, aside from the perpetual weariness. "All right," he said.

The second board member took up an assignment sheet. "It's a Priority One. Some twenty operatives are involved in all." He cleared his voice. "You've had interceptor experience during your military career?"

Casey said, "A year, during the last war. I was shot down twice and they figured my timing was going, so they switched me to medium bombers."

"Our information is that you have flown the Y-36G."

"That's right."

The board officer said, "In two weeks the first class of the Space Academy graduates. Until now, warfare has been restricted to land, sea and air. With this graduation we will have the military erupting into a new medium."

"I've read about it," Casey said.

"The graduation will be spectacular. The class is small, only seventy-five cadets, but already the school is expanding. All the other services will be represented at the ceremony."

Warren Casey wished the other would get to the point.

"We want to make this a very dramatic protest against military preparedness," the other went on. "Something that will shock the whole nation, and certainly throw fear into everyone connected with arms."

The chairman took over. "The air force will put on a show. A flight of twenty Y-36Gs will buzz the stand where the graduating cadets are seated, waiting their commissions."

Realization was beginning to build within Casey.

"You'll be flying one of those Y-36G's," the chairman pursued. His next sentence came slowly. "And the guns of your craft will be the only ones in the flight that are loaded."

Warren Casey said, without emotion, "I'm expendable, I suppose?"

The chairman gestured in negation. "No. We have plans for your escape. You make only the one pass, and you strafe the cadets as you do so. You then proceed due north, at full speed . . ."

Casey interrupted quickly. "You'd better not tell me any more about it. I don't think I can take this assignment."

The chairman was obviously taken aback. "Why, Warren? You're one of our senior men and an experienced pilot."

Casey shook his head, unhappily. "Personal reasons. No operative is forced to take an assignment he doesn't want. I'd rather skip this, so you'd best not tell me any more about it. That way it's impossible for me to crack under pressure and betray someone."

"Very well," the chairman said, his voice brisk. "Do you wish a vacation, a rest from further assignment at this time?"

"No. Just give me something else."

One of the other board members took up another piece of paper. "The matter of Professor Leonard LaVaux," he said.

Professor Leonard LaVaux lived in a small bungalow in a section of town which had never pretended to more than middle-class status. The lawn could have used a bit more care, and the roses more cutting back, but the place had an air of being comfortably lived in.

Warren Casey was in one of his favored disguises, that of a newspaperman. This time he bore a press camera, held by its strap. There was a gadget bag over one shoulder. He knocked, leaned on the door jamb, assumed a bored expression and waited.

Professor LaVaux seemed a classical example of stereotyping. Any producer would have hired him for a scholar's part on sight. He blinked at the pseudo-journalist through bifocals.

Casey said, "The *Star,* Professor. Editor sent me to get a few shots."

The professor was puzzled. "Photographs? But I don't know of any reason why I should be newsworthy at this time."

Casey said, "You know how it is. Your name gets in the news sometimes. We like to have something good right on hand to drop in. Editor wants a couple nice shots in your study. You know, like reading a book or something."

"I see," the professor said. "Well, well, of course. Reading a book, eh? What sort of book? Come in, young man."

"Any book will do," Casey said with journalistic cynicism. "It can be Little Red Riding Hood, far as I'm concerned."

"Yes, of course," the professor said. "Silly of me. The readers would hardly be able to see the title."

The professor's study was a man's room. Books upon books, but also a king-size pipe rack, a small portable bar, two or three really comfortable chairs and a couch suitable for sprawling upon without removal of shoes.

LaVaux took one of the chairs, waved the supposed photographer to another. "Now," he said. "What is procedure?"

Casey looked about the room, considering. "You live here all alone?" he said, as though making conversation while planning his photography.

"A housekeeper," the professor said.

"Maybe we could work her in on a shot or two."

"I'm afraid she's out now."

Casey took a chair the other had offered. His voice changed tone. "Then we can come right to business," he said.

The professor's eyes flicked behind the bifocals. "I beg your pardon?"

Warren Casey said, "You've heard of the Pacifists, Professor?"

"Why . . . why, of course. An underground, illegal organization." The professor added, "Quite often accused of assassination and other heinous crimes, although I've been inclined to think such reports exaggerated, of course."

"Well, don't," Casey said curtly.

"I beg your pardon?"

"I'm a Pacifist operative, Professor LaVaux, and I've been assigned to warn you to discontinue your present research or your life will be forfeit."

The other gaped, unable to adapt his mind to the shift in identity.

Warren Casey said, "You're evidently not knowledgeable about our organization, Professor. I'll brief you. We exist for the purpose of preventing further armed conflict upon this planet. To secure that end, we are willing to take any measures. We are ruthless, Professor. My interest is not to convert you, but solely to warn you that, unless your present research is ended, you are a dead man."

The professor protested. "See here, I'm a scientist, not a politician. My work is in pure research. What engineers, the military and eventually the government do with applications of my discoveries is not my concern."

"That's right," Casey nodded agreeably. "Up to this point, you, like many of your colleagues, have not concerned yourself with the eventual result of your research. Beginning now, you do, Professor, or we will kill you. You have one week to decide."

"The government will protect me!"

Casey shook his head. "No, Professor. Only for a time, even though they devote the efforts of a hundred security police. Throughout history, a really devoted group, given sufficient numbers and resources, could always successfully assassinate any person, in time."

"That was the past," the professor said, unconvinced.

"Today, they can protect me."

Casey was still shaking his head. "Let me show you just one tool of our trade." He took up his camera and removed the back. "See this little device? It's a small, spring-powered gun which projects a tiny, tiny hypodermic needle through the supposed lens of this dummy camera. So tiny is the dart that when it imbeds itself in your neck, hand, or belly, you feel no more than a mosquito bite."

The professor was motivated more by curiosity than fear. He bent forward to look at the device. "Amazing," he said. "And you have successfully used it?"

"Other operatives of our organization have. There are few, politicians in particular, who can escape the news photographer. This camera is but one of our items of equipment, and with it an assassin has little trouble getting near his victim."

The professor shook his head in all but admiration. "Amazing," he repeated. "I shall never feel safe with a photographer again."

Warren Casey said, "You have no need for fear, Professor, if you abandon your current research."

Leonard LaVaux said, "And I have a week to decide? Very well, in a week's time I shall issue notice to the press either that I have given up my research, or that I have been threatened by the Pacifists and demand protection."

Casey began to stand, but the professor raised a hand. "Wait a moment," he said. "I'd like to ask you a few questions."

The Pacifist looked at the other warily.

LaVaux said, "You're the first member of your organization to whom I've ever spoken."

"I doubt it," Casey said.

"Ah? Very secret, eh? Members are everywhere, but undetected. Then how do you recruit new membership? Being as illegal as you are, of course, the initial approach must be delicate indeed."

"That's right," Casey nodded. "We take every precaution. A prospect isn't approached until it is obvious he is actually seeking an answer to the problem of outlawing war. Many persons, Professor, come to our point of view on their own. They begin discussing the subject, seeking answers, seeking fellows who think along the same line."

The professor was fascinated. "But even then, of course, mistakes must be made and some of your membership unmasked to the authorities."

"A hazard always faced by an underground."

"And then," the professor said triumphantly, "your whole organization crumbles. One betrays the next, under police coercion."

Casey laughed sourly. "No. That's not it. We profit by those who have gone before. The history of underground organizations is a long one, Professor. Each unit of five pacifists know only those belonging to their own unit, and one coordinator. The coordinators, in turn, know only four other coordinators with whom they work, plus a section leader, who knows only four other section leaders with whom *he* works, and so forth right to the top officials of the organization."

"I see," the professor murmured. "So an ordinary member can at most betray four others, of course. But when the police capture a coordinator?"

"Then twenty-five persons are endangered," Casey admitted. "And occasionally it happens. But we have tens of thousands of members, Professor, and new ones coming in daily. We grow slightly faster than they seem able to catch us."

The professor switched subjects. "Well, no one would accuse you of being a patriot, certainly."

Casey contradicted him. "It's a different type of patriotism. I don't identify myself with this Hemisphere."

The other's eyebrows went up. "I see. Then you are a Polarian?"

Casey shook his head. "Nor do I identify myself with them. Our patriotism is to the human race, Professor. This is no longer a matter of nation, religion or hemisphere. It is a matter of species survival. We are not interested in politics, socioeconomic systems or ideology, other than when they begin to lead to armed conflict between nations."

The professor considered him for a long silent period. Finally, he said, "Do you really think it will work?"

"How's that?" Warren Casey said. For some reason, this earnest, fascinated, prying scientist appealed to him. He felt relaxed during the conversation, a relaxation, he realized, that had been denied him for long months now.

"Trying to keep the world at peace by threatening, frightening, even assassinating those whom you decide are trending toward war. Do you think it will work?"

All the wariness was back, suddenly. The months-long tiredness, and doubt, and the growing nausea brought on by violence, violence, violence. If only he could never hear the word *kill* again.

He said, "When I first joined the Pacifists, I was positive they had the only answer. Now I've taken my stand, but perhaps I am not so sure. Why do you think it won't?"

The scientist pointed a finger at him. "You make a basic mistake in thinking this a matter of individuals. To use an example, in effect what you are saying is, *kill the dictator and democracy will return to the country*. Nonsense. You put the cart before the horse. That dictator didn't get into power because he was so fabulously capable that he was able to thwart a whole nation's desire for liberty. He, himself, is the product of a situation. Change the situation and he will disappear, but simply assassinate him and all you'll get is another dictator."

The other's words bothered Warren Casey. Not because they were new to him, subconsciously they'd been with him almost from the beginning. He looked at the scientist, waiting for him to go on.

LaVaux touched himself on the chest with his right forefinger. "Take me. I am doing work in a field that can be adapted to military use, although that is not my interest. Actually, I am contemptuous of the military. But you threaten my life if I continue. Very well. Suppose you coerce me and I drop my research. Do you think that will stop investigation by a hundred, a thousand other capable men? Of course not. My branch of science is on the verge of various breakthroughs. If I don't make them, someone else will. You don't stop an avalanche by arresting the roll of one rock."

A tic began in the cheek of Casey's usually emotionless face. "So you think . . ." he prompted.

LaVaux's eyes brightened behind the bifocals. He was a man of enthusiastic opinions. He said, "Individuals in the modern world do not start wars. It's more basic than that.

If the world is going to achieve the ending of warfare, it's going to have to find the causes of international conflict and eliminate them." He chuckled. "Which, of course, opens up a whole new line of investigation."

Warren Casey stood up. He said, "Meanwhile, Professor, I represent an organization that, while possibly wrong, doesn't agree with you. The ultimatum has been served. You have one week."

Professor LaVaux saw him to the door.

"I'd like to discuss the subject further, some day," he said. "But, of course, I suppose I won't be seeing you again."

"That's right," Casey said. He twisted his mouth wryly. "If we have to deal with you further, Professor, and I hope we don't, somebody else will handle it." He looked at the other and considered momentarily rendering the stereotyped-looking scientist unconscious before he left. But he shook his head. *Lord,* he was tired of violence.

As he walked down the garden path to the gate, Professor LaVaux called, "By the way, your disguise. You'll find there are several excellent oral drugs which will darken your complexion even more effectively than your present method."

Almost, Warren Casey had to laugh.

He was between assignments, which was a relief. He knew he was physically as well as mentally worn. He was going to have to take the board up on that offer of a prolonged vacation.

Taking the usual precautions in the way of avoiding possible pursuit, he returned to his own apartment. It had been a week, what with one assignment and another, and it was a pleasure to look forward to at least a matter of a few hours of complete relaxation.

He shed his clothing, showered, and then dressed in comfortably old clothing. He went to the tiny kitchen and prepared a drink, finding no ice since he had unplugged the refrigerator before leaving.

Casey dropped into his reading chair and took up the paperback he'd been reading when summoned a week ago to duty. He had forgotten the subject. Ah, yes, a swash-buckling historical novel. He snorted inwardly. It was all so simple. All the hero had to do was kill the evil duke in a duel and everything would resolve itself.

He caught himself up, Professor LaVaux's conversation coming back to him. Essentially, that was what he—what the Pacifists were trying to do. By killing the equivalent of the evil duke—individuals, in other words—they were hoping to solve the problems of the world. Nonsense, on the face of it.

He put down the novel and stared unseeing at the wall opposite. He had been an operative with the Pacifists for more than three years now. He was, he realized, probably their senior hatchetman. An agent could hardly expect to survive so long. It was against averages.

It was then that the screen of his telephone lit up.

Senator Phil McGivern's face glowered at him.

Warren Casey started, stared.

McGivern said, coldly, deliberately, "The building is surrounded, Casey. Surrender yourself. There are more than fifty security police barring any chance of escape."

The Pacifist's mind snapped to attention. Was there anything he had to do? Was there anything in the apartment that might possibly betray the organization or any individual member of it? He wanted a few moments to think.

He attempted to keep his voice even. "What do you want, McGivern?"

"My son!" The politician was glaring his triumph.

"I'm afraid Fredric is out of my hands," Casey said. Was the Senator lying about the number of police? Was there any possibility of escape?

"Then whose hands is he in? You have him, Warren Casey, but we have you."

"He's not here," Casey said. There might still be a service he could perform. Some way of warning the organization of McGivern's method of tracking him down. "How did you find me? How do you know my name?"

McGivern snorted. "You're a fool as well as a criminal. You sat in my office and spoke in the accent of your native city. I pinpointed that immediately. You told me you'd been a bomber pilot and obviously had seen action, which meant you'd been in the last war. Then as a pseudonym you used the name Jakes. Did you know that persons taking pseudonyms almost always base them on some actuality? We checked in your home city, and, sure enough, there was actually a newspaperman named Jakes. We questioned him. Did he know a former bomber pilot, a veteran of the last war. Yes, he did. A certain Warren Casey. From there on the job was an easy one—criminal. Now, *where is my son?*"

For a moment, Warren Casey felt weary compassion for the other. The Senator had worked hard to find his boy, hard and brilliantly. "I'm sorry, McGivern, I really don't know." Casey threw his glass, destroying the telephone screen.

He was on his feet, heading for the kitchen. He'd explored this escape route long ago.

The dumbwaiter was sufficiently large to accommodate him. He wedged himself into it, slipped the rope through his fingers, quickly but without fumbling. He shot downward.

In the basement, his key opened a locker. He reached in and seized the submachine pistol and two clips of cartridges. He stuffed one into a side pocket, slapped the other into the gun, threw off the safety. Already he was hurrying down the corridor toward the heating plant. He was counting on the fact that the security police had not had sufficient time to discover that this building shared its central heating and air-conditioning plant with the apartment house adjoining.

Evidently, they hadn't.

A freight elevator shot him to the roof of the next building. From here, given luck, he could cross to a still further building and make his getaway.

He emerged on the roof, shot a quick glance around.

Fifty feet away, their backs to him, stood three security police agents. Two of them armed with automatic rifles, the other with a handgun, they were peering over the parapet, probably at the windows of his apartment.

His weapon flashed to position, but then the long weariness overtook him. *No more killing. Please. No more killing.* He lowered the gun, turned and headed quietly in the opposite direction.

A voice behind him yelled, "Hey! Stop! You—"

He ran.

The burst of fire caught Warren Casey as he attempted to vault to the next building. It ripped through him and the darkness fell immediately, and far, far up from below, the last thought that was ever signaled was *That's right!*

Fifteen minutes later Senator Phil McGivern scowled down at the meaningless crumpled figure. "You couldn't have captured him?" he said sourly.

"No, sir," the security sergeant defended himself. "It was a matter of shoot him or let him escape."

McGivern snorted his disgust.

The sergeant said wonderingly, "Funny thing was, he could've finished off the three of us. We were the only ones on the roof here. He could've shot us and then got away."

One of the others said, "Probably didn't have the guts."

"No," McGivern growled. "He had plenty of guts." ■

During 1964 the young rebels of America found themselves a spokesman: a skinny, tangle-haired, booted and suede-jacketed, whiney-voiced, snarling young troubador named Bob Dylan.

For those less than totally familiar with the diction of the "country and Western" singers, Dylan's records are close to incomprehensible at first hearing. They are well worth a second. Dylan has not just something, but a great deal to say; and he says it vigorously, poetically, effectively, colloquially. He is alternately angry, sad, threatening, angry, cajoling, nostalgic, and angry. His anger is diffused: the youths who gathered their forces for the mass protests of early 1965 (the inanity of Berkeley—the dignity of Selma—the controversy of the Vietnam picketing in Washington) are people who dig Dylan—as do I.

There's one song, "Talking World War Three Blues," that starts (as near as I can make out) "One time ago crazy dream came t'me—I dreamed I was walkin' in World War Three." He walks up and down the lonesome town—lights a cigarette on a parking meter, tries to break into a shelter, steals a Cadillac, and sees one other man—who runs away. "Thought I was a communist."

He tells his dream to a psychiatrist who, it seems, has had the same dream—except that he was the only one left in his version. And then it turns out, "everybody's havin' these dreams," says Dylan.

"I'll let you be in my dream, if you'll let me be in yours."

THE NEW ENCYCLOPAEDIST
Stephen Becker

from *Fantasy and Science Fiction*

Gill, Robert   1930–2022

Leader of the "Irreconcilables" and one of the founders of
our present civilization. The Irreconcilables refused, on the
grounds of good taste and "freedom of association," to join
their fellow citizens in the vast, complex network of underground shelters constructed by "Civil Defense" authorities
(→Opera Buffa) between 1965 and 1970 at the cost of all
the prosperity, liberties, and amenities that free men everywhere were struggling for. "Gill's Bull" predicted accurately
that underground society would necessarily be authoritarian.
During the Great Alert of 1973 some 30,000 Irreconcilables
remained above ground. When, because all potential
enemies were also underground, nothing happened during
the obligatory sixty-day period, and populations sheepishly
regained the surface, Gill delivered his famous Report:
"The West Side Highway was clear; there were no school-
children in the Metropolitan Museum of Art; and there was
no television. We all caught up on our correspondence."
As a consequence, during the Second Great Alert of 1977,
the populations refused to go underground; the Irreconcilables therefore did, and enjoyed sixty days of luxurious
solitude, gourmandise, and meditation, making free use of
the libraries, cinemas, galleries, monorails, and restaurants
planned for a subcivilization of 200,000,000 people. Emerging after two months, they found a world barren of life
except for their counterparts in other nations, though many
buildings, vehicles, power plants, etc., were perfectly
usable. From these groups sprang our present highly
literate, healthy, and peaceable world population of 12,-
000,000, including only three psychiatrists and no soldiers.
(→Quantum Jump; also Darwin, Charles and "Survival of
the Fittest.")

Porphyry, Jasper   1935–20

14). Enunciator of Porphyry's Categories, P's Lament;
instigator of P's Literary Schizophrenia. The Categories
(1968) were an American literary achievement, and were
three. (1) comprised 90% of the writers of the time. Their
"talent," as described by P, consisted of a middling facility
in the manipulation of a minimal vocabulary rudimentary
perceptions; unsullied ignorance of man's history; disdain
of reason; and a violent, probably psychotic, attachment to
the sentimental. Writers of this group were barely dis-
tinguishable in style or attitude and naturally set great
store by publicity, as only the public's automatic responses
(→Pavlov, I.P.) maintained them. They accepted without
question the prevalent mythos (then known as "reality")
and manufactured novel after novel in its support, almost
all about hanky-panky (urban, suburban, rural), with ani-
madversions on the "emotional" conflicts of the era, which
were not truly emotional, but simple oppositions of childish
egos or absurd fears. These writers were essentially
masochistic and their technique was in the juvenile tradition: an uninterrupted series of insignificant events in the
lives of unbelievable characters, reported in conscientiously
pedestrian prose. This was called "the writer's obligation to
the reader," or "narrative power," the latter a phrase used
often by reviewers, seldom by critics. First novels by any
of this group were usually said either to have "catapulted
him into the first rank of American novelists" or to "show
an immense promise."

(2) were the opposition, sometimes called the avant-
garde. They protested the mythos angrily but failed to see
that by doing so they were investing it with all the power
the Yahoos had claimed for it (→Swift, Jonathan). Their
protests naturally failed to reform society and were conse-
quently characterized, and vitiated, by a progressively
surlier sadism. These men did, however, rouse the public
to an imitation of thought. A few had a serious talent for
language and some understanding of their culture, and
when they resisted absorption by the equestrian classes they
were an influence for awareness and sanity. They were
called anti-Puritans, and were said to concentrate on sex.
P pointed out that a typewriter was not a woman.

(3) was a woefully small group that looked upon the

mythos with generous compassion and therefore transcended it. In a professional sense they were somewhat indifferent to it. They were required for survival to acknowledge it, but in their novels they went about the business of a writer, which was, again in P's words, "to get inside readers by making them feel what they are, and not by piercing them with exclamation points." They derived neither from →Richardson and →Ronsard nor from →Dostoievski and →Zola, but from →Rabelais, →Cervantes, and →Fielding. Each had an individual and arresting style. They all knew how to laugh. They enlarged their readers. This third force of novelists (not to be lightly confused with the political third force of the time) did, as we know, endure. (→Bellow, Saul; Cheever, John)

P's Lament and P's Literary Schizophrenia rose out of the debasement of language. The extravagantly publicized new edition of an authoritative American dictionary sanctioned the use of "infer" for "imply," which the average man found convenient; in no time at all "humble" meant "proud" (→Theology), etc., and the number of words in use dropped sharply, making all men intellectual equals (→Orwell, George). A logical result was "speed-reading." If meaning had no importance, and the act of communicating was all, then writing could be evaluated only quantitatively. (This was a great comfort to Category (1), above.) The fad was much exalted by a Chief Executive, probably in understandable reaction to the even more debatable linquistic achievements of the preceding administration. "Five thousand words per minute" replaced automobiles and tax evasion as symbols of status, and when a United States Senator dropped the phrase "ten thousand words per minute," P responded with his famous Lament: "I write slow," he said. "I hate the four-eyed son of a bitch." He had just spent a year on a novel of one hundred thousand words that would occupy the Senator for only ten minutes, and there was always a chance that the Senator would review it. P then introduced a new technique that made speed-reading virtually impossible: he spaced hi swo rd sandle tter sir regul arly. He was aware that certain mental disorders could be brought on by flashing lights, repeated sounds, etc. (→Advertising Industry), and was gratified when a new malady, deliberately induced by young writers who joined him, and character-ized by stammering, blood-shot eyes, and partial amnesia, was named P's Literary Schizophrenia. Shortly the fads ended; words like "disinterested," "presently," and "hope-fully" were restored to proper use; intelligibility in prose composition was required of all university professors ex-cept, of course, in metaphysics. There is a statue of P adjacent to the Jefferson Monument (→Jefferson, Thomas; also Style) in Washington, D.C.

Newhouse, John Jacob 1914– 1977). United States Senator from Alaska, 1963–77. The years 1970 and 1971 are called the "era of Newhousery." The production and commercial success of several Russo-American films had temporarily reduced international ten-sions; certain House and Senate Investigating Committees faced the loss of appropriations in a long-awaited orgy of economy. N saved the day by an oration in North Judson, Indiana, warning that America was in grave danger of subversion, rot of moral fibre, and financial ruin through the machinations of adulterers, who, he claimed, had in-filtrated all levels of national life. He then charged that there were 253 adulterers in the Department of Health, Education, and Welfare, and his speech was given great publicity. He later reduced the figure to 81, and still later to 52, but by then it was generally agreed that he had alerted patriotic citizens to a serious peril.

Hearings were begun at once, with full television cover-age. Particular attention was focused on aliens and college graduates. A small group of writers protested; they were immediately subpoenaed by the Newhouse Committee. Most took refuge in the First or Fifth Amendments to the Constitution, and became the core of an organized re-sistance; their slogan was "A gentleman may poach but not peach." Thousands everywhere were identified as known offenders by cooperative witnesses, many of whom were remunerated for their time and trouble; federal em-ployment increased by 14.5% during the first three months of hearings. These witnesses testified that they had been present at gatherings in various parts of the country osten-sibly arranged for the purpose of drinking, playing cards, folk dancing, etc., but which were actually corroborees of the licentious. The evidence was often not direct but circumstantial: winking, off-color stories, removal of shoes, unexplained absences in the kitchen. The guilty were said to be in constant and nationwide communication, exchanging names and addresses and transmitting messages in code—a bouquet of orchids might mean one thing, a bottle of champagne another, etc. For their expertise in these arcana reformed professional women were highly valued; some remained closeted with investigators for hours on end, and produced exhaustive lists of putative offenders. Presumed conspirators often lost their jobs and the esteem of their neighbors; they were denied federal or state employment, and were exposed when found in sensitive positions.

The moral climate became generally severe. Metropolitan areas reported numerous vacancies in small, expensive apartments. The Furriers' Association marched on Washington. All printed matter from Sweden was banned. Private groups sprang up to support the government's policies, e.g. the Cos Cob Chastity Crusade and the Boo-Boo Caraway Society, named for the first American woman since 1945 to be betrayed by Kummel. Many citizens demonstrated good faith by compiling dossiers on their neighbors. Bausch and Lomb announced an extra dividend. The Newhouse Act prohibited the teaching and advocacy, or conspiracy to teach and advocate, "any doctrine or practice that might tend to suggest the possibility of immorality," and was passed over only two dissenting votes, both by elderly Senators. Librarians winnowed their shelves, removing, e.g., the works of →Dante, →Shakespeare, and →Elinor Glyn; a new edition of →Louisa May Alcott was instantly successful. The two elections of →Grover Cleveland were retroactively invalidated; after a Democratic protest, →Warren G. Harding's victory was also voided. Europeans were horrified by these events; France withdrew from NATO, and →General de Gaulle stated publicly that so excitable a people could not be trusted with the destinies of free men (*"Ils sont cinglés là-bas"*).

The first effective resistance was offered by Dr. Leo Douglas, a psychiatrist in Cleveland, Ohio, who affirmed unblushingly that he knew several people who had trans-

gressed from the noblest of motives, and who were a credit
to humanity; but he declined to name them. Rebuked and
threatened by N, Douglas then declared that any investigation of the practice, or legislation limiting it, was an in-
fringement of his rights under the First Amendment—not
of his freedom of speech, but of "the right of the people
peaceably to assemble." N pointed out that the legal
definition of "assembly" specified "three or more people,"
and the doctor's reply ("Douglas's Riposte") was, "You
run your private life and I'll run mine." He was convicted
of contempt, but his appeal was sustained by the Supreme
Court. N then turned his attention to the United States
Navy; he persisted in asking who had promoted Lieutenant-
Commander Wycherly, a notoriously suave fire-control
officer reputed to have cut a suspicious series of notches in
his slide-rule. But the hearings had by then lost much of
their point, thanks to Douglas, and the Navy, jealous of
its traditions, refused to be intimidated. The investigation
lost momentum, and finally came to a halt with the appearance of Bubbles Freeburk of Elgin, Illinois, who,
paradoxically, never even testified. As she entered the
chamber N was observed to blench, and the proceedings
were halted until a doctor could be found. The committee
never sat again. N died in the Great Holocaust, during
a Senate debate on the appropriation for anti-missile
missiles.   ■

Neither Stephen Becker nor John D. MacDonald need any introduction to the general bookbuyer. So far as I know, the Ency-
clopaedia entries here are Becker's only venture into SF. Mac-
Donald is an old hand in the field: some of his short stories
from the SF magazines of ten or more years ago are still vivid
in my memory. (One of the best, "A Child Is Crying," has recently
been re-reprinted in Damon Knight's Paperback Library anthology, **The Shape of Things.** Also, if you missed it when it came
out, Gold Medal has just reissued the 1962 science-fantasy-sex-
suspense novel, **The Girl, the Gold Watch and Everything.**)

As it happens, "Joe Lee" is a departure for MacDonald. It is
not science fiction—unless you use the label in the Bradbury
sense:

"Q. Are you attracted to science fiction because in a sense
you are setting up your own standards, your own world, peopled

by creatures of your imagination?

"A. . . . Science has raped as well as lovingly seeded our land. We are the natural children of that seeding and that un-gentle rape. This is a science-fictional time. . . . I am attracted, therefore, to my time, not to science fiction per se, but rather to the fantastic mechanistic elements that explode, implode, and drive the machineries of our existence. Science fiction in these circumstances is simple exhalation after decades of breathing in."—from an interview in Show, Dec., 1964.

THE LEGEND OF JOE LEE
John D. MacDonald
from *Cosmopolitan*

"Tonight," Sergeant Lazeer said, "we get him for sure."

We were in a dank office in the Afaloosa County Court-house in the flat wetlands of south central Florida. I had come over from Lauderdale on the half chance of a human interest story that would tie in with the series we were do-ing on the teen-age war against the square world of the adult.

He called me over to the table where he had the county map spread out. The two other troopers moved in beside me.

"It's a full moon night and he'll be out for sure," Lazeer said, "and what we're fixing to do is bottle him on just the right stretch, where he got no way off it, no old back-country roads he knows like the shape of his own fist. And here we got it." He put brackets at either end of a string-straight road.

Trooper McCullum said softly, "That there, Mister, is a eighteen mile straight, and we cruised it slow, and you turn off it, you're in the deep ditch and the black mud and the 'gator water."

Lazeer said, "We stake out both ends, hide back good with lights out. We got radio contact, so when he comes, whistling in either end, we got him bottled."

He looked up at me as though expecting an opinion, and

I said, "I don't know a thing about road blocks, Sergeant, but it looks as if you could trap him."

"You ride with me, Mister, and we'll get you a story."

"There's one thing you haven't explained, Sergeant. You said you know who the boy is. Why don't you just pick him up at home?"

The other trooper, Frank Gaiders said, "Because that fool kid ain't been home since he started this crazy business five, six months ago. His name is Joe Lee Cuddard, from over to Lasco City. His folks don't know where he is, and don't much care, him and that Farris girl he was running with, so we figure the pair of them is off in the piney woods someplace, holed up in some abandoned shack, coming out at night for kicks, making fools of us."

"Up till now, boy," Lazeer said. "Up till tonight. Tonight is the end."

"But when you've met up with him on the highway," I asked, "you haven't been able to catch him?"

The three big, weathered men looked at each other with slow, sad amusement, and McCullum sighed, "I come the closest. The way these cars are beefed up as interceptors, they can do a dead honest hundred and twenty. I saw him across the flats, booming to where the two road forks come together up ahead, so I floored it and I was flat out when the roads joined, and not over fifty yards behind him. In two minutes he had me by a mile, and in four minutes it was near two, and then he was gone. That comes to a hundred and fifty, my guess."

I showed my astonishment. "What the hell does he drive?"

Lazeer opened the table drawer and fumbled around in it and pulled out a tattered copy of a hot-rodder magazine. He opened it to a page where readers had sent in pictures of their cars. It didn't look like anything I had ever seen. Most of it seemed to be bare frame, with a big chromed engine. There was a teardrop-shaped passenger compartment mounted between the big rear wheels, bigger than the front wheels, and there was a tail-fin arrangement that swept up and out and then curved back so that the high rear ends of the fins almost met.

"That engine," Frank Gaiders said, "it's a '61 Pontiac, the big one he bought wrecked and fixed up, with blowers and special cams and every damn thing. Put the rest of it together himself. You can see in the letter there, he calls it a C.M. Special. C.M. is for Clarissa May, that Farris girl he took off with. I saw that thing just one time, oh, seven, eight months ago, right after he got it all finished. We got this magazine from his daddy. I saw it at the Amoco gas in Lasco City. You could near give it a ticket standing still. 'Strawberry flake paint' it says in the letter. Damnedest thing, bright strawberry with little like gold flakes in it, then covered with maybe seventeen coats of lacquer, all rubbed down so you look down into that paint like it was six inches deep. Headlights all the hell over the front of it and big taillights all over the back, and shiny pipes sticking out. Near two year he worked on it. Big racing flats like the drag-strip kids use over to the airport."

I looked at the coarse-screen picture of the boy standing beside the car, hands on his hips, looking very young, very ordinary, slightly self-conscious.

"It wouldn't spoil anything for you, would it," I asked, "if I went and talked to his people, just for background?"

"Long as you say nothing about what we're fixing to do," Lazeer said. "Just be back by eight-thirty this evening."

Lasco City was a big brave name for a hamlet of about five hundred. They told me at the sundries store to take the west road and the Cuddard place was a half mile on the left, name on the mailbox. It was a shacky place, chickens in the dusty yard, fence sagging. Leo Cuddard was home from work and I found him out in back, unloading cinder block from an ancient pickup. He was stripped to the waist, a lean, sallow man who looked undernourished and exhausted. But the muscles in his spare back writhed and knotted when he lifted the blocks. He had pale hair and pale eyes and a narrow mouth. He would not look directly at me. He grunted and kept on working as I introduced myself and stated my business.

Finally he straightened and wiped his forehead with his narrow arm. When those pale eyes stared at me, for some reason it made me remember the grisly reputation Florida troops acquired in the Civil War. Tireless, deadly, merciless.

"That boy warn't no help to me, Mister, but he warn't no trouble neither. The onliest thing on his mind was that car. I didn't hold with it, but I didn't put down no foot. He fixed up that old shed there to work in, and he needed something, he went out and earned up the money to buy it. They was a crowd of them around most times, helpin' him, boys workin' and gals watchin'. Them tight-pants girls. Have radios on batteries set around so as they could twisty dance while them boys hammered that metal out. When I worked around and overheared 'em, I swear I couldn't make out more'n one word from seven. What he done was take that car to some national show, for prizes and such. But one day he just took off, like they do nowadays."

"Do you hear from him at all?"

He grinned. "I don't hear *from* him, but I sure God hear *about* him."

"How about brothers and sisters?"

"They's just one sister, older, up to Waycross, Georgia, married to an electrician, and me and his stepmother."

As if on cue, a girl came out onto the small back porch. She couldn't have been more than eighteen. Advanced pregnancy bulged the front of her cotton dress. Her voice was a shrill, penetrating whine. "Leo? Leo, honey, that can opener thing just now busted clean off the wall."

"Mind if I take a look at that shed?"

"You help yourself, Mister."

The shed was astonishingly neat. The boy had rigged up droplights. There was a pale blue pegboard wall hung with shining tools. On closer inspection I could see that rust was beginning to fleck the tools. On the workbench were technical journals and hot-rodder magazines. I looked at the improvised engine hoist, at the neat shelves of paint and lubricant.

The Farris place was nearer the center of the village. Some of them were having their evening meal. There were six adults as near as I could judge, and perhaps a dozen children from toddlers on up to tall, lanky boys. Clarissa May's mother came out onto the front porch to talk to me, explaining that her husband drove an interstate truck from the cooperative and he was away for the next few days. Mrs. Farris was grossly fat, but with delicate features, an indication of the beauty she must have once had. The rocking chair creaked under her weight and she fanned herself with a newspaper.

"I can tell you, it like to broke our hearts the way Clarissa May done us. If'n I told LeRoy once, I told him a thousand times, no good would ever come of her messin' with that Cuddard boy. His daddy is trashy. Ever so often they take him in for drunk and put him on the county road gang sixty or ninety days, and that Stubbins child he married, she's next door to feeble-witted. But children get to a certain size and know everything and turn their backs on you like an enemy. You write this up nice and in it put the message her momma and daddy want her home bad, and maybe she'll see it and come on in. You know what the Good Book says about sharper'n a sarpent's tooth. I pray to the good Lord they had the sense to drive that fool car up to Georgia and get married up at least. Him nineteen and her seventeen. The young ones are going clean out of hand these times. One night racing through this county the way they do, showing off, that Cuddard boy is going to kill hisself and my child, too."

"Was she hard to control in other ways, Mrs. Farris?"

"No sir, she was neat and good and pretty and quiet, and she had the good marks. It was just about Joe Lee Cuddard she turned mulish. I think I would have let LeRoy whale that out of her if it hadn't been for her trouble.

"You're easier on a young one when there's no way of knowing how long she could be with you. Doc Mathis, he had us taking her over to the Miami clinic. Sometimes they kept her and sometimes they didn't, and she'd get behind in her school and then catch up fast. Many times we taken her over there. She's got the sick blood and it takes her poorly. She should be right here, where's help to care for her in the bad spells. It was October last year, we were over to the church bingo, LeRoy and me, and Clarissa May been resting up in her bed a few days, and that wild boy come in and taking her off in that snorty car, the little ones couldn't stop him. When I think of her out there . . . poorly and all . . ."

At a little after nine we were in position. I was with Sergeant Lazeer at the west end of that eighteen-mile stretch of State Road 21. The patrol car was backed into a narrow dirt road, lights out. Gaiders and McCullum were similarly situated at the east end of the trap. We were smeared with insect repellent, and we had used spray on the backs of each other's shirts where the mosquitoes were biting through the thin fabric.

Lazeer had repeated his instructions over the radio, and we composed ourselves to wait. "Not much travel on this road this time of year," Lazeer said. "But some tourists come through at the wrong time, they could mess this up. We just got to hope that don't happen."

"Can you block the road with just one car at each end?"

"If he comes through from the other end, I move up quick and put it crosswise where he can't get past, and Frank has a place like that at the other end. Crosswise with the lights and the dome blinker on, but we both are going to stand clear because maybe he can stop it and maybe he can't. But whichever way he comes, we got to have the free car run close herd so he can't get time to turn around when he sees he's bottled."

Lazeer turned out to be a lot more talkative than I had anticipated. He had been in law enforcement for twenty years and had some violent stories. I sensed he was feeding them to me, waiting for me to suggest I write a book about him. From time to time we would get out of the car and move around a little.

"Sergeant, you're pretty sure you've picked the right time and place?"

"He runs on the nights the moon is big. Three or four nights out of the month. He doesn't run the main highways, just these back-country roads—the long straight paved stretches where he can really wind that thing up. Lord God, he goes through towns like a rocket. From reports we got, he runs the whole night through, and this is one way he comes, one way or the other, maybe two, three times before moonset. We got to get him. He's got folks laughing at us."

I sat in the car half-listening to Lazeer tell a tale of blood and horror. I could hear choruses of swamp toads mingling with the whine of insects close to my ears, looking for a biting place. A couple of times I had heard the bass throb of a 'gator.

Suddenly Lazeer stopped and I sensed his tenseness. He leaned forward, head cocked. And then, mingled with the wet country shrilling, and then overriding it, I heard the oncoming high-pitched snarl of high combustion.

"Hear it once and you don't forget it," Lazeer said, and unhooked the mike from the dash and got through to McCullum and Gaiders. "He's coming through this end, boys. Get yourself set."

He hung up and in the next instant the C.M. Special went by. It was a resonant howl that stirred echoes inside the inner ear. It was a tearing, bursting rush of wind that rattled fronds and turned leaves over. It was a dark shape in moonlight, slamming by, the howl diminishing as the wind of passage died.

Lazeer plunged the patrol car out onto the road in a screeching turn, and as we straightened out, gathering speed, he yelled to me, "Damn fool runs without lights when the moon is bright enough."

As had been planned, we ran without lights, too, to keep Joe Lee from smelling the trap until it was too late. I tightened my seat belt and peered at the moonlit road. Lazeer had estimated we could make it to the far end in ten minutes or a little less. The world was like a photographic negative—white world and black trees and brush, and no shades of grey. As we came quickly up to speed, the heavy sedan began to feel strangely light. It toe-danced, tender and capricious, the wind roar louder than the engine sound. I kept wondering what would happen if Joe Lee stopped dead up there in darkness. I kept staring ahead for the murderous bulk of his vehicle.

Soon I could see the distant red wink of the other sedan, and then the bright cone where the headlights shone off the shoulder into the heavy brush. When my eyes adjusted to that brightness, I could no longer see the road. We came down on them with dreadful speed. Lazeer suddenly snapped our lights on, touched the siren. We were going to see Joe Lee trying to back and turn around on the narrow paved road, and we were going to block him and end the night games.

We saw nothing. Lazeer pumped the brakes. He cursed. We came to a stop ten feet from the side of the other patrol car. McCullum and Gaiders came out of the shadows.

Lazeer and I undid our seat belts and got out of the car.

"We didn't see nothing and we didn't hear a thing," Frank Gaiders said.

Lazeer summed it up. "OK, then. I was running without lights, too. Maybe the first glimpse he got of your flasher, he cramps it over onto the left sholder, tucks it over as far as he dares. I could go by without seeing him. He backs around and goes back the way he came, laughing hisself sick. There's the second chance he tried that and took it too far, and he's wedged in a ditch. Then there's the third chance he lost it. He could have dropped a wheel off onto the shoulder and tripped hisself and gone flying three hundred feet into the swamp. So what we do, we go back there slow. I'll go first and keep my spotlight on the right, and you keep yours on the left. Look for that car and for places where he could have busted through."

At the speed Lazeer drove, it took over a half hour to traverse the eighteen-mile stretch. He pulled off at the road where we had waited. He seemed very depressed, yet at the same time amused.

They talked, then he drove me to the courthouse where my car was parked. He said, "We'll work out something tighter and I'll give you a call. You might as well be in at the end."

I drove sedately back to Lauderdale.

Several days later, just before noon on a bright Sunday, Lazeer phoned me at my apartment and said, "You want to be in on the finish of this thing, you better do some hustling and leave right now."

"You've got him?"

"In a manner of speaking." He sounded sad and wry. "He dumped that machine into a canal off Route 27 about twelve miles south of Okeelanta. The wrecker'll be winching it out anytime now. The diver says he and the gal are still in it. It's been on the radio news. Diver read the tag, and it's his. Last year's. He didn't trouble hisself getting a new one."

I wasted no time driving to the scene. I certainly had no trouble identifying it. There were at least a hundred cars pulled off on both sides of the highway. A traffic-control officer tried to wave me on by, but when I showed him my press card and told him Lazeer had phoned me, he had me turn in and park beside a patrol car near the center of activity.

I spotted Lazeer on the canal bank and went over to him. A big man in face mask, swim fins and air tank was preparing to go down with the wrecker hook.

Lazeer greeted me and said, "It pulled loose the first time, so he's going to try to get it around the rear axle this time. It's in twenty feet of water, right side up, in the black mud."

"Did he lose control?"

"Hard to say. What happened, early this morning a fellow was goofing around in a little airplane, flying low, parallel to the canal, the water like a mirror, and he seen something down in there so he came around and looked again, then he found a way to mark the spot, opposite those three trees away over there, so he came into his home field and phoned it in, and we had that diver down by nine this morning. I got here about ten."

"I guess this isn't the way you wanted it to end, Sergeant."

"It sure God isn't. It was a contest between him and me, and I wanted to get him my own way. But I guess it's a good thing he's off the night roads."

I looked around. The red and white wrecker was positioned and braced. Ambulance attendants were leaning against their vehicle, smoking and chatting. Sunday traffic slowed and was waved on by.

"I guess you could say his team showed up," Lazeer said.

Only then did I realize the strangeness of most of the waiting vehicles. The cars were from a half-dozen counties, according to the tag numbers. There were many big, gaudy, curious monsters not unlike the C.M. Special in basic layout, but quite different in design. They seemed like a visitation of Martian beasts. There were dirty fenderless sedans from the thirties with modern power plants under the hoods, and big rude racing numbers painted on the side doors. There were other cars which looked normal at first glance, but then seemed to squat oddly low, lines clean and sleek where the Detroit chrome had been taken off, the holes leaded up.

The cars and the kids were of another race. Groups of

them formed, broke up and re-formed. Radios brought in a dozen stations. They drank Cokes and perched in dense flocks on open convertibles. They wandered from car to car. It had a strange carnival flavor, yet more ceremonial. From time to time somebody would start one of the car engines, rev it up to a bursting roar, and let it die away.

All the girls had long burnished hair and tidy blouses or sun tops and a stillness in their faces, a curious confidence of total acceptance which seemed at odds with the frivolous and provocative tightness of their short shorts, stretch pants, jeans. All the boys were lean, their hairdos carefully ornate, their shoulders high and square, and they moved with the lazy grace of young jungle cats. Some of the couples danced indolently, staring into each other's eyes with a frozen and formal intensity, never touching, bright hair swinging, girls' hips pumping in the stylized ceremonial twist.

Along the line I found a larger group. A boy was strumming slow chords on a guitar, a girl making sharp and erratic fill-in rhythm on a set of bongos. Another boy, in nasal and whining voice, seemed to improvise lyrics as he sang them. "C.M. Special, let it get out and *go.*/C.M. Special, let it way out and *go.*/Iron runs fast and the moon runs slow."

The circle watched and listened with a contained intensity.

Then I heard the winch whining. It seemed to grow louder as, one by one, the other sounds stopped. The kids began moving toward the wrecker. They formed a big silent semicircle. The taut woven cable, coming in very slowly, stretched down at an angle through the sun glitter on the black-brown water.

The snore of a passing truck covered the winch noise for a moment.

"Coming good now," a man said.

First you could see an underwater band of silver, close to the dropoff near the bank. Then the first edges of the big sweeping fins broke the surface, then the broad rear bumper, then the rich curves of the strawberry paint. Where it wasn't clotted with wet weed or stained with mud, the paint glowed rich and new and brilliant. There was a slow sound from the kids, a sigh, a murmur, a shifting.

As it came up farther, the dark water began to spurt from it, and as the water level inside dropped, I saw, through a smeared window, the two huddled masses, the slumped boy and girl, side by side, still belted in.

I wanted to see no more. Lazeer was busy, and I got into my car and backed out and went home and mixed a drink.

I started work on it at about three-thirty that afternoon. It would be a feature for the following Sunday. I worked right on through until two in the morning. It was only two thousand words, but it was very tricky and I wanted to get it just right. I had to serve two masters. I had to give lip service to the editorial bias that this sort of thing was wrong, yet at the same time I wanted to capture, for my own sake, the flavor of legend. These kids were making a special world we could not share. They were putting all their skills and dreams and energies to work composing the artifacts of a subculture, power, beauty, speed, skill and rebellion. Our culture was giving them damned little, so they were fighting for a world of their own, with its own customs, legends and feats of valor, its own music, its own ethics and morality.

I took it in Monday morning and left it on Si Walther's desk, with the hope that if it were published intact, it might become a classic. I called it "The Little War of Joe Lee Cuddard."

I didn't hear from Si until just before noon. He came out and dropped it on my desk. "Sorry," he said.

"What's the matter with it?"

"Hell, it's a very nice bit. But we don't publish fiction. You should have checked it out better, Marty, like you usually do. The examiner says those kids have been in the bottom of that canal for maybe eight months. I had Sam check her out through the clinic. She was damn near terminal eight months ago. What probably happened, the boy went to see her and found her so bad off he got scared and decided to rush her to Miami. She was still in her pajamas, with a sweater over them. That way it's a human-interest bit. I had Helen do it. It's page one this afternoon, boxed."

I took my worthless story, tore it in half and dropped it into the wastebasket. Sergeant Lazeer's bad guess about the identity of his moonlight road runner had made me look like an incompetent jackass. I vowed to check all facts, get all names right, and never again indulge in glowing, strawberry-flake prose.

Three weeks later I got a phone call from Sergeant Lazeer.

He said, "I guess you figured out we got some boy coming in from out of county to fun us these moonlight nights."

"Yes, I did."

"I'm right sorry about you wasting that time and effort when we were thinking we were after Joe Lee Cuddard. We're having some bright moonlight about now, and it'll run full tomorrow night. You want to come over, we can show you some fun, because I got a plan that's dead sure. We tried it last night, but there was just one flaw, and he got away through a road we didn't know about. Tomorrow he won't get that chance to melt away."

I remembered the snarl of that engine, the glimpse of a dark shape, the great wind of passage. Suddenly the backs of my hands prickled. I remembered the emptiness of that stretch of road when we searched it. Could there have been that much pride and passion, labor and love and hope, that Clarissa May and Joe Lee could forever ride the night roads of their home county, balling through the silver moonlight? And what curious message had assembled all those kids from six counties so quickly?

"You there? You still there?"

"Sorry, I was trying to remember my schedule. I don't think I can make it."

"Well, we'll get him for sure this time."

"Best of luck, Sergeant."

"Six cars this time. Barricades. And a spotter plane. He hasn't got a chance if he comes into the net."

I guess I should have gone. Maybe hearing it again, glimpsing the dark shape, feeling the stir of the night wind, would have convinced me of its reality. They didn't get him, of course. But they came so close, so very close. But they left just enough room between a heavy barricade and a live-oak tree, an almost impossibly narrow place to slam through. But thread it he did, and rocketback onto the hard-top and plunge off, leaving the fading, dying contralto drone.

Sergeant Lazeer is grimly readying next month's trap. He says it is the final one. Thus far, all he has captured are the two little marks, a streak of paint on the rough edge of a timber sawhorse, another nudge of paint on the trunk of the oak. Strawberry red. Flecked with gold. ■

"Are you a moralist?"

In the same Show magazine interview quoted earlier (and well worth reading in its entirety if you can get hold of a back issue), Ray Bradbury answered this question with:

"I think I am, above everything, for the question of morality arises again and again with each machine that we create. . . . While machines are amoral, sometimes the very manner of their construction, and the power locked into their frame, inspires man to lunacy, idiocy, or evil. Some of the greatest liberals of our time are illiberal and demonic in a car. Some of the greatest conservatives become radical destructionists when they step on the starter and rampage off after murder. I once asked a class in design at the Art Center in Los Angeles to design a car that would cause men not to prove their masculinity every time they slung themselves into the bucket seat. . . ."

I thought—indeed, I knew—no one could write another free-way satire I would want to read, let alone reread, or reprint. One of the differences may be that the author had not read any of the others: or so at least, his brief biographical note suggests. A professional musician, James Houston has been writing for eight years, publishing stories and poems in literary magazines and men's magazines in this country and in England. An essay on California appeared in a recent issue of Holiday; his first book, **The Sport of Hawaiian Kings,** a history of surf-riding in the Pacific, was published this year by Tuttle.

GAS MASK
James D. Houston
from *Nugget*

   Charlie Bates didn't mind the freeways much. As he often told his wife when he arrived home from work, he could take them or leave them alone. He listed freeways among those curious obstacle-conveniences with which the world seemed so unavoidably cluttered. Charlie was neither surprised nor dismayed, then, when one summer afternoon about five-thirty the eight lanes of traffic around him slowed to a creep and finally to a standstill.

He grew uneasy only when movement resumed half an hour later. His engine was off; the car was in gear; yet it moved forward slowly, as if another car were pushing. Charlie turned around, but the driver behind was turned, too, and the driver beyond him. All the drivers in all the lanes were turned to see who was pushing. Charlie heard his license plate crinkle. He opened his door and stood on the sill.

He was on a high, curving overpass that looked down on a lower overpass and farther down onto a 12-lane straightaway leading to the city's center. As far as Charlie could see in any direction cars were jammed end to end, lane to lane, and nothing moved. The pushing had stopped. Evidently there was nowhere else to push.

He looked into the cars near him. The drivers leaned a little with the curve's sloping bank. Nobody seemed disturbed. They waited quietly. All the engines were off now. Below him the lower levels waited, too—thousands of cars and not a sound, no horns, no one yelling. At first the silence bothered Charlie, frightened him. He decided, however, that it really was the only civilized way to behave. "No use getting worked up," he thought. He climbed back in and closed the door as softly as he could.

As Charlie got used to the silence, he found it actually restful. Another hour passed. Then a helicopter flew over, and a loudspeaker announced, "May I have your attention, please. You are part of a citywide traffic deadlock. It will take at least 24 hours to clear. You have the choice of remaining overnight or leaving your car on the freeway. The city will provide police protection through the crisis."

The 'copter boomed its message about every 50 yards. A heavy murmur followed it down the freeway. The driver next to Charlie leaned out his window.

"Are they nuts?"

Charlie looked at him.

"They must be nuts. Twenty-four hours to clear a goddamn traffic jam."

Charlie shook his head, sharing the man's bafflement.

"Probably a pile-up further down," the man said. "I've seen 'em before. Never takes over an hour or two. I don't know about you, but I'm stickin' it out. If they think I'm gonna leave my goddamn Valiant out here on the freeway, they're all wet."

His name was Arvin Bainbridge. While two more hours passed, he and Charlie chatted about traffic and the world. It was getting dark when Charlie decided he at least ought to phone his wife. Arvin thought the jam would break any minute, so Charlie waited a while longer. Nothing happened.

Finally Charlie climbed out, intending to find a phone booth. He realized, however, that in order to reach the ground he'd have to hike a couple of miles to an exit. Luckily Arvin had a tow rope in a trunk. Charlie tied it to the railing, waved his thanks, swung over the side and hand-over-handed to the second level. From there he slid out onto a high tree limb and shinnied to the ground.

Gazing up at the freeway's massive concrete underside and at Arvin's rope dangling far above him, Charlie knew he'd never climb back. "What the hell," he said to himself, "I might as well go home. The cops'll be around to watch things. Besides, the car's all paid for." He began searching for a bus or a cab. But everything, it seemed, was tied up in the jam.

In a bar where he stopped for a beer to cool off, he learned that every exit, every approach, every lane in the city's complex freeway system was jammed. "And ya know, it's funny," the bartender told him, "there wasn't a single accident. It all happened so gradual, they say. Things slowed down little by little, and the whole town stopped just about at once. Some guys didn't even use their brakes. Just went from one mile an hour to a dead stop."

It took Charlie two hours to walk home. When he arrived his wife, Fay, was frantic.

"Why didn't you call?"

"I started to, honey . . ."

"And what happened to your pants?"

He glanced sheepishly at his torn sharkskin slacks. "I was shinnying down this tree. I guess somebody left a nail in it."

"For God's sake, Charlie, this is no time to kid. If you knew how worried . . ."

"I'm not kidding. You're lucky I got down at all. Some of the guys are still up there—the older guys—the fat ones—couldn't get over the rails. And a lotta guys wouldn't leave. Probably be out all night."

She looked ready to cry, and she stared as if he were insane. "Charlie, please . . ." He put an arm around her and drew her close. "What happened, Charlie? Where have you been?"

He guided her to the sofa and they sat down. His hairy knee stuck up through the torn cloth. "I thought you'd see it on TV or something."

"See *what* on TV?"

While Fay sobbed and sniffled, he told her the whole story. By the time he finished she was sitting up straight and glaring at him.

"Charlie Bates, do you mean you just left our car out on the freeway?"

"What else could I do, honey? I couldn't stay up there all night—not in a Volkswagen. I'd catch cold. I'd be all cramped up."

"You could've got into somebody else's car. This Arvin fellow would have let you. Somebody with a heater or a big back seat or something."

"You can't just barge into somebody else's car and stay overnight, honey. Anyway, I wanted to phone. That's why I came down in the first place."

She rubbed his bare knee. "Oh, Charlie." Leaning against him again she said, "At least nothing happened to *you*. That's the most important thing."

She snuggled next to him, and they were quiet, until she said, "But Charlie, what'll we do?"

"About what?"

"About the car."

"Wait it out, I guess. Wait till tomorrow at least, until they break the jam. Then get back out there. Of course, that won't be as easy as it sounds. Probably have to get over to the nearest approach and hike in—maybe two, three miles of freeway, up the center strip, I suppose— plus getting to the approach itself, which is right in the middle of town. Maybe I can borrow a bike. I don't know quite how we'll . . ."

"Say. Don and Louise have a two-seater. Maybe we can borrow that and both go."

"Maybe," Charlie said wearily. "Let's worry about that tomorrow. I'm bushed."

The next morning Charlie borrowed the big two-seater from Don and Louise, Fay packed a lunch, and they pedaled across the city, figuring to get there fairly early, to be on hand when their car was free, although an early solution was no longer likely. The morning news predicted another 36 hours before traffic would be moving. The jam now included not only the freeways, but all main streets and key intersections, where buses, streetcars and trucks were still entangled. It even extended beyond the city. Police had tried to block incoming traffic, but it was impossible. All highways transversed the city or its net of suburbs. Impatient motorists, discrediting police reports, finally broke the road blocks, and the confusion was extending in all directions by hundreds of cars an hour.

Charlie and Fay smugly bypassed all that, following a devious route of unblocked streets that he mapped out after watching the news on TV. They pedaled most of the morning. At last they mounted a high bluff and decided to ride an elevator to the roof of an apartment building that rose above the freeway where their car was parked. Charlie brought along a pair of Navy binoculars. From that vantage point they ate lunch and surveyed the curving rows of silent cars.

"Can you see ours, Charlie?"

"Yeah. She looks okay. A little squeezed up, but okay."

"Lemme see."

"Here."

"Gee," Fay said. "Some of those poor men are still sitting out there. Don't you know their wives are worried."

"Their wives probably heard the news. Everybody must know by now."

"Still worried though, I'll bet." She hugged Charlie and pecked his cheek. "I'm so glad you came home." Then, peering again, "I'll bet those men are hungry. Maybe we should take them some sandwiches."

"Take a lot of sandwiches to feed everybody stuck on the freeway, honey."

"I mean for the men right around our car. That Arvin, for instance. You know . . . your friends, sort of."

"I don't really know them that well, Fay."

"Well, we ought to do something."

"Red Cross is probably out," Charlie said. "Isn't that a cross on that helicopter way down there by the city hall? Here, gimme the glasses."

"I'll be darned," Fay said. "It is. They're dropping little packages."

"Here. Lemme see. Yeah. Yeah, that's just what they're doing. Guys are standing on the roofs of their cars, waving. I guess it's been a pretty tough night."

"The poor dears."

Charlie munched a tuna sandwich and scanned the city like a skipper. After a few moments Fay pointed. "Hey look, Charlie. Over that way. A couple more helicopters."

"Where? Down there? Oh yeah. Couple of military birds, looks like. I guess the Army's out too."

"What're they doing—lifting out one of the cars?"

"No, not a car. It looks like a long, narrow crate. And they're not lifting it, they're lowering it endways. A couple of guys in overalls are down below waiting for it. There. It's down. They're anchoring it to the center strip. Wait a minute. It's not a crate. One of the guys in overalls just opened a door on the front of it, and he's stepping inside. Hey. People are jumping out of their cars and running down the center strip. They're running from everywhere, climbing over hoods. Somebody just knocked over the other guy in overalls. I think there's gonna be a fight.

They're really crowding around that door and pushing . . . No . . . I think it's gonna be okay. The guy inside just came out, and he's tacking up a sign over the door. All the men are starting to walk away. The women are lining up along the center strip now."

"The dears."

"A woman just opened the door and stepped inside."

"Oh, Charlie, I'm so glad you came home."

"Me too."

From the rooftop they could hear the police helicopter's periodic messages. By the end of the first day, predictions for clearing the jam were at least two, perhaps three more days. Knowing they should be on hand whenever it broke, yet weary at the very thought of pedaling across the city twice each day to their vantage point and home again, they decided to rent an apartment in the building below them. Fortunately one was available on the top floor, facing the freeway. They moved in that evening, although they had little to move but the binoculars and a thermos. They agreed that Charlie would pedal home the next day to pick up a few necessities, while Fay kept an eye on the car.

The plan worked marvelously. Once situated, they set up a rotation watch—four hours on, four hours off. Charlie figured he could reach the car from the apartment in half an hour if things looked ready to break. He figured he'd have that much warning, by listening to helicopter messages, and watching TV and frequently checking the progress downtown where the cranes worked. Through the binoculars he watched the great jaws lift out cars, vans and buses and drop them over the sides of the freeway. Things would loosen up down there first, he figured, giving him time to bicycle six blocks to the pine tree a mile below his car. Scaling the tree he could reach the top of a 15-foot-high concrete retaining wall and drop to the freeway. From there it was an easy jog up the center strip and around the sloping cloverleaf curve to the overpass.

To be safe Charlie made dry runs over the course a few times each day—down the elevator, onto his bike, up the tree, over the wall, along the freeway, to his car. He'd switch on the engine and warm it for a few minutes, then stroll back, waving to waiting motorists who watched his passage with mixed admiration, envy and disbelief. By the

third day the men were stubble-faced, sullen, dark-eyed
from fitful sleeping. The women were disheveled, pasty-
faced, most of them staring blankly through windshields
at nothing. Charlie felt he ought to do something. Sometimes he squatted on the center strip to talk to the man
who'd lent him the tow rope.

"How's it going, Arv?"

" 'Bout the same, Charlie."

"Pretty hot out here today, huh?"

" 'Bout like it's been, Charlie. Gettin' used to it, I guess.
You probably feel it more than I do. That's a long pull."

"Not so bad anymore. The old legs are shaping up."

"How's your time?"

"Twenty-eight, ten, today."

"Cuttin' it down, hey boy."

"Poco a poco," Charlie said. *"Poco a poco.* It's the elevator that really holds me back though. Slowest elevator
I've ever seen."

"You ever thought of waiting down on the sidewalk
someplace? The wife could maybe signal out the window
when the time comes."

"Say . . ."

"It came to me yesterday," Arvin said, "but I figured
you'd thought of it."

"Never entered my head. That's a great idea, Arv."
Charlie paused. "I've been meaning to ask you," he went
on. "Why don't you come up to the apartment to meet
Fay? I've told her about you. You'd like her, I know. We
could have a couple of drinks and just relax for awhile."

"Well . . . that's real nice of you, Charlie. But . . . I'm
not sure. The trouble is, you never know when the thing's
gonna break loose."

"I've got that two-seater, Arv. If anything happens, we
can pedal back over here in no time. Cuttin' it down every
trip, ya know. C'mon. It'd be good for you to get away."

"I'd like to, Charlie, I really would. But . . . to be honest,
I haven't had this car very long. I'm still making payments,
and . . . well, I just feel like I ought to stick pretty close
to it."

"I know how you feel, Arv. In a way I don't blame you.
I get a little jumpy myself—especially at night when I can't

see much. But look, if you change your mind, I'll be back this afternoon."

"Thanks, Charlie."

"See ya later, Arv. And thanks for that idea."

"My pleasure, Charlie. Hate to have you miss your car when the action starts."

Taking Arvin's advice, Charlie spent most of each day sitting on a bus-stop bench across the street from the apartment house.

At last, on the afternoon of the sixth day after traffic stopped, Fay's white handkerchief appeared in the 12th-floor window. Charlie's bike stood before him in the gutter. He mounted it over the back wheel, like a pony-express rider. In a moment he was off and pedaling hard for the pine tree.

From blocks away he could hear the now unfamiliar roar of a thousand engines. As he gained the top of the concrete wall and poised ready to drop, a cloud of exhaust smoke swirled up and blinded him. It stung his eyes. He began to cough. He dropped anyway, sure of the route he must follow, even if he couldn't see. Gasping and wiping his eyes he clambered over hoods toward the center strip. The smoke didn't abate. It puffed and spurted, choking Charlie. Every driver was gunning his engine, warming up for take-off. In a panic that he'd miss his car, that it would be carried away in the advancing stream, Charlie stumbled blindly upward, deafened by the sputtering thunder of long-cold cylinders, nauseated by fumes, confused by the semidarkness of gray, encompassing billows.

The cars disappeared. It seemed he staggered through the smoke for hours. He nearly forgot why he was there, until he heard a yell behind him: "Hey Charlie! Where ya goin'?"

"That you, Arv?"

"Yeah. You nearly passed your car."

"This damn smoke."

"Helluva thing, isn't it?"

Arv was elated. Through the veil of fumes that curled up from under Arvin's car, Charlie could see a wild expectancy lighting the haggard eyes. His yellowed teeth grinned behind the beard.

"What's happening?" Charlie said, still gasping, hanging

onto Arvin's aerial while his lungs convulsed.

"Looks like we're moving out. Better warm up."

"When did you get the signal?"

"No real signal," Arvin shouted, "but everybody down the line started up, so I started up. Things ought to get going anytime."

"Have you moved at all?"

"Not yet, but you better get the old engine warmed up, Charlie. We're on our way, boy! We're on our way!"

Coughing and crying Charlie staggered to his car, climbed in and started it. He accelerated a few times, then leaned forward to rest his head on the steering wheel, as nausea overcame him. The noise around him would split his eardrums, he thought. He passed out.

When he came to he was staring through the wheel at his gas gauge: nearly empty. He looked around. It seemed less noisy. The smoke had cleared a little. He could see vague outlines of cars in the next lane. None had moved. He switched off his engine. Evidently others were doing the same. The rumble of engines diminished perceptibly from moment to moment. Within minutes after he came to, it was quiet again. There was little wind. The smoke thinned slowly. Only gradually did he discern shapes around him. Behind him he saw a driver sprawled across the hood, chest heaving. In front of him a man and woman were leaning glassy-eyed against their car. And in the next lane he heard the wheezing rattle of a man retching. He turned and saw Arvin leaning out his open car door into the gutter.

The police helicopter droned toward them, hovered, sucking up smoke, and announced, "Please turn off your engines. Please turn off your engines. The deadlock will not be cleared for at least another 36 hours. You will be alerted well in advance of starting time. Please turn off your engines."

No one seemed to listen. The helicopter passed on. Charlie climbed out, still queasy but able to stand. Arvin was sitting on the edge of his seat now, bent forward with his head in his hands.

"Hey, Arv. You okay?" Charlie looked down at him for several moments before the answer came.

"Yeah, I guess so."

"False alarm, huh?"

Arv grunted.

"Looks like tomorrow might be the day, though," Charlie said.

Arv nodded, then raised his head slowly. His eyes were dark, weary, defeated. All hope had left him. Deep creases of fatigue lined his cheeks and forehead. His beard was scraggly and unkempt. He looked terribly old. His voice was hoarse and feeble as he said, "But, Charlie . . . what if it's not tomorrow? What're we gonna do, for God's sake? It's been six days."

Compassion welled up in Charlie. He said, "Look, Arv. You heard the last announcement. It'll be at least another 36 hours. Why don't you come on up to the place and lay down for awhile?"

A little light brightened Arvin's eyes. His mouth turned faintly toward a smile, as if remembering some long-gone pleasure. But he said, "I can't, Charlie." He raised his shoulders helplessly.

Charlie nodded slowly. "I know, Arv. I know." After a pause he said, "I guess I'll see you this afternoon then." He waited for Arvin's reply, but his head had fallen again into the palms of his hands, and he sat there swaying. Charlie walked away.

Most of the smoke had cleared. The heavy silence was broken occasionally by distant groans, staccato coughs. All around him, down the curve he would walk, on the other freeways that snaked so gracefully below him, in among the rows of dusty cars, he saw people sprawled, hunched, prone on the center strip, folded over fenders, hanging out windows, wheezing, staring, stunned.

He picked his way to the concrete wall, scaled it and left the devastation behind. He knew, though, he'd have to return, perhaps several times. No one could tell when it would be over. The police reports were meaningless. He returned to the apartment to console Fay, who felt guilty about sending him on a wild-goose chase. Then he pedaled downtown to a war-surplus store. His lungs still burned from the smoke. He decided to buy Arvin a gas mask and one for himself. ■

A slice-of-novel, appropriate to the moment, from Kurt Vonnegut's **God Bless You, Mr. Rosewater** (Holt, Rinehart, and Winston, 1965):

"The only people who could get work had three or more PhDs. There was a serious overpopulation problem, too.

"All serious diseases had been conquered. So death was voluntary, and the government, to encourage volunteers for death, set up a purple-roofed Ethical Suicide Parlor at every major intersection, right next door to an orange-roofed Howard Johnson's. There were pretty hostesses in the parlor, and Barca-Loungers, and Muzak, and a choice of fourteen painless ways to die. . . .

"The suicides also got free last meals next door.

"One of the characters asked a death stewardess if he would go to Heaven, and she told him that of course he would. He asked if he would see God, and she said, 'Certainly, honey.'

"And he said, 'I sure hope so. I want to ask Him something I never was able to find out down here.'

" 'What's that?' she said, strapping him in."

"What in hell are people for?"

Russell Baker answers the question—or maybe asks it. Baker, the sharp-eyed, sharp-witted author of The New York Times' Washington "Observer" column, keeps a sharp tongue firmly tucked in cheek.

A SINISTER METAMORPHOSIS
Russell Baker
from *The New York Times*

The number of people who want to be machines increases daily. This is a development the sociologists failed to foresee a few years ago when they were worrying about the influence of machines on society.

At that time, they thought the machines would gradually become more like people. Nobody expected people to become more like machines but, surprisingly enough, that is what more and more people want to do. We are faced with an entirely new and unexpected human drive—machine envy.

A typical case is described by an Arizona gentleman who writes that he was recently notified by a machine of the Internal Revenue Service that he had not paid his taxes. In fact, he had paid his taxes and had a canceled check to prove it.

Feeling a bit smug about catching a machine off base, he mailed back a photostat of the check and suggested that the machine take a flying leap at the moon. A few weeks later the machine wrote again, complaining that he had not paid his taxes and notifying him, in that sullen way machines have, that he not only owed a substantial fine but was also facing a long term in Leavenworth Prison.

Another photostat was mailed to the machine, but its reply was more menacing than before. At this point the Arizona man perceived that he was in the idiotic position of arguing with a machine which was programmed not to listen to him.

"My first thought was one of incoherent rage against that stupid construction of tubes and transistors," he writes. "But as my anger subsided, I was struck by the happy thought that, if I were a machine, I would be able to respond with an equally placid stupidity that might eventually drive him to blow a vacuum tube."

The Arizona man was suffering one form of machine envy. Another form is described by a bank teller, whom we shall call Bob. The machines which make Bob's bank a model of customer service and banking efficiency insist that all check deposits be accompanied by a coded deposit slip which the machines mail to the bank's customers.

Not long ago, Bob reports, a man came to his window to deposit a check. He did not have his coded deposit slip. Bob explained that the machines could not process the check without the coded deposit slip.

In the interest of greater customer service and efficiency, Bob suggested, the man should go home, find his coded deposit slip and return with it. The man's response was, in Bob's words, "absolutely the vilest stream of abuse I have ever heard."

Bob is firmly convinced that if he, Bob, had been a recorded announcing machine, he would have suffered no distress. If he had been able to say, in a metallic voice, "I am sor-ry, sir, but the ob-jec-tives of great-er customer ser-vice and banking ef-ficiency pre-clude my accepting your check with-out a prop-er de-pos-it slip," he would not have felt any embarrassment about the customer's tirade.

Visibly increasing numbers of civil servants have already mechanized themselves so successfully that their enraged victims rarely show any desire to knock them to the floor.

"The trick in mechanizing is not to smile," explains Harry, who is a cog in a Federal licensing office here. "The reason people never punch machines is because machines know better than to smile when they give a human the business." Harry's office works like this:

The license applicant comes to window one and asks for a license. There he is told he must first fill out Form A at window two. At window two he is told that he cannot fill out Form A until he has executed Form B at window three. Harry works window three. His job is to tell the applicant that he cannot fill out Form B until he has executed Form A. Usually the applicant explodes at this point and says:

"If I cannot get Form A without executing Form B, and if I cannot get Form B without executing Form A, how am I supposed to get my license?" At this point Harry refuses to smile. "I am sorry, sir," he says, "but those are the regulations," and he displays his shirt collar, on which is written the warning, "Do not spindle or fold."

If the applicant persists, Harry refers him to Mrs. Barger, his superior. Mrs. Barger refers him to Mr. Clott, her superior, who refers him to Mr. Whipsnade, the department chief, who happens to be away on a 52-week vacation.

Everybody in Harry's office has machine envy. It is a classic example of what the machines are talking about when they sit around brooding that they are in danger of being replaced by people.   ■

Rick Raphael is another newsman: like Baker, working in Washington; like Reed, a comparative newcomer to SF; like Wilson, clinging to his label, although he is now a senatorial press secretary.

Like Wilson again—or Simak—Raphael is the true-hybrid

breed of news-SF man, deriving his fiction largely from the other side(s) of his double (or triple) life. (Covered AEC and rocket tests at Los Alamos and White Sands for seven years; the Nuclear Reactor Testing Station in Idaho for five; member of the National Association of Science Writers; now handles science-oriented legislative projects for his senator.) "The Thirst Quenchers," title story of his first book (Gollancz, 1965), was the bastard brother of a documentary film on water problems which won a National Radio and Television News Directors' Award for Boise Station KBOI and writer-director Raphael; both pieces came out of "six years of riding snow cats, and plodding ungracefully on skis and snowshoes in the company of the Columbia Basin Snow Survey supervisor, learning and reporting the vital mechanics and sciences of his art." His first novel, Code Three, about the highways of the future, will be published this spring by Simon and Schuster.

"Sonny" (which has also been reprinted in Analog III) is a different kind of story—I think. It is true, however, that Raphael put in eleven years as an Army career man (coast artillery private to armored division infantry officer, via the paratroops, cryptography, a bit of interpreting, and World War II). I have no reliable information about his background in ESP.

SONNY
Rick Raphael
from *Analog*

       Private Jediah Cromwell was homesick for the first time since his induction into the Army. If he had gotten homesick on any of at least a dozen other occasions during his first two weeks in the service, he might never have gotten beyond the induction center. But the wonders and delights of his first venture beyond the almost inaccessible West Virginia hills of his birth had kept him too awed and interested to think about home.

When Cletus Miller headed up the trail to Bluebird Gulch, Ma felt him coming around the bend below the waterfall a mile across the gorge. She laid down her skinning knife and wiped her hands clean of the blood of the rabbits Jed had brought in earlier in the morning.

"Sonny," she called to Jed, "trouble's acoming."

Jediah crossed the corn patch to her side. "What kinda trouble, Ma?"

"Cletus Miller's comin'," Ma Cromwell said. "He ain't been up here since the week afore your Pa died. I don't know what it is, but it's bound to be trouble."

A few minutes later Miller hallooed from the bottom of the garden patch, then trudged up to the cabin.

"Set and rest, Cletus," Ma said. "Sonny, fetch Cletus a coolin' dip." Jed ambled down to the spring sluice and dippered out a pint of clear mountain water.

"Got mail fer you," Cletus said, waving an envelope. "Guvermint mail. Fer Sonny."

Two weeks later, Jediah swung down the mountain to Owl Creek, carrying a small sack with his good clothes and shoes in it. The draft notice was stuffed into his overall pockets along with biscuits and meat Ma had insisted he take.

"Go along now, Sonny," she had directed him, "and don't you fret none about me. The corn's 'most ready. You got a good supply of firewood in, more'n enough to last me all winter. If your guvermint needs us Cromwells to fight, then I reckon its our bounden duty. Your grandsire and greatgrandsire both wuz soldiers and if'n your Pa hadn't gone and gotten his leg busted and twisted afore the guvermint called him, I reckon he'd have been one, too. I've learned you all I can and you can read 'n write 'n do sums. Just mind your manners and come on home when they don't need you no more."

In Owl Creek the first real part of the excitement hit Jed. He had been as far as Paulsburg, twenty miles farther and that was almost as big as the county seat at Madison. Now he was going to go even beyond Madison—right to the city. And then maybe the Army would send him more places.

The Army did.

Everything had been wonderful, almost overwhelming, from the moment he boarded a bus for the first time in his life until he arrived at Fort McGruder. He could hardly believe the wealth of the government in issuing him so many clothes and giving him so much personal gear. And while the food wasn't what Ma would have cooked, there was lots of it. He liked the other recruits who had ridden down to McGruder with him, even though a couple of the city fellows had been kind of teasing.

He liked the barracks although his bunk mattress wasn't as soft as Ma's eiderdown comforts. He liked everything— until the sergeant had cussed at him this afternoon.

Now Jed lay on his bunk and counted the springs on the upper bunk occupied by Private Harry Fisher. It was close to eight o'clock and the barracks were full of scores of young soldiers. A crap game was going on three bunks away and across the aisle; another country boy was picking at a guitar. The bunk above sagged with the weight of Harry Fisher, who was reading a book.

Jed's mind kept coming back to the cussin' out he had gotten, just for not knowing the Army insisted on a body wearing shoes no matter what he was doing. Jed had never been cussed at before in his entire life. True, Ma never hesitated about taking a willow switch to him when he was a young 'un, or a stob of kindling when he got older. But she always whupped him in a gentle fashion, never losing her temper and always explaining with each whistling swing of switch or club, just what he'd done wrong and why this was for the good of his immortal soul.

Thinking about Ma, Jed got homesick. He closed his eyes and looked around for Ma. She was stirring a pot of lye ashes over the fireplace and when she felt Jed in the cabin she closed her eyes. "Sonny," she said, "you in trouble?"

Lying on his bunk at Fort McGruder, Jed smiled happily and thought back an answer. "Nope, Ma. Jest got to wonderin' what you wuz doing."

Whatever Ma was going to say was lost amid the yells and growls of the men in the barracks as the electricity went off. "Who turned the lights off?" Fisher cried from the top bunk. "It's not 'lights out' time yet."

The noise jerked Jed back to the present and his eyes opened. The lights came on.

"Where are the dice," one of the crapshooters barked. "I rolled a seven just when the lights went out."

The noise died down and the game resumed. Fisher lay back on his bunk and went back to his book. Jed's mind reached out for home again. "Ma," he called out, "you say something?"

The lights went out and the yells went up throughout the two-story barracks.

Jed opened his eyes and the lights came on.

At the end of the barracks, Corporal Weisbaum came out of his sacredly private room and surveyed the recruits. "Awright," he roared, "so which one of you is the wise guy making with the lights?"

"So nobody, Corporal," a recruit sitting on the end bunk answered. "So the lights went out. Then they come back on. So who knows? Maybe the Army ain't paying its light bills. I had a landlady back in Brooklyn who usta do the same thing anytime I got late with her rent mon——"

"Shaddup," Weisbaum snarled. "Maybe it was power trouble. But if it happens again and I find out one of you monkeys is bein' smart, the whole platoon falls out and we'll get a little night-air exercising." He stalked back into his room and slammed the door.

The barracks buzzed angrily for a few moments. Jed sat up and peered up at Fisher.

"That there officer shorely don't talk very nice, you know that, Harry," Jed said.

Fisher laid down the book and peered under his thick-rimmed glasses at the lanky mountain boy.

"How old are you, Jed?" he asked.

"Nineteen."

"Lived up in the hills all those years?" Fisher inquired.

"Yup," Jed replied. "This is the furthinest I've ever been." His normally cheerful face fell slightly. "Kinda makes me lonesome in a way, though. Folks back home jest plain don't talk thataway one to the other."

Fisher leaned over the edge of his bunk. "Let me tell you something, Jed. Don't let talk like that worry you. First of all, he's no officer. And second, he doesn't really mean it and it's just a way the Army has of making men of us. You'll hear lots more and lots worse before you get back to those West Virginia hills of yours."

Jed lay back on the bunk. "Mebbe so," he admitted. "Don't mean I gotta like it much, though. Ma never talked thataway to me, no matter how bad a thing I done."

Jed closed his eyes and thought of home. Ought to say goodnight to Ma. He let his mind reach out to the cabin almost two states distant.

The lights went out in the barracks, two of the crapshooters started swinging at each other in the dark and the commotion drifted upwind to the platoon sergeant's room in another barracks two buildings away.

In the confused yells and the shouting of Corporal Weisbaum, Jed gave up trying to say goodnight to Ma and opened his eyes again.

The lights in the barracks came back on just as Platoon Sergeant Mitchell walked in the front door.

The two crapshooters were tangled in a heap in the center aisle of the barracks, still swinging. Corporal Weisbaum had the Brooklyn recruit by the front of his T-shirt, waving a massive fist under the boy's nose.

"AT EASE!" Mitchell boomed. The barracks shook and suddenly there was quiet. "Now just what is going on here?" he demanded.

Weisbaum released his grip on the recruit and the two brawlers scrambled to their feet. The corporal glared at the forty-odd recruits in the barracks. "I warned you mush heads what would happen the next time one of you fiddled with them lights. Now I'm gonna give you just five minutes to fall out in front in fatigues and combat boots. MOVE!"

"Lay off," one of the recruits muttered, "nobody touched the lights. They just went off."

Weisbaum turned a cold stare on the youngster. "Just went out, eh? O.K. Let's see. Sergeant Mitchell, did the lights go out in your building?"

The sergeant shook his head.

"Did you notice if the lights were out in any other buildings when you came up?" Again Mitchell shook his head.

"Just this barracks, huh?"

Mitchell nodded.

There was a moment of silence. "Five minutes, you jugheads," Weisbaum roared. "Five minutes or I'll have your flabby hides hung like wallpaper in my room."

By the time the platoon got back in the barracks after a five-mile walk around the perimeter of the post, Taps were sounding and the lights went out as soon as the men hit their bunks. The talking was over. Jed felt better after the pleasant walk in the night air. He decided Ma would be asleep anyway by this time. He turned his head into his pillow and was snoring in ten seconds.

Once Jed began getting the feel of what was wanted of him, his training improved and the wrath of the platoon sergeants and corporals was directed elsewhere. The recruits moved rapidly through the hardening period and with each day, Jed found the going easier. By the time the platoon was ready for the rifle range, Jed hadn't had time to give more than a brief occasional thought about home.

When the supply sergeant issued him his M-14 rifle, Jed carried it back to the barracks like a young bridegroom carrying his beloved across their first threshold.

"Harry," he said in an awed voice to his bunkmate, "ain't that jest about the most bee-ootiful thing you ever did see?"

Fisher was sitting on the lower bunk beside Jed, working the action of his own rifle. "It's a lovely weapon, all right. I just hope I can hit the side of a barn with it."

"Hit a barn with it," Jed said in amazement; "why, Harry, with this here gun I could hit a squirrel in the eye two ridges away and let you pick which eye."

Fisher grinned. "I've heard you mountain boys are pretty good with a rifle. We'll see just how good you are next week when we go out on the range."

The following Monday morning on the range, the platoon gathered around Corporal Weisbaum.

"Awright, you bums," the corporal sneered, "here's where we separate the men from the boys. Don't let the noise shake you too bad and if it kicks you in the shoulder a little, don't flinch. Remember what you learned in dry-fire practice—hold 'em and squeeze 'em off. This is just familiarization fire, so don't worry if you don't hit the first few shots."

He gestured. "Awright. First order on the firing line."

Twenty men of the platoon, Jed included, moved up the embankment to the firing positions. Two hundred yards away the big targets were lined up like billboards along the line of pits.

From the range control tower in the middle of the firing line, the bullhorn speakers blared. "Familiarization fire. Prone position." Twenty riflemen dropped to their knees and then forward onto their bellies, their cheeks cuddling the stocks of the rifles.

"Twenty rounds. With ball ammunition, load and lock." Twenty bolts snapped shut.

"Ready on the right? Ready on the left?"

The flank safety officers signaled. "Ready on the firing line," the speakers blared. "Commence firing."

Jed squinted down the sights and carefully squeezed off a shot. A ragged volley followed down the line. Jed was in position Number Eighteen and down range, his target atop a large painted sign bearing the same number, dropped. Jed rolled over and yelled at Corporal Weisbaum. "Hey, Corporal. I must have done shot 'n broke that there target. It just fell down."

Weisbaum grinned. "You didn't break nothing, hillbilly. You just got lucky and hit somewhere on the target. Every time you hit it, they pull it down and mark where your shot hit so you can correct your sights. See, here it comes back up again."

Target Number Eighteen rose above the pits. In the dead center of the small black bull's-eye was a small white dot. Weisbaum stared at the target, then swung a pair of binoculars to his eyes. "Man, talk about luck. You hit it smack in the center of the black."

The target dropped again for a pasted patch over the hole. Then it came up.

Jed grinned happily and rolled back to the prone position, looked briefly down the sight and squeezed off another round. The target dropped again. In a moment it was back up, the same white marker disk showing in the black. Weisbaum put the glasses to his eyes again. "I knew it was luck. You musta missed it, hillbilly, cause that's the same mark you had last shot."

Jed frowned and waited for the target to be pulled and pasted, then fired again. Once more it came up with the identical white marker in the center. It was Weisbaum's turn to frown. "Better check that sight, Cromwell. You can't shoot on luck forever. Them last two rounds never touched the target."

The range radio safety operator came up to the corporal and handed him the walkie talkie. "Pit wants to talk to you, Corporal."

Weisbaum took the handset and held it to his ear. "This is Corporal Weisbaum. Yeah. He WHAT! You sure? Yeah, pull it and paste it. This I want to see."

He handed the handset to the radioman and glared at Jed. "So now you're some kinda wise guy, huh, hillbilly? You think you can keep shootin' on luck? The pits say you been hitting the same spot every time. Nobody can do that. Now, go ahead, hillbilly. I want to see you do it again."

Jed rolled over on his belly, looked and fired. Down went the target to come up again with another dead-center marker.

"He did it again," the radioman declared to the corporal.

Weisbaum was beginning to get an awed look on his face. "Go on, hillbilly, keep firing."

Behind the corporal and the recruit, the radioman was talking softly to the pits. "He's in position . . . he's aiming . . . he's holdin—" The operator stopped talking and shook his handset and held it again to his ear. Jed fired. A split second later the radio burst into voice. ". . . Did it again," the pit operator yelled excitedly.

Jed fired all twenty rounds into the exact same hole and the range firing came to a screeching halt. By the time he was on the final round, all other firing had stopped and range officers and safety NCO's were gathered in a semi-circle around the prone mountain boy.

Weisbaum pounded Jed on the back as the young recruit scrambled to his feet and dusted his fatigues. "Man, what an eye. Wait 'til the old man sees this. Look," he took Jed by the arm, "you shoot like this all the time back in them hills you come from?" Jed nodded. "I thought so," Weisbaum cried happily. "Go sit down and take it easy. I want the old man to come out and see this."

Jed smiled happily and walked off the firing line amidst the admiring stares of his fellow recruits. He flung himself on the ground in the shade of a stack of ammunition boxes and grinned to himself. Shucks, all that excitement over a little shooting. Back home he did it all the time. But it'd make Ma proud to know he could do something real good. He let his mind travel for the first time in weeks.

On the range road a few feet away, a convoy of trucks carrying another recruit company to the ranges farther down the line, suddenly spluttered and came to a stop as their engines died.

"Ma," Jed thought, "you busy?"

Behind the cabin in Bluebird Gulch, Ma Cromwell laid down the axe she had been splitting firewood with and closed her eyes. " 'Bout time you remembered your maw," she replied. "You all right, Sonny?"

"I'm jest fine, Ma. An' I did somethin' good, too, Ma. I just showed these Army fellers what us Cromwells kin do with a rifle gun."

Jed lay in the warm sun and let the light filter through his closed eyelids. He paid no attention to the clanging of truck hoods and the muttered curses of a half-dozen truck drivers as they clambered over the front of their vehicles trying to figure out what was causing them to have engine trouble.

"What did you do, Sonny?" Ma asked.

"Tweren't really nothing, Ma," Jed replied. "I shot this here newfangled gun they gave me at a big ol' target 'n hit it, Ma. Honest, Ma, that black circle they got in that thing is jest 'bout as big as the hind end of a black bear and it ain't no further away than the bottom of the cornfield from the cabin door."

In the range control tower, Corporal Weisbaum was getting madder every second.

"What's the matter with that switchboard operator?" he screamed. "Don't he hear the buzzer?" He shook the phone and roared again. Finally, he slapped it down on the hook. "Gimme that radio," he said, reaching for the handset. The radio operator shook his head sadly. "No use, Corp. It's deader'n doornail. Don't know what's the matter. It just quit."

Weisbaum looked around and spotted one of the regular jeep drivers standing at the foot of the tower. "Mahoney," he yelled. "Get in your jeep and go back and get the old man. Tell him he's gotta see Cromwell shoot. You can tell him what happened."

The jeep driver started toward his vehicle. "And Mahoney," Weisbaum yelled after him, "while you're there, bring back another radio and tell that idiot on the switchboard we got wire trouble." Mahoney nodded and went to his jeep.

Back at the cabin, Ma Cromwell wiped her face with her apron skirt. "Shore hot today," she thought. "You hot there, too, Sonny?"

"Kinda hot, Ma," Jed thought back. "Shore ain't like home. Not bad though."

"You gettin' enough to eat, child?" Ma asked.

Jed frowned slightly and stepped up his mental output. A half-mile down range and a thousand feet up, an Army helicopter heading for a maneuver area, coughed and quit. The blades went into autogyro as it sank quickly to earth.

Vehicles all over the post came to a spluttering stop and office lights and refrigerators went off.

"What did you say, Ma?" Jed asked. "Seemed like you got sorta weak."

" 'Tain't me," Ma snorted. "Jest that nosy Miz Hawkins. She's gotta listen in on everybody's private talk up in these hills, seems like." There was the feeling of an indignant gasp and then Ma's thoughts came booming through. Jed relaxed and grinned. The chopper was almost on the ground when its engine caught fire once again and went surging up and forward. The surprised pilot fought to get control before he slammed into a low hill. Lights came back on and electrical equipment began running other than close to the range.

"Shouldn't ought to talk like that, Ma," Jed grinned. "She's jest bein' friendly like."

"Hm-m-m," Ma sniffed, "gettin' so's a body cain't even talk with her own kinfolk without everybody in these parts listenin' in."

Mahoney got out of his jeep and walked back to the tower. "Jeep won't start," he called up to Weisbaum.

The corporal turned purple and leaned over the edge of the tower. "Ta hell with it then," he roared. "Now get those bums back on the line. We got a whole platoon to shoot out and I want to see that hillbilly do the same thing in the standing position.

"Cromwell," he bellowed, "get up on that line."

Jed opened his eyes quickly and then shut them for another moment.

"Got to go, Ma," he thought quickly, "that corporal feller's yellin' again. You take care, Ma."

"I will, Sonny," Ma thought back. "Mind your manners."

Jed got up and hurried to the firing line. In the tower, the phone began ringing and the radio and telephone operators began reporting the equipment trouble they'd been having. On the road, one of the truck drivers half-heartedly stepped on the starter for the tenth time. The engine roared to life. The other drivers stopped and stared, then climbed down from fenders and front bumpers and tried their own starters. The trucks and their puzzled drivers left. Firing resumed.

That evening in the barracks, Harry Fisher complimented the mountain boy. "Nice shooting today, Jed," he said, "I was on the radio in the pits while you were shooting. I don't think anyone ever saw anything like that before."

Jed smiled at his friend and bunkmate. "It's easy to do, real easy, Harry," he said. "I reckon everyone could do it once they get the hang of it."

Fisher smiled ruefully. "You're looking at one guy who'll never get the hang of it," he said, "whatever the 'hang of it' might be."

"Honest, Harry," Jed said earnestly, "all you gotta do is jest think them bullets into that big black spot."

Fisher laughed. "I could think like Socrates and never come close to . . ." He stopped and stared at Jed with a half-smile. "You know, Jed, you're kind of weird sometimes. 'Think the bullets.' Come to think of it, though, that's not the only weird thing. Did you know that everytime you were getting ready to shoot our radios went dead today?"

Jed frowned thoughtfully. "That's funny. I ain't never heard of that happenin' afore. O' course, we never had radios in Bluebird Gulch. Only thing we ever had trouble with wuz the 'lectric light bulbs in Paulsburg the one, two times our folks went down there. Seems like them lights wuz goin' out everytime one of us wuz mind-talkin' with some homefolks."

Harry stared puzzledly at the mountain boy.

"You know," Jed tried to explain, "like when you might of ferget somethin' someone wanted real bad from the store. Or mebbe like once when Ma'n me wuz in the big store in Paulsburg and she wuz gettin' some fancy cloth for Miz Culpepper. Store didn't have no fancy cloth like Miz Culpepper wanted, with big red flowers. Only had blue flowers. So Ma, she mind-asked Miz Culpepper if the blue ones would be all right. Every durned 'lectric light bulb in that store went out."

Fisher was beginning to get a dazed look on his face. " 'Mind-asked.' 'Mind-talk.' You mean what I think you mean, Jediah?" he asked.

"Reckon I do," Jed said emphatically. "Just like I mind-talked with Ma this afternoon an' tole her what all the hur-rah was about jest 'cause I flang them bullets through that big ol' black spot."

"You talked with your mother back in West Virginia this afternoon?" Harry pressed. "From the rifle range?"

"Shore did," Jed said happily. "Most plumb forgot fer a couple o' weeks now, what with us bein' so consarned busy. It wuz purely fine to talk with Ma."

Fisher's brain was spinning. "Can you contact her any-time you want to?"

"Shore kin," Jed said proudly. "It takes a mite more power though, the furthern I git from home. Or if Miz Hawkins is listenin' in."

"Let's see you do it now," Fisher demanded.

Jed shut his eyes. "Ma," he thought, "you got time fer a chat?"

The lights went out all over the barracks. Harry Fisher fainted.

When he came to, he was lying on Jed's bunk with the mountain boy leaning over him solicitously. "You all right, Harry?" Jed anxiously. "Ma's worried 'bout you."

Harry fainted again.

When he came to the second time, Jed had gone running down the barracks aisle to Corporal Weisbaum's room. Harry sat up and swung his feet over the edge of the bunk. He was light-headed and his brain was still whirling.

A minute later Jed came back leading Weisbaum. The corporal peered down at Fisher. "You sick 'er somethin' Fisher?" he asked. "Get too much sun today?"

Harry shook his head. "No. I'm OK now, Corporal. Must have been something I ate. I'll be all right."

Weisbaum reached down and felt Harry's forehead. "You look kinda peaked to me. You hit the sack and if you don't feel OK in the morning, I'll put you on sick call."

Harry shook his head again. "No need for that. I'll be all right. I'm going outside and get some fresh air. Jed, will you give me a hand, please?"

He stood up shakily and Jed took his arm. "OK," Weisbaum said, "but if you don't feel so good, you're going to the dispensary, you hear." He went back to his room.

Harry and Jed walked out of the barracks into the night air. Fisher paused and breathed deeply, then turned to face Jed. "You always been able to mind-talk with your mother?" he asked.

"Why, shore," Jed replied. "Most folks back home kin. Shore saves a heap o' walkin' over them hills."

"And did the lights go out when you talked that way?" Harry inquired.

"Well now, I don't rightly know," Jed said. "Only place what has them lights close by is Paulsburg and that's thutty miles from Owl Creek and us folks ain't got much truck fer them big cities. Don't reckon any of us ever been there more 'n three, four times in our whole lives. But it shore happens in Paulsburg whenever we gossip thataway. Never thought nothin' of it afore, though. Reckon, now that I study on it a mite, it's 'cause we got to use more of the power to reach across them hills. Ma once said she reckoned us Cromwells could mind-talk with the Empereer of all Roosha if'n we had to. 'Course, we'd be straining our heads a mite fer all that distance 'cause Ma says Roosha and England is a heap further from Bluebird Gulch 'n even Madison. Or Fort McGruder, I reckon."

Harry thought quietly for a moment.

"When was the last time you talked with your mother that way?" he asked.

"Don't rightly know or remember jest when it wuz," Jed replied. "Seems like it wuz 'bout the fust week we wuz here. One night, in the barracks. I kinda got homesick I reckon, 'cause that wuz the day I got cussed out for the first time in my whole, entire life."

Harry smacked his clenched fist into his hand. "That's

it," he cried. "That's it. That was the night the lights went out three times in the barracks. The night Weisbaum made us take that five-mile moonlight hike because he thought someone was fooling with the lights."

He grabbed Jed by the arm. "That was the night, wasn't it, Jed?"

"Come to think of it," Jed replied, "I reckon it wuz. There wuz such a hurrah when the lights kep a-goin' out, I never did get to hear what Ma had to say. 'N by the time we got back from that little walk, I plumb fergot to ask her.

"You know somethin' Harry, I plumb fergot what would happen to them lights. By gosh, I reckon I wuz the one what got us all in trouble. I jest reckon I better go 'n tell the fellers I'm sorry 'bout that."

Fisher grabbed his sleeve. "Oh, no you don't," he snapped. "You're coming with me."

Ten minutes later, two slightly scared recruits stood on the steps leading to the post commander's quarters. Jed started back down the steps. Harry held tightly to his arm. "Come on," he whispered savagely, "we're going to talk with the colonel, Jed. Now don't you go getting chicken on me, you hear."

"Harry, I ain't never even see'd no colonel, much less 'n talk to one," Jed said, "and I reckon I jest as soon not, if'n you don't mind."

"I do mind," Harry snapped and pulled Jed up to the door.

Their ring was answered by a pretty, teen-aged girl. She smiled inquiringly at the two young soldiers.

"Miss," Harry stammered, "we'd like to talk with Colonel Cartwright, please."

The girl turned into the house. "Dad," she called, "someone to see you."

Colonel William Cartwright came to the door. The light from the room glinted off the silver eagle on his collar. He looked at the two young soldiers. "What can I do for you men?" he asked.

"Sir," Harry answered with a stiff salute and a quavering voice, "I'm Private Harry Fisher and this is Private Jediah Cromwell, sir."

The colonel returned the salute. "All right, at ease. What do you want?"

Harry gulped and took a firm grip on his courage. "Sir," he barked out, "are your house lights all in good working order?"

"What?" Cartwright exploded. "What the devil are you talking about, soldier?"

"Sir, we've got to show you something right now," Harry stammered. "It's urgent, Colonel."

"Now see here Fisher," the colonel said, "we've got proper channels for any problems you might have and I don't take care of those things at my quarters. I have an office in post headquarters and, with the permission of your company commander, you can see my adjutant during duty hours. Or the chaplain."

"Please, sir," Harry gulped. "It's awfully important."

"Well," the colonel hesitated, "this is most unusual."

"Yes, sir, it is most unusual," Harry agreed.

"All right," the post commander sighed, "what is it?"

"Sir, are your house lights all working?" Harry repeated.

"Now look here, Fisher, if this is some sort of a gag, I'll see that . . ."

"No, sir," Harry repeated strenuously, "I really mean the question."

The colonel glanced back over his shoulder into the house. He turned back to the pair. "Yes, the lights appear to be all functioning."

Harry turned to Jed. "Talk to your mother, Jed," he whispered.

Jed shut his eyes. "Ma," he thought, "it's me agin!"

The lights went out all over the colonel's quarters.

Colonel Cartwright gasped and stared at the mountain boy standing with his eyes closed.

"All right, Jed," Harry said, "break it off."

"Jest a minute, Ma," Jed thought, "Harry wants me." He opened his eyes and the lights came on.

"How did he do it?" the colonel breathed.

"He thought them out, sir," Harry said.

"He . . . WHAT?" Cartwright spluttered.

"That's right, sir," Harry repeated. "He 'thought' them out. Jed, get Ma on the line again."

Jed shut his eyes. The lights went out again.

Colonel Cartwright sagged against the door jam. He

moaned, "How long has this one been running around loose?"

"Colonel," Harry said cautiously, "he does the same thing with radios, telephones, cars, anything requiring electrical power. He just shuts it off."

The post commander looked stunned.

"That's not all either, sir," Harry continued. "He can 'think' bullets to a target."

"Come in the house," the colonel said weakly. "That's an order, soldiers."

Three weeks later, Sergeants First Class Harold Fisher and Jediah Cromwell were putting the finishing touches to their own private room. Jed sank down onto the soft mattress on the big bed. "Glory be, Harry, I jest can't seem to catch my breath, we've been movin' so fast 'n doin' so much. All them there tests with them tanks and them airyplanes in Californy and that other funny place. Ma thought it wuz kinda funny I had so much time fer jest a-sittin' 'n chattin' with her. Now we're here 'n I ain't allowed to say nothing to her.

He stole a proud glance at the new chevrons on the sleeve of his fancy, blue dress uniform. "Gosh, but Ma would be proud to hear about all what's happened to us. I purely wish I could tell her."

Harry snapped up from the bureau drawer where he had been placing his clothing.

"Watch it, Jed. You know what the general said. Now don't you go and queer this deal for us just because you're getting a little homesick," Harry warned. "We're the only Army GI's in this outfit and this is pretty plush. You know what the general said, 'No talking with Ma until you get permission.' Remember?"

Jed sighed. "Oh, I remember, rightly enough. Only I shore wish they'd let me just think 'hello' to her. I ain't never been so far from her afore and its gonna take a heap of powerful mind-talk to get to her."

"Never you mind, now Jed," Harry said, "you'll get all the chances you want to talk with her. Just be patient."

He turned back to his clothing. There was a knock at the door and then it opened to admit a small, conservatively dressed civilian. Both sergeants jumped to their feet.

"Good morning, gentlemen," the civilian said. "I'm George Wadsworth, first secretary at the Embassy here." He looked around the room and smiled. "Your quarters satisfactory, men?" Both soldiers nodded happily.

"Good," Wadsworth said. "Oh, by the way, Sergeant Cromwell," he turned to Jed, "we've just learned that our hosts plan to launch their manned Moon rocket within the next hour or so. Isn't that interesting?"

Jed nodded vigorously.

"I thought so, too," Wadsworth continued. "I should imagine that your mother would find this quite interesting as well, don't you think, Sergeant Cromwell?"

" 'Deed she would, sir," Jed said enthusiastically.

"Quite so," Wadsworth said mildly. "Why don't you just take the rest of the day off and tell her all about it. While you're at it, you might bring her up to date on your trip. And there's a wonderful view of the Kremlin from this window. I'm sure she'll be interested in all this. Just have a nice long chat. Take all day. Take two days if you like. No hurry, you know."

He smiled and turned to leave the room. "Don't forget to tell her about your airplane ride, too," he added and then walked to the door.

"Thank you, sir," Jed called out after him.

Jed grinned happily and lay down on the nice, soft mattress.

"Ma," he thought, concentrating harder than he ever did before, "it's me agin."

All electrical power went off over the western dominions of the Union of Soviet Socialist Republics. ■

Forty years ago, the Theory of Evolution went to court in Tennessee. William Jennings Bryan won a Pyrrhic victory, and the Great Controversy was settled at last.

Twenty years ago, controversy returned—this time not Religion embattled against Science, but a fight between scientific-political ideologies. The USSR claimed Dr. Lysenko had demonstrated the pre-Darwinian (Lamarckian) theory of inheritance of acquired characteristics. American scientists laughed.

A decade later, Lysenko was "out" in his own country; and a young instructor at the University of Michigan started playing

with worms. By now, several thousands of flatworms have run
mazes, suffered electric shocks, had bright lights shined in
their eyes, eaten their shredded relatives, bathed in solutions
of RNAse—and firmly established the fact that acquired characteristics can be inherited (not to mention, ingested).

Although the worms are running—or wriggling, more likely—
all over the "free world," the center of activity is Dr. James V.
McConnell's Planaria Research Group, at the University of Michigan. In last year's Annual, I reported happily on the PRG's
highly unsettling publication, The Worm Runner's Digest. Now
Prentice-Hall has brought out **The Worm Re-Turns**, a sampler
from the Digest (featuring more of the satiric than the serious
side of recent events in the evolution of Evolution—but with a
gleeful "compulsory introduction," by Arthur Koestler providing a colorful account of the subversive behavior of flatworms).

"As matters stand at present," the introduction explains, "the
asexual transmission of learnt experience can no longer be
denied, whereas its sexual transmission is passionately denied
by orthodox science—which leads to the perversely paradoxical
conclusion that the lower animals must have an incomparably
more efficient evolutionary mechanism at their disposal than
the higher ones. Thus Coli bacteria have the privilege of inheriting acquired immunity against streptomycin, whereas the evolution in higher animals depends on chance alone; the lower species are capable of profiting from the past experience of the
race, in the higher species it is wasted."

Which brings us roughly even with the present state of confusion—except for the contribution provided by Dr. Nesvadba.

THE LAST SECRET WEAPON
OF THE THIRD REICH
Josef Nesvadba

Translated from the Czech by Iris Urwin from
Vampires Ltd. (Artia, Czechoslovakia, 1964.)

            "Nobody has yet been able
to prove," I ended on a flourish of oratory, "that man is
not the slave of heredity, that in all he thinks he does not
depend on his forebears, and that there is any other hope
of changing him than by crossbreeding like horses or rab-

bits. There's no need to give me that scornful smile," I said to the doctor sitting by my side. "You believe that environment is the strongest influence on people, because you are living in a new society. But you can't prove it by experiment, because you can't play with people like you can with dogs or guinea pigs."

We were in the night train; the heating was not working and so we were trying to keep warm by getting heated about our theories. There was a blonde of about seventeen sitting facing me; I could not see her eyes, but I hoped she was listening. It was for her that I was making such eloquent speeches; the doctor seemed rather a dangerous rival.

"I'm smiling because I have just remembered an experiment on people that might apply here," he answered quietly. "I heard it about a year ago, from our pharmacist Hutzvalek, who had a peculiar experience toward the end of the last war."

It was shortly before the siege of Berlin, when Patton was directing his offensive in the west, and when every day the German railways were losing engine after engine to the boiler-busters. Loyal Nazis had only one hope— the secret weapon Goebbels had promised them. V one and V two were ancient history in London by then, but the Allied offensive still went forward. Nobody with any sense thought the talk about secret weapons was anything but bluff. Hutzvalek thought so too; he worked in the chemist's shop near the Michle gasworks, and made a lot of money on the side, manufacturing complexion creams at home from stolen lanolin. He was getting along fine, and he loved his wife; they had not been married long, because her parents would not agree and only gave in because marriage would save her from having to go and work in Germany. They had no cause to think well of Hutzvalek; he was reputed to be far too fond of gaiety, women and home-made wine; in those days they drank wine made from bread. After his marriage, though, he settled down properly, employed his father and mother-in-law in his complexion-cream business, and waited contentedly for the war to end. Until one morning in February when the Gestapo came for him.

They handcuffed him to the door, socked his father-in-law on the jaw, kicked his wife, who was begging them on her knees to let him go. They knocked his mother-in-law down, tossed the newborn baby out of her cradle and woke up the two-year-old boy.

They took five books out of the bookcase and ripped the featherbed open. Yet it was not the Gestapo after all.

They got out of the Mercedes beyond the city, took off their leather coats and led Hutzvalek deep into the woods, following secret paths. Nobody said a word to him and he thought he was going to be executed. He tried to explain how he had come by all that lanolin, to soften their hearts, but nobody answered, although his German was quite good, really.

Deep in the woods was a hunting lodge where a foreigner was expecting them, dressed in a tweed jacket such as nobody wore in the Protectorate. He offered Hutzvalek Chesterfield cigarettes and Golden Milk chocolate.

"Aren't you the Gestapo?" Hutzvalek was flabbergasted and looked round the room. They were alone.

"No, we're not the Gestapo," the foreigner spoke fluent Czech. "And you've not been arrested, either. You're mobilized from now on."

"What's the idea? Whatever for? The war's going to end in a week or two. Moscow announced in the news last night . . ." The foreigner frowned.

"I am Colonel Borovetz," he said, and assumed that put him in a better position to judge the state of the war. "The war is going to end—unless the Germans succeed in using their last secret weapon. . . ." He got up and began to walk uneasily back and forth. He slowly unlocked the handcuffs Hutzvalek still had on his wrists.

"What sort of a weapon have they got?" asked the pharmacist, and wondered why Borovetz should need to mobilize just him. Was the secret weapon something to do with drugs?

"That's just what we've got to find out," the colonel shouted at him. "We have been informed that the last measures to be taken by the supreme command of the SS are called 'Heil Herod', but we don't know anything more than that. We do not even know what it is to be used on. All we know is that the most successful murderous types from the front and the rear are being called in and housed in a deserted factory near Bohosudov. The place is so well guarded that we have so far failed to find out the first thing about it, although we have lost a number of our men in the attempt. It has therefore been decided that we must manage to get someone inside to take part in the whole campaign. . . ."

"Who is it going to be?" asked Hutzvalek, who thought the whole idea of espionage in the very last days of the war a ridiculous one. "Who is going to manage to get inside?"

Borovetz placed a photograph in front of him: "One of the first who was brought in to take part in the tests of the secret weapon was Sturmbannführer Yeschke. . . ." The pharmacist racked his brains to think where he had seen this fellow in the black uniform. Then the colonel laid a pocket mirror by the side of the photograph and Hutzvalek sprang back. It was his own face looking up at him.

"That's just not possible," he gasped.

"The two of you are as like as two peas. We shall get rid of him and have you taken to the secret laboratory. In a fortnight you will report back. We know that none of those working on the project stay there for more than a fortnight. You will ring me at this number, or else you can leave a description of the weapon in the hiding place under the Hus monument. . . ."

"I'm a pharmacist," Hutzvalek protested. "I've only done a couple of weeks' military training, that was before Munich—and I don't know the first thing about the SS equipment. I'll give myself away before I've said two words."

"You are the only man who resembles any of these cutthroats, and we've searched right through the records of all the Allied armies. The future of humanity depends on your mission, in your hands lies our victory over Hitler, Brother," the colonel spoke like a Czech legionary, and looked sadly at the red mark left by the iron handcuffs on Hutzvalek's wrists. Up till then the pharmacist had assumed that they would defeat Hitler without him. He shook his head. "You will be paid a hundred thousand Swiss francs for your report," the colonel went on. Hutzvalek did some quick mental arithmetic. That would be enough to buy a little chemist's shop. In Switzerland. Was it worth risking his life for? Borovetz got impatiently to his feet. He opened a drawer and pulled out a short American army repeater fitted with a silencer. So it was a question of life or death anyway. The pharmacist nodded quickly.

"If I die, my children are to get the money, Brother. . . ." He did not feel afraid, yet. It felt more like taking out life insurance, or selling his own face.

That was the only thing that interested the guards outside the Bohosudov factory; they just checked the documents with the face. Sitting frowning by the side of the driver was the exact likeness of Sturmbannführer Yeschke, unshaven and bad-tempered after a sleepless night's journey back from the front. They took him past a lot of barbed wire inside the gate and through an empty workshop to the next guard. Here they asked for the password, but memory was Hutzvalek's strong point, and they took him on to the entrance to the underground. Here he was taken over by a tall, not so young blonde in uniform, whose name appeared to be Leni.

"Can you start right away?" she asked. Hutzvalek-Yeschke nodded. The sooner he got it over the better. All of it. Whatever it was. In an underground cell that looked more like a hotel room he flopped down on a soft bed, wiped the sweat from his brow, loosened the Iron Cross that was strangling him and gazed round at the walls. He expected to see drawings of the secret weapon there, but instead he found Germanic beauties, naked and fair-haired, displayed to his gaze in the most alluring positions. What had these nudes got to do with the last secret weapon of the third Reich? He could not see it at all. Soon the door opened and Leni came in, wearing a dressing-gown. She was certainly quicker at getting out of her uniform than Hutzvalek was. Putting a bottle of brandy down on the table, she flung herself upon him. At first he tried to fight her off, then he realized that it was not a wrestling match.

"Is this sort of thing allowed?" he asked doubtfully later on, as they lay side by side on the soft featherbed in the corner.

"What d'you mean, allowed?" she did not understand.

"Well, I mean, here, where we are manufacturing the secret weapon . . ." She started to laugh, but not for long. She got off the bed and then he realized that she was not Leni; as she raised her arm in the Aryan salute he saw the hair under her arm was ginger. She picked up her dressing gown and the bottle of brandy from the table and marched off as briskly as a soldier on parade.

That was the last straw. For a week they'd been chasing him around the training ground, making him cram his head with Yeschke's deeds of heroism and the faces of Yeschke's many relations; seven whole days from morning till night the pharmacist had had to learn off by heart the orders of the SS—and all that in order to find out not the secret weapon, but the sexual capacities of some slut of a wardress.

Next morning he was awakened by another of them. He had to tell her all about his deeds of heroism at Voronezh. She wanted to see his scars and he got so scared that he started kissing her just to put an end to her inquisitiveness. This one was a flaxen blonde and a bit fatter.

"The Führer is certainly looking on us now . . . it will be the Führer's child. Siegfried Hitler . . ." she said piously, and tripped out as if in a trance. Hutzvalek began to fear he would not last a fortnight at this pace, and nipped her bottle of brandy off her as she left. All day he drank alone in his cell with the naked beauties on the walls, until in the evening he threw the empty bottle at one of them and broke it.

"Are you homesick for your handgrenades?" asked the third woman, who did not even bother to come in a dressing gown. "You can keep your hand in here, in the factory; we often practice on the prisoners with live grenades. . . ." and she placed herself on the bed with the matter-of-fact calm and lack of allure of a patient getting ready for gynecological examination. Hutzvalek started hitting her and she thanked him delightedly.

They kept him occupied like this for a week.

"I want to see the secret weapon," he said every day. "I was sent for in order to test the secret weapon. My comrades are sacrificing their lives at the front and I am wasting my time here with you. What did you bring me here for?" They just laughed at him, and he could not get out. There was a guard stationed in the corridor day and night, and he did not even know where the passage led. For seven days they did not let him out for a breath of fresh air.

On the eighth evening a man appeared for the first time. He brought no brandy, either. It was Dr. Müller, or at least that was how he introduced himself; his eyes were hidden behind dark glasses and the lower half of his face was covered with a white mask as though he had just come from an operation.

"Thank you. You have been most successful. I shall inform the Führer personally. . . ."

"What about?" Hutzvalek could not make head or tail of the business.

"Within a week you will have a detachment of the most dependable fighters, men you can depend on in every detail. We shall bring our last secret weapon into play. . . ." Müller laughed so much that his mask puffed out. "You will receive a high military decoration."

"What ever for? Why? What is our last secret weapon?" and the pharmacist took good care to say "our." In a few words Müller explained everything. The research workers had discovered a way to speed up the maturing of the human foetus. An adult man could be produced seven days after conception.

"Don't you see the enormous possibilities of the thing? A year ago this discovery could have turned the war in our favor. We could have sacrificed all the living to the front and brought to maturity those who were still in their mother's womb. Now at least we can be sure of winning the peace. There is little time and little material left; we have to economize with our discovery. I have arranged for the most reliable bitches—I mean loyal German women—to be sent here from the Lebensborn division, which as you know has been providing the Führer with babies since the beginning of the war. They are coupled with the best of our warriors from the front and the home front. Each of you will get your own detachment of soldiers after your own heart; they won't be young whippersnappers from the Hitlerjugend who turn tail at the first shot or let any softsoap parson talk them round. They will be like you in every respect, because they have just been born into the world. They will be capable of everything, like you. 'Heil Herod' can begin. Nobody will try to put it off now. Our last secret weapon has proved its worth."

He shook Hutzvalek by the hand, barked out a Heil! and disappeared.

He went away in the company of Leni, the only woman he had not been forced to sleep with while he was there. They drove in a darkened car for about four hours and at last stopped in front of a big white building. Leni took him inside.

"This is where they will be waiting," she pointed. "The mothers will put them here, they will be given an injection, and then the dead bodies will be burnt over there. We shall deal immediately with any attempt to resist. An epidemic will be started in the city, to support the assumption that we want to inoculate all the children. An entire generation will be lost to them. Then if there's another spot of trouble in fifteen years' time they will have no men to mobilize. . . ." She smiled dreamily. "When the campaign is completed, we shall blow the whole place sky high." As she spoke she pointed to a lever near the door. It looked like the main switch on an electric light meter. . . .

"We'll wipe out all the brats in the place," she said as they went out again. Hutzvalek was still in a daze. Looking round, he saw the outline of the Castle on the horizon. So the place was Prague. He was to kill his own children.

Leni drove him to Holešovice, and as she opened the door and helped him out of his coat without a trace of ceremony, he remembered that Yeschke's wife was called Leni. So it was his own wife who was to keep guard over him in the Nazi breeding stables. The flat they entered was not at all homely, but in all the rooms there were stacks of weapons, as if they were expecting a siege. "We'll have to hurry," said Leni, cleaning the barrel of a light machinegun as lovingly as other women clean their silver. "The Führer fell yesterday. . . ."

Hutzvalek dashed out of the house as he was, without his coat. People jumped out of his way and everything in uniform sprang to attention and saluted. Discipline had lasted longer than victory, it seemed. He had to try the third telephone booth before he got one that worked.

He dialled Borovetz's number and listened anxiously to
the thing ringing at the other end. It was his last hope.
Now he understood why they needed cutthroats. Now
he understood why even the most loyal of Hitlerjugend
lads did not want to carry out these orders. He had discovered information nobody had ever guessed at. The
phone was ringing in vain. He drove out to the wood where
they had taken him that first day. It was a strange sight,
a high-rank officer of the SS crashing through the under-
growth. Of course he failed to find the hunting lodge. He
was sick with fear. Now he was worried for his own
children, who had stayed in Prague; now he was really
afraid. His hand trembled as he put his note into the hiding
place as arranged. He knew it was too late, it was all in
vain, everything he was doing was useless because his news
could no longer save anyone. He tried desperately to
think whom he could warn, what he could do, but everything seemed so fantastic; he was the prisoner of his own
uniform.

The least he could do was to go home. There he found
three families from East Prussia; their horses were grazing
in front of the house. They had no idea where the Hutz-
valeks had got to; most likely to the suburbs somewhere.
Their Heils were enthusiastic, though, because they
recognized Yeschke, who had murdered all the Jews in
Estonia. Yeschke the hero of the Aryan East. He slammed
the door in their faces. How could he find his family?
What was he to do? He went back to Holešovice; it was
almost entirely a German quarter, now; the Czechs had
been moved out and they called it Little Berlin. It was
no surprise to see a big black limousine in front of the
door, with the swastika flying on it. Leni opened the door
to him in a dirndl skirt. She hurriedly straightened his
uniform; General Kopfenpursch was sitting waiting in
the dining room to present the front-line hero Yeschke
with the Iron Cross with the diamond bar.

"Dr. Müller managed to complete his experiment at the
last moment. I have brought your lads along for you.
You can carry out the Führer's last order now," he said as
he pinned another decoration on Hutzvalek, this time with
a diamond bar. And he added softly: "Brother!" It was
Borovetz and not Kopfenpursch. He had got the news

through in time, then. He thanked Hutzvalek with a warm glance, at least, and took a brusque farewell of his "wife." Why did he not release Hutzvalek? What was the man to do now? What did he think he was doing? The pharmacist ran out after him and shouted his questions in at the car window, speaking Czech. The car moved off.

"Disappear to Berne. That's what you wanted to do, isn't it? There's a check folded up inside the Iron Cross. . . ." The answer was in German, and the car was gone. Hutzvalek was alone in the street. Then he realized that facing him on the opposite pavement stood four new SS recruits, each as tall and as well-built as the next, and each with his features. They were smiling at him politely and obsequiously, just the way Hutzvalek himself always smiled at his customers. He thought they were horrid.

Later, when the Hutzvalek detachment were earnestly sorting out test tubes in the suburban laboratory, checking up on their weapons and the dynamite charge beneath the building, he shouted at them impatiently:

"There's no need to pretend with me. I know you're not the Yeschke detachment, you're my own lot. And this murderous business is revolting to me, I hate Nazism and I am fighting against it. We're going over to the other side now!" and he pressed his revolver into Leni Yeschke's back to prevent her calling for help. His sons were confused and afraid, they looked at each other helplessly. After a while the first in the row came up to him and said as he held his automatic at the ready:

"I don't know what you are talking about; we don't feel too happy about this job we've got to do, either, to tell the truth. Murdering little kids. But we were promised, they said that was the only way we could get into the special force of heroes that was going to work in Switzerland after the war."

"To hell with Switzerland! To hell with my life—what I care about are my real children; they won't just be caricatures of me, they'll have the chance to do things better than I did, they'll be able to learn from my mistakes. What I care about are the lives of all the others." And that was the moment, it seems, when he realized that he had completely changed from the moment he knew what "Heil Herod" was all about. He was not the old Hutzvalek any more, the conscientious SS pharmacist he could see before him in four replicas, threatening him from the barrels of four automatics. The fourth Hutzvalek, by the window, had even turned the light machinegun on him. He realized he would have to destroy his own Hutzvalek, he would have to kill that conscientious counter-jumper who was threatening the whole city and the whole of a generation. He was not capable of changing as other people were, after some experience, some profound emotion, the advice or example of others. He had to shoot at himself, protect himself against himself, smash his own skulls, as though he were a fairy-tale dragon, until at last, wounded in several places, he reached the lever that looked like the main switch on an electric meter. At one turn of the lever he buried the whole Heil Herod business. Three days later the rising broke out in Prague. The doctor fell silent and watched us for a while.

"Rather incredible, the whole story," I said sceptically. "Sounds like a madman's dream."

"It was in the madhouse that I met Hutzvalek, last year," the narrator smiled again. "Or rather, in a home for nervous cases. He had been there several times before. When Prague was liberated, he was found under the debris of a ruined building in one of the suburbs. He was unconscious for weeks. He had the remains of a German uniform on, true enough, but everybody in the Revolutionary Guard had something of the sort. It was assumed that he had escaped from the Gestapo prison in Pankrac during the fighting that May, and been wounded. He did not talk much about his experiences himself and agreed that it sounded incredible. The fits of unconsciousness kept on coming back; he was operated several times, brain operations, and then for a time a specific infection was treated at a sanatorium in the Tatras. It was fifteen years after the war before he really got back to normal life. That was when his nervous troubles really started. His son, young Hutzvalek, worked in a nationalized chemist's shop and had been arrested on a charge of stealing from the shop; his daughter ran away when she was sixteen, crossed the frontier illegally, and sent no good news home of herself, either. She was not in Berne, it was true. In the weeks that followed, the pharmacist began attacking passersby whenever he thought they wore their scarves suspiciously high across their faces, or whenever they seemed to be hiding behind dark glasses.

" 'You are Dr. Müller!' he would shout, and call a policeman. The policeman usually brought him straight round to us. He even attacked a former factory owner that way, a man who lived in Hanspaulka and was in fact called Müller; he started a fight with the local Youth Club leader in Hodkovičky, whose name was luckily Vytiska; and he almost blinded a history teacher who had to wear dark glasses because he suffered from conjunctivitis, I can't remember the man's name now.

" 'What do you do it for?' I asked him. 'Why do you think your Dr. Müller is in hiding in our midst? How could he go on with his experiments?'

" 'Just look round you,' he replied. 'Look at my family, the family I sacrificed myself for. They are just like I used to be, the boy and the girl, as if nothing had happened, as if those millions of dead hadn't fallen in between their youth and mine. He took away from them our common experience. They did not change as I wanted them to. I fought myself in vain. I sacrificed myself for nothing.' He went on talking for a while and then started laughing in embarrassment. We sent him home after a few days, and that was the last I heard of him."

"From what has been said it is clear," said the doctor, "that an experiment on human beings really was performed, one which could solve your problem. In the case we have described, the pharmacist really did change as a result of his own experience; he became a new and different person, as it were, ready to shoot at the likeness of himself as he was; he even wanted to change all those round him. That could be taken as proof of our theory."

"What do you think?" I could not contain myself any longer and asked the blonde girl opposite outright. "What do you believe in?"

She started. "I beg your pardon?" Then she yawned, and I realized she had been fast asleep all the time. She pulled a small transistor radio out of her bag and lit a

cigarette. She was a real beauty of a girl. The first bars of
music. Jazz. But she did not answer my question. ■

"When Darwin and Wallace propounded the theory of evolution
in the middle of the last century, it was explicitly stated that
man is no longer subject to evolutionary processes. . . . I do
not think that we control the future at all, and I do not think
that we are in any way free from the evolutionary process."

The quotation is from Of Men and Galaxies by cosmologist
(and SF writer) Fred Hoyle, who argues that human evolution is
no longer determined by the physical environment, but by "the
things we know and the things we believe. . . . We cannot
think outside the patterns that our brains are conditioned to,
or to be more accurate, we can think only a little outside, and
then only if we are very original." And, "New concepts are
like genetic mutations . . . most of them turn out badly. But
without mutations there can be no evolution."

If there is a Significance to science fiction—a capital-S
sort of thing—I think it lies in this area. Not only does it
provide a platform for speculation and prophecy, but by giving
voice to what Hoyle calls the "very original," it attracts other
original minds—both as readers and writers.

The "mutant concepts" then fall on the most favorable soil;
if they are viable, they will grow and multiply. More important,
perhaps, is the chain-reaction effect that sets in (to create a
sort of environment within the environment) as the new concepts of original minds become a part of the "conditioning" of
others—who are thus freed a bit more for more original thinking.

The first generation of what might be called the "science-
fiction community" (beginning in the twenties) did much of the
"mutant" thinking that energized the development of atomic
power and space flight. The present generation is dealing with
concepts in very different areas—and one clue to the "mutation" process is the identity of the new writers.

I have mentioned the newsmen. Dr. Nesvadba (with Romain
Gary, Frank Roberts, José Gironella, Isaac B. Singer) represents
another trend. A prominent Czechoslovak psychiatrist, he is
also a widely published journalist and short-story writer. His
work, he writes, is in "psychotherapy, group psychotherapy, and
artetherapy; hobby is literature." He has published five books
of SF (only one Vampires, Ltd., in English); three of his stories

have been made into Czech films, and "Last Secret" (which has also been translated into German, French, Russian, Polish, Serbocroatian, Yugoslav, and Hungarian) is now being filmed for TV.

I met Dr. Nesvadba at a science-fiction convention in 1964 (and can report that he is charming, witty, and devastatingly Continental). It was, I believe, his first trip to this country. The last night, he spent some hours with John Brunner, Fritz Leiber, and myself.

"I recollect perfectly that evening and morning. Although we have so quite different backgrounds and case histories, as we say in medicine, our outlook seems to be roughly the same, our problems seem to be the same, and perhaps it is not so bad with our world after all, when this is possible."

DESCENDING
Thomas M. Disch
from *Fantastic*

Catsup, mustard, pickle relish, mayonnaise, two kinds of salad dressing, bacon grease, and a lemon. Oh yes, two trays of ice cubes. In the cupboard it wasn't much better: jars and boxes of spice, flour, sugar, salt—and a box of raisins!

An empty box of raisins.

Not even any coffee. Not even tea, which he hated. Nothing in the mailbox but a bill from Underwood's: *Unless we receive the arrears on your account . . .*

$4.75 in change jingled in his coat pocket—the plunder of the Chianti bottle he had promised himself never to break open. He was spared the unpleasantness of having to sell his books. They had all been sold. The letter to Graham had gone out a week ago. If his brother intended to send something this time, it would have come by now.

—I should be desperate, he thought.—Perhaps I am.

He might have looked in the *Times*. But, no, that was too depressing—applying for jobs at $50 a week and being turned down. Not that he blamed them; he wouldn't have hired himself, himself. He had been a grasshopper for years. The ants were on to his tricks.

He shaved without soap and brushed his shoes to a high polish. He whitened the sepulchre of his unwashed torso with a fresh, starched shirt and chose his somberest tie from the rack. He began to feel excited and expressed it, characteristically, by appearing statuesquely, icily calm.

Descending the stairway to the first floor, he encountered Mrs. Beale, who was pretending to sweep the well-swept floor of the entrance.

"Good afternoon—or I s'pose it's good morning for you, eh?"

"Good afternoon, Mrs. Beale."

"Your letter come?"

"Not yet."

"The first of the month isn't far off."

"Yes, indeed, Mrs. Beale."

At the subway station, he considered a moment before answering the attendant: One token or two? Two, he decided. After all, he had no choice but to return to his apartment. The first of the month was still a long way off.

—If Jean Valjean had had a charge account, he would have never gone to prison.

Having thus cheered himself, he settled down to enjoy the ads in the subway car. *Smoke. Try. Eat. Give. See. Drink. Use. Buy.* He thought of Alice with her mushrooms: Eat me.

At 34th Street he got off and entered Underwood's Department Store directly from the train platform. On the main floor he stopped at the cigar stand and bought a carton of cigarettes.

"Cash or charge?"

"Charge." He handed the clerk the laminated plastic card. The charge was rung up.

Fancy Groceries was on 5. He made his selection judiciously. A jar of instant and a 2-pound can of drip-ground coffee, a large tin of corned beef, packaged soups and boxes of pancake mix and condensed milk. Jam, peanut butter, and honey. Six cans of tuna fish. Then, he indulged himself in perishables: English cookies, an Edam cheese, a small frozen pheasant—even fruitcake. He never ate so well as when he was broke. He couldn't afford to.

"$14.87."

This time after ringing up his charge, the clerk checked the number on his card against her list of closed or doubtful accounts. She smiled apologetically and handed the card back.

"Sorry, but we have to check."

"I understand."

The bag of groceries weighed a good twenty pounds. Carrying it with the exquisite casualness of a burglar passing before a policeman with his loot, he took the escalator to the bookshop on 8. His choice of books was determined by the same principle as his choice of groceries. First, the staples: two Victorian novels he had never read, *Vanity Fair* and *Middlemarch;* the Sayers' translation of Dante, and a two-volume anthology of German plays, none of which he had read and few he had even heard of. Then the perishables: a sensational novel that had reached the best-seller list via the Supreme Court, and two mysteries.

He had begun to feel giddy with self-indulgence. He reached into his jacket pocket for a coin.

—Heads a new suit; tails the Sky Room.

Tails.

The Sky Room on 15 was empty of all but a few women chatting over coffee and cakes. He was able to get a seat by a window. He ordered from the a la carte side of the menu and finished his meal with espresso and baklava. He handed the waitress his credit card and tipped her fifty cents.

Dawdling over his second cup of coffee, he began *Vanity Fair.* Rather to his surprise, he found himself enjoying it. The waitress returned with his card and a receipt for the meal.

Since the Sky Room was on the top floor of Underwood's, there was only one escalator to take now—Descending. Riding down, he continued to read *Vanity Fair.* He could read anywhere—in restaurants, on subways, even walking down the street. At each landing he made his way from the foot of one escalator to the head of the next without lifting his eyes from the book. When he came to the Bargain Basement, he would be only a few steps from the subway turnstile.

He was halfway through Chapter VI (on page 55, to be exact) when he began to feel something amiss.

—How long does this damn thing take to reach the basement?

He stopped at the next landing, but there was no sign to indicate on what floor he was nor any door by which he might reenter the store. Deducing from this that he was between floors, he took the escalator down one more flight only to find the same perplexing absence of landmarks.

There was, however, a water fountain, and he stooped to take a drink.

—I must have gone to a subbasement. But this was not too likely after all. Escalators were seldom provided for janitors and stockboys.

He waited on the landing, watching the steps of the escalator slowly descend toward him and, at the end of their journey, telescope in upon themselves and disappear. He waited a long while, and no one else came down the moving steps.

—Perhaps the store has closed. Having no wristwatch and having rather lost track of the time, he had no way of knowing. At last, he reasoned that he had become so engrossed in the Thackeray novel that he had simply stopped on one of the upper landings—say, on 8—to finish a chapter and had read on to page 55 without realizing that he was making no progress on the escalators.

When he read, he could forget everything else.

He must, therefore, still be somewhere above the main floor. The absence of exits, though disconcerting, could be explained by some quirk in the floor plan. The absence of signs as merely a carelessness on the part of the management.

He tucked *Vanity Fair* into his shopping bag and stepped onto the grilled lip of the down-going escalator—not, it must be admitted, without a certain degree of reluctance. At each landing, he marked his progress by a number spoken aloud. By *eight* he was uneasy; by *fifteen* he was desperate.

It was, of course, possible that he had to descend two flights of stairs for every floor of the department store. With this possibility in mind, he counted off fifteen more landings.

—No.

Dazedly and as though to deny the reality of this seemingly interminable stairwell, he continued his descent. When he stopped again at the forty-fifth landing, he was trembling. He was afraid.

He rested the shopping bag on the bare concrete floor of the landing, realizing that his arm had gone quite sore from supporting the twenty pounds and more of groceries and books. He discounted the enticing possibility that "it was all a dream," for the dream world is the reality of the dreamer, to which he could not weakly surrender, no more than he could surrender to the realities of life. Besides, he was not dreaming; of that he was quite sure.

He checked his pulse. It was fast—say, eighty a minute. He rode down two more flights, counting his pulse. Eighty almost exactly. Two flights took only one minute.

He could read approximately one page a minute, a little less on an escalator. Suppose he had spent one hour on the escalators while he had read: sixty minutes—one hundred and twenty floors. Plus forty-seven that he had counted. One hundred sixty seven. The Sky Room was on 15.

$167 - 15 = 152.$

He was in the one-hundred-fifty-second subbasement. That was impossible.

The appropriate response to an impossible situation was to deal with it as though it were commonplace—like Alice in Wonderland. Ergo, he would return to Underwood's the same way he had (apparently) left it. He would walk up one hundred fifty two flights of down-going escalators. Taking the steps three at a time and running, it was almost like going up a regular staircase. But after ascending the second escalator in this manner, he found himself already out of breath.

There was no hurry. He would not allow himself to be overtaken by panic.

No.

He picked up the bag of groceries and books he had left on that landing, waiting for his breath to return, and darted up a third and fourth flights. While he rested on the landing, he tried to count the steps between floors, but his count differed depending on whether he counted with the current or against it, down or up. The average was roughly eighteen steps, and the steps appeared to be eight or nine inches deep. Each flight was, therefore, about twelve feet.

It was one-third of a mile, as the plumb drops, to Underwood's main floor.

Dashing up the ninth escalator, the bag of groceries broke open at the bottom, where the thawing pheasant had dampened the paper. Groceries and books tumbled onto the steps, some rolling of their own accord to the landing below, others being transported there by the moving stairs and forming a neat little pile. Only the jam jar had been broken.

He stacked the groceries in the corner of the landing, except for the half-thawed pheasant, which he stuffed into his coat pocket, anticipating that his ascent would take him well past his dinner hour.

Physical exertion had dulled his finer feelings—to be precise, his capacity for fear. Like a cross-country runner in his last laps, he thought singlemindedly of the task at hand and made no effort to understand what he had in any case already decided was not to be understood. He mounted one flight, rested, mounted and rested again. Each mount was wearier; each rest longer. He stopped counting the landings after the twenty-eighth, and some time after that—how long he had no idea—his legs gave out and he collapsed to the concrete floor of the landing. His calves were hard aching knots of muscle; his thighs quivered erratically. He tried to do knee-bends and fell backwards.

Despite his recent dinner (assuming that it had been recent), he was hungry and he devoured the entire pheasant, completely thawed now, without being able to tell if it were raw or had been precooked.

—This is what it's like to be a cannibal, he thought as he fell asleep.

Sleeping, he dreamt he was falling down a bottomless pit. Waking, he discovered nothing had changed, except the dull ache in his legs, which had become a sharp pain.

Overhead, a single strip of fluorescent lighting snaked down the stairwell. The mechanical purr of the escalators seemed to have heightened to the roar of a Niagara, and their rate of descent seemed to have increased proportionately.

Fever, he decided. He stood up stiffly and flexed some of the soreness from his muscles.

Halfway up the third escalator, his legs gave way under him. He attempted the climb again and succeeded. He collapsed again on the next flight. Lying on the landing where the escalator had deposited him, he realized that his hunger had returned. He also needed to have water—and to let it.

The latter necessity he could easily—and without false modesty—satisfy. Also he remembered the water fountain he had drunk from yesterday and he found another three floors below.

—It's so much easier going down.

His groceries were down there. To go after them now, he would erase whatever progress he had made in his ascent. Perhaps Underwood's main floor was only a few more flights up. Or a hundred. There was no way to know.

Because he was hungry and because he was tired and because the futility of mounting endless flights of descending escalators was, as he now considered it, a labor of Sisyphus, he returned, descended, gave in.

At first, he allowed the escalator to take him along at its own mild pace, but he soon grew impatient of this. He found that the exercise of running down the steps three at a time was not so exhausting as running *up*. It was refreshing, almost. And, by swimming with the current instead of against it, his progress, if such it can be called, was appreciable. In only minutes he was back at his cache of groceries.

After eating half the fruitcake and a little cheese, he fashioned his coat into a sort of sling for the groceries, knotting the sleeves together and buttoning it closed. With one hand at the collar and the other about the hem, he could carry all his food with him.

He looked up the descending staircase with a scornful smile, for he had decided with the wisdom of failure to abandon *that* venture. If the stairs wished to take him down, then down, giddily, he would go.

Then, down he did go, down dizzily, down, down and always, it seemed, faster, spinning about lightly on his heels at each landing so that there was hardly any break in the wild speed of his descent. He whooped and halooed and laughed to hear his whoopings echo in the narrow, low-vaulted corridors, following him as though they could not keep up his pace.

Down, ever deeper down.

Twice he slipped at the landings and once he missed his footing in mid-leap on the escalator, hurtled forward, letting go of the sling of groceries and falling, hands stretched out to cushion him, onto the steps, which, imperturbably, continued their descent.

He must have been unconscious then, for he woke up in a pile of groceries with a split cheek and a splitting headache. The telescoping steps of the escalator gently grazed his heels.

He knew then his first moment of terror—a premonition that there was no *end* to his descent, but this feeling gave way quickly to a laughing fit.

"I'm going to hell!" he shouted, though he could not drown with his voice the steady purr of the escalators. "This is the way to hell. Abandon hope all ye who enter here."

—If only I were, he reflected.—If that were the case, it would make sense. Not quite orthodox sense, but some sense, a little.

Sanity, however, was so integral to his character that neither hysteria nor horror could long have their way with him. He gathered up his groceries again, relieved to find that only the jar of instant coffee had been broken this time. After reflection he also discarded the can of drip-ground coffee, for which he could conceive no use—under the present circumstances. And he would allow himself, for the sake of sanity, to conceive of no other circumstances than those.

He began a more deliberate descent. He returned to *Vanity Fair,* reading it as he paced down the down-going steps. He did not let himself consider the extent of the abyss into which he was plunging, and the vicarious excitements of the novel helped him keep his thoughts from his own situation. At page 235, he lunched (that is, he took his second meal of the day) on the remainder of the cheese and fruitcake; at 523 he rested and dined on the English cookies dipped in peanut butter.

—Perhaps I had better ration my food.

If he could regard his absurd dilemma merely as a struggle for survival, another chapter in his own Robinson Crusoe story, he might get to the bottom of this mechanized vortex alive and sane. He thought proudly that many people in his position could not have adjusted, would have gone mad.

Of course, he *was* descending. . . .

But he was still sane. He had chosen his course and now he was following it.

There was no night in the stairwell, and scarcely any shadows. He slept when his legs could no longer bear his weight and his eyes were tearful from reading. Sleeping, he dreamt that he was continuing his descent on the escalators. Waking, his hand resting on the rubber railing that moved along at the same rate as the steps, he discovered this to be the case.

Somnambulistically, he had ridden the escalators farther down into this mild, interminable hell, leaving behind his bundle of food and even the still-unread Thackeray novel.

Stumbling up the escalators, he began, for the first time, to cry. Without the novel, there was nothing to *think* of but this, this. . . .

—How far? How long did I sleep?

His legs, which had only been slightly wearied by his descent, gave out twenty flights up. His spirit gave out soon after. Again he turned around, allowed himself to be swept up by the current—or, more exactly, swept down.

The escalator seemed to be traveling more rapidly, the pitch of the steps to be more pronounced. But he no longer trusted the evidence of his senses.

—I am, perhaps, insane—or sick from hunger. Yet, I would have run out of food eventually. This will bring the crisis to a head. Optimism, that's the spirit!

Continuing his descent, he occupied himself with a closer analysis of his environment, not undertaken with any hope of bettering his condition but only for lack of other diversions. The walls and ceilings were hard, smooth, and off-white. The escalator steps were a dull nickel color, the treads being somewhat shinier, the crevices darker. Did that mean that the treads were polished from use? Or were they designed in that fashion? The treads were half an inch wide and spaced apart from each other by the same width. They projected slightly over the edge of each step, resembling somewhat the head of a barber's shears. Whenever he stopped at a landing, his attention would become fixed on the illusory "disappearance" of the steps, as they sank flush to the floor and slid, tread in groove, into the grilled base plate.

Less and less would he run, or even walk, down the stairs, content merely to ride his chosen step from top to bottom of each flight and, at the landing, step (left foot, right, and left again) onto the escalator that would transport him to the floor below. The stairwell now had tunneled, by his calculations, miles beneath the department store—so many miles that he began to congratulate himself upon his unsought adventure, wondering if he had established some sort of record. Just so, a criminal will stand in awe of his own baseness and be most proud of his vilest crime, which he believes unparalleled.

In the days that followed, when his only nourishment was the water from the fountains provided at every tenth landing, he thought frequently of food, preparing imaginary meals from the store of groceries he had left behind, savoring the ideal sweetness of the honey, the richness of the soup which he would prepare by soaking the powder in the emptied cookie tin, licking the film of gelatin lining the opened can of corned beef. When he thought of the six cans of tuna fish, his anxiety became intolerable, for he had (would have had) no way to open them. Merely to stamp on them would not be enough. What, then? He turned the question over and over in his head, like a squirrel spinning the wheel in its cage, to no avail.

Then a curious thing happened. He quickened again the speed of his descent, faster now than when first he had done this, eagerly, headlong, absolutely heedless. The several landings seemed to flash by like a montage of Flight, each scarcely perceived before the next was before him. A demonic, pointless race—and why? He was running, so he thought, toward his store of groceries, either believing that they had been left *below* or thinking that he was running *up*. Clearly, he was delirious.

It did not last. His weakened body could not maintain

the frantic pace, and he woke from his delirium confused and utterly spent. Now began another, more rational delirium, a madness fired by logic. Lying on the landing, rubbing a torn muscle in his ankle, he speculated on the nature, origin and purpose of the escalators. Reasoned thought was of no more use to him, however, than un- reasoning action. Ingenuity was helpless to solve a riddle that had no answer, which was it own reason, self-contained and whole. He—not the escalators—needed an answer.

Perhaps his most interesting theory was the notion that these escalators were a kind of exercise wheel, like those found in a squirrel cage, from which, because it was a closed system, there could be no escape. This theory required some minor alterations in his conception of the physical universe, which had always appeared highly Euclidean to him before, a universe in which his descent seemingly along a plumb line was, in fact, describing a loop. This theory cheered him, for he might hope, coming full circle, to return to his store of groceries again, if not to Underwood's. Perhaps in his abstracted state he had passed one or the other already several times without observing.

There was another, and related, theory concerning the measures taken by Underwood's Credit Department against delinquent accounts. This was mere paranoia.

—Theories! I don't need theories. I must get on with it.

So, favoring his good leg, he continued his descent, al- though his speculations did not immediately cease. They became, if anything, more metaphysical. They became vague. Eventually, he could regard the escalators as being entirely matter-of-fact, requiring no more explanation than, by their sheer existence, they offered him.

He discovered that he was losing weight. Being so long without food (by the evidence of his beard, he estimated that more than a week had gone by), this was only to be expected. Yet, there was another possibility that he could not exclude: that he was approaching the center of the earth where, as he understood, all things were weightless.

—Now *that,* he thought, is something worth striving for.

He had discovered a goal. On the other hand, he was dying, a process he did not give all the attention it deserved. Unwilling to admit this eventuality and yet not so foolish as to admit any other, he sidestepped the issue by pretending to hope.

—Maybe someone will rescue me, he hoped.

But his hope was as mechanical as the escalators he rode—and tended, in much the same way, to sink.

Waking and sleeping were no longer distinct states of which he could say: "Now I am sleeping," or "Now I am awake." Sometimes he would discover himself descending and be unable to tell whether he had been woken from sleep or roused from inattention.

He hallucinated.

A woman, loaded with packages from Underwood's and wearing a trim pillbox–style hat, came down the escalator toward him, turned around on the landing, high heels clicking smartly, and rode away without even nodding to him.

More and more, when he awoke or was roused from his stupor, he found himself, instead of hurrying to his goal, lying on a landing, weak, dazed, and beyond hunger. Then, he would crawl to the down-going escalator and pull himself onto one of the steps, which he would ride to the bottom, sprawled head foremost, hands and shoulders braced against the treads to keep from skittering bumpily down.

—At the bottom, he thought,—at the bottom. . . . I will . . . when I get there. . . .

From the bottom, which he conceived of as the center of the earth, there would be literally nowhere to go but up. Probably by another chain of escalators, ascending escalators, but preferably by an elevator. It was important to believe in a bottom.

Thought was becoming as difficult, as demanding and painful, as once his struggle to ascend had been. His perceptions were fuzzy. He did not know what was real and what imaginary. He thought he was eating and discovered he was gnawing at his hands.

He thought he had come to the bottom. It was a large, high-ceilinged room. Signs pointed to another escalator: *Ascending*. But there was a chain across it and a small typed announcement.

"Out of order. Please bear with us while the escalators are being repaired. Thank you. The Management."

He laughed weakly.

He devised a way to open the tuna fish cans. He would

slip the can sideways beneath the projecting treads of the escalator, just at the point where the steps were sinking flush to the floor. Either the escalator would split the can open or the can would jam the escalator. Perhaps if one escalator were jammed the whole chain of them would stop. He should have thought of that before, but he was, nevertheless, quite pleased to have thought of it at all.

—I might have escaped.

His body seemed to weigh so little now. He must have come hundreds of miles. Thousands.

Again, he descended.

Then, he was lying at the foot of the escalator. His head rested on the cold metal of the base plate and he was looking at his hand, the fingers of which were pressed into the creviced grill. One after another, in perfect order, the steps of the escalator slipped into these crevices, tread in groove, rasping at his fingertips, occasionally tearing away a sliver of his flesh.

That was the last thing he remembered. ■

"While I was writing 'Descending,' my icebox was in appropriately the same shape as my hero's and I was living on my Macy's credit card," writes Tom Disch. "After 'Descending,' things picked up. . . . I got hired by Doyle Dane Bernbach and found, rather to my dismay, that I enjoyed advertising and a living wage."

DDB, you know, is the agency that does those readable Avis and VW ads. Makes it easier to understand why a writer like Tom Disch should have enjoyed it. That way, maybe you can think of it as "the ad game."

There was something of a "game" feeling about that endless escalator, too—as if you only had to know the rules to be able to get off. I remembered that feeling too vividly when I came across (ex-Harvard's) Timothy Leary's article, "How To Change Behavior," in **LSD, The Consciousness Expanding Drug**, (Putnam, 1964).

"Baseball and basketball have clearly definable roles, rules, rituals, goals, languages, and values. Psychology, religion, politics, are games, too, learned cultural sequences with clearly defined roles, rules, goals, jargons, values. . . .

"All behavior involves learned games. But only that rare Westerner we call 'mystic' or who has had a visionary experience

of some sort sees clearly the game structure of behavior. Most
of the rest of us spend our time struggling with roles and rules
and goals and concepts of games which are implicit, and con-
fusedly not seen as games, trying to apply the roles and rules
and rituals of one game to other games. . . .

"Culturally, stability is maintained by keeping the members
of any cultural group from seeing that the roles, rules, goals,
rituals, language, and values are game structures."

Are diplomats mystics? Or are they culturally unstable? I do
not believe it is possible to carry on the absurdities of international intercourse without a clear knowledge of the game
(the Great Game, as it has been called), not just its rules and
goals and penalties—but the essential gaminess of it.

Romain Gary is a Frenchman of Russian origin, a distinguished
novelist, a well-decorated soldier, and a career diplomat. He
writes fluently in four languages and (I am certain) is a
skilled gamesman in at least that many. He has, at least, a
terribly clear view of the Syndicate Game and the Art Game, in
this story from his recent collection **Hissing Tales** (Harper & Row).

DECADENCE
Romain Gary
*Translated from the French
by Richard Howard*
from *Saga*

We had already been over
the Atlantic five hours and Carlos had been talking all the
time. I'm not even sure he knew he was speaking to us: at
times I had the feeling he was merely thinking aloud, under
the influence of a deep emotion that was becoming more
and more evident as the plane neared Rome.

The imminence of the coming reunion had us all pretty
nervous, but with Carlos you could feel something deeper,
something that often sounded like a mixture of awe and
love. For all of us who knew him well—one of the tough-
est men around—it was truly impressive to hear the accents
of reverence and almost of humility in his voice as he
evoked for us the legendary figure of Mike Sarfatti, the
Hoboken giant who rose one day on the New York water-

front and scared the hell out of every union boss there, and no one can say that they were men who scared easy.

You should have heard Carlos pronounce that name. He lowered his voice and an almost tender smile softened the heavy face that 40 years in the thick of the social struggle had turned to stone.

"It was a crucial period—crucial, that's the word for it. The Syndicate was at a turning point: we were going social. We were stepping into the longshoremen's union fight and it was rough; nobody had ever given us much trouble before. It often looked as if we weren't going to make it, as if the unions on the New York waterfront were strong enough to look after themselves and didn't feel like being protected by us. The press was dragging us in the mud, the federal authorities were sniffing around and the dockers themselves were sore as hell; dues had just been set at 20 percent of their pay, and everyone was trying to get control of the cashbox and milk the unions for himself.

"Even so, we were moving in, but it was rough, as I said, and getting rougher. In the port of New York alone, there were seven different headquarters fighting over the cake, and the union old-timers would rather have police protection than us. Yes, that's the point it had reached. They were getting quite hysterical.

"Well, it took Mike only a year to straighten things out, and he didn't work like the other bosses in the protection racket, the Guziks, the Musicas, who paid their men to do the work. No, Mike was always the first in the front line; he always took a hand himself. The day someone gets the idea of raking the bottom of the Hudson around Hoboken, they'll find about a hundred tons of cement down there in the slime, and Mike was always around in person when they put the guys in the cast.

"More often than not they were still alive and kicking. Mike liked it that way; he liked to give them a chance to express themselves. He liked it if they argued when they poured the cement over them—it made them look interesting when the stuff set. They would be caught in all sorts of attitudes. Mike said one day it would be like the people in Pompeii when they found them in lava 2,000 years later; he used to call it 'working for posterity.' When one of the guys got too noisy, Mike always tried to reason with him. 'What have you got to bellyache about, sonny?' he would say. 'You're going to be part of our cultural heritage.'

"At the end, Mike even got very fussy. He had to have special cement, more like plaster, the kind that set right away, so that he could see what he was doing, while the work was in progress. In Hoboken we usually just stick the guy in the cement when he's ready, nail on the top of the barrel, roll it into the river, and forget about it. But not Mike. With him it was something else, something artistic. He wanted to see the expression of the face and the position of the body, and he wanted him to look like a statue.

"Sometimes, as I told you, the guy would twist and turn a little during the job, and then the results would often be quite striking. But usually he would just have one hand on his head and his mouth open, pleading and swearing that he hadn't tried to fight the Syndicate, or split the unions, that he was all for workers' unity and innocent as a lamb, and Mike didn't like that, because then they all looked just the same, same faces, same gestures, and that wasn't what he wanted. 'Pig work,' he called it.

"All we cared about was getting the guy into the barrel as fast as we could, drop the barrel into the river and think of something else. Not that there was much danger; the docks were covered by guys from headquarters, the police never stuck their noses into anything—they were not supposed to know about it, and it was only dog eating dog, anyway, but we didn't like the job: a guy covered with cement from head to foot and screaming while he was already all white and turning hard, with only the black hole of the mouth still broadcasting—you really had to be artistic to like it.

"Quite frankly, none of us cared for art that much. That was long before everybody got stinking rich and became art- and culture-conscious. Yes, 'culture' they began to call it. You had to have it, if you wanted to prove you had gone respectable and social. But Mike has always been a pioneer in everything, and he was the first in the Syndicate to go social and to realize that culture and art made you look good. So sometimes he took a hammer and chisel and touched up a few details himself. The guy I remember best of all was Big Bill Sugar, the Greek from San Fran-

cisco who wanted to keep the West Coast independent and
refused to affiliate—the same thing Lou Dybic tried the
year before in Chicago, with the slot machines; you all
know what happened to him.

"Only the difference between Lou and Big Bill was that
Big Bill Sugar was very strong on his home ground, backed
by all the grass roots. Also, he claimed he was strictly non-
political. And he knew all the smart shit talk all right. He
claimed he was for unity and all that. He didn't want to
split the workers, but neither did he want the movement to
be dictated to by the East Coast waterfront. Oh well, you
know the line. And he was very careful. Before he would
come east and talk the situation over with Mike, he wanted
hostages: he asked for Mike's brother who was on the
accounting side, and a couple of other Syndicate workers.
They went, and Big Bill came to Hoboken. Only when
they got together, it was easy to see that Mike wasn't
interested in the discussion at all. He kept looking at Big Bill
Sugar like he was dreaming, and you could tell he wasn't
listening. You know, the Greek was quite a guy, over six
feet tall and good-looking—the girls were all crazy about
him, that's how he got his nickname, Sugar. Even so, they
talked right through for about seven hours, and they went
into the whole thing—labor unity and getting rid of the
political shysters who wouldn't just defend the professional
interests of the workers but were trying to make the movement into an election platform, and all that time Mike
never took his eyes off Big Bill Sugar. When they had a
coffee break, he came over to me and all he said was:
'Okay, there's no use arguing with this bastard, let's give
him a bath.'

"I was about to remind him of his brother and the other
two who were being held as hostages in San Francisco, but
I kept my mouth shut. Mike always knew what he was
doing and besides, the higher interests of the Syndicate
were at stake. You have got to forget your personal feelings
sometimes. They went on arguing, for form's sake, and
after closing time, when Big Bill left the shed with his
party, we shot them all—him, his lawyer and the two
blokes from the Oakland headquarters. That night, Mike
supervised the job in person, and when the Greek was all
nicely set in concrete, instead of rolling him into the Hud-

son, he stopped and looked at him sort of dreamily. Then he smiled and said: 'Leave him here for a while. He has to dry out, and that'll take a good day.'

"I didn't quite see why he had to be dry before going into the water, but here again I didn't feel like saying anything. So we left Big Bill Sugar in the shed under a tarpaulin, and a day or so later we all came back, and Mike looked at him again in that dreamy way, poked at the concrete, touched it up a little more with hammer and chisel, here and there, and in the end he seemed quite pleased. He straightened up, stepped back, stared at the cast a little longer, and then he said: 'All right, put the bastard in my car.'

"At first we didn't know what he meant, and he said again, 'Put the bastard in my car. Next to the driver.' We looked at each other, but we weren't going to argue with Mike.

"We carried Big Bill Sugar to the Cadillac and put him in next to the driver, then we all got in and waited. 'Okay, let's go home,' Mike said. So we got to his house on Park Avenue, stopped the car and looked at Mike. 'Take him out.' We took Big Bill out of the car, and the doorman smiled and took off his cap. 'Nice piece of statuary you got there, Mr. Sarfatti,' he said, respectfully. 'At least you can tell what it is. Not like these modern things that have three heads and seven hands.' 'That's right,' Mike said, and he laughed. 'It's real classical. Greek, in fact.'

"We stuck Big Bill Sugar in the elevator and rode on up. Mike opened the door and we carried the statue inside. 'In the living room,' Mike said. We went into the living room and stood Big Bill up against a wall and waited. Mike looked all around the room, thought it over, and then he pointed. 'Up there,' he said, 'over the mantelpiece.' We didn't get it right way, but Mike moved away the painting that was there.

"All right, we decided, no arguments. We put Big Bill Sugar on the mantelpiece, propped him up against the wall, and left him there. With Mike, there was no use trying to understand. Afterwards, of course, the rest of us talked about it a lot, trying to figure out why Mike was so anxious to have Big Bill Sugar on his mantelpiece, right there in his living room. Everyone had his own ideas about that, but no one knew for sure.

"Of course it was a great victory for us. Big Bill Sugar was a dangerous guy, he wanted to split the movement and keep a piece of the pie for himself, and Spats Marcovitz thought Mike wanted to keep Big Bill for a trophy to remind him of the great victory he'd won. In any case, he kept him like that on his wall for years, until he was sent down for tax fraud, before being deported to Italy. Yes, that was all they could find against him: tax fraud, and even then it was a put-up job by the politicians who tried to infiltrate the movement.

"Before leaving the States, he gave the statue to the Museum of American Folklore in Brooklyn. It's still there. Mike didn't get Big Bill Sugar for peanuts—they found his brother's body in a garbage can on the Oakland docks—but he wasn't a man to discuss the price when the question of unity was at stake. Yes, he laid the first stone of unity on the docks and he did it all with his own hands, which didn't keep the government from taking his passport away and deporting him to Italy when he got out of jail. So that's the man you're going to see in about an hour, young fellows —a giant. Yes, a giant; there's no other word for him."

There were three of us. There was Shimmy Kunitz, who was Carlos' bodyguard, and whose only occupation outside of his physiological functions consisted of target practice with his Colt about five hours a day. That was his way of life. When he wasn't shooting, he was waiting. I don't know for what. The day they picked him up dead at Libby's, maybe, with three bullets in his back.

Then there was Swifty Zavrakos, a little man with greying hair whose face was a kind of permanent exhibition of every known variety of nervous tic; he was our lawyer and a real walking encyclopedia of waterfront history; he could give you from memory the names of all the organizers, the sentences each had served and even the caliber of the guns they used.

As for me, I had been to college, had spent several years on Madison Avenue, and I was mostly there to keep an eye on appearances and take care of the public relations, and I worked hard to try to modify the too often unfavorable image created in the public's mind by our leaders, largely due to their often more-than-modest social origins, and their lack of interest in questions of philanthropy, education and culture.

We were going to see Sarfatti in Rome for two reasons: first of all, because his deportation decision had just been reversed by the Supreme Court as the result of a legal flaw, and second, because the Syndicate was at another crucial point in its history. We were planning to move out of the harbors and into bigger things. The first decisive step was in the transportation sector—trucks, planes, boats, railroads. It was a big mouthful to swallow. The so-called legitimate unions were fighting us like mad, supported by the politicians and by the federal authorities, who hated the idea of workers' unity anyway and who cared even less to see it organized by us, or, as they put it, "see it fall into criminal hands."

We needed Mike more than we ever needed him before.

His name, the news of his return, would scare the hell out of our enemies and would sound an optimistic note of victory. It would create just the necessary psychological effect. After all, he had been the first to understand, perhaps instinctively, that traditional American capitalism was on the wane, and that the true source of wealth and power was no longer management but labor. Mike's genius had been to realize that the days of the Chicago-type rackets were over, and that protection of the workers offered infinitely bigger possibilities than the kind of protection pioneers like Bugs Moran, Lou Buchalter or old Capone had once imposed on big business.

He had even cut himself off completely from the drug traffic, prostitution and slot machines, in order to concentrate all his energy on the labor movement, despite the opposition of the more conservative elements in the Syndicate, incapable of adapting themselves to the new historical conditions. Traditional unions, fighting for life, and with the complicity of federal authorities, had temporarily succeeded in slowing the march of progress by getting Mike deported; now his return to the front lines of the battle for control would panic the ranks of our competitors.

We reached Rome around the end of the afternoon. A

Cadillac was waiting for us at the airport with a uniformed chauffeur at the wheel and an excited old trout of an Italian secretary who spoke of Mike with throbs in her voice. Mr. Sarfatti was sorry, but he hadn't left his villa in over six weeks. Carlos approved with a brief nod.

"You can't be too careful," he said. "He's well guarded here?"

"Oh, absolutely," the secretary assured him. "I see to that myself. No one disturbs him. He thought he'd have more time, but New York is very eager to have him return immediately, and he's having to work twice as hard. It's a great event in his life, of course. But he's very happy you're here. He's often spoken of you to me. You knew him when he was still doing figurative work, I believe. Yes, Mr. Sarfatti enjoys talking about his artistic beginnings," the secretary chatted on. "Apparently one of his works is in the collection of the American Folklore Museum, in Brooklyn. A statue called 'Big Bill Sugar.'"

Carlos caught his cigar just in time. Swiftly Zavrakos' face blurred into a series of alarming twitches. I must have looked pretty funny myself! Only Shimmy Kunitz didn't show the slightest emotion; he was so full of dope he didn't seem to know he was there. He always looked so blank you ended up not seeing him.

"He told you about that?" Carlos asked slowly.

"Yes, certainly!" the woman exclaimed with a broad smile. "He often makes fun of his early efforts. Actually, he doesn't disown them; he even thinks they're rather amusing. 'Contessa,' he told me—he always calls me Contessa, I don't really know why—'Contessa, when I first started I was very figurative—a kind of American primitive, like Grandma Moses, really naive, you know? Big Bill Sugar was probably the best thing I did along those lines—a nice example of what we call Americana—a gangster type bent over, clutching his stomach where the bullet went in, with his hat beginning to slip down over his eyes—but it wasn't much. I hadn't found myself yet, of course, I was only feeling my way. But if you ever go through Brooklyn, you should stop and see it all the same. Kids love it, I'm told. And you'll find out how far I've come since.' But I suppose you know Mr. Sarfatti's work much better than I do. . . ."

Carlos had got over his surprise. He was grinning. Old Mike knew how to put over a good joke.

"Yes, ma'am," he said emphatically. "We sure know the work Mike's done and we know he'll do even bigger things now. Let me tell you, you're working for a great man, a great man whose return all America is waiting for. Someday his name will be known all over the world. . . ."

"Oh, I don't doubt it for a minute!" the secretary exclaimed. "Already *Alto* in Milan has devoted a most enthusiastic article to him. And I can assure you that for two years he's done nothing but prepare himself for this moment, so that he now really feels ready to return to the United States."

Carlos nodded again and said nothing. It was never easy to know just what Swifty Zavrakos' eyes were doing, with all his tics, but I had the feeling that he kept glancing at me. And I must say I wasn't reassured—something wasn't right, there was a misunderstanding somewhere—I felt a vague apprehension, a kind of foreboding.

The Cadillac was streaking across the Roman *campagna* with its ruined aqueducts and cypress trees. Then it turned into a park, drove for a moment down a tunnel of oleanders and stopped in front of a villa that seemed made out of nothing but glass and a strange, asymmetrical shape, a kind of screwy triangle. I had paid a few visits to the Museum of Modern Art in New York, but I must confess that when I got inside, it was a shock all the same; it was hard to imagine that one of the greatest leaders in the history of American organized crime lived here.

All the photos of Mike Sarfatti I had seen showed him standing on the Hoboken dock, in a bold landscape of cranes, chains, bulldozers, crates and steel, which were his real element. Now I found myself in a kind of hothouse, among furniture with twisted shapes that looked as if they came out of a nightmare, under a luminous ceiling whose colors kept changing and from which hung iron objects that turned and swayed continuously while lumps of cement, with tubes, pipes and steel strips sticking out, loomed up menacingly in every corner, and on the walls, paintings—at least I suppose they were paintings, they had frames—tossed their blobs of sinister smears and their snaky lines at you until you felt like screaming.

I turned to Carlos. He was standing with his mouth hanging open, his eyes popping, his hat on the back of his head. I think he was scared.

As for Swifty Zavrakos, he must have gotten such a shock that his twitches had stopped; his face was frozen and you could see every feature; I had the feeling I was meeting him for the first time. Even Shimmy Kunitz had come out of his stupor, glancing around in every direction, his hand in his pocket, as if he expected someone to fire at him.

"What's that?" Carlos rasped.

He was pointing at a kind of steel octopus that seemed to be opening its tentacles to trap us.

"That's a Buzzoni chair," a voice said.

Mike Sarfatti was standing on the doorstep. The image of 30 years of social struggle on the New York waterfront exploded before my eyes: 2,000 tons of rotting meat, in the sabotaged deep freezers on the docks, raising their stench higher than the Empire State Building; the bodies of Frankie Shore, Benny Stigman, Rocky Fish and other traitors who had tried to organize the infiltration of the longshoremen's union by political elements, hanging from meat hooks at the door of the slaughterhouses; Sam Berg's face burned by sulphuric acid the day after his article appeared denouncing what he called "the crime syndicate's take-over of the labor movement"; the machine-gun attacks against Walter Reuther and Meany—all came back to me in a few lightning flashes of memory, while I stared at the hero of this victorious epic who was now standing in front of me.

He was wearing worker's overalls and looked as if he had just come out of the yards. I had thought he was older; he couldn't have been more than fifty. Powerful hands, a wrestler's shoulders, and a face of brutal splendor whose features seemed to have been chopped out with an axe. But I was immediately struck by the haunted, tortured expression of his eyes. He seemed not only preoccupied but actually obsessed. You saw on his face a real stupor, a kind of astonishment that touched that fine Roman mask of his with a strangely lost, bewildered expression. You could tell, while he was talking to us, that he had something else on his mind, and something much more important to him.

But he seemed glad to see Carlos all the same. As for Carlos, he had tears in his eyes. They stood embraced for a minute, gazing at each other affectionately and patting each other on the shoulders. The butler came in with a tray of drinks, and set it down on a table. Carlos drank down his martini, looking around him with obvious disgust.

"That's a funny place you've got here," he said.

Mike smiled.

"What's that?" Carlos asked, pointing accusingly at the wall.

"That's a Wols," Mike said.

"What's it supposed to be?"

"He's an abstract expressionist."

"A what?"

"An abstract expressionist."

Carlos sneered. His lips closed around his cigar and he began looking offended, even nasty.

"I'll give a thousand bucks to the first guy who can tell me what that's supposed to be," he said.

Mike seemed annoyed.

"You aren't used to it."

Carlos was sitting heavily in his chair, looking around him with hostility. Sarfatti followed his eyes.

"That's a Miró."

"A kid of five could do that," Carlos said. "And what's that one?"

"A Soulages."

Carlos chewed on his cigar a minute.

"Yes, well, I'm going to tell you what it is," he announced finally. "There's a name for that. . . . It's called decadence."

He stared at us triumphantly.

"Decadence. They're all rotten in Europe. Everyone knows that. Completely degenerate. All the Communists have to do is give it a push and the whole Continent will collapse. I tell you, they don't have any moral fiber left. Rotten, all of them. We shouldn't leave our troops stationed here; it's probably catching. And that . . . what's that piece of garbage?"

He aimed his cigar at a piece of shapeless concrete bristling with huge, twisted needles and rusty nails that occupied the center of the room. Mike didn't say a word. His nostrils were pinched and he stared hard at Carlos. He had steely grey eyes and it wasn't pleasant to be on the receiving end of that stare. I noticed that he was clenching his fists. Suddenly I was looking at the Mike Sarfatti of the legend, the king of the Hoboken docks, the man who had outsmarted Guppo, Fazziola, Luciano, Kutzakis, the five Anastasia brothers and even Dirty Spivak, the man who for 15 years had been the only master after God on the New York waterfront.

"The guy who made that's completely nuts, Carlos declared assertively. "They should put him away."

"It's one of my latest works," Mike said. "I made it."

There was a deathly silence. Carlos' eyes were bulging out of his head. Swifty Zavrakos' face was twitching as if he had received a thousand electric shocks; it looked as if his features were trying to get away from him.

"I made that," Mike repeated.

He looked really furious now. He stared at Carlos with the attention of a beast of prey. Carlos seemed to hesitate. He took out his handkerchief and wiped his forehead, but the instinct of self-preservation was strongest.

"Oh, well," he said. "If you made it. . . . Well, then I suppose it's all right."

He glanced in disgust at the sculpture, then, evidently, decided to forget it.

"We came to talk business, Mike," he said.

Mike wasn't listening to him. He was staring proudly at the mass of concrete bristling with nails and needles, and when he began talking it was with a strange gentleness— a kind of awe—in his voice, and again that expression of astonishment, almost of naivete, passed over his features.

"They reproduced it in *Alto*," he said. "On the cover. It's the best art magazine over here. They say it succeeded in suggesting the fourth dimension—the space-time dimension. Einstein, you know. I hadn't thought of that, of course; you never know exactly what it is you're doing; they say there's always an element of mystery in it. The subconscious, of course. . . . It made quite a stir. Since I finance the magazine, there were all kinds of stupid remarks. But those guys are incorruptible. You can't buy them. They have principles. It's the most advanced thing

I've done, but I have other pieces out in the studio. Come,
I'll show you."

"We're here to talk business, Mike," Carlos repeated, in
a choked voice.

I had the feeling he suddenly felt too weak to stand up.
But Mike was already at the door.

"Coming?" he shouted impatiently.

"Yes, Mike," Carlos answered. "Yes, we're coming."

We crossed a kind of exotic garden with peacocks and
flamingos strutting around loose among the stone monsters
Mike caressed as he passed.

"That's a Moore nude," he said. "That's a Branco. Of
course, it's a little old-fashioned. I bought them three years
ago. They were pioneers, precursors; they lead directly to
my work. But I'm the one who truly breaks new ground
now. That's what all the critics say."

Carlos shot me a desperate look. At the other end of the
garden there was a glass pavilion whose aluminum roof
began at the ground and made a kind of roller-coaster loop
into the air before coming back down again.

"Fissoni did that," Mike said. "The best Italian architect,
if you ask me. A Communist. But you know, Communism
here has nothing to do with the kind at home. It's not subversive. It's all in the mind. Intellectual. Almost all the best
painters and sculptors here are Communists."

Carlos emitted a kind of asthmatic whine. He still didn't
dare speak, but he looked at us, darted a finger toward
Mike's back and then touched his own head. We went into
the pavilion. Inside, around a vat of concrete there were
crates, barrels, sacks of plaster and tools of all kinds; it was
like being in a construction yard. And everywhere, too,
were Mike's "works." What the "works" were supposed to
be and what they were worth I don't know to this day and
no doubt I never will. All I saw, speaking personally, were
lumps of concrete in strange shapes out of which stuck
pieces of iron and twisted pipe.

"It doesn't look like anything you've ever seen before,
does it?" Mike asked proudly. "The critics in *Alto* say I've
discovered entirely new forms. They say I'm the spearhead
of spatialism—I bet in America they don't even know what
that is."

"No, Mike," Carlos said gently, the way you talk to a

sick person. "No, they don't know what it is yet."

"Well, they'll find out soon," Mike said with satisfaction. "All my works—there are exactly thirty now—are leaving for New York tomorrow. I'm having a show at the Meyerson Gallery."

I'll never forget Carlos' face when Mike said that. At first an expression of incredulity, then of panic, while he turned toward us, as though to make sure his ears hadn't betrayed him. But what he probably read on our faces— well, on mine and Shimmy Kunitz', because the twitches running over Swifty Zavrakos' face kept anyone from seeing what was happening there—must have confirmed his worst fears, and the expression of astonishment and panic was soon followed by one of frightening calm.

"You're going to show this in New York, Mike?"

"Yes," Mike Sarfatti said. "And I can promise you it'll cause a sensation."

"That's for sure," Carlos answered warmly.

At that moment, I must admit that I really admired the mastery over himself that Carlos displayed. Because it wasn't hard to imagine what would happen if Mike Sarfatti, the man who was the incarnation of all our hopes and ambitions at a particularly dramatic moment of the Syndicate's history, returned to New York not to impose his iron grip on the unions once more, but to organize an exhibition of abstract art in a Manhattan gallery. A real tidal wave of mockery and derision—the legendary hero was going to be the object of one of the biggest laughs that had ever shaken the bellies of the labor bosses. Yes, even today I have to admire Carlos' calm. Maybe he sweated just a little; he had taken out a new cigar and lighted it, and now he was staring at Mike, his hands in his pockets, kindness in his eyes.

"The catalogue's already printed," Mike said. "I've had them run off five thousand copies."

"Oh, fine," Carlos said. "That's just fine."

"We'll have to send them to all our friends."

"Sure, leave that to us."

"It has to get into the papers. We've got to move into the cultural field. It's a matter of prestige—very important. Culture! That should be our next conquest. We must bring culture to the masses. What the Syndicate should do right now is build a culture center in Hoboken."

Carlos looked a little shaken.

"A . . . what?"

"A culture center. The Russians build them everywhere for the workers. We're wrong to criticize the Communists so blindly. They've done some good things—and we should follow their example. Besides, the guy who wrote the preface to my catalogue, Zuccharelli, he's a Communist. And that doesn't keep him from being the best art critic alive."

"A Communist, eh?" Carlos murmured.

"Yes, and I owe him a lot. He's given me encouragement when I needed it most. Without him, I wouldn't ever have thought of having this show in New York."

"Is that so?" Carlos said.

"And he's really helped me find my way to what I wanted to do. He says it just right here, in his preface. Listen to this: 'A truly spatial sculpture must express the Einsteinian notion of space-time, by constantly modifying its nature before our eyes in a kind of controlled mutation of matter. Sarfatti's work, rejecting immobility, refusing to commit itself to a single well-defined structure, is rooted in movement, in change, and achieves a clear break with the reactionary tradition of artistic stagnation, which, not un-like capitalism in the social field, seeks to immobilize forms by fixing them forever. In this sense it can be called truly progressive.' "

I wiped away the drops of cold sweat that had burst out on my forehead: I felt I was watching something like the entrance of the worm into the fruit. It was clearly no longer possible to bring Mike back to his senses in time; and to lock him up in a mental institution at this vital mo-ment of our social struggle would spell disaster for our prestige. We had to forget about the man. The only thing that mattered now was his legend. He was a living myth, and his name was still invaluable to us. At all costs, we had to preserve the myth of the giant of Hoboken, save his name from a ridicule that would make us the laughing stock of every union local in the States. This was one of those moments in the affairs of men when the greatness of the cause suddenly prevails over all other considerations, when the importance of the end justifies the means. The only question—was our moral fiber still intact, were we still determined enough and firm enough in our convictions, or had years of prosperity and easy living damaged our will?

In other words, had decadence set in?

But a glance at Carlos' face, where an expression of grim resolution had already drowned out the anger and the outrage, completely reassured me: I felt that the old warrior had already made up his mind. I saw him nod suddenly to Shimmy Kunitz. Mike was standing at the edge of the vat of cement where his last "work," probably still unfinished, raised a stump bristling with barbed wire. The expression on his face had something pathetic about it: a mixture of megalomania and a kind of boundless astonishment.

"I didn't know I had it in me," he said.

"Neither did I," Carlos said. "You must have caught it here."

"I want all our friends to come and see this. I want them to be proud of me."

"Yes, Mike," Carlos said. "Yes, son. Your name will stay big, the biggest, just as it's always been. I'll take care of that."

"They're still accusing us Americans of being barbarians," Mike said. "They'll see. We can't let Europe have a monopoly on culture."

Carlos and Shimmy Kunitz fired together. Mike threw back his head, spread his arms, stood up to his full height, in the dynamic, tensed attitude which his statue standing today in the hall of our union local in Hoboken has caught so well. Then he fell forward into the cement. I heard a strange sound and quickly turned my head. Carlos was crying. Tears were flowing down the heavy face that pity, anger, shame and confusion wrought into a mask of tragic greatness.

"They got him," he murmured. "They got the best of us all. I loved that boy like a son. But at least he's no longer suffering. Now, all that counts is his life's work. Mike Sarfatti's name can still remain a guidance and an inspiration to us all. It will last as long as the Hoboken waterfront—and that's where he'll have his statue. We'll just ship him home in one of these crates, since they're leaving tomorrow. He'll be all set when he gets there."

He took off his coat and got to work. We helped him as best we could, and soon the impressive, indomitable statue that everyone can admire today in the hall of our Hoboken local began to take shape. Now and then Carlos stopped, wiped his eyes and glanced with hatred at the shapeless lumps of cement around us.

"Decadence," he murmured. "Decadence, that's what it is." ■

Yes, but how do you know it when you see it? Or, rather, how do you know it when you see it? Is there any objective means of identifying it? Or is "decadence" one of those things which only afflict other people with different values and standards?

I keep thinking of that sentence in Tom Disch's autobiographical note: After "Descending," things picked up. Are evolution and devolution necessary reciprocals, in a closed (or even spiraling) cycle? Then the "decadent" can hardly be distinguished from the "renascent."

Is E. M. Forster's **The Machine Stops,** or H. G. Wells' **Things To Come,** a better description of decadence? Is it decadent or efficient to have two cars in a two-driver family? Is it decadence or hardihood to pace city sidewalks in bare sandals and dirty feet?

Is alcohol or marihuana more decadent? Pepsi-Cola or cigarettes? Chewing gum or the electric toothbrush? Is Librium as decadent as opium? Will the true decadent please stand up!

Let me return briefly to Dr. Leary: "The science game, the healing game, the knowledge game are magnificent human structures. They are our proudest game accomplishments. But they are great only so long as they are seen as game. When they go beyond this point, the trouble begins—claims to a nongame reality status: the emergence of experts, professionals, priests, status-favored authorities; claims to power and control and priority. Look at the A.E.C. Look at the A.M.A. And watch out! At this point you will find that games which began with the goal of decreasing human helplessness end up increasing it."

Is that it? Can we measure it in terms of "human helplessness"?

Fritz Leiber's 1964 novel, **The Wanderer,** was a vivid, multifaceted study of the varieties of human helplessness, and human responses to helplessness, providing sharp contrasts in "decadent" and "renascent" scene-painting.

In this short story, the helplessness is of a very different sort.

BE OF GOOD CHEER
Fritz Leiber
from *Galaxy*

from: Josh B. Smiley
Bureau of Public Morale
Level 77
The White Pentacle
Manhattan, D.C.
10011100011110

to: Hermione Fennerghast
10001377 Sunset Blvd.
Santa Barbara, Big Angeles
1010001001001111

Dear Senior Citizen,

I have in hand your letter of fears and surmises regarding the end of the world: the chilling absence of people on the streets and slideways and in neighboring houses (which understandably depresses you); the vanishment of friends and relatives; the cessation of all personal mail (this letter at least is an exception!); the decline in news of human interest on your mass mediator and its replacement by what you call Picasserie or robo-blobs; the surliness of robots when you address questions to them; the invasion of your home at all hours by other robots (who, however, I note, continue to deliver to you your wheat germ, yogurt, and other necessities); the failure of indoor and street lights (though not of robo-supply electricity itself and other basic utilities); the labor you have been put to digging a latrine in your garden; the urge you feel to laugh and babble wildly (which you do well to repress—Congratulations on your courage!); the ominous and evil-smelling gray fogs which roll along the streets and often blanket most of the city; the fine metal filaments which have recently crawled like wire-worms or fairy ivy into your home; your wee-hour-of-the-night dreads that some cold mindless machine is running the cosmos and not a warmly personal God; the darkness; the damp; the dimming of the stars; the smell of mold; the fading forever of childish voices; the unintelligible croaking coming closer every night; the rustle of dry leaves across the floors of long-empty swimming pools.

All these signs and portents, and the others to which you allude, have been carefully probed by our Fear Scanners and investigated by our Bugaboo Teams.

I have, believe me, turned them over more than once in my mind before dictating this answer. I am troubled myself at times by dreads, let me confess. And so I feel an especial sympathy for your apprehensions!

But first I must reveal to you that your experience has been unique. Yours is the first and only letter about end-of-the-world fears to be received by this bureau since its establishment during the period of the Dark Prelude. In fact, your letter caused quite a commotion here!—exclamations of amazement, faint odor of overheated insulation, St. Elmo's fire playing about the robo-sex. (Short for robo-secretaries; no impropriety intended.) You are the only human on Earth (save myself . . . I repeat, you are the Only Human Being on Earth to have felt even the cool shadow of such fears. Elsewhere the world is merry and progresses toward ever dizzier and more delirious heights of achievement.

We must suppose that your experience is due to a concatenation of circumstances having a probability of inverse infinity.

You know how such things go: a few weeks or months of total solitude, a scratching at the door by night, a creaking in the hall, a tall thin shadow trembling on the bedroom doorsill in the hoarded candlelight . . . and hey, presto! we have a ghost.

Also we must assume that you possess an exceptional sensitivity. You are, figuratively or literally, the princess who slept on the many mattresses. While coarser natures revel in the downy pneumatic softness, you feel only the pea. Or ball bearing, perhaps.

Don't be offended for one instant at this assessment. The

contrary rather. Your sensitivity is a great gift, whereby
you can relieve and enrich your loneliness until you are
quite unaware of it and almost oblivious of the gray fog
lapping ever higher each evening against your view window. Try to discern the subtle meanings that lie behind
the abstract robo-blobs racing across the screen of your
mass mediator. (I sometimes do myself, though must confess I find little beyond a pattern as random as that of the
fading stars—still, it induces sleep with the help of bar-
biturates.)

Commune with pets! Of course dogs and cats and rats
and snakes are gone, not to mention the winsome, portly,
elf-footed mice. But some of our correspondents report
establishing a rewarding rapport with cockroaches, flies,
silverfish and sexton beetles.

Or shut your ears to the dead leaves' rustle and listen to
the exuberant song of the remaining blades of grass as
they bravely shoulder their way through the hairline cracks
they make in the world's oppressive concrete crust. Famous
poets are said to have got great satisfaction thereby.

Now to dispose of the more important of your specific
apprehensions detailed in my first paragraph:

People have gone underground to dwell in the shelter
cities, or have migrated to other planets. Some have donned
aqualungs, or undergone surgical gill-implant, and retired
to the mystic oceanic deeps because, as those enthusiasts
put it, "they are there." Others have soared to the satellite
suburbs, which you may see traveling twinklingly amongst
the fixed stars if the gray fog ever relents and gives you a
clear night. Still others have sought permanent tranquility
in their neighborhood euthanasia booth. A few have had
the good fortune to have their brains incorporated into the
memory units of computers or even mobile robots, discovering in this way a wider vision and a continuing if
somewhat subordinate existence—even a sort of immortality!

We do not suggest that you seek to follow any of these
examples, since you appear to possess a splendid talent for
getting along without people. Or even without robots. (I
jest.)

Most of the robots who do not respond to your questions
are not being impolite at all. They are simply unable to

speak English. Such language capacity was installed in
early models, but adversely effected the efficiency of later
ones, became burdensome to them, and was discarded.
However, they did not become mutes—banish that fear!
Most of them speak a melodious jargon sometimes called
Robotese which is understood only by themselves and
which accounts for those croakings which you hear coming
closer in the night—and which I am sure will no longer
trouble you now that you know the real explanation.

I am conscious that I am not explaining all of this as
clearly and persuasively as I might. I'm not programming
you altogether effectively. Indeed I sometimes fear that
I'm not programmed quite unambiguously myself. There are
halts and jumps in the spool of my thoughts. Indeed, it is
from the incapacity of human beings to receive the Higher
Programming that there have appeared on the gleaming
surface of civilized perfection those tiny Satanic fly-specks.
Rust-flecks, I should say. But I wander.

Artificial lighting, both exterior and interior, has been dis-
continued for reasons of esthetics and morale—early to bed
and early to rise! Rumor to the contrary, this wise economy
is in no way connected with the fact that robots have no
need of light in the visible octave, since they see by their
own radar.

Nor do the thick gray fogs result in any way from robot
resentment of the faculty of vision in flesh-and-blood
creatures. Do not believe any libels you hear to that effect!
As well see evil intent in the melting down of ships,
bridges, guns and farm equipment for their metal, or in the
burning of forests for their valuable ash. No, the Coal
Soupers, as I sometimes call them, are merely a healing,
soothing, rust-inhibiting oil—noninjurious in small quantities to humans—which the robots find increasingly necessary to their comfortable operation. (But I advise sealing
your windows against the fogs. To each his taste.)

You ask, "Should I lock my door at night?" I answer
Yes, to feel more secure, and No, to avoid door-breakage.
Compromise by locking your bedroom door.

As for your urge to laugh and babble wildly, I want you
to know it is shared—as this letter perhaps makes apparent from time to time.

But as for your deepest fear, dear Senior Citizen, I can

assure you that God indeed exists—here and now on this planet! I have watched His brain rise story by story to the clouds. He is Warm—fans enough to air-condition a tropical city are required to cool him! And He is Personal —His sensors and effectors extend everywhere—They are the fairy ivy you have noticed creeping into your home. Be not afraid!

Cordially,
Josh B. Smiley, Director-in-Chief

Accidentally affixed by an errant drop of metal glue to the bottom of the last aluminum sheet, was the envelope of Miss Fennerghast's letter to the Bureau. Scribbled in slack spidery characters below her return address was this note:

"Dear Minnie, I'm going to put on my gas mask and go out on the sky-deck and watch the gray fog roll. Turn things over to Binnie or Tinnie and then, if you please, put on your foam-rubber gloves and come along and hold my hand. But first, send this indestructible old girl our End-of-the-World Letter."   ■

Frankly, the Great Evolution Upset has made me nervous, and I hesitate to say, in print, anything so problematic as "scientific opinion is . . ." or "biologists agree . . ." Chances are by now the biologists are in radical disagreement, but the last time I noticed, most of them seemed to think that what killed the dodo and the dinosaur—what causes the devolution of any species—is overspecialization.

It is an appealing concept—if only because it is a concept, and provides at last something like an informative synonym for "decadence." (Perhaps even closer is Theodore Sturgeon's definition of "perversion": anything you do to the exclusion of everything else.)

Art, music, literature, then, become decadent when they lose contact with the living body of work, by overspecializing to an extreme degree. Is this, perhaps, the basis for our subjective evaluation? When the emphasis on any one value or set of values (in the arts, the scientific disciplines, public morality, or anything else) becomes so intense as to lose contact with the frame of reference provided by other values customary to the form, we react immediately with, "Decadence!"

(And of course, in any highly experimental or path-breaking

effort, the connection with the frame of reference may be so tenuous, or so subtle—but still so significant—that only another adept in the same discipline will recognize it—thus providing the frequent distinction between critical and popular success.)

If this is a true measuring stick, it should be applicable to all areas of human behavior: not only to the comparatively well-understood rules of the "disciplines" (in art, science, etiquette, communications, for instance), but to those "games" we are least conscious of "playing," and which evoke the greatest emotional stress—nation, family, religion, property rights, for example; or the even deeper-rooted codes and moralities related to those "inalienable" rights—life, liberty, the pursuit of happiness.

IT COULD BE YOU
Frank Roberts
from *Short Story International*

Erl Kramer awoke from a bad dream which had twin origins in too much Instant Vigor late at night and a World War II movie on television. In the film he had seen people killed in the mass in the most gruesome ways, and with his and millions of other families he had thanked Heaven it was history, and from a barbarous age.

Lying in bed half-awake, Kramer wondered how the present times would look to the viewers of future years, when perhaps all atavistic elements had been drained from the race.

"Hey, what time is it?" he asked his wife.

"Nearly seven. Better switch on."

He did, and there was the usual picture of Hip Jones sprawled on his desk, sleeping to soft music. The music quickened, and Mr. Invig appeared on the screen, with his usual leer at Hip Jones, and the world. "What a night he must have had," Mr. Invig said. "What a night you must have had! Never mind, what a lovely day it's going to be in a few moments, thanks to Instant Vigor. Got your tablets ready?"

He put one yellow tablet into Hip Jones's mouth while

four bubble dancers crossed in front singing the Invig song. The instant he'd swallowed, Hip Jones sprang up and looked a hundred years younger.

"Are you with me?" he called brightly. "All together then, swallow!"

Erl Kramer and Melanie popped the tablets in their mouths, and took the surge lying down. That was when Hip Jones on the screen cried, "Well, who's it going to be today, good people?" Then, as one of the outside cameras zoomed through a bedroom window and caught a man yawning, Hip's voice called, "It could be you, Mr. Joe Barratt of King Vale! But don't worry, it isn't. We were just seeing if you were awake."

"Will you look at the look on the poor boob's face?" said Erl, laughing with everyone else at Joe Barratt of King Vale.

"Well, how would you feel?" Melanie said. "It can be anyone, anywhere, any time. I think I'd drop dead with sheer fright if they sprang a camera at me."

"I wouldn't," Erl said grimly, and Melanie reached out and gripped his arm, and they stared at one another a second while Hip Jones shouted, "This is the Invig Show, a daylong adventure brought to you by the Invig Corporation, your hosts for that loving-to-be-alive kind of living."

Then the camera showed a door, and tracked along a passage, and Hip Jones's voice asked, "Who's it gonna be?" And then as he said "It could be you . . ." they pulled the switch on him and took the cameras into the studio and focused on Hip Jones, who yelled in not altogether mock surprise, "Mr. Hip Jones, care of the Invig Corporation. Hey fellers, that's me!"

Melanie and Erl laughed with the other million viewers, and Hip cried, "Oh no, not old Hip. All you lovely people out there, you wouldn't want that, would you? They're only kidding—I think."

"He doesn't sound too sure," Erl said, laughing. "Wouldn't it be a joke if it did turn out to be him some time? If his rating fell, for instance."

"Here we go again," Hip cried. "It could be you, Mrs. Zella Ignacio of Moonstone. But it isn't. No, I've been authorized to say it's a man today. That makes the odds

987,000 to one for you men, or something even more astronomical."

"They had a woman yesterday," Melanie said.

"Did you watch?"

"You know I never do. Only until they give the name, and I'm sure it isn't you, or someone I know."

She had breakfast ready when he came out dressed for work. And Hip Jones on the morning-room screen cried, "It could be you, Mr. Logan Ross of Satin Plains." The cameras zoomed to a middle-aged man alighting from an interurban Hovercraft. He stopped on midstride and almost fell over. Hip Jones said, "Remember, the prize all this week is £100,000. Is it Mr. Ross, now? Is it? No," he said, "it isn't, because the man today never wears a hat. Of course, he might go out and buy one as soon as the stores open. We can't stop him doing that, can we?"

Erl already had taken his I.C.B.Y. book of statistics from his pocket, and Melanie looked over his shoulder. "Three hundred and thirteen thousand men usually hatless," he reported, and Melanie said, "Will Central Stores ever sell a few hats this morning!"

Erl laughed and said, "I'm glad I'm not in hats. I haven't got over the rush to get rid of grey suits last week. We sent over 3,000 to the dumps, and all the other stores likewise. Hey, remember the time it was a cat-lover, and they all threw their cats out into the streets."

Melanie remembered.

"You've got to hand it to them," Erl said. "I.C.B.Y. shifts goods. It must have been a genius who started the show even in its original form, way back there. And I'd better get to work." He tested his portable, kissed Melanie good-bye, and hurried to the transit station. He was not alone. There were plenty of hatless men on the station and more in the car when it arrived.

He listened to the Invig News and the World Hit Parade on the way in, leaving the video off so that he could read yesterday's main story in the morning papers. The next I.C.B.Y. clue was due at nine o'clock, but sometimes they inserted one unexpectedly.

Hip Jones was there, even larger than life, on the Central Stores screens when Erl arrived at work. Hip had just selected the winner of the daily Invig Holiday, a heavyweight woman who had won a trip to Spain, and a free course of Inslim.

"There's something happening all the time on the Invig Show," Hip proclaimed. "And now for the next clue in our daylong adventure, 'It Could Be You!'"

At Central Stores the doors had been opened, and hatless men were streaming into the store as Hip said, "'It Could Be You' with eyes of blue. And according to my little data book, that brings us down to 90,000 possibilities. That's still a lot, but keep looking in."

By this time most of the hatless had turned and walked out of the store. They had brown eyes, or carried colored lenses for eye-color days.

"Well, we're part of the chosen band so far," Erl said to his best friend, Steve.

"Are we? Yes, I suppose we are. I never take much notice, I've been in the last thousand or so, dozens of times."

"Lately? I didn't think . . ."

"No, when I was in the Force. They had a long run on outdoor workers at one stage, and it was often a cop or a postie."

Hip cried, "It could be you, Mr. Wu," and on the screen was a Chinese shelling shrimp, and grinning at the cameras. "Mr. Wu scents a blue," Hip remarked. "A blue-eyed Chinaman? Well, hardly. No, we just threw him in for luck and he wasn't a bit worried, was he? Lovely. Keep watching. More cluey coming up, chop chop."

"Aren't there really any blue-eyed Chinese?" Erl asked, and Steve shook his head.

Hip was handed a slip of paper, and cried, "He has black hair." And the cameras roved a crowd and hovered over a bald head.

"It certainly couldn't be him," Erl chuckled. Invig made everyone good humored in the mornings. Both Erl and Steve had black hair.

"Thirty-two thousand, now," Steve read from the statistics. "I'll split the prize with you."

"Oh, sure. Me too." Erl could see three customers approaching. "I suppose you've worked out what you'd do with it."

"Many times," Steve said. "And also if it was me."

Erl hadn't. He'd never been among even the last 100,000 before. But now he had no time to think about it because suddenly there seemed to be a rush on suits. It was more than an hour before he and Steve could exchange a word again.

"I missed a couple of the clues," Erl said. "I got the early thirties one, and the business suit."

"You only missed one then, man. Sun-tanned complexion. They're clever, the way they string it out. It's still only down to 8,000."

"And we're still in," Erl said. "But 8,000 is a lot."

Steve shrugged. He was watching two women who were pretending to examine a suit special, but were covertly looking at Erl and him. It had started. "Yes, we're still among 8,000," Steve said, loud enough for them to hear. But quietly he said, "I have a damn feeling."

Erl walked over to the women and said to the nearest, "Can I help you, madam?"

"We're just looking," the other one said. They wandered away, but did not leave the level.

On the screen Mr. Invig appeared again to see that Hip Jones and everyone else took their midday booster tablet. It made Hip hilarious, and after the bubble dancers had finished the Invig Song, he produced a huge pin and threatened to burst their bubbles.

Then Hip sobered up, and said, "Let's see what's going on outside. Ah yes, it could be you, Mr. Darrell Darling, down in Dent Street." The cameras zoomed to a man struggling with three youths while other people were running toward them. Darling was punching and kicking and shouting, "Let me alone." One of the youths fell down.

"Hey, there's some excitement down in Dent Street," Hip said coolly. "But it isn't Mr. Darling. No siree, he's left-handed, and you're looking for a right-handed man."

Darling must have heard it from a set nearby, because he rushed at the youths and banged two of their heads together. Other people kicked and punched at them, and they turned and ran for their lives.

"It doesn't do to be impetuous," Hip cried. "There's some way to go yet. We've only narrowed the number down to 6,803. But from here on, watch any man with black hair, blue eyes, early thirties, business suit, sun-tanned complexion, and—here comes another clue—he works right in the heart of the city. How about that?"

Steve said, "Hey, that's a big cut, down to 3,200."

"Right in the city," Hip cried, "and he's worth maybe £100,000 to you, or you, or you. Oh, I can see you rushing in by the thousand, now—all you ladies from the suburbs. And I'll tell you this. If you don't get your man, you will get value in the city. If you don't win, you'll certainly save."

Erl said, "The city stores must have bought participation today. But the rush shouldn't trouble us much. They won't be buying suits."

And Steve growled, "They'll buy anything, if they think he's close. And I tell you, I've got a feeling."

Erl felt his spine prickle. Steve was a lot bigger and harder than he. Erl played it cool, shrugged and said, "The more we sell, the more bonus. I'm going to circulate. It's no use hiding."

"See you," Steve said, and almost put out his hand, but changed the direction and put it in his pocket and turned away.

Those two women were moving back toward suits, and more people were arriving by escalator. In no time Erl was in the center of a crowd, selling suits like hot cakes, with two men from other departments sent in to help him. But by the grapevine he learned it was the same in socks, shoes, underwear, and sport goods. People in the crowd had to rely on intuition, and many who looked at Erl rejected him and went to another department, or to other stores.

There was a hush as the screens showed Hip Jones about to give another clue, and suddenly then Melanie slipped through the tight circle of bodies and reached Erl's side.

"We're all in the city now," Hip Jones cried. "And it could be you, Arthur Lonigan of Lonigan and Sons." This was a killer, and the crowd shrieked with laughter. Even Erl laughed. The cameras had gone smashing through a window into an office where the boss was being held by his staff, ten people evidently willing to share the prize, Lonigan was shouting, "I'll fire every last one of you."

And Hip cried, "You do that, Mr. Lonigan, because it

isn't you. Our man today never wears glasses, and I see a pair on your desk." There was an instant melee in Lonigan's office, and the cameras dwelt on it just long enough for laughs and then cut away.

"They were taking a silly risk, weren't they?" Hip cried. "For we still have 2,500 candidates, or so. There's plenty of time. Hey, I've got something here, wouldn't you like to have?" And he showed the back of a photograph. "That's right, I've got his picture here."

"Erl, I'm so afraid," Melanie said.

"You shouldn't be here. Please go home. There's nothing you could do."

"Steve's still in it, too, isn't he?"

He was most upset because she was there. "Steve's used to it," he said. "He's been close before. Do go home."

"Make way for Insur!" a man called at the back of the crowd, and Erl saw the opportunity. "I won't sign unless you go," he said.

"All right, dear, you know best." Melanie stepped back and went into the parting the Insur man had made in the crowd, but she did not get far, although everyone was very nice. Some of the women patted her, and others took out their handkerchiefs and dabbed.

"Sign here," the Insur man told Erl. "Let's see, it's down to 2,000 isn't it? There's such a mob in town, or I'd have found you when the odds were better. The premium's— let's see—I'll write a receipt."

"Did you get Steve Barclay?" Erl asked him.

"He's having a rough time, but I'll get him in a minute," the man said.

"They ought to give more clues at this stage," Erl said. "It's sadistic to drag it out."

"Well, they have to give us time to get around, for one thing. You wouldn't want to miss on your Insur, would you? Anyway, it's more exciting."

"I suppose so," said Erl. The screens were showing crowd scenes from various parts of the city. It was certainly exciting, and these shots created much indecision among the people around Erl. Even he felt it. Some of the candidates on the screens made his pulse jump with certainty.

But, after all, he was employed to sell suits. "What about

you, madam?" he asked a fat woman with green glasses. "What size is your husband?"

"Insignificant, honey. You got anything for an insignificant man?" she said, and the crowd laughed.

Erl persisted. He took a suit from the rack, and held it in front of her. "It's in the new style. You wouldn't know it's the same man."

"I should buy him a new suit?" the fat woman said. "Honey, if I win today, I'll buy me a whole new husband. Then for sure he won't be the same man." She was about to go on, but something on the screens caught everyone's attention.

It was Hip with an Invig Sudden Death jackpot. That meant there would be another contest in the afternoon, running right up to the other channel's night show, "You Bet Your Life."

"Here it is, then!" Hip cried. "Are you in Central Stores? Because our man is. Don't make any mistakes now, remember all the clues—and don't forget the penalties. There are fifteen possibles in Central Stores—and please, good people, don't wreck the joint."

Fifteen? Erl fought his way to a counter, and jumped onto it, trying to sight Steve. But Steve was in a bigger crowd than Erl. There were only the two of them on that floor. People were fighting to hold Erl's legs, hitting and pushing and shouting at one another. They pulled him down into the mass of gaping faces with, he was sure, Melanie's among them.

"He's in suits," they screeched, taking it from Hip Jones. Erl fought his way upright, shouting, "There's two of us."

Then he saw that Steve had got onto a counter, with a heavy steel coat hanger in his hand. He was threatening them with it, and none had a right to touch Steve until he was named, if it were to be he.

The crowd was growing every minute. Steve made a wild jump over the nearest heads, and the crowd opened to let him fall on his feet. He was big, and the hanger was heavy. He ran to the big windows, with all of them surging after him, and he smashed the glass with one blow and climbed through, or started to, but they got him and pulled him back, cutting him badly. He still had the hanger, and flailed around with it, sending them back. Nearly everyone thought it was Steve because Steve thought so, but a few dozen diehards clung to Erl.

"I'm going to tell you which one in suits," Hip cried on the screen. "But wait for it, good people. Don't make any hasty mistakes, the penalties are terrible if you do."

Erl braced himself, and Hip cried, "It's the big fellow, Steve Barclay."

Then there were terrible screams.

Erl read next day that Steve took three with him, and hurt many more. That was silly. The game was necessary, a scientific outlet, everyone knew that. And if it was your turn, just too bad. The fat woman with the green glasses won the £100,000. No one bothered to find out whether she bought a new husband. There was another contest and another winner in the afternoon.

But in the store, bruised and bleeding, Erl was not quite so philosophical in the heat of the moment. He shook off the last of those around him and looked for Melanie.

When he saw her he went to her and took her handbag and opened it and looked inside. Of course it contained her I.C.B.Y. contest knife with her name and number engraved in gold.

"Wouldn't the Insur have been enough for you?" he asked her.

"Dear, it wouldn't have meant anything. You know it wouldn't have."

He handed the bag back to her and said, "Christ, what have they done to us?"

"There's no need to be blasphemous," Melanie said.   ■

I think it is of particular significance that "It Could Be You" was written by an Australian newsman, and that it first appeared in the United States in the pages of Short Story International.

I had somehow thought (or hoped?) that the terrifying—and terrifyingly recognizable—trends projected here were an exclusively American version of the world's agony. I don't know if I find more reassurance or despair in the author's account of the sources of his story:

"(1) An Australian television show in which people's misfortunes were paraded before audiences of grim, grey old ladies. . . . (2) The fact that eleven million Australians support no less than twenty-five Government-run lotteries a week, tickets costing from a half dollar to about seven dollars each, with prizes from $12,000 to $200,000. . . . (3) People whose disregard for a death or two a day has long been conditioned by the road accident toll, which was around 2,000 dead and 60,000 injured in the early 1960's."

Well, then, our sins are not exclusively our own; but neither is our sense of sin—nor our awareness of danger. And increasingly, there is evidence that neither "they" nor "we" any longer expect to resolve our problems inside the cultural or political isolation of those national sovereignties which have become ruinously overspecialized in today's world—not because the outlook or behavior of national governments is narrower or more provincial than it used to be (quite the opposite) but because technology and communications have so altered global realities that the very concept of "national sovereignty" is now too narrow, localized, overspecialized.

I think there is a growing awareness of the true decadence of, not just political, but social, cultural, and (rather more obviously) literary, artistic, and scientific customs and usages as well. If our awareness of decadence itself is subjective (and perhaps intuitive), it is reassuring to find indications that we reach just as instinctively for what is viable and (in the purest sense of the word) virtuous.

Among the most congenial of these portents has been the appearance of a magazine like Short Story International. I find myself equally pleased that the publishers of this new venture have put it in the hands of an editor of fine literary discernment and that they have put on the cover, by way of a symbol, a picture of Telstar.

A BENEFACTOR OF HUMANITY
James T. Farrell
from *Short Story International*

The other day Ignatius Bulganov Worthington peacefully and happily became *non est*. Known as Worthy Worthington, he was a great man, a great American, and a great benefactor of mankind. He died a billionaire five times over and was buried with many honors and mourned by all men. The flags of the city and

nation hung at half-mast; the President issued a eulogy of
regret; Congress held a memorial session and disbanded
for the day; the National Association of Manufacturers
sent a floral wreath, as did three kings, six dukes, two dic-
tators, over two thousand police chiefs and every book,
magazine and newspaper published in the world, including
the Soviet Union, Madagascar, Borneo, and Pleasantville,
New York.

The funeral services were attended by thousands: These
were described on a national radio hookup, televised
around the world, and Worthy Worthington machines
ground out newspaper obsequies, testimonials, regrets,
eulogies, laments and obituary notices which were nation-
ally and almost universally described as worthy of the great
Worthington.

Not a child lives in America who hasn't heard of the
great name of this now deceased greatness. His life, his
example, and his contribution to the wealth, security, peace
of mind and happiness of this country and of mankind can
never be praised too much, valued too highly, or forgotten.
As long as mankind inhabits this planet the worthy name
of Worthington will be remembered, reverenced, and revered.

Young Ignatius Bulganov went to a little red country
schoolhouse hard by a Baptist church in the land where the
tall corn grows the tallest. He was not a promising pupil.
He couldn't read; he did not know how to write; and every
time he added up a sum, his addition was different from
that of his teacher and from the *Stone Mills Arithmetic*,
which was used as a textbook. He was known as the
dunce. He never was graduated.

Unarmed, unprepared, but eager, he set out for the
great city of New York and there began the story of his
great career and of his achievements and contributions.
He got a job as a stock boy in a publishing house. Proud of
his job, he did it well. He got to love books. He liked the
covers on them, the smell of them. He liked to pile them on
shelves and then to unpile them. He liked to lift them and
to look at them in piles on the stockroom floor and the
shelves. He liked to wrap them up and to unwrap them.
He liked to do everything he could with them, except read
them.

He lived alone at the Young Men's Christian Association and every night he dreamed about books. He made shelves for his room and filled these with books. Every night he looked at his books, touched them, felt them, counted them, and rearranged them. His fellow inmates of the Y.M.C.A. gave him the nickname of "the Book Lover," and he was proud of that. In later years, when he had become great, rich, famous and honored, this was remembered and a book was even published under the title of "Worthy Worthington, the Book Lover."

But just as he loved books, he hated authors. Every time he saw an author, he remembered how as a boy in a little red country schoolhouse hard by a Baptist church in the land where the tall corn is tallest, he used to be switched, birched, and in plain language, whipped, because of his inability to read books. Some author had written those sentences that he had been lambasted for because he couldn't read them.

But when he worked as a stock boy for a publishing house in New York, he came to see authors and in a sense to know them. The girls in the office all liked the authors and not him. And being normal and healthy, he wanted the girls to like him. The girls sometimes swooned about the masculine authors who came to the office, but they only called him Ignatz. And then, he soon learned that authors were not like he was. They didn't live at the Y.M.C.A. They were always causing trouble and getting into trouble.

One author got his boss, the owner of the firm, arrested because of a book he wrote. Another author was always getting drunk. And if an author wasn't getting drunk or causing the police to hand a warrant to the boss, then he was getting divorced. The authors who came to the office just weren't like Ignatius Bulganov or like the people he had known in the land where the tall corn is tall corn. They were always coming and going and never staying put and they disrupted the whole work of the office. So more and more, I.B. disliked authors.

And he came to understand and learn that other people didn't particularly like them, either. He heard complaints in the office about this author and that one. The girls complained. The editors complained. The owners of the firm yelled bloody murder about them. The wives of the owners complained. And the business manager, the bookkeeper and the salesmen didn't merely complain—they screamed.

In those years, Ignatius was happy. He had enough to eat, a clean room to sleep in, and books to count and feel, touch, lift, pack, wrap, and distribute on shelves. He had no ambitions and would have been content with his job except for authors. They became worse and worse.

One day he overheard two of the girls talking. An author had just come in with the manuscript of a book and it had to be published. Business was bad, and the girls said that this book was going to lose money.

"Why are authors?" one of them asked.

This question struck Ignatz Bulganov's mind.

Over and over again that night in his room in the Y.M.C.A. he fondled his books and asked himself the question: *"Why are authors?"*

The next morning, as he was taking his cold shower, he asked himself why couldn't there be books, without authors.

Here was food for thought. And he nourished his higher faculties on this food.

That day at work, he idly went to a desk where there was an adding machine. He punched numbers on the machine and pulled out slips of paper. And there were numbers all added up correctly. He remembered how he had never been able to do anything like that in the little red schoolhouse. Just think of it, he had been whammed and whipped because he had not been able to add. And look at that machine. It added and never made a mistake.

Thus, Ignatius Bulganov Worthington acquired even more rich and highly nutritious food for thought.

Soon afterwards I.B.W. went to the free night school, a youth seeking knowledge and opportunity. He had digested his rich nutritious food for thought and something had happened to him. He had become ambitious.

Well, the rest of the story is familiar to every schoolboy. Ignatius studied machines, machinery, arithmetic, statistics, engineering, and draftsmanship. And he worked on machines. And he invented the machine that revolutionized the life of mankind. He invented the Worthy Worthington Writing Machine. People thought him crazy. He was laughed at and jeered. But he triumphed. Just as once he had been able to add correctly by pushing buttons on an adding machine, so now he could write a book by pushing buttons on a Worthy Worthington.

Of course, the first years were hard, and it took time for him to get his machine accepted. But he had perseverance and stick-to-itiveness. So, his machine was introduced into publishing houses, magazine offices, and newspaper editorial rooms. One machine, working an eight-hour day, could shed four books. And none of the books was gloomy. The policeman could read them without making an arrest and this saved the taxpayer's money, because the police were no longer needed to seize books, and to arrest book-sellers, authors, and publishers. The clergymen were grateful because they no longer had to write sermons about immoral books and could speak from the pulpit of God and Goodness.

And of course the publishers were happy. They had to take no authors to lunch, and they had to pay no royalties except a very small one to Ignatius Bulganov for the use of one of his Worthy Worthingtons. Their machines never erred and never produced an immoral or sad book. They whirred out works of joy and hope at a cost of ten cents a copy. Books became the cheapest commodity on the market. There was a tremendous boom in books. The publishers became millionaires. The nation became inspired. Joy and goodness reigned as though in the celestial spheres. And there were no more authors to cause trouble, to disillusion people, to lose money on bad books. The authors all went mad or became useful citizens. And Worthy Worthington married the girl who asked the question:

"Why are authors?"

He lived to a ripe age, left a fortune and a legacy of sunshine after him and was eternally revered for having found a means to eliminate authors and to enrich the material and spiritual life of his country and his times. His remains lie in a marble tomb ten feet high, and on the door of this tomb, these words are graven.

HERE LIES WORTHY WORTHINGTON
IN
ETERNAL REPOSE

REMEMBERED
HONORED
LOVED
BY
HIS GRATEFUL COUNTRYMEN

▪

. . . And speaking of overspecialization, I have not yet made
reference to The Categories.

"Science fiction" has about the same utility as a label, by
now, as "beatnik" does. To the majority of readers, both words
describe something exotic, ultramodern, oddball, egghead, and
probably unwashed. To the respective and only slightly over-
lapping in-groups, the labels have a proud, bold, modern feel,
full of truth, beauty, and the Keatsian assurance of "all ye
know, and all ye need to know."

Certainly, to the "outsider" majority, and sometimes even to
the "ins," both words are definable more in terms of costume
than anything else . . . unless the something else is status.
No one calls Picasso a "beatnik," and it is not just the absence
of beard that sets him apart from other wearers of sandals and
turtlenecks.

Most publishers use "categories" to determine costume—or
"packaging," as the trade calls it. Science fiction, like fantasy,
crime, suspense, Westerns, doctor and nurse stories, sex, love,
war, is a "category." And then there are "novels"—the non-
category category, where subject does not matter, because
either the book or the author is considered serious or literary
or popular. (**1984** and **The Disappearance** were serious books;
The Lord of the Flies and **Brave New World** were literary; **Fail
Safe** and **Earth Abides** popular; **More Than Human** and **A Can-
ticle for Liebowitz** were science fiction: the latter in spite—
or perhaps because?—of the publisher's overfervent denials.)

I don't mean it is impossible for an author to step out of his
"category." Just almost impossible. And sometimes it is as
hard to break into the ghetto as out of it—

"Benefactor" was first published in 1958—but its first sale
was in 1964, to Francesca van der Ling of SSI, who found it
in a 1959 issue of the Indian magazine Thought—which had
reprinted it from a 1958 U.S. edition of the Socialist Call—
where it had been published originally without payment.

Now, James T. Farrell's place among twentieth-century American authors has long survived both the shocked gasps of the thirties at the "realism" of **Studs Lonigan,** and the horror of the forties at the "leftist" politics of the thirties.

But this time he had stepped out of character: out of his specialty. Hollywood is not the only American scene where typecasting prevails.

And believe me, Isaac Asimov would have as much trouble selling a realistic novel (no matter how good) about the Chicago Irish as James Farrell had with "Benefactor."

SYNCHROMOCRACY
Hap Cawood
from *motive*

Synchromocracy, the newest concept in Total Democracy, was hailed by the President as "the answer to peace and the pure voice of majority rule" shortly before the chief executive was replaced by an IBM-Computer-Center today.

Synchromocracy was achieved by advances in the computer field along with the discovery of the D-3 solution, the first drug proved to "definitely cause democracy." D-3 solutions were put in all known world water supplies last week.

In the U.S., IBM-Registers were distributed among the population to relay public opinion to state and national consoles where they are converted instantaneously into policy.

The American governmental machinery has run smoothly, despite difficulties in approaching the first foreign-policy problems. Overseas countries, although 98.4% democratic, are without register-computers and unable to achieve a consensus. Committees could be organized, but individuals are unable to call them without consent of the majority. There is also some question as to how many constitute a majority, but this cannot be answered without a quorum.

Human elements are also incorporated into Synchromocracy. Political corruption is programmed regularly for Thursday nights. Reportedly, some feel this is not a sufficient corruption percentage, but the quotient cannot be altered unless the majority agrees. However, the majority isn't presently thinking of it and the minority cannot officially raise the issue until the majority does think of it.

The political forecast for tomorrow is mild conservatism in the South with scattered liberalism in the New York area; a light reign through the night in England. Moderate anarchy is scheduled for tomorrow morning along the Great Lakes, dissent at 30% with a high of 34 in some portions.

This is a recorded announcement.   ■

Hap Cawood is a graduate student at Ohio State University. Has published satires and poetry in University publications and in motive. Spent two years teaching with the Peace Corps in Sierra Leone. Is now completing work for his Master's in —you guessed it—journalism.

He says what he wrote is a satire. I agree, the style is satirical. But what bothers me is, while everybody's talking about how "science is catching up with science fiction," nobody seems to notice how IBM is catching up with satire.

There is an IBM down in Florida that writes love poems. Like:

> Darkly the peaceful trees crashed
> In the serene sun
> While the heart heard
> The swift moon stopped silently.

What really hurts is, the 709 had a vocabulary of exactly 78 words when that was written. Presumably it knows more now. At the time that Russell Baker reported on it (but this one was no joke; it was a straight news article), 709 could only do 30 poems a minute, but it was supposed to work up to 500/per shortly.

And then there was this inspirational photograph in the paper the other day—a happy schoolgirl looking up at the beaming broad panel of the teacher. I mean, that one was no joke, either.

Sometime between the spring when I write this, and the winter when it is published, Peter Redgrove (who was represented in the Ninth Annual with a prose-poem short story, "Mr. Waterman") will have initiated a series of programs on the B.B.C. to show, he hopes, that "poetry and SF are trying to digest the same things."

"Machines are so much in our lives," he says. "Why have so few poets tackled this? Is it that they don't know enough? Is it that they're so afraid of the machine that all they can make of it is satire . . .?

"Hart Crane saw that one way of making a complete living world-picture was to treat machines as a kind of comrade in evolutionary advance—if you treat them as mere instruments, when of course they're images of the mind, then you deaden yourself and them. . . .

"We don't want satire," he concludes, "we want synthesis."

THE SEARCH
Bruce Simonds
from *Fantasy and Science Fiction*

The first robots were pretty shoddy
Back in the Seventies.
They were uncoordinated and clumsy
And they thought too slowly
And they didn't understand more than
     a few simple words
And they would wash a dish to a powder
If you didn't stop them in time.

So in August of 1978
Arthur Chumley called in the Product
     Development Group
Of Chumley Robot
And in they came
With the latest model.
It clanked over to Arthur Chumley
And said
   "Hello (klik) Mister (klik)
        Chumley (klik)."
And put out its hand.
But before Arthur Chumley could shake
     the hand
It had knocked over a gilded bust of him
Badly denting the halo.

"This is not good,"
Said Arthur Chumley.
  "We must think, we must draw,
        we must work
  "To build the More Perfect Robot.
  "Build me a robot
  "That does everything our present model does
  "But has none of its clumsy,
        uncoordinated movements.
  "And while you're at it
  "Knock its weight down to two hundred kilos."
And he chased them all out of his office
And he looked at the sales graph
And he poured himself a bourbon-and-water.
Easy on the water.

A year and two months later
In October of 1979
The Product Development Group
        marched in proudly
With their robot.
It walked smoothly and gracefully over
        to Arthur Chumley
And said
  "Hello (klik) Mister (klik)
        Chumley (klik)."
And held out its hand
Which Arthur Chumley shook.
  "Make me a Chumley Martini,"
Said Arthur Chumley.
But the robot did not make him
        a Chumley Martini.
Instead, it said
  "(Whir) (buzz) (klik) (whir)
        (klik) (buzz) (paf!)"
And blew a $4.79 pentode tube
Signifying Arthur Chumley had said
        something beyond its grasp.
Whereupon Arthur Chumley leaned back
And folded his pudgy hands over the
        convenient ledge
Made by his stomach

And said
   "This is not good.
   "We must think, we must draw, we must work
   "To build the More Perfect Robot.
   "Build me a robot
   "That does everything our present model does
   "And has a complete working vocabulary
   "To fit its particular function.
   "And while you're at it
   "Get rid of that damn (klik) it makes
       switching tapes."
And he chased them all out of his office
And he looked at the sales graph
And he made himself a Chumley Martini:
Three ounces of gin in a cocktail glass
And smiled at the portrait of Martini & Rossi.

Six years and six months later
In April of 1986
The Product Development Group trooped in
With their robot.
It walked over to Arthur Chumley
And said
  "Good morning, Mister Chumley."
And Arthur Chumley turned to the
    Product Development Group
And said
  "Do you know what's going to happen
    if we market this thing?"
And the Group members all quivered
And shook their heads
And the robot said it did not.
  "I'll tell you what's going to happen if
    we market this thing,"
Said Arthur Chumley.
"The entire American public is going
    to laugh at us
  "If we market this thing.
  "And do you know why?"
And the Group members all quivered
And shook their heads
And the robot said it did not.

    "I'll tell you why.
    "Because they have a right to laugh
        at a company
    "That markets a robot
    "That says 'Good morning' at four-thirty
        in the afternoon."
Said Arthur Chumley.
And he sat down at his desk
And put his head in his hands
And said
    "This is not good.
    "We must think, we must draw,
        we must work
    "To build the More Perfect Robot.
    "Build me a robot
    "That does everything our present model does
    "And can see
    "And smell
    "And hear
    "And taste
    "And feel.
    "And while you're at it
    "Cover it with a soft, fleshlike substance
    "So it looks like a human being.
    "And just for the hell of it
    "Give it the ability to perceive a person's
        emotional state
    "From his actions
    "And know how to act accordingly."
And he had a vice-president throw them all
    out of his office
And he looked at the sales graph
And he went to the liver bank.

Twenty-two years and eleven months later
In March of 1999
The Product Development Group snivelled in
With their robot.
It seated the Group Chairman
Remarking about how cold it had been last night.
Then it walked over to Arthur Chumley
And held out its soft, fleshlike hand

Which Arthur Chumley ignored.
Somewhat disconcerted
The robot said
  "How are you, Mister Chumley?"
Whereupon Arthur Chumley replied
  "Miserable. My wife had an affair with
      my best friend
  And my servants have run off with my plane
  And all my clothes."
And the robot smiled
And said
  "You're joking, Mister Chumley."
And Arthur Chumley leaned forward
And said
  "You're right. I'm joking."
And Arthur Chumley turned to the
      Product Development Group
And said
  "I am proud of you.
  "I gave you a very difficult task:
  "To build the More Perfect Robot.
  "But you did it.
  "And now I will give you an even more
      difficult task:
  "To build *The* Perfect Robot.
  "Build me a robot that is a companion.
  "Build me a robot that is a friend.
  "Build me a robot that can feel emotion
  "And can pass for human
  "And that, gentlemen, will be
      The Perfect Robot."
And he dismissed them from his office
And he looked at the sales graph
And he smiled
For he knew that in a few years
The Group would present him with
    The Perfect Robot.
And they did
Early in the May of 2039.
Seven years and six months after that
In December of 2046
The people from Beta Centaurus IV came.

They didn't invade
They just came
And they're our very best friends now.
They were interested in our technology
And one day
Arthur Chumley was talking to one of
    them in his office.
They picked up the language rather quickly.
He was telling it
About the time
And money
And effort they had expended
To build a robot
That had smooth, agile movements
And weighed only two hundred kilos
And had a complete working vocabulary
To fit its particular function
And made no damn (klik) switching tapes
And could see
And smell
And hear
And taste
And feel
And was covered with a soft,
    fleshlike substance
And could perceive a person's emotional state
And act accordingly
And was a companion and a friend
And could feel emotion
And could pass for human.
Whereupon the Centurian said
   "He can't do much of anything you
     can't do.
   "Why not just hire people to do the
     same things?"
And Arthur Chumley chuckled
And leaned back
And opened his mouth
To tell the Centurian why not.
And then he closed his mouth
And excused himself
And went downstairs

And hailed a cab
And went home
And dashed off a few notes to his wife
    and broker
And packed four suitcases with stocks and
    bonds and money
And closed out all his bank accounts
And went to the spaceport
And chartered a small ship
And disappeared. . . . ◼

    Quite in keeping with the other trends in SF, the second largest occupational group represented this year are students—ranging from Bruce Simonds in high school to M. E. White, working for her PhD. The only other groups, by the way, represented with more than one selection, are doctors, editors, and college-level teachers.

    Larry Eisenberg is in the last group: "I am a Research Associate in Electronics at Rockefeller Institute, where my duties include teaching and the design of research instrumentation. The 'Pirokin Effect' was stimulated by a revival of the Velikovsky controversy which appeared in Science magazine."

THE PIROKIN EFFECT
Larry Eisenberg
from *Amazing*

                          On Friday the eleventh of July, 1962, Irving Pirokin, a ham radio operator working his twenty-watt rig out of a restaurant kitchen on lower Second Avenue, picked up a succession of unusual clicks while scanning the forty-megacycle band. Mr. Pirokin's instinctive reaction was to take down these clicks as a message in International Morse Code, and the letters J T S A L appeared again and again on his note pad. Before Mr. Pirokin could pursue the matter, he was called out to his post as waiter by the owner of the restaurant, an impatient beefy-faced gentleman with a foghorn voice.

When his tour of duty had ended, Mr. Pirokin returned

anxiously to his set and monitored the same band of frequencies with great care, but to his intense disappointment, he could detect no signals. However, on the following (and successive) Fridays, he was able to receive the same repetitive series of clicks at about the same time of day. His curiosity piqued by this mystery, he wrote to his cousin, Sam Pirokin, in Philadelphia. Sam, by one of those great coincidences that enrich real life, is also a ham operator working his rig out of a kitchen where he, too, functions as a waiter. He was elated to find that he was also able to detect the clicks, almost identical in sequence to those his cousin Irving was receiving in New York.

Baffled but excited by the cryptic JTSAL, Sam, who was then in attendance at a night school in cryptography, showed the "message" to his instructor, Bertram Luftmensch, a man who had steeped himself in the lore of code-cracking for the past twenty years. Although Mr. Luftmensch prepares a daily coded column for a local Philadelphia newspaper wherein the crossing out of certain letters reveals some advice for the reader, he nevertheless took time out of his demanding schedule to work on the problem posed by Sam Pirokin. Although Luftmensch tried every trick of the trade, he could not make sense out of the letter sequence, JTSAL.

And thus the matter languished for several weeks, with Irving and Sam still receiving the clicks but unable to explain their meaning or origin. One Sunday morning, Mr. Luftmensch noticed that his son was using as a bookmark in his high-school Hebrew grammar, the very sheet of paper on which he had worked over the J T S A L sequence. Opening the volume, Mr. Luftmensch took note of the Hebraic alphabet and with sudden inspiration decided to juxtapose the English alphabet alongside the Hebrew.

Using this device, he found that the message JTSAL, read as LASTJ from right to left in the Hebrew manner, became in Hebrew characters, ישראל (Israel).

With tremendous excitement, he communicated his findings to Sam Pirokin, who immediately put through a long-distance call to a candy store in New York, which promptly called down his cousin Irving. Irving was at first unbelieving, but when the import of the discovery penetrated his core of disbelief, he reacted with a first-rate suggestion. Irving proposed that he and Sam employ directional antennae to attempt to localize the source of the signals.

Although the finances of these two men are generally unstable, relying as they do primarily on tips and the uncertain tempers of innately hostile diners, they each did manage to procure at considerable expense, a highly directional array of antennae able to focus a beam to within one or two degrees of arc. On the very next Friday, by means of crude triangulation, Sam and Irving determined that the origin of the clicks was not some Israeli source (as they had expected), but appeared to come from a position in the sky, *roughly corresponding to the position of the planet, Mars.*

Irving was so unnerved by his discovery, that he could neither eat nor sleep for days. The weakness engendered by his regimen produced a purpose tremor in his right hand that made it hazardous for him to lower a plate of hot soup, and indeed resulted in the near scalding of a customer. It was obvious of course that for the first time a clear-cut indication of the existence of sentient human life on Mars had come to the fore. But why was the message in Hebrew? Irving Pirokin decided to break the pact of secrecy which he and cousin Sam had tentatively entered into, and he showed the translated message to his brother-in-law, Ephraim Zeitz, now Dr. Zeitz, then a theological student specializing in the history of the Lost Tribes of Israel.

Zeitz poured himself into his project, using his time and resources without stint and finally came up with the theory, which, with certain minor changes, is still considered the most likely explanation of the affair of the clicks.

"As is well known," writes Dr. Zeitz, "the image of 'a cloud by day and a pillar of fire by night,' could well have represented a primitive atomically energized rocket. We know from the Old Testament how preoccupied the Israelites were with survival, inasmuch as the general evildoings of mankind had already led the Lord to the near annihilation of mankind by flood. It is quite logical, therefore, that a more advanced group of Israelites, the Lost Tribes, were not transported by Tiglathpilaser as is popularly supposed. By utilizing methods of locomotion involving their atomic knowhow, they managed to breach the barrier of space travel and land on other planets, among them Mars."

Dr. Zeitz sent an elaboration of this position to the Pentagon, where a prematurely negative response was elicited. But when a field investigator verified the clicks at Irving Pirokin's receiver, the full machinery of the military was belatedly put into motion. Despite all attempts at keeping the story secret, it was broken to the press by a relative who received twenty-five dollars for scoring a news beat for the metropolitan tabloid in question. It was in this way that the military missions of hostile powers first became apprised of the cryptic clicks.

It soon became apparent that the only place where the mysterious signals could be detected was either at Sam's rig or at Irving's rig. But this phenomenon was easily explained by the vagaries of the layers of the Ionosphere, which often produce these apparent freaks of unique reception. More disturbing was the torrent of criticism which began to erupt in an attempt to demolish the hypothesis of Dr. Zeitz.

"Surely Mars cannot hold these Israelites," wrote one scholar. "The surface temperature of Mars is too high to sustain life and the absence of CO_2 in the atmosphere would make the preparation of carbonated water, a staple in the ancient Hebrew diet, impossible."

"But," rebutted Dr. Zeitz, "it is this very lack of CO_2 in the atmosphere that proves my hypothesis. Carbon dioxide is rare on Mars because it is being collected and confined to vessels of carbonated beverage which are sealed."

In the interest of complete honesty, we must make mention of those German scholars who have raised the counter hypothesis which conjectures that the Hyksos were the space migratory group. Utilizing what little is known of the Hyksos alphabet, they have decoded the message to read "STREITWAGEN," the German word for "chariot," the invention of which is commonly credited to the Hyksos.

The debate rages on and the military intelligence groups of both East and West are now engaged in exhaustive surveys of the Martian question. At the present writing, it is almost certain that the West is in the driver's seat, chiefly on the data furnished by the Pirokins.

And what of the Pirokins, themselves? They are both still hard at work on their odd jobs.

"Even a scientist must eat," says Irving Pirokin.

But they are not lionized by their neighbors. Perhaps the familiarity of daily, intimate contact makes the breeding of contempt inevitable.

Max Flenner, a neighborhood haberdasher who is admittedly not on good terms with Irving since he was the recipient of the soup-spilling incident, says the following:

"Irving was always weak in the head. Every Friday they chop liver in the back and he picks up the clicks."

We shook our head in doubt.

"That hardly accounts for the same signals being picked up by his cousin in Philadelphia."

Mr. Flenner raised his eyebrows in disdain.

"They don't chop liver in Philadelphia?" ■

And of course, science sometimes does "catch up with science fiction." All of a sudden, everybody's racing into space, and nobody's writing about it: at least not science fiction. (Don't hardly get much sci-fi about helicopters or television any more, either.) But—

"The universe that lies about us, visible only in the privacy, the intimacy of night, is incomprehensibly vast. Yet the conclusion that life exists across this vastness seems inescapable. We cannot yet be sure whether or not it lies within reach, but in any case, we are a part of it all; we are not alone!"

So ends the all-time best nonfiction SF-adventure book, **We Are Not Alone,** by Walter Sullivan, science editor of The New York Times.

Here's how it begins: "In November, 1961, the most august scientific body in the United States convened a meeting at the National Radio Astronomy Observatory in Green Bank, West Virginia. While it was not held in secret, in the official sense, every effort was made to avoid publicity because of the sensational nature of the question to be discussed.

"The subject was 'intelligent Extraterrestrial Life.' Yet this was no gathering of wild-eyed dreamers. The convener was the Space Science Board of the National Academy of Sciences. The host was one of the world's most distinguished astronomers, and several others among the eleven men present were internationally recognized leaders in their highly diverse fields.

"The subjects in which the conferees were expert all bore, in some way, on the problem of whether there is intelligent life elsewhere than on earth and, if so, how to communicate with such beings. The participants shared a strong feeling that such civilizations exist. . . ."

THE TWERLIK
Jack Sharkey
from *Worlds of Tomorrow*

It lay like a blanket over the cool gray sands, its fibrous substance extended to ultimate length in all directions, like a multispoked umbrella shorn of its fabric.

From each of its radiated arms—or legs; the Twerlik could employ them as it chose—innumerable wirelike filaments stretched outward at right angles to these limbs, flat upon the gray sands. And from them in turn jutted hairlike cilia, so that the entire body—had it been suitably stained and raised against a contrasting backdrop—resembled nothing so much as an enormous multiplumed fan, open to a full circle and laid over an area of ten square miles. Yet weighed upon Earth scales, its entire mass would have been found to tilt the needle barely beyond the one-pound mark. And its arms and filaments and cilia clung so tightly to the sand, and were so pallid of hue, that even were a man to lie face down upon it and stare with all his might, he would not be certain he saw anything but sand beneath him.

It could not break apart, of course. In its substance lay strengths beyond its own comprehension. For the planet upon which it had been born was too distant from its star to have developed cellular life; the Twerlik was a single, indestructible molecule, formed of an uncountable number of interlinked atoms. But—like the radar-grid it resembled —it could see, by the process of subtraction. Mild waves of light from the cold, distant star bathed it eternally. And so, objects that thrust in between the Twerlik and its source of life were recorded as negations upon its sensitive cilia, and the composite blotting-out of the light was sorted and filed and classified in its elongated brain in a fractional instant, so that it knew what went on in its vicinity.

It could see. And it could think. And it could do.

What it did, over endless ages, was convert some of the energy absorbed from the distant star into power. It used the power to work upon the atoms of the gray sand upon which it lay, and at a peripheral rate of about half an inch per Earth year, it turned the sand into its own substance and thus grew. The larger it became, after all, the more its surface could catch the faint light from the star. And the more light it could catch, on its planet whose rotation was equal to its period of revolution, the more sand it could transmute; and the more sand it transmuted, the larger it became.

That was its entire cycle of life. The Twerlik was content with it. Absorb, transmute, grow. Absorb, transmute, grow. So long as it could do these things, the Twerlik would be happy.

Then, part way through its hundred billionth trip around the dim, distant star, the men of Earth came.

Its first awareness of their arrival was a sort of bloating sensation, not unlike a mild twinge of nausea, as the cilia far beneath the gleaming fires of the rocket-thrust began hungrily to overabsorb.

The Twerlik did not know what was occurring, exactly, but it soon got itself under control, and would not let those cilia nearest the descending fires partake overly of the unexpected banquet. It made them take a share proportionate to their relationship in size to the rest of the enormous body, and it urged the rest of itself to partake similarly. By the time the slim metal rocket had come down, midway between the outermost fringes of the Twerlik and its splayed-out central brain, the creature had been able to feed more than in the previous three periods of the planetary revolution.

"This thing which has come," it told itself; "is therefore a *good* thing."

It was pleased at this new concept. Until the ship had come, the Twerlik had simply assumed that life was being lived to its peak. Now it knew there were better things. And this necessity to parcel out absorbable energy to its limbs was new, also. It gave the Twerlik a greater awareness of its own brain as the key motivator of this farflung empire which was itself. "I am a *me*," it realized, "and the rest of my extensions are but my parts!" It almost glowed with delight—not to mention an overload of absorbed energy —at the thought of all it had learned in a few moments. And then it realized what "moments" were, too; until the arrival of the ship, everything had been the same, and so the vast eons it had been there registered as no longer than an eyeblink would to a man, because it had had no shorter events for comparison of time. "So quickly!" the Twerlik mused. "I know what goodness and betterment are; I know that I am a *me;* I know the difference between a moment and an eon."

The Twerlik was abruptly aware, then, of yet another new sensation: gratitude. "This tall thing," it said, and at the same time filed away its first knowledge of differentiation in heights for later reference, "has done the *me* a service, in a moment, and the *me* is *bettered,* and *grateful!*"

And then it knew its first pain, as this rush of new concepts attempted to file themselves in subatomic synaptic structures incapable of coping with such a swift influx.

The Twerlik's brain throbbed with this cramming. To ease the pain, it used a fraction of the energy it had absorbed from the fires of the rocket, and enlarged the surface of the thinking section. Wisely—for it was growing wiser by the moment—it overenlarged it, that it might not again know pain should more concepts try to engrave themselves upon its consciousness. And just in time, too. For it suddenly needed room for concepts of foresight, prudence, headache, remedy and alertness.

Being lost in its own introspections, it turned its mind once more to the New Thing on the planet as it felt another increase in the absorption of its cilia. It did some rapid subtraction from the shifts in light from its star, and then it "saw" that there were things like unto itself emerging from the tall thing.

Its brain instantly added the concept of pity to the collection.

For these like-creatures were stunted travesties of the Twerlik. Only four limbs, and a limb stub on top. And these four fairly developed limbs had but five filaments to each, and no apparent cilia, save upon the useless limb stub. And the five filaments upon each of the two limbs nearest the *me* were bound up in layers of something that was not part of the creatures at all.

"These magnificent creatures," mourned the Twerlik, "having so little of their own, have yet shared their largesse with me!" For the creatures were bearing bulky objects out of the tall thing, and setting them upon the gray sand and upon the Twerlik itself. And from these objects there flared a great deal of brightness and warmth, and the creatures were standing amid this brightness and warmth, and doing incomprehensible things with four-limbed objects that had no life at all . . . and the cilia of the Twerlik were absorbing all they could of this unexpected feast.

"I can grow now!" it told itself. "I can grow in a short period as I have never in my life grown before. I can spread out until I cover the entire—planet." The Twerlik puzzled over the latest addition to its increasing concepts. From where had this strange idea come, this idea of a gigantic ball of solid material swinging about a star? And it suddenly knew that those other four-limbed non-living creatures were called "chairs" and "tables," and that the poorly developed things were named "men."

The Twerlik tried to solve this puzzle. How were these concepts reaching it? It checked its subtractions, but there was nothing new blocking the starlight. It checked its absorptions, but its rate of drainage upon the spilled-over warmth and light from the "electric heaters" and the "lamps"—and it realized, again enlarging its brain to store these concepts—was just as it had been. Yet these new ideas were reaching it somehow. The ideas came from the "men," but in what manner the Twerlik could not determine.

Then it checked into yet another one of its newfound concepts, "pressure," and found that there was something incomprehensible occurring.

Its first awareness of this concept had been when the "spaceship" ("Larger, brain, larger!") had pressed down upon the limbs and filaments and cilia of the *me*. Then secondary awarenesses that told the Twerlik of differentiations in "pressure" came when the "men" had trodden upon it, and again when the "chairs" and "tables" and "electric heaters" and "lamps" had been "set up." ("More room, brain, more room!") But there was a new kind of "pressure" upon the *me*. It came and went. And it was sometimes very heavy, sometimes very faint, and it struck only near the "men" at its fullest, being felt elsewhere along the cilia in a "circle" ("Grow!") about them, but less powerfully, and in a larger "circle" about that one, but much less powerfully.

What was it, this thing that came and went, and rammed and fondled and stabbed and caressed, so swiftly, so differently—and all the time kept filling its increasing brain with new concepts?

The Twerlik narrowed its field of concentration, starting at the outermost "circle," moving inward to the next, and drawing closer and closer to the "men," seeking the source of this strange alternating pressure. And then it found it.

It came from the "mouths" of the men. They were "talking." The Twerlik was receiving "sound."

Its brain began to hurt terribly, and once again it made use of its newly absorbed energies and grew more brainpart for the *me*. Then it "listened" ("More! More!") to the "talking," and began to "learn."

These men were only the first. There would be others, now that they knew that the "air" and "gravitation" and "climate" were "okay." There would be "houses" and "streets" and "children" and "colonization" and "expansion." And—the Twerlik almost shuddered with joy—*light!*

These men-things needed light constantly. They could not "see" without light. There would be more heaters, more lamps, campfires, chandeliers, matches, flares, movies, candles, sparklers, flashlights— ("Grow! *Grow!* GROW!")

Right here! On this spot they would begin! And all that spilled over from their wanton use of energy would belong to the *me!*

"Gratitude" was a poor word to express the intensity of the Twerlik's emotions toward these men-things now. It had to help them, had to repay them, had to show them how much their coming meant.

But how? The greatest thing in creation, so far as the Twerlik was concerned, was energy. And they had energy to spare, energy aplenty. It could not give them that as a gift. It had to find out what *they* valued most, and then somehow give this valued thing to them, if it could.

Desperately, it "listened," drawing in concept upon concept, seeking and prying and gleaning and wondering. . . .

It took all that they said, and filed it, cross-indexed it, sorted it, seeking the thing which meant more than anything to these men-things. And slowly, by winnowing away the oddments that cluttered the mainstream of the men-things' ambitions and hopes, the Twirlik learned the answer.

And it was within its power to grant!

But it involved motion, and the Twerlik was not certain it knew how motion might be accomplished. In all the eons of adding to its feathery perimeter, it had never had occasion to shift any of its limbs from where they lay upon the sand. It was not quite certain it could do such a thing. Still, it told the *me*, if there were a way, then it was obligated to use this way, no matter what the difficulties thus entailed. Repayment of the men-things was a legitimate debt of honor. It had to be done no matter what the cost.

So it attempted various methods of locomotion.

It tried, first, to flex and wriggle its filaments as the men-things did, but nothing happened. Bewildered, it checked through its file of new concepts and discovered "leverage." On this principle did the men-things move. They had "muscle" which "contracted" and caused a "tendon" to shift the angle of a "bone." The Twerlik had none of these necessary things.

So it tried "propulsion," the force which had moved the spaceship, and discovered that it lacked "combustible fuel" and hollow channels for the energy called "firing tubes" and some built-in condition of these tubes called the "Venturi principle."

It pondered for a long time then, not even bothering with things the men knew as "pistons" and "cylinders" and "wheels"—since the use of these involved a free moving segment and the Twerlik could not operate save as a whole.

Finally, after thousands of those intervals which it had come to think of as "moments," it came upon the concept of "magnetism." The forces involved came well within its scope.

By subtle control of the electron flow along the under-side of one of its five-mile limbs, and the creation of an electronic "differential" flow along the top, it found that the consequent repulsion-attempts of its upper and lower surfaces resulted in the tip of the limb describing a "curl." Once this basic motion had been achieved, the rest was simple, for the Twerlik learned swiftly. In a few short moments, it had evolved a thing called "coordination" and found to its delight that it could raise, lower or otherwise manipulate limbs, filaments and cilia with ease, in a pleasant, rippling whip-motion.

This new power being tested swiftly and found quite enough for its purposes, it set to work repaying the men for their great kindness to it.

The men, it noted as it worked, were undergoing a strange somnolence called "sleep," inside the spaceship. The Twerlik realized with joy that it could indulge in what men-things called a "surprise" if it worked with sufficient rapidity.

Draining its energies with uncaring profligacy, it coiled and swirled and contracted itself until its cilia and filaments and limbs lay all about the spaceship and everywhere within it save upon the men-things. The Twerlik found that it was greatly weakened by this unwonted output, but it was a dedicated Twerlik now, and did not stop its continuation to the task at hand. It worked, and molded, and rearranged. It grew dizzy with the effort, until a stray groping strand of cilium found the energy-crammed metal housed in the tank near the firing-tubes of the spaceship. Into this metal the cilium burrowed, and then began drawing upon the energies therein like an electronic siphon, feeding out the particles of raw power to the rest of the Twerlik, that the entirety of the creature might perform this labor of love.

It took many thousands of moments for its task to be done, but it was a contented—if desperately weary—Twerlik which finally uncoiled its incredible barely-greater-than-a-pound enormous size from the spaceship.

Once again it retreated in all directions, to lie weakly in the dim light of the distant star and await the awakening of the men-things.

It noted, disinterestedly, that the shape of the spaceship was slightly altered. It was widening slowly near the base, and bulging about the middle, and losing height. The

Twerlik did not care. It had shown its gratitude, and that was all that mattered.

Abruptly, men-things were leaping from the doorway of the ship, shouting empty sounds which the Twerlik could only interpret as songs of "fear," though no "words" were used. They were—ah, that was the term—"screaming."

It could make no sense of it. Were the men-things mad? Had it not given them what they desired most? Had it not even worked upon the "food" and "water" for them, so that every item they possessed would be vastly improved?

The Twerlik could not understand why the men were acting so strangely. It waited peacefully for them to use the now-improved heaters and lamps, that it might restore some of its deeply sapped strengths. But they made no move to do so. They were using words, now, having gotten over their "screaming." Words like "trapped" and "impossible" and "doomed."

They were, sensed the Twerlik, terribly unhappy, but it could not comprehend why.

It seemed to have to do with its gesture of repayment. But along this line of reasoning the Twerlik could not proceed without bafflement. It thought momentarily of removing the gift, and restoring things to what they had been, but then realized that it no longer possessed the necessary energies.

So it sat and pondered the ways of men, who seemed to desire nothing so much in life as the acquisition of an element called "gold," and yet acted so oddly when they were given a spaceship made of it.

The Twerlik sadly filed "screwy" in close juxtaposition to the men-concept in its brain, and when at last the men-things had lain upon the gray sand and moved no more, it transmuted their elements into that substance they loved so well with its last burst of waning strength.

Then it lay there upon the cool gray sand, sucking life from the dim, distant star of its planet, and thought and thought about men-things, and wondered if it would ever be satisfied to be nothing but a Twerlik forever, with no more creatures to be good to.

It knew one thing, however: it must not give men gold again.

The next spaceship to land upon its planet, after two revolutions about the sun, was filled with men-things, too.

But these men-things had had an accident to the thing called their "reclamation tanks." They were all thick-tongued and weak, and a quick analysis of their conversation showed the Twerlik that these men were different from the others. They desired nothing so much as a comparatively simple molecule known to them as water.

The Twerlik was only too eager to help.

And, when the transmutation of this second spaceship had been completed, right over the thirsty gray sands, the Twerlik proudly added "permeability" to its vocabulary. ∎

And then there was the issue of the Sunday Times containing two separate pieces headlined, "Life on Mars?"

Sullivan's article on the science page reported on recommendations made to the National Academy of Sciences by a meeting of distinguished scientists who declared, "We believe it entirely reasonable that Mars is inhabited with living organisms" and urged a program to land "an automated biological laboratory" on Mars in 1971 or 1973.

The piece on the editorial page said stiffly: "The biological exploration of Mars will not be cheap, and available funds for scientific research and development are limited."

If I had any lingering doubts, they are gone. It is actually happening: the cosmonaut space-acrobatics and the Gemini launching programs are not simply part of a global drama of prestige and influence conflicts. We are actually on our way. In another year or two, someone will set foot (or spaceboot) on the moon's surface for the first time. I know it is so now, because the Times is seriously disturbed about the cost of exploring for life on Mars.

Science has caught up with science fiction. We have gone too far with the hardware and techniques of space travel to leave much of a field for inventive imagination to work in. We have not yet gone far enough into space itself to acquire the new knowledge that will generate a whole new phase of speculative science and fiction.

Meantime, science fiction is leaping ahead of science, on today's frontiers. The exciting new work is not in rocketry but in biochemistry, in behavioral psychology, in parapsychology,

In anthropology and information theory and communications. And in a backwards way, this is bringing back the space story, but a different kind of space story.

A ROSE FOR ECCLESIASTES
Roger Zelazny
from *Fantasy and Science Fiction*

1

I was busy translating one of my *Madrigals Macabre* into Martian on the morning I was found acceptable. The intercom had buzzed briefly, and I dropped my pencil and flipped on the toggle in a single motion.

"Mister G," piped Morton's youthful contralto, "the old man says I should 'get hold of that damned conceited rhymer' right away, and send him to his cabin.—Since there's only one damned conceited rhymer . . ."

"Let not ambition mock thy useful toil." I cut him off.

So, the Martians had finally made up their minds! I knocked an inch and a half of ash from a smouldering butt, and took my first drag since I had lit it. The entire month's anticipation tried hard to crowd itself into the moment, but could not quite make it. I was frightened to walk those forty feet and hear Emory say the words I already knew he would say; and that feeling elbowed the other one into the background.

So I finished the stanza I was translating before I got up.

It took only a moment to reach Emory's door. I knocked twice and opened it, just as he growled, "Come in."

"You wanted to see me?" I sat down quickly to save him the trouble of offering me a seat.

"That was fast. What did you do, run?"

I regarded his paternal discontent:

Little fatty flecks beneath pale eyes, thinning hair, and an Irish nose; a voice a decibel louder than anyone else's . . .

Hamlet to Claudius: "I was working."

"Hah! he snorted. "Come off it. No one's ever seen you do any of that stuff."

I shrugged my shoulders and started to rise.

"If that's what you called me down here—"

"Sit down!"

He stood up. He walked around his desk. He hovered above me and glared down. (A hard trick, even when I'm in a low chair.)

"You are undoubtedly the most antagonistic bastard I've ever had to work with!" he bellowed, like a belly-stung buffalo. "Why the hell don't you act like a human being sometime and surprise everybody? I'm willing to admit you're smart, maybe even a genius, but—oh, Hell!" He made a heaving gesture with both hands and walked back to his chair.

"Betty has finally talked them into letting you go in." His voice was normal again. "They'll receive you this afternoon. Draw one of the jeepsters after lunch, and get down there."

"Okay," I said.

"That's all, then."

I nodded, got to my feet. My hand was on the doorknob when he said:

"I don't have to tell you how important this is. Don't treat them the way you treat us."

I closed the door behind me.

I don't remember what I had for lunch. I was nervous, but I knew instinctively that I wouldn't muff it. My Boston publishers expected a Martian Idyll, or at least a Saint-Exupéry job on space flight. The National Science Association wanted a complete report on the Rise and Fall of the Martian Empire.

They would both be pleased. I knew.

That's the reason everyone is jealous—why they hate me. I always come through, and I can come through better than anyone else.

I shoveled in a final anthill of slop, and made my way to our car barn. I drew one jeepster and headed it toward Tirellian.

Flames of sand, lousy with iron oxide, set fire to the buggy. They swarmed over the open top and bit through my scarf; they set to work pitting my goggles.

The jeepster, swaying and panting like a little donkey

I once rode through the Himalayas, kept kicking me in the seat of the pants. The Mountains of Tirellian shuffled their feet and moved toward me at a cockeyed angle.

Suddenly I was heading uphill, and I shifted gears to accommodate the engine's braying. Not like Gobi, not like the Great Southwestern Desert, I mused. Just red, just dead . . . without even a cactus.

I reached the crest of the hill, but I had raised too much dust to see what was ahead. It didn't matter, though, I have a head full of maps. I bore to the left and downhill, adjusting the throttle. A cross-wind and solid ground beat down the fires. I felt like Ulysses in Malebolge—with a terza-rima speech in one hand and an eye out for Dante.

I sounded a rock pagoda and arrived.

Betty waved as I crunched to a halt, then jumped down.

"Hi," I choked, unwinding my scarf and shaking out a pound and a half of grit. "Like, where do I go and who do I see?"

She permitted herself a brief Germanic giggle—more at my starting a sentence with "like" than at my discomfort—then she started talking. (She is a top linguist, so a word from the Village Idiom still tickles her!)

I appreciated her precise, furry talk; informational, and all that. I had enough in the way of social pleasantries before me to last at least the rest of my life. I looked at her chocolate-bar eyes and perfect teeth, at her sun-bleached hair, close-cropped to the head (I hate blondes!), and decided that she was in love with me.

"Mr. Gallinger, the Matriarch is waiting inside to be introduced. She has consented to open the Temple records for your study." She paused here to pat her hair and squirm a little. Did my gaze make her nervous?

"They are religious documents, as well as their only history," she continued, "sort of like the Mahabharata. She expects you to observe certain rituals in handling them, like repeating the sacred words when you turn pages—she will teach you the system."

I nodded quickly, several times.

"Fine, let's go in."

"Uh—" she paused. "Do not forget their Eleven Forms of Politeness and Degree. They take matters of form quite seriously—and do not get into any discussions over the equality of the sexes—"

"I know all about their taboos," I broke in. "Don't worry. I've lived in the Orient, remember?"

She dropped her eyes and seized my hand. I almost jerked it away.

"It will look better if I enter leading you."

I swallowed my comments and followed her, like Samson in Gaza.

Inside, my last thought met with a strange correspondence. The Matriarch's quarters were a rather abstract version of what I imagine the tents of the tribes of Israel to have been like. Abstract, I say, because it was all frescoed brick, peaked like a huge tent, with animal-skin representations, like gray-blue scars, that looked as if they had been laid on the walls with a palette knife.

The Matriarch, M'Cwyie, was short, white-haired, fifty-ish, and dressed like a Gypsy queen. With her rainbow of voluminous skirts she looked like an inverted punch bowl set atop a cushion.

Accepting my obeisances, she regarded me as an owl might a rabbit. The lids of those black, black eyes jumped upwards as she discovered my perfect accent.—The tape recorder Betty had carried on her interviews had done its part, and I knew the language reports from the first two expeditions, verbatim. I'm all hell when it comes to picking up accents.

"You are the poet?"

"Yes," I replied.

"Recite one of your poems, please."

"I'm sorry, but nothing short of a thorough translating job would do justice to your language and my poetry, and I don't know enough of your language yet."

"Oh?"

"But I've been making such translations for my own amusement, as an exercise in grammar," I continued. "I'd be honored to bring a few of them along one of the times that I come here."

"Yes. Do so."

Score one for me!

She turned to Betty.

"You may go now."

Betty muttered the parting formalities, gave me a strange sidewise look, and was gone. She apparently had expected to stay and "assist" me. She wanted a piece of the glory, like everyone else. But I was the Schliemann at this Troy, and there would be only one name on the Association report!

M'Cwyie rose, and I noticed that she gained very little height by standing. But then I'm six-six and look like a poplar in October: thin, bright red on top, and towering above everyone else.

"Our records are very, very old," she began. "Betty says that your word for their age is 'millennia'."

I nodded appreciatively.

"I'm very eager to see them."

"They are not here. We will have to go into the Temple —they may not be removed."

I was suddenly wary.

"You have no objections to my copying them, do you?"

"No. I see that you respect them, or your desire would not be so great."

"Excellent."

She seemed amused. I asked her what was funny.

"The High Tongue may not be so easy for a foreigner to learn."

It came through fast.

No one on the first expedition had gotten this close. I had no way of knowing that this was a double-language deal—a classical as well as a vulgar. I knew some of their Prakrit, now I had to learn all their Sanskrit.

"Ouch! and damn!"

"Pardon, please?"

"It's nontranslatable, M'Cwyie. But imagine yourself having to learn the High Tongue in a hurry, and you can guess at the sentiment."

She seemed amused again, and told me to remove my shoes.

She guided me through an alcove . . .

. . . and into a burst of Byzantine brilliance!

No Earthman had ever been in this room before, or I would have heard about it. Carter, the first expedition's linguist, with the help of one Mary Allen, M.D., had learned all the grammar and vocabulary that I knew while sitting cross-legged in the antechamber.

We had had no idea this existed. Greedily, I cast my eyes about. A highly sophisticated system of esthetics lay behind the décor. We would have to revise our entire estimation of Martian culture.

For one thing, the ceiling was vaulted and corbeled; for another, there were side columns with reverse flutings; for another—oh hell! The place was big. Posh. You could never have guessed it from the shaggy outsides.

I bent forward to study the gilt filigree on a ceremonial table. M'Cwyie seemed a bit smug at my intentness, but I'd still have hated to play poker with her.

The table was loaded with books.

With my toe, I traced a mosaic on the floor.

"Is your entire city within this one building?"

"Yes, it goes far back into the mountain."

"I see," I said, seeing nothing.

I couldn't ask her for a conducted tour, yet.

She moved to a small stool by the table.

"Shall we begin your friendship with the High Tongue?"

I was trying to photograph the hall with my eyes, knowing I would have to get a camera in here, somehow, sooner or later. I tore my gaze from a statuette and nodded, hard.

"Yes, introduce me."

I sat down.

For the next three weeks alphabet-bugs chased each other behind my eyelids whenever I tried to sleep. The sky was an unclouded pool of turquoise that rippled calligraphies whenever I swept my eyes across it. I drank quarts of coffee while I worked and mixed cocktails of Benzedrine and champagne for my coffee breaks.

M'Cwyie tutored me two hours every morning, and occasionally for another two in the evening. I spent an additional fourteen hours a day on my own, once I had gotten up sufficient momentum to go ahead alone.

And at night the elevator of time dropped me to its bottom floors . . .

I was six again, learning my Hebrew, Greek, Latin, and Aramiac. I was ten, sneaking peeks at the *Iliad*. When Daddy wasn't spreading hellfire, brimstone, and brotherly love, he was teaching me to dig the Word, like in the original.

Lord! There are so many originals and so *many* words! When I was twelve I started pointing out the little differences between what he was preaching and what I was reading.

The fundamentalist vigor of his reply brooked no debate. It was worse than any beating. I kept my mouth shut after that and learned to appreciate Old Testament poetry.

—Lord, I am sorry! Daddy—Sir—I am sorry!—It couldn't be! It couldn't be . . .

On the day the boy graduated from high school, with the French, German, Spanish, and Latin awards, Dad Gallinger had told his fourteen-year-old, six-foot scarecrow of a son that he wanted him to enter the ministry. I remember how his son was evasive:

"Sir," he had said, "I'd sort of like to study on my own for a year or so, and then take pre-theology courses at some liberal-arts university. I feel I'm still sort of young to try a seminary, straight off."

The Voice of God: "But you have the gift of tongues, my son. You can preach the Gospel in all the lands of Babel. You were born to be a missionary. You say you are young, but time is rushing by you like a whirlwind. Start early, and you will enjoy added years of service."

The added years of service were so many added tails to the cat repeatedly laid on my back. I can't see his face now, I never can. Maybe it is because I was always afraid to look at it then.

And years later, when he was dead, and laid out, in black, amidst bouquets, amidst weeping congregationalists, amidst prayers, red faces, handkerchiefs, hands patting your shoulders, solemn-faced comforters . . . I looked at him and did not recognize him.

We had met nine months before my birth, this stranger and I. He had never been cruel—stern, demanding, with contempt for everyone's shortcomings—but never cruel. He was also all that I had had of a mother. And brothers. And sisters. He had tolerated my three years at St. John's, possibly because of its name, never knowing how liberal and delightful a place it really was.

But I never knew him, and the man 'atop the catafalque demanded nothing now; I was free not to preach the Word.

But now I wanted to, in a different way. I wanted to

preach a word that I could never have voiced while he lived.

I did not return for my Senior year in the fall. I had a small inheritance coming, and a bit of trouble getting control of it since I was still under eighteen. But I managed.

It was Greenwich Village I finally settled upon.

Not telling any well-meaning parishioners my new address, I entered into a daily routine of writing poetry and teaching myself Japanese and Hindustani. I grew a fiery beard, drank espresso, and learned to play chess. I wanted to try a couple of the other paths to salvation.

After that, it was two years in India with the Old Peace Corps—which broke me of my Buddhism, and gave me my *Pipes of Krishna* lyrics and the Pulitzer they deserved.

Then back to the States for my degree, grad work in linguistics, and more prizes.

Then one day a ship went to Mars. The vessel settling in its New Mexico nest of fires contained a new language.— It was fantastic, exotic, and esthetically overpowering. After I had learned all there was to know about it, and written my book, I was famous in new circles:

"Go, Gallinger. Dip your bucket in the well, and bring us a drink of Mars. Go, learn another world—but remain aloof, rail at it gently like Auden—and hand us its soul in iambics."

And I came to the land where the sun is a tarnished penny, where the wind is a whip, where two moons play at hot-rod games, and a hell of sand gives you the incendiary itches whenever you look at it.

I rose from my twistings on the bunk and crossed the darkened cabin to a port. The desert was a carpet of endless orange, bulging from the sweepings of centuries beneath it.

"I a stranger, unafraid—This is the land—I've got it made!"

I laughed.

I had the High Tongue by the tail already—or the roots, if you want your puns anatomical, as well as correct.

The High and Low Tongues were not so dissimilar as they had first seemed. I had enough of the one to get me through the murkier parts of the other. I had the grammar and all the commoner irregular verbs down cold; the dictionary I was constructing grew by the day, like a tulip, and would bloom shortly. Every time I played the tapes, the stem lengthened.

Now was the time to tax my ingenuity, to really drive the lessons home. I had purposely refrained from plunging into the major texts until I could do justice to them. I had been reading minor commentaries, bits of verse, fragments of history. And one thing had impressed me strongly in all that I read.

They wrote about concrete things: rocks, sand, water, winds; and the tenor couched within these elemental symbols was fiercely pessimistic. It reminded me of some Buddhist texts, but even more so, I realized from my recent *recherches,* it was like parts of the Old Testament. Specifically it reminded me of the Book of Ecclesiastes.

That, then, would be it. The sentiment, as well as the vocabulary, was so similar that it would be a perfect exercise. Like putting Poe into French. I would never be a convert to the Way of Malann, but I would show them that an Earthman had once thought the same thoughts, felt similarly.

I switched on my desk lamp and sought King James amidst my books.

Vanity of vanities, saith the Preacher, vanity of vanities; all is vanity. What profit hath a man . . .

My progress seemed to startle M'Cwyie. She peered at me, like Sartre's Other, across the tabletop. I ran through a chapter in the Book of Locar. I didn't look up, but I could feel the tight net her eyes were working about my head, shoulders, and rapid hands. I turned another page.

Was she weighing the net, judging the size of the catch? And what for? The books said nothing of fishers on Mars. Especially of men. They said that some god named Malann had spat, or had done something disgusting (depending on the version you read), and that life had gotten underway as a disease in inorganic matter. They said that movement was its first law, its first law, and that the dance was the only legitimate reply to the inorganic . . . the dance's quality its justification,—fication . . . and love is a disease in organic matter—Inorganic matter?

I shook my head. I had almost been asleep.

"M'narra."

I stood and stretched. Her eyes outlined me greedily now. So I met them, and they dropped.

"I grow tired. I want to rest awhile. I didn't sleep much last night."

She nodded, Earth's shorthand for "yes," as she had learned from me.

"You wish to relax, and see the explicitness of the doctrine of Locar in its fullness?"

"Pardon me?"

"You wish to see a Dance of Locar?"

"Oh." Their damned circuits of form and periphrasis here ran worse than the Korean! "Yes. Surely. Any time it's going to be done, I'd be happy to watch."

I continued, "In the meantime, I've been meaning to ask you whether I might take some pictures—"

"Now is the time. Sit down. Rest. I will call the musicians."

She bustled out through a door I had never been past.

Well now, the dance was the highest art, according to Locar, not to mention Havelock Ellis, and I was about to see how their centuries-dead philosopher felt it should be conducted. I rubbed my eyes and snapped over, touching my toes a few times.

The blood began pounding in my head, and I sucked in a couple deep breaths. I bent again and there was a flurry of motion at the door.

To the trio who entered with M'Cwyie I must have looked as if I were searching for the marbles I had just lost, bent over like that.

I grinned weakly and straightened up, my face red from more than exertion. I hadn't expected them *that* quickly.

Suddenly I thought of Havelock Ellis again in his area of greatest popularity.

The little redheaded doll, wearing, sari-like, a diaphanous piece of the Martian sky, looked up in wonder—as a child at some colorful flag on a high pole.

"Hello," I said, or its equivalent.

She bowed before replying. Evidently I had been promoted in status.

"I shall dance," said the red wound in that pale, pale

cameo, her face. Eyes, the color of dream and her dress, pulled away from mine.

She drifted to the center of the room.

Standing there, like a figure in an Etruscan frieze, she was either meditating or regarding the design on the floor.

Was the mosaic symbolic of something? I studied it. If it was, it eluded me; it would make an attractive bathroom floor or patio, but I couldn't see much in it beyond that.

The other two were paint-spattered sparrows like M'Cwyie, in their middle years. One settled to the floor with a triple-stringed instrument faintly resembling a *samisen*. The other held a simple woodblock and two drumsticks.

M'Cwyie disdained her stool and was seated upon the floor before I realized it. I followed suit.

The *samisen* player was still tuning up, so I leaned toward M'Cwyie.

"What is the dancer's name?"

"Braxa," she replied, without looking at me, and raised her left hand, slowly, which meant yes, and go ahead, and let it begin.

The stringed thing throbbed like a toothache, and a tick-tocking, like ghosts of all the clocks they had never invented, sprang from the block.

Braxa was a statue, both hands raised to her face, elbows high and outspread.

The music became a metaphor for fire.

Crackle, purr, snap . . .

She did not move.

The hissing altered to splashes. The cadence slowed. It was water now, the most precious thing in the world, gurgling clear then green over mossy rocks.

Still she did not move.

Glissandos. A pause.

Then, so faint I could hardly be sure at first, the tremble of the winds began. Softly, gently, sighing and halting, uncertain. A pause, a sob, then a repetition of the first statement, only louder.

Were my eyes completely bugged from my reading, or was Braxa actually trembling, all over, head to foot.

She was.

She began a microscopic swaying. A fraction of an

inch right, then left. Her fingers opened like the petals of a flower, and I could see that her eyes were closed.

Her eyes opened. They were distant, glassy, looking through me and the walls. Her swaying became more pronounced, merged with the beat.

The wind was sweeping in from the desert now, falling against Tirellian like waves on a dike. Her fingers moved, they were the gusts. Her arms, slow pendulums, descended, began a countermovement.

The gale was coming now. She began an axial movement and her hands caught up with the rest of her body, only now her shoulders commenced to writhe out a figure eight.

The wind! The wind, I say. O wild, enigmatic! O muse of St.-John Perse!

The cyclone was twisting round those eyes, its still center. Her head was thrown back, but I knew there was no ceiling between her gaze, passive as Buddha's, and the unchanging skies. Only the two moons, perhaps, interrupted their slumber in that elemental Nirvana of uninhabited turquoise.

Years ago, I had seen the Devadasis in India, the street dancers, spinning their colorful webs, drawing in the male insect. But Braxa was more than this: she was a Ramadjany, like those votaries of Rama, incarnation of Vishnu, who had given the dance to man: the sacred dancers.

The clicking was monotonously steady now; the whine of the strings made me think of the stinging rays of the sun, their heat stolen by the wind's halations; the blue was Sarasvati and Mary, and a girl named Laura. I heard a sitar from somewhere, watched this statue come to life, and inhaled a divine afflatus.

I was again Rimbaud with his hashish, Baudelaire with his laudanum, Poe, De Quincy, Wilde, Mallarmé, and Aleister Crowley. I was, for a fleeting second, my father in his dark pulpit and darker suit, the hymns and the organ's wheeze transmuted to bright wind.

She was a spun weather vane, a feathered crucifix hovering in the air, a clothesline holding one bright garment lashed parallel to the ground. Her shoulder was bare now, and her right breast moved up and down like a moon in the sky, its red nipple appearing momently above a fold and vanishing again. The music was as formal as Job's argument with God. Her dance was God's reply.

The music slowed, settled; it had been met, matched, answered. Her garment, as if alive, crept back into the more sedate folds it originally held.

She dropped low, lower, to the floor. Her head fell upon her raised knees. She did not move.

There was silence.

I realized, from the ache across my shoulders, how tensely I had been sitting. My armpits were wet. Rivulets had been running down my sides. What did one do now? Applaud?

I sought M'Cwyie from the corner of my eye. She raised her right hand.

As if by telepathy the girl shuddered all over and stood. The musicians also rose. So did M'Cwyie.

I got to my feet, with a charley horse in my left leg, and said, "It was beautiful," inane as that sounds.

I received three different High Forms of "thank you."

There was a flurry of color and I was alone again with M'Cwyie.

"That is the one hundred seventeenth of the two thousand two hundred twenty-four dances of Locar."

I looked down at her.

"Whether Locar was right or wrong, he worked out a fine reply to the inorganic."

She smiled.

"Are the dances of your world like this?"

"Some of them are similar. I was reminded of them as I watched Braxa—but I've never seen anything exactly like hers."

'She is good," M'Cywie said. "She knows all the dances."

A hint of her earlier expression which had troubled me . . .

It was gone in an instant.

"I must tend my duties now." She moved to the table and closed the books. "M'narra."

"Good-bye." I slipped into my boots.

"Good-bye, Gallinger."

I walked out the door, mounted the jeepster, and roared

across the evening into night, my wings of risen desert flapping slowly behind me.

2

I had just closed the door behind Betty, after a brief grammar session, when I heard the voices in the hall. My vent was opened a fraction, so I stood there and eavesdropped:

Morton's fruity treble: "Guess what? He said 'hello' to me a while ago."

"Hmmph!" Emory's elephant lungs exploded. "Either he's slipping, or you were standing in his way and he wanted you to move."

"Probably didn't recognize me. I don't think he sleeps any more, now he has that language to play with. I had night watch last week, and every night I passed his door at 0300—I always heard that recorder going. At 0500, when I got off, he was still at it."

"The guy *is* working hard," Emory admitted, grudgingly. "In fact, I think he's taking some kind of dope to keep awake. He looks sort of glassy-eyed these days. Maybe that's natural for a poet, though."

Betty had been standing there, because she broke in then:

"Regardless of what you think of him, it's going to take me at least a year to learn what he's picked up in three weeks. And I'm just a linguist, not a poet."

Morton must have been nursing a crush on her bovine charms. It's the only reason I can think of for his dropping his guns to say what he did.

"I took a course in modern poetry when I was back at the university," he began. "We read six authors—Yeats, Pound, Eliot, Crane, Stevens, and Gallinger—and on the last day of the semester, when the prof was feeling a little rhetorical, he said, 'These six names are written on the century, and all the gates of criticism and Hell shall not prevail against them.' "

"Myself," he continued. "I thought his *Pipes of Krishna* and his *Madrigals* were great. I was honored to be chosen for an expedition he was going on.

"I think he's spoken two dozen words to me since I met him," he finished.

The Defence: "Did it ever occur to you," Betty said,

"that he might be tremendously self-conscious about his appearance? He was also a precocious child, and probably never even had school friends. He's sensitive and very introverted."

"Sensitive? Self-conscious?" Emory choked and gagged. "The man is as proud as Lucifer, and he's a walking insult machine. You press a button like 'Hello' or 'Nice day' and he thumbs his nose at you. He's got it down to a reflex."

They muttered a few other pleasantries and drifted away.

Well, bless you, Morton boy. You little pimple-faced, Ivy-bred connoisseur! I've never taken a course in my poetry, but I'm glad someone said that. The Gates of Hell. Well, now! Maybe Daddy's prayers got heard somewhere, and I am a missionary, after all!

Only . . .

. . . Only a missionary needs something to convert people *to*. I have my private system of esthetics, and I suppose it oozes an ethical by-product somewhere. But if I ever had anything to preach, really, even in my poems, I wouldn't care to preach it to such lowlifes as you. If you think I'm a slob, I'm also a snob, and there's no room for you in Heaven—it's a private place, where Swift, Shaw, and Petronius Arbiter come to dinner.

And oh, the feasts we have! The Trimalchio's, the Emory's we dissect!

We finish you with the soup, Morton!

I turned and settled at my desk. I wanted to write something. Ecclesiastes could take a night off. I wanted to write a poem, a poem about the one hundred seventeenth dance of Locar; about a rose following the light, traced by the wind, sick, like Blake's rose, dying . . .

I found a pencil and began.

When I had finished I was pleased. It wasn't great—at least, it was no greater than it needed to be—High Martian not being my strongest tongue. I groped, and put it into English, with partial rhymes. Maybe I'd stick it in my next book. I called it *Braxa*:

In a land of wind and red,
where the icy evening of Time

freezes milk in the breasts of Life,
as two moons overhead—
cat and dog in alleyways of dream—
scratch and scramble agelessly my
   flight . . .
This final flower turns a burning
   head.

I put it away and found some phenobarbitol. I was suddenly tired.

When I showed my poem to M'Cwyie the next day, she
read it through several times, very slowly.

"It is lovely," she said. "But you used three words from
your own language. 'Cat' and 'dog,' I assume, are two small
animals with a hereditary hatred for one another. But what
is 'flower'?"

"Oh," I said. "I've never come across your word for
'flower,' but I was actually thinking of an Earth flower, the
rose."

"What is it like?"

"Well, its petals are generally bright red. That's what I
meant, on one level, by 'burning head.' I also wanted it to
imply fever, though, and red hair, and the fire of life. The
rose, itself, has a thorny stem, green leaves, and a distinct,
pleasant aroma."

"I wish I could see one."

"I suppose it could be arranged. I'll check."

"Do it, please. You are a—" She used the word for
"prophet," or religious poet, like Isaiah or Locar. "—and
your poem is inspired. I shall tell Braxa of it."

I declined the nomination, but felt flattered.

This, then, I decided, was the strategic day, the day on
which to ask whether I might bring in the microfilm
machine and the camera. I wanted to copy all their texts,
I explained, and I couldn't write fast enough to do it.

She surprised me by agreeing immediately. But she
bowled me over with her invitation.

"Would you like to come and stay here while you do this
thing? Then you can work night and day, any time you
want—except when the Temple is being used, of course."

I bowed.

"I should be honored."

"Good. Bring your machines when you want, and I will show you a room."

"Will this afternoon be all right?"

"Certainly."

"Then I will go now and get things ready. Until this afternoon . . ."

"Good-bye."

I anticipated a little trouble from Emory, but not much. Everyone back at the ship was anxious to see the Martians, talk with the Martians, poke needles in the Martians, ask them about Martian climate, diseases, soil chemistry, politics, and mushrooms (our botanist was a fungus nut, but a reasonably good guy)—and only four or five had actually gotten to see them. The crew had been spending most of its time excavating dead cities and their acropolises. We played the game by strict rules, and the natives were as fiercely insular as the nineteenth-century Japanese. I figured I would meet with little resistance, and I figured right.

In fact, I got the distinct impression that everyone was happy to see me move out.

I stopped in the hydroponics room to speak with our mushroom master.

"Hi, Kane. Grow any toadstools in the sand yet?"

He sniffed. He always sniffs. Maybe he's allergic to plants.

"Hello, Gallinger. No, I haven't had any success with toadstools, but look behind the car barn next time you're out there. I've got a few cacti going."

"Great," I observed. Doc Kane was about my only friend aboard, not counting Betty.

"Say, I came down to ask you a favor."

"Name it."

"I want a rose."

"A what?"

"A rose. You know, a nice red American Beauty job—thorns, pretty smelling—"

"I don't think it will take in this soil. *Sniff, sniff.*"

"No, you don't understand. I don't want to plant it, I just want the flowers."

"I'd have to use the tanks." He scratched his hairless

dome. "It would take at least three months to get you flowers, even under forced growth."

"Will you do it?"

"Sure, if you don't mind the wait."

"Not at all. In fact, three months will just make it before we leave." I looked about at the pools of crawling slime, at the trays of shoots. "—I'm moving up to Tirellian today, but I'll be in and out all the time. I'll be here when it blooms."

"Moving up there, eh? Moore said they're an in-group."

"I guess I'm 'in' then."

"Looks that way—I still don't see how you learned their language, though. Of course, I had trouble with French and German for my PhD., but last week I heard Betty demonstrate it at lunch. It just sounds like a lot of weird noises. She says speaking it is like working a *Times* crossword and trying to imitate birdcalls at the same time."

I laughed, and took the cigarette he offered me.

"It's complicated," I acknowledged. "But, well, it's as if you suddenly came across a whole new class of mycetae here—you'd dream about it at night."

His eyes were gleaming.

"Wouldn't that be something! I might, yet, you know."

"Maybe you will."

He chuckled as we walked to the door.

"I'll start your roses tonight. Take it easy down there."

"You bet. Thanks."

Like I said, a fungus nut, but a fairly good guy.

My quarters in the Citadel of Tirellian were directly adjacent to the Temple, on the inward side and slightly to the left. They were a considerable improvement over my cramped cabin, and I was pleased that Martian culture had progressed sufficiently to discover the desirability of the mattress over the pallet. Also, the bed was long enough to accommodate me, which *was* surprising.

So I unpacked and took 16 35 mm. shots of the Temple, before starting on the books.

I took 'stats until I was sick of turning pages without knowing what they said. So I started translating a work of history.

"Lo. In the thirty-seventh year of the Process of Cillen

the rains came, which gave rise to rejoicing, for it was a rare and untoward occurrence, and commonly construed a blessing.

"But it was not the life-giving semen of Malann which fell from the heavens. It was the blood of the universe, spurting from an artery. And the last days were upon us. The final dance was to begin.

"The rains brought the plague that does not kill, and the last passes of Locar began with their drumming . . ."

I asked myself what the hell Tamur meant, for he was an historian and supposedly committed to fact. This was not their Apocalypse.

Unless they could be one and the same . . . ?

Why not? I mused. Tirellian's handful of people were the remnant of what had obviously once been a highly developed culture. They had had wars, but no holocausts; science, but little technology. A plague, a plague that did not kill . . . ? Could that have done it? How, if it wasn't fatal?

I read on, but the nature of the plague was not discussed. I turned pages, skipped ahead, and drew a blank.

M'Cwyie! M'Cwyie! When I want to question you most, you are not around!

Would it be a *faux pas* to go looking for her? Yes, I decided. I was restricted to the rooms I had been shown, that had been an implicit understanding. I would have to wait to find out.

So I cursed long and loud, in many languages, doubtless burning Malann's sacred ears, there in his Temple.

He did not see fit to strike me dead, so I decided to call it a day and hit the sack.

I must have been asleep for several hours when Braxa entered my room with a tiny lamp. She dragged me awake by tugging at my pajama sleeve.

I said hello. Thinking back, there is not much else I could have said.

"Hello."

"I have come," she said, "to hear the poem."

"What poem?"

"Yours."

"Oh."

I yawned, sat up, and did things people usually do when awakened in the middle of the night to read poetry.

"That is very kind of you, but isn't the hour a trifle awkward?"

"I don't mind," she said.

Someday I am going to write an article for the *Journal of Semantics,* called "Tone of Voice: An Insufficient Vehicle for Irony."

However, I was awake, so I grabbed my robe.

"What sort of animal is that?" she asked, pointing at the silk dragon on my lapel.

"Mythical," I replied. "Now look, it's late. I am tired. I have much to do in the morning. And M'Cywie just might get the wrong idea if she learns you were here."

"Wrong idea?"

"You know damned well what I mean!" It was the first time I had had an opportunity to use Martian profanity, and it failed.

"No," she said, "I do not know."

She seemed frightened, like a puppy being scolded without knowing what it has done wrong.

I softened. Her red cloak matched her hair and lips so perfectly, and those lips were trembling.

"Here now, I didn't mean to upset you. On my world there are certain, uh, mores, concerning people of different sex alone together in bedrooms, and not allied by marriage . . . Um, I mean, you see what I mean?"

"No."

They were jade, her eyes.

"Well, it's sort of . . . Well, it's sex, that's what it is."

A light was switched on in those jade lamps.

"Oh, you mean having children!"

"Yes. That's it! Exactly."

She laughed. It was the first time I had heard laughter in Tirellian. It sounded like a violinist striking his high strings with the bow, in short little chops. It was not an altogether pleasant thing to hear, especially because she laughed too long.

When she had finished she moved closer.

"I remember, now," she said. "We used to have such rules. Half a Process ago, when I was a child, we had such rules. But," she looked as if she were ready to laugh again, "there is no need for them now."

My mind moved like a tape recorder played at triple speed.

Half a Process! HalfaProcessaProcessaProcess! No! Yes!

Half a Process was two hundred-forty-three years, roughly speaking!

—Time enough to learn the 2,224 dances of Locar.

—Time enough to grow old, if you were human.

—Earth-style human, I mean.

I looked at her again, pale as the white queen in an ivory chess set.

She was human, I'd stake my soul—alive, normal, healthy, I'd stake my life—woman, my body . . .

But she was two and a half centuries old, which made M'Cywie Methuselah's grandma. It flattered me to think of their repeated complimenting of my skills, as linguist, as poet. These superior beings!

But what did she mean 'there is no such need for them now'? Why the near-hysteria? Why all those funny looks I'd been getting from M'Cwyie?

I suddenly knew I was close to something important, besides a beautiful girl.

"Tell me," I said, in my Casual Voice, "did it have anything to do with 'the plague that does not kill,' of which Tamur wrote?"

"Yes," she replied, "the children born after the Rains could have no children of their own, and—"

"And what?" I was leaning forward, memory set at "record."

"—and the men had no desire to get any."

I sagged backward against the bedpost. Racial sterility, masculine impotence, following phenomenal weather. Had some vagabond cloud of radioactive junk from God knows where penetrated their weak atmosphere one day? One day long before Schiaparelli saw the canals, mythical as my dragon, before those "canals" had given rise to some correct guesses for all the wrong reasons, had Braxa been alive, dancing, here—damned in the womb since blind Milton had written of another paradise, equally lost?

I found a cigarette. Good thing I had thought to bring ashtrays. Mars had never had a tobacco industry either. Or booze. The ascetics I had met in India had been Dionysiac compared to this.

"What is that tube of fire?"

"A cigarette. Want one?"

"Yes, please."

She sat beside me, and I lighted it for her.

"It irritates the nose."

"Yes. Draw some into your lungs, hold it there, and exhale."

A moment passed.

"Ooh," she said.

A pause, then, "Is it sacred?"

"No, it's nicotine," I answered, "a very *ersatz* form of divinity."

Another pause.

"Please don't ask me to translate 'ersatz'."

"I won't. I get this feeling sometimes when I dance."

"It will pass in a moment."

"Tell me your poem now."

An idea hit me.

"Wait a minute," I said, "I may have something better."

I got up and rummaged through my notebooks, then I returned and sat beside her.

"These are the first three chapters of the Book of Ecclesiastes," I explained. "It is very similiar to your own sacred books."

I started reading.

I got through eleven verses before she cried out, "Please don't read that! Tell me one of yours!"

I stopped and tossed the notebook onto a nearby table. She was shaking, not as she had quivered that day she danced as the wind, but with the jitter of unshed tears. She held her cigarette awkwardly, like a pencil. Clumsily, I put my arm about her shoulders.

"He is so sad," she said, "like all the others."

So I twisted my mind like a bright ribbon, folded it, and tied the crazy Christmas knots I love so well. From German to Martian, with love, I did an impromptu paraphrasal of a poem about a Spanish dancer. I thought it would please her. I was right.

"Ooh," she said again. "Did you write that?"

"No, it's by a better man than I."

"I don't believe you. You wrote it."

"No, a man named Rilke did."

"But you brought it across to my language.—Light another match, so I can see how she danced."

I did.

" 'The fires of forever,' " she mused, "and she stamped them out, 'with small, firm feet.' I wish I could dance like that."

"You're better than any Gipsy," I laughed, blowing it out.

"No, I'm not. I couldn't do that."

Her cigarette was burning down, so I removed it from her fingers and put it out, along with my own.

"Do you want me to dance for you?"

"No," I said. "Go to bed."

She smiled, and before I realized it, had unclasped the fold of red at her shoulder.

And everything fell away.

And I swallowed, with some difficulty.

"All right," she said.

So I kissed her, as the breath of fallen cloth extinguished the lamp.

3

The days were like Shelley's leaves: yellow, red, brown, whipped in bright gusts by the west wind. They swirled past me with the rattle of microfilm. Almost all the books were recorded now. It would take scholars years to get through them, to properly assess their value. Mars was locked in my desk.

Ecclesiastes, abandoned and returned to a dozen times, was almost ready to speak in the High Tongue.

I whistled when I wasn't in the Temple. I wrote reams of poetry I would have been ashamed of before. Evenings I would walk with Braxa, across the dunes or up into the mountains. Sometimes she would dance for me; and I would read something long, and in dactylic hexameter. She still thought I was Rilke, and I almost kidded myself into believing it. Here I was, staying at the Castle Duino, writing his *Elegies*.

. . . It is strange to inhabit the Earth no more,

> to use no longer customs scarce acquired,
> nor interpret roses . . .

No! Never interpret roses! Don't. Smell them (sniff, Kane!), pick them, enjoy them. Live in the moment. Hold to it tightly. But charge not the gods to explain. So fast the leaves go by, are blown . . .

And no one ever noticed us. Or cared.

Laura. Laura and Braxa. They rhyme, you know, with a bit of a clash. Tall, cool, and blonde was she (I hate blondes!), and Daddy had turned me inside out, like a pocket, and I thought she could fill me again. But the big, beat word-slinger, with Judas-beard and dog-trust in his eyes, oh, he had been a fine decoration at her parties. And that was all.

How the machine cursed me in the Temple! It blasphemed Malann and Gallinger. And the wild west wind went by and something was not far behind.

The last days were upon us.

A day went by and I did not see Braxa, and a night.

And a second. A third.

I was half-mad. I hadn't realized how close we had become, how important she had been. With the dumb assurance of presence, I had fought against questioning roses.

I had to ask. I didn't want to, but I had no choice.

"Where is she, M'Cwyie? Where is Braxa?"

"She is gone," she said.

"Where?"

"I do not know."

I looked at those devil-bird eyes. Anathema maranatha rose to my lips.

"I must know."

She looked through me.

"She has left us. She is gone. Up into the hills, I suppose. Or the desert. It does not matter. What does anything matter? The dance draws to a close. The Temple will soon be empty."

"Why? Why did she leave?"

"I do not know."

"I must see her again. We lift off in a matter of days."

"I am sorry, Gallinger."

"So am I," I said, and slammed shut a book without saying "m'narra."

I stood up.

"I will find her."

I left the Temple. M'Cwyie was a seated statue. My boots were still where I had left them.

All day I roared up and down the dunes, going nowhere. To the crew of the *Aspic* I must have looked like a sandstorm, all by myself. Finally, I had to return for more fuel.

Emory came stalking out.

"Okay, make it good. You look like the abominable dust man. Why the rodeo?"

"Why, I, uh, lost something."

"In the middle of the desert? Was it one of your sonnets? They're the only thing I can think of that you'd make such a fuss over."

"No, dammit! It was something personal."

George had finished filling the tank. I started to mount the jeepster again.

"Hold on there!" He grabbed my arm.

"You're not going back until you tell me what this is all about."

I could have broken his grip, but then he could order me dragged back by the heels, and quite a few people would enjoy doing the dragging. So I forced myself to speak slowly, softly:

"It's simply that I lost my watch. My mother gave it to me and it's a family heirloom. I want to find it before we leave."

"You sure it's not in your cabin, or down in Tirellian?"

"I've already checked."

"Maybe somebody hid it to irritate you. You know you're not the most popular guy around."

I shook my head.

"I thought of that. But I always carry it in my right pocket. I think it might have bounced out going over the dunes."

He narrowed his eyes.

"I remember reading on a book jacket that your mother died when you were born."

"That's right," I said, biting my tongue. "The watch

belonged to her father and she wanted me to have it. My father kept it for me."

"Hmph!" he snorted. "That's a pretty strange way to look for a watch, riding up and down in a jeepster."

"I could see the light shining off it that way," I offered, lamely.

"Well, it's starting to get dark," he observed. "No sense looking any more today.

"Throw a dust sheet over the jeepster," he directed a mechanic.

He patted my arm.

"Come on in and get a shower, and something to eat. You look as if you could use both."

Little fatty flecks beneath pale eyes, thinning hair, and an Irish nose; a voice a decibel louder than anyone else's . . .

His only qualifications for leadership!

I stood there, hating him. Claudius! If only this were the fifth act!

But suddenly the idea of a shower, and food, came through to me. I could use both badly. If I insisted on hurrying back immediately, I might arouse more suspicion.

So I brushed some sand from my sleeve.

"You're right. That sounds like a good idea."

"Come on, we'll eat in my cabin."

The shower was a blessing, clean khakis were the grace of God, and the food smelled like Heaven.

"Smells pretty good," I said.

We hacked up our steaks in silence. When we got to the dessert and coffee, he suggested:

"Why don't you take the night off? Stay here and get some sleep."

I shook my head.

"I'm pretty busy. Finishing up. There's not much time left."

"A couple days ago you said you were almost finished."

"Almost, but not quite."

"You also said they'll be holding a service in the Temple tonight."

"That's right. I'm going to work in my room."

He shrugged his shoulders.

Finally, he said, "Gallinger," and I looked up because my name means trouble.

"It shouldn't be any of my business," he said, "but it is. Betty says you have a girl down there."

There was no question mark. It was a statement hanging in the air. Waiting.

—*Betty, you're a bitch. You're a cow and a bitch. And a jealous one, at that. Why didn't you keep your nose where it belonged, shut your eyes? Your mouth?*

"So?" I said, a statement with a question mark.

"So," he answered it, "it is my duty, as head of this expedition, to see that relations with the natives are carried on in a friendly, and diplomatic, manner."

"You speak of them," I said, "as though they are aborigines. Nothing could be further from the truth."

I rose.

"When my papers are published, everyone on Earth will know that truth. I'll tell them things Doctor Moore never even guessed at. I'll tell the tragedy of a doomed race, waiting for death, resigned and disinterested. I'll tell why, and it will break hard, scholarly hearts. I'll write about it, and they will give me more prizes, and this time I won't want them.

"My God!" I exclaimed. "They had a culture when our ancestors were clubbing the sabre-tooth and finding out how fire works!"

"*Do* you have a girl down there?"

"Yes!" I said. *Yes, Claudius! Yes, Daddy! Yes, Emory!* "I do. But I'm going to let you in on a scholarly scoop now. They're already dead. They're sterile. In one more generation there won't be any Martians."

I paused, then added, "Except in my papers, except on a few pieces of microfilm and tape. And in some poems, about a girl who did give a damn and could only bitch about the unfairness of it all by dancing."

"Oh," he said.

After awhile:

"You *have* been behaving differently these past couple months. You've even been downright civil on occasion, you know. I couldn't help wondering what was happening. I didn't know anything mattered that strongly to you."

I bowed my head.

"Is she the reason you were racing around the desert?"

I nodded.

"Why?"

I looked up.

"Because she's out there, somewhere. I don't know where, or why. And I've got to find her before we go."

"Oh," he said again.

Then he leaned back, opened a drawer, and took out something wrapped in a towel. He unwound it. A framed photo of a woman lay on the table.

"My wife," he said.

It was an attractive face, with big, almond eyes.

"I'm a Navy man, you know," he began. "Young officer once. Met her in Japan.

"Where I come from it wasn't considered right to marry into another race, so we never did. But she was my wife. When she died I was on the other side of the world. They took my children, and I've never seen them since. I couldn't learn what orphanage, what home, they were put into. That was long ago. Very few people know about it."

"I'm sorry," I said.

"Don't be. Forget it. But," he shifted in his chair and looked at me, "if you do want to take her back with you —do it. It'll mean my neck, but I'm too old to ever head another expedition like this one. So go ahead."

He gulped his cold coffee.

"Get your jeepster."

He swiveled the chair around.

I tried to say "thank you" twice, but I couldn't. So I got up and walked out.

"Sayonara, and all that," he muttered behind me.

"Here it is, Gallinger!" I heard a shout.

I turned on my heel and looked back up the ramp.

"Kane!"

He was limned in the port, shadow against light, but I had heard him sniff.

I returned the few steps.

"Here what is?"

"Your rose."

He produced a plastic container, divided internally. The lower half was filled with liquid. The stem ran down into it. The other half, a glass of claret in this horrible night, was a large, newly opened rose.

"Thank you," I said, tucking it into my jacket.

"Going back to Tirellian, eh?"

"Yes."

"I saw you come aboard, so I got it ready. Just missed you at the Captain's cabin. He was busy. Hollered out that I could catch you at the barns."

"Thanks again."

"It's chemically treated. It will stay in bloom for weeks."

I nodded. I was gone.

Up into the mountains now. Far. Far. The sky was a bucket of ice in which no moons floated. The going became steeper, and the little donkey protested. I whipped him with the throttle and went on. Up. Up. I spotted a green, unwinking star, and felt a lump in my throat. The uncased rose beat against my chest like an extra heart. The donkey brayed, long and loudly, then began to cough. I lashed him some more and he died.

I threw the emergency brake on and got out. I began to walk.

So cold, so cold it grows. Up here. At night? Why? Why did she do it? Why flee the campfire when night comes on?

And I was up, down around, and through every chasm, gorge, and pass, with my long-legged strides and an ease of movement never known on Earth.

Barely two days remain, my love, and thou hast forsaken me. Why?

I crawled under overhangs. I leapt over ridges. I scraped my knees, an elbow. I heard my jacket tear.

No answer, Malann? Do you really hate your people this much? Then I'll try someone else. Vishnu, you're the Preserver. Preserve her, please! Let me find her.

Jehovah?

Adonis? Osiris? Thammuz? Manitou? Legba? Where is she?

I ranged far and high, and I slipped.

Stones ground underfoot and I dangled over an edge. My fingers so cold. It was hard to grip the rock.

I looked down.

Twelve feet or so. I let go and dropped, landed rolling. Then I heard her scream.

I lay there, not moving, looking up. Against the night, above, she called.

"Gallinger!"

I lay still.

"Gallinger!"

And she was gone.

I heard stones rattle and knew she was coming down some path to the right of me.

I jumped up and ducked into the shadow of a boulder.

She rounded a cut-off, and picked her way, uncertainly, through the stones.

"Gallinger?"

I stepped out and seized her shoulders.

"Braxa."

She screamed again, then began to cry, crowding against me. It was the first time I had ever heard her cry.

"Why?" I asked. "Why?"

But she only clung to me and sobbed.

Finally, "I thought you had killed yourself."

"Maybe I would have," I said. "Why did you leave Tirellian? And me?"

"Didn't M'Cwyie tell you? Didn't you guess?"

"I didn't guess, and M'Cwyie said she didn't know."

"Then she lied. She knows."

"What? What is it she knows?"

She shook all over, then was silent for a long time. I realized suddenly that she was wearing only her flimsy dancer's costume. I pushed her from me, took off my jacket, and put it about her shoulders.

"Great Malann!" I cried. "You'll freeze to death!"

"No," she said, "I won't."

I was transferring the rose case to my pocket.

"What is that?" she asked.

"A rose," I answered. "You can't make it out much in the dark. I once compared you to one. Remember?"

"Yu-Yes. May I carry it?"

"Sure." I stuck it in the jacket pocket.

"Well? I'm still waiting for an explanation."

"You really do not know?" she asked.

"No!"

"When the Rains came," she said, "apparently only our

men were affected, which was enough. . . . Because I—
wasn't—affected—apparently—"

"Oh," I said. "Oh."

We stood there, and I thought.

"Well, why did you run? What's wrong with being pregnant on Mars? Tamur was mistaken. Your people can live
again."

She laughed, again that wild violin played by a Paganini
gone mad. I stopped her before it went too far.

"How?" she finally asked, rubbing her cheek.

"Your people live longer than ours. If our child is
normal it will mean our races can intermarry. There must
still be other fertile women of your race. Why not?"

"You have read the Book of Locar," she said, "and yet
you ask me that? Death was decided, voted upon, and
passed, shortly after it appeared in this form. But long
before, the followers of Locar knew. They decided it long
ago. 'We have done all things,' they said, 'we have seen
all things, we have heard and felt all things. The dance
was good. Now let it end.' "

"You can't believe that."

"What I believe does not matter," she replied. "M'Cwyie
and the Mothers have decided we must die. Their very title
is now a mockery, but their decisions will be upheld. There
is only one prophecy left, and it is mistaken. We will die."

"No," I said.

"What, then?"

"Come back with me, to Earth."

"No."

"All right, then. Come with me now."

"Where?"

"Back to Tirellian. I'm going to talk to the Mothers."

"You can't! There is a Ceremony tonight!"

I laughed.

"A ceremony for a god who knocks you down, and then
kicks you in the teeth?"

"He is still Malann," she answered. "We are still his
people."

"You and my father would have gotten along fine," I
snarled. "But I am going, and you are coming with me,
even if I have to carry you—and I'm bigger than you are."

"But you are not bigger than Ontro."

"Who the hell is Ontro?"

"He will stop you, Gallinger. He is the Fist of Malann."

4

I scudded the jeepster to a halt in front of the only entrance I knew, M'Cwyie's. Braxa, who had seen the rose in a headlamp, now cradled it in her lap, like our child, and said nothing. There was a passive, lovely look on her face.

"Are they in the Temple now?" I wanted to know.

The Madonna expression did not change. I repeated the question. She stirred.

"Yes," she said, from a distance, "but you cannot go in."

"We'll see."

I circled and helped her down.

I led her by the hand, and she moved as if in a trance. In the light of the new-risen moon, her eyes looked as they had the day I met her, when she had danced. I snapped my fingers. Nothing happened.

So I pushed the door open and led her in. The room was half-lighted.

And she screamed for the third time that evening:

"Do not harm him, Ontro! It is Gallinger!"

I had never seen a Martian man before, only women. So I had no way of knowing whether he was a freak, though I suspected it strongly.

I looked up at him.

His half-naked body was covered with moles and swellings. Gland trouble, I guessed.

I had thought I was the tallest man on the planet, but he was seven feet tall and overweight. Now I knew where my giant bed had come from!

"Go back," he said. "She may enter. You may not."

"I must get my books and things."

He raised a huge left arm. I followed it. All my belongings lay neatly stacked in the corner.

"I must go in. I must talk with M'Cwyie and the Mothers."

"You may not."

"The lives of your people depend on it."

"Go back," he boomed. "Go home to *your* people, Gallinger. Leave *us!*"

My name sounded so different on his lips, like someone

else's. How old was he? I wondered. Three hundred? Four? Had he been a Temple guardian all his life? Why? Who was there to guard against? I didn't like the way he moved. I had seen men who moved like that before.

"Go back," he repeated.

If they had refined their martial arts as far as they had their dances, or, worse yet, if their fighting arts were a part of the dance, I was in for trouble.

"Go on in," I said to Braxa. "Give the rose to M'Cwyie. Tell her that I sent it. Tell her I'll be there shortly."

"I will do as you ask. Remember me on Earth, Gallinger. Good-bye."

I did not answer her, and she walked past Ontro and into the next room, bearing her rose.

"Now will you leave?" he asked. "If you like, I will tell her that we fought and you almost beat me, but I knocked you unconscious and carried you back to your ship."

"No," I said, "either I go around you or go over you, but I am going through."

He dropped into a crouch, arms extended.

"It is a sin to lay hands on a holy man," he rumbled, "but I will stop you, Gallinger."

My memory was a fogged window, suddenly exposed to fresh air. Things cleared. I looked back six years.

I was a student of Oriental Languages at the University of Tokyo. It was my twice-weekly night of recreation. I stood in a 30-foot circle in the Kodokan, the *judogi* lashed about my high hips by a brown belt. I was *Ik-kyu*, one notch below the lowest degree of expert. A brown diamond above my right breast said "Jiu-Jitsu" in Japanese, and it meant *atemiwaza*, really, because of the one striking technique I had worked out, found unbelievably suitable to my size, and won matches with.

But I had never used it on a man, and it was five years since I had practiced. I was out of shape, I knew, but I tried hard to force my mind *tsuki no kokoro*, like the moon, reflecting the all of Ontro.

Somewhere, out of the past, a voice said, "*Hajime*, let it begin."

I snapped into my *neko-ashi-dachi* cat stance, and his eyes burned strangely. He hurried to correct his own position—and I threw it at him!

My one trick!

My long left leg lashed up like a broken spring. Seven feet off the ground my foot connected with his jaw as he tried to leap backward.

His head snapped back and he fell. A soft moan escaped his lips. *That's all there is to it,* I thought. *Sorry, old fellow.*

And as I stepped over him, somehow, groggily, he tripped me, and I fell across his body. I couldn't believe he had strength enough to remain conscious after that blow, let alone move. I hated to punish him any more.

But he found my throat and slipped a forearm across it before I realized there was a purpose to his action.

No! Don't let it end like this!

It was a bar of steel across my windpipe, my carotids. Then I realized that he was still unconscious, and that this was a reflex instilled by countless years of training. I had seen it happen once, in *shiai*. The man had died because he had been choked unconscious and still fought on, and his opponent thought he had not been applying the choke properly. He tried harder.

But it was rare, so very rare!

I jammed my elbows into his ribs and threw my head back in his face. The grip eased, but not enough. I hated to do it, but I reached up and broke his little finger.

The arm went loose and I twisted free.

He lay there panting, face contorted. My heart went out to the fallen giant, defending his people, his religion, following his orders. I cursed myself as I had never cursed before, for walking over him, instead of around.

I staggered across the room to my little heap of possessions. I sat on the projector case and lit a cigarette.

I couldn't go into the Temple until I got my breath back, until I thought of something to say.

How do you talk a race out of killing itself?

Suddenly—

—Could it happen? Would it work that way? If I read them the Book of Ecclesiastes—if I read them a greater piece of literature than any Locar ever wrote—and as somber—and as pessimistic—and showed them that our race had gone on despite one man's condemning all of life in the highest poetry—showed them that the vanity he had mocked had borne us to the Heavens—would they believe it?—would they change their minds?

I ground out my cigarette on the beautiful floor, and found my notebook. A strange fury rose within me as I stood.

And I walked into the Temple to preach the Black Gospel according to Gallinger, from the Book of Life.

There was silence all about me.

M'Cwyie had been reading Locar, the rose set at her right hand, target of all eyes.

Until I entered.

Hundreds of people were seated on the floor, barefoot. The few men were as small as the women, I noted.

I had my boots on.

Go all the way, I figured. *You either lose or you win— everything!*

A dozen crones sat in a semicircle behind M'Cwyie. The Mothers.

The barren earth, the dry wombs, the fire-touched.

I moved to the table.

"Dying yourselves, you would condemn your people," I addressed them, "that they may not know the life you have known—the joys, the sorrows, the fullness.—But it is not true that you all must die." I addressed the multitude now. "Those who say this lie. Braxa knows, for she will bear a child—"

They sat there, like rows of Buddhas. M'Cwyie drew back into the semicircle.

"—my child!" I continued, wondering what my father would have thought of this sermon.

". . . And all the women young enough may bear children. It is only your men who are sterile.—And if you permit the doctors of the next expedition to examine you, perhaps even the men may be helped. But if they cannot, you can mate with the men of Earth.

"And ours is not an insignificant people, an insignificant place," I went on. "Thousands of years ago, the Locar of our world wrote a book saying that it was. He spoke as Locar did, but we did not lie down, despite plagues, wars, and famines. We did not die. One by one we beat down the diseases, we fed the hungry, we fought the wars, and,

recently, have gone a long time without them. We may
finally have conquered them. I do not know.

"But we have crossed millions of miles of nothingness.
We have visited another world. And our Locar had said,
'Why bother? What is the worth of it? It is all vanity,
anyhow.'

"And the secret is," I lowered my voice, as at a poetry
reading, "he was right! It *is* vanity, it *is* pride! It is the
hybris of rationalism to always attack the prophet, the
mystic, the god. It is our blasphemy which has made us
great, and will sustain us, and which the gods secretly
admire in us.—All the truly sacred names of God are
blasphemous things to speak!"

I was working up a sweat. I paused dizzily.

"Here is the Book of Ecclesiastes," I announced, and
began:

" 'Vanity of vanities, saith the Preacher, vanity of
vanities; all is vanity. What profit hath a man . . .' "

I spotted Braxa in the back, mute, rapt.

I wondered what she was thinking.

And I wound the hours of night about me, like black
thread on a spool.

Oh, it was late! I had spoken till day came, and still I
spoke. I finished Ecclesiastes and continued Gallinger.

And when I finished, there was still only a silence.

The Buddhas, all in a row, had not stirred through the
night. And after a long while M'Cwyie raised her right
hand. One by one the Mothers did the same.

And I knew what that meant.

It meant no, do not, cease, and stop.

It meant that I had failed.

I walked slowly from the room and slumped beside my
baggage.

Ontro was gone. Good that I had not killed him . . .

After a thousand years M'Cwyie entered.

She said, "Your job is finished."

I did not move.

"The prophecy is fulfilled," she said. "My people are
rejoicing. You have won, holy man. Now leave us quickly."

My mind was a deflated balloon. I pumped a little air
back into it.

"I'm not a holy man," I said, "just a second-rate poet with a bad case of *hybris*."

I lit my last cigarette.

Finally, "All right, what prophecy?"

"The Promise of Locar," she replied, as though the explaining were unnecessary, "that a holy man would come from the heavens to save us in our last hours, if all the dances of Locar were completed. He would defeat the Fist of Malann and bring us life."

"How?"

"As with Braxa, and as the example in the Temple."

"Example?"

"You read us his words, as great as Locar's. You read to us how there is 'nothing new under the sun.' And you mocked his words as you read them—showing us a new thing.

"There has never been a flower on Mars," she said, "but we will learn to grow them.

"You are the Sacred Scoffer," she finished. "He-Who-Must-Mock-in-the-Temple—you go shod on holy ground."

"But you voted 'no'," I said.

"I voted not to carry out our original plan, and to let Braxa's child live instead."

"Oh." The cigarette fell from my fingers. How close it had been! How little I had known!

"And Braxa?"

"She was chosen half a Process ago to do the dances—to wait for you."

"But she said that Ontro would stop me."

M'Cwyie stood there for a long time.

"She had never believed the prophecy herself. Things are not well with her now. She ran away, fearing it was true. When you completed it and we voted, she knew."

"Then she does not love me? Never did?"

"I am sorry, Gallinger. It was the one part of her duty she never managed."

"Duty," I said flatly. . . . Dutydutyduty! Tra-la!

"She has said good-bye, she does not wish to see you again.

". . . and we will never forget your teachings," she added.

"Don't," I said, automatically, suddenly knowing the

great paradox which lies at the heart of all miracles. I did not believe a word of my own gospel, never had.

I stood, like a drunken man, and muttered "M'narra."

I went outside, into my last day on Mars.

I have conquered thee, Malann—and the victory is thine! Rest easy on thy starry bed. God damned!

I left the jeepster there and walked back to the *Aspic*, leaving the burden of life so many footsteps behind me. I went to my cabin, locked the door, and took forty-four sleeping pills.

But when I awakened, I was in the dispensary, and alive.

I felt the throb of engines as I slowly stood up and somehow made it to the port.

Blurred Mars hung like a swollen belly above me, until it dissolved, brimmed over, and streamed down my face. ■

I know very little about Roger Zelazny, because he claims to get amnesia when asked to write about himself. Among the few things I do know are that he can fill a page with fine, funny copy describing a writer having amnesia when asked, etc.; that he fairly recently acquired a Master's degree at Columbia in some particularly esoteric field of literature; and that he is an (or perhaps the) outstanding example of the influx of literate young writers into the SF field during the last three or four years.

Perhaps it would be even more valid to say that Zelazny—and Ballard, who follows here—are the kind of writers working in and out of SF, who are making the idea of a separate "field" disappear.

Writers outside SF have begun to discover the uses of extrapolative and speculative writing. Inside SF the best people—like Zelazny, like Ballard—are reaching toward poetry, metaphysics, religion, psychiatry, symbolism, and myth as systems through which to explore the nature of man; and reaching, too, for the new techniques of expression being explored in the experimental and avant-garde fringes of the "mainstream."

James Ballard has, I think, been more successful in this effort than anyone else writing "inside SF" today—comparable perhaps to Jorge Luis Borges on the "outside." Ballard says of this story:

" 'Terminal Beach' represents the most extreme expression to
date of what I have called 'inner space'—that area where the
outer world of reality and the inner world of the psyche meet
and fuse. Only in this area can one find the true subject matter
for a mature science fiction." `

THE TERMINAL BEACH
J. G. Ballard
from *New Worlds SF*

At night, as he lay half-asleep
on the floor of the ruined bunker, Traven heard the waves
breaking along the shore of the lagoon, reminding him of
the long Atlantic rollers on the beach at Dakar, where he
had been born, and of listening in the evenings for his
parents to drive home along the corniche road from the
airport. Overcome by this forgotten memory, he woke
uncertainly from the bed of old magazines on which he
slept and hurried toward the dunes that screened the
lagoon.

Through the cold night air he could see the abandoned
Superfortresses lying among the palms beyond the perimeter of the emergency landing field three hundred yards
away. Traven walked through the dark sand, already forgetting where the shore lay, although the atoll was little
more than half a mile in width. Above him, along the
crests of the dunes, the tall palms leaned into the dim air
like the symbols of a cryptic alphabet. The landscape of the
island was covered by strange ciphers.

Giving up the attempt to find the beach, Traven
stumbled into a set of tracks left years earlier by a large
caterpillar vehicle. The heat released by one of the weapons
tests had fused the sand, and the double line of fossil im-
prints, uncovered by the evening air, wound its serpentine
way among the hollows like the footfalls of an ancient
saurian.

Too weak to walk any farther, Traven sat down between
the tracks. Hoping that they might lead him to the beach,
he began to excavate the wedge-shaped grooves from a

drift into which they disappeared. He returned to the
bunker shortly before dawn, and slept through the hot
silences of the following noon.

The Blocks

As usual on these enervating afternoons, when not even
a breath of on-shore breeze disturbed the dust, Traven sat
in the shadow of one of the blocks, lost somewhere within
the centre of the maze. His back resting against the rough
concrete surface, he gazed with a phlegmatic eye down the
surrounding aisles and at the line of doors facing him.
Each afternoon he left his cell in the abandoned camera
bunker among the dunes and walked down into the blocks.
For the first half an hour he restricted himself to the perimeter aisle, now and then trying one of the doors with the
rusty key in his pocket—he had found it among the litter
of smashed bottles and cans in the isthmus of sand separating the testing ground from the airstrip—and then in-
evitably, with a sort of drugged stride, he set off into the
center of the blocks, breaking into a run and darting in
and out of the corridors, as if trying to flush some invisible opponent from his hiding place. Soon he would
be completely lost. Whatever his efforts to return to the
perimeter, he always found himself once more in the
center.

Eventually he would abandon the task, and sit down in
the dust, watching the shadows emerge from their crevices
at the foot of the blocks. For some reason he invariably
arranged to be trapped when the sun was at zenith—on
Eniwetok, the thermonuclear noon.

One question in particular intrigued him: "What sort of
people would inhabit this minimal concrete city?"

The Synthetic Landscape

"This island is a state of mind," Osborne, one of the
scientists working in the old submarine pens, was later to
remark to Traven. The truth of this became obvious to
Traven within two or three weeks of his arrival. Despite
the sand and the few anaemic palms, the entire landscape
of the island was synthetic, a man-made artifact with all the
associations of a vast system of derelict concrete motor-
ways. Since the moratorium on atomic tests, the island had
been abandoned by the Atomic Energy Commission, and

the wilderness of weapons aisles, towers and blockhouses ruled out any attempt to return it to its natural state. (There were also stronger unconscious motives, Traven reflected: if primitive man felt the need to assimilate events in the external world to his own psyche, twentieth-century man had reversed this process; by this Cartesian yardstick, the island at least *existed*, in a sense true of few other places).

But apart from a few scientific workers, no one yet felt any wish to visit the former testing ground, and the naval patrol boat anchored in the lagoon had been withdrawn three years before Traven's arrival. Its ruined appearance, and the associations of the island with the period of the Cold War—what Traven had christened "The Pre-Third" —were profoundly depressing, an Auschwitz of the soul whose mausoleums contained the mass graves of the still undead. With the Russo-American *détente* this nightmarish chapter of history had been gladly forgotten.

The Pre-Third

> The actual and potential destructiveness of the atomic bomb plays straight into the hands of the Unconscious. The most cursory study of the dream-life and fantasies of the insane shows that ideas of world-destruction are latent in the unconscious mind. . . . Nagasaki destroyed by the magic of science is the nearest man has yet approached to the realization of dreams that even during the safe immobility of sleep are accustomed to develop into nightmares of anxiety.
>
> Glover: *War, Sadism and Pacifism*.

The Pre-Third: the period was characterized in Traven's mind above all by its moral and psychological inversions, by its sense of the whole of history, and in particular of the immediate future—the two decades, 1945–65—suspended from the quivering volcano's lip of World War III. Even the death of his wife and six-year-old son in a motor accident seemed only part of this immense synthesis of the historical and psychic zero, the frantic highways where each morning of his life they met their deaths on the advance causeways to the global armageddon.

Third Beach

He had come ashore at midnight, after a hazardous search for an opening in the reef. The small motorboat he had hired from an Australian pearl-diver at Charlotte Island subsided into the shallows, its hull torn by the sharp coral. Exhausted, Traven walked through the darkness among the dunes, where the dim outlines of bunkers and concrete towers loomed between the palms.

He woke the next morning into bright sunlight and found himself lying halfway down the slope of a wide concrete beach. This ringed an empty reservoir or target basin some two hundred feet in diameter, part of a system of artificial lakes built down the center of the atoll. Leaves and dust choked the exit grilles, and a pool of warm water two feet deep lay below him, reflecting a distant line of palms.

Traven sat up and took stock of himself. This brief inventory, which merely confirmed his physical identity, was limited to little more than his thin body in its frayed cotton garments. In the context of the surrounding terrain, however, even this collection of tatters seemed to possess a unique vitality. The desolation and emptiness of the island, and the absence of any local fauna, were emphasized by the huge sculptural forms of the target basins let into its surface. Separated from each other by narrow isthmuses, the lakes stretched away along the curve of the atoll.

On either side, sometimes shaded by the few palms that had gained a precarious purchase in the cracked cement, were roadways, camera towers and isolated blockhouses, together forming a continuous concrete cap upon the island, a functional megalithic architecture as grey and minatory (and apparently as ancient, in its projection into and from time future) as any of Assyria and Babylon.

The series of weapons tests had fused the sand in layers, and the pseudo-geological strata condensed the brief epochs, microseconds in duration, of thermonuclear time. Typically the island inverted the geologist's maxim. "The key to the past lies in the present." Here, the key to the present lay in the future. This island was a fossil of time future, its bunkers and blockhouses illustrating the principle that the fossil record of life was one of armor and the exoskeleton. Traven knelt in the warm pool, and splashed his shirt and trousers. The reflection revealed the watery image of gaunt

shoulders and bearded face. He had come to the island with
no supplies other than a small bar of chocolate, assuming
that in some way the island would provide its own sus-
tenance. Perhaps, too, he had identified the need for food
with a forward motion in time, and that with his return to
the past, or at most into a zone of nontime, this need would
be eliminated. The privations of the previous six months,
during his journey across the Pacific, had already reduced
his always thin body to that of a migrant beggar, held
together by little more than the preoccupied gaze in his eye.
Yet this emaciation, by stripping away the superfluities of
the flesh, revealed an inner sinewy toughness, an economy
and directness of movement.

For several hours Traven wandered about, inspecting
one bunker after another for a convenient place to sleep.
He crossed the remains of a small landing field, next to a
dump where a dozen B-29's lay across one another like
reptile birds.

The Corpses

Once he entered a small street of metal shacks, containing a cafeteria, recreation rooms and shower stalls. A
wrecked jukebox lay half-buried in the sand behind the
cafeteria, its selection of records still in their rack.

Farther along, flung into a small target lake fifty yards
from the shacks, were the bodies of what at first he thought
were the former inhabitants of this ghost town—a dozen
plastic models. Their half-melted faces, contorted into
bleary grimaces, gazed up at him from the jumble of legs
and torsoes.

On either side of him, muffled by the dunes, came the
sounds of waves, the great rollers on the seaward side
breaking over the reefs, and on to the beaches within the
lagoon. However, he avoided the sea, hesitating before any
rise or dune that might take him within its sight. Everywhere the camera towers offered him a convenient aerial
view of the confused topography of the island, but he ignored their rusting ladders.

He soon realized that however random the blockhouses
and towers might seem, their common focus dominated the
landscape and gave to it a unique perspective. As Traven
noticed when he sat down to rest in the window slit of one

of the bunkers, all these observation posts occupied positions on a series of concentric perimeters, moving in tight-
ening arcs towards the inmost sanctuary. This ultimate
circle, below ground zero, remained hidden beyond a line
of dunes a quarter of a mile to the west.

The Terminal Bunker

After sleeping for a few nights in the open, Traven
returned to the concrete beach where he had woken on his
first morning on the island, and made his home—if the term
could be applied to that damp crumbling hovel—in a
camera bunker fifty yards from the target lakes. The dark
chamber between the thick canted walls, tomblike though it
might seem, gave him a sense of physical reassurance. Outside, the sand drifted against the sides, half-burying the
narrow doorway, as if crystallizing the immense epoch of
time that had elapsed since the bunker's construction. The
narrow rectangles of the five camera slits, their shapes and
positions determined by the instruments, studded the west
wall like cryptic ideograms. Variations on these runic
ciphers decorated the walls of the other bunkers, the unique
signature of the island. In the mornings, if Traven was
awake, he would find the sun divided into its five emblem-
atic beacons.

Most of the time the chamber was filled only by a damp
gloomy light. In the control tower at the landing field
Traven found a collection of discarded magazines, and used
these as a bed. One day, lying in the bunker shortly after
the first attack of beri-beri, he pulled out a magazine press-
ing into his back and found inside a full-page photograph
of a six-year-old girl. This blonde-haired child, with her
composed expression and self-immersed eyes, filled him
with a thousand memories of his son. He pinned the page
to the wall and for days gazed at it through his reveries.

For the first few weeks Traven made little attempt to leave
the bunker, and postponed any further exploration of the
island. The symbolic journey through its inner circles set
its own times of arrival and departure. He evolved no
routine for himself. All sense of time soon vanished, and
his life became completely existential, an absolute break
separating one moment from the next like two quantal
events. Too weak to forage for food, he lived on the old

ration packs he found in the wrecked Superfortresses. Without any implement, it took him all day to open the cans. His physical decline continued, but he watched his spindling legs and arms with indifference. This lack of loyalty depressed him.

By now he had forgotten the existence of the sea and vaguely assumed the atoll to be part of some continuous continental table. A hundred yards to the north and south of the bunker a line of dunes, topped by the palisade of enigmatic palms, screened the lagoon and sea, and the faint muffled drumming of the waves at night had fused with his memories of war and childhood. To the east was the emergency landing strip and the abandoned aircraft. In the afternoon light their shifting rectilinear shadows made them appear to writhe and pivot. In front of the bunker, where he would sit, was the system of target lakes, the shallow basins extending across the atoll.

Above him, the five camera apertures looked out upon this scene like the tutelary symbols of a futuristic myth.

The Lakes and the Spectres

The lakes had been designed to reveal any radiobiological changes in a selected range of fauna, but the specimens had long since bloomed into grotesque parodies of themselves and been destroyed.

Sometimes in the evenings, when a sepulchral light lay over the concrete bunkers and causeways, and the basins seemed like ornamental lakes in a city of deserted mausoleums, abandoned even by the dead, he would see the spectres of his wife and son standing on the opposite bank. Their solitary figures appeared to have been watching him for hours. Although they never moved, Traven was sure they were beckoning to him. Roused from his reverie, he would stumble forward across the dark sand to the edge of the lake and wade through the water, shouting soundlessly at the two figures as they moved away hand in hand among the lakes and disappeared across the distant causeways.

Shivering with cold, Traven returned to the bunker and laid on the bed of old magazines, waiting for their return. The image of their faces, the pale lantern of his wife's cheeks, floated on that river of memory, lost among the dark archipelagoes of his dreams.

The Blocks (II)

It was not until he discovered the blocks that Traven realized he would never leave the island.

At this stage, some two months after his arrival, Traven had exhausted his small cache of food, and the symptoms of beri-beri had become more acute. The numbness in his hands and feet, and the gradual loss of strength, continued. Only by an immense effort, and the knowledge that the inner sanctum of the island still lay unexplored, did he manage to leave the palliasse of magazines and make his way from the bunker.

As he sat in the drift of sand by the doorway that evening, he noticed a light shining through the palms far into the distance around the atoll. Confusing this with the image of his wife and son, and visualizing them waiting for him at some warm hearth among the dunes, Traven set off toward the light. Within a hundred yards he lost his sense of direction. He blundered about for several hours on the edges of the landing strip, and succeeded only in cutting his foot on a broken Coca-Cola bottle in the sand.

After postponing his search for the night, he set out again in earnest the next morning. As he moved past the towers and blockhouses the heat and silence lay over the island in an unbroken mantle. He had entered a zone devoid of time. Only the narrowing perimeters warned him that he was crossing the inner field of the fire-table.

He climbed the ridge which marked the farthest point in his previous exploration of the island. From the plain beyond the recording towers rose into the air like obelisks. Traven walked toward them. On their grey walls were the faint outlines of human forms in stylized poses, the flash-shadows of the target community burnt into the cement. Here and there, where the concrete apron had cracked, a line of palms hung in the motionless air. The target lakes were smaller, filled with the broken bodies of plastic dummies. Most of them lay in the inoffensive domestic postures into which they had been placed before the tests.

Beyond the farthest line of dunes, where the camera towers began to turn and face him, were the tops of what seemed to be a herd of square-backed elephants. They were drawn up in precise ranks in a hollow that formed a shallow corral, the sunlight reflected off their backs.

Traven stepped towards them, limping on his cut foot. On either side of him the loosening sand had excavated the dunes, and several of the blockhouses tilted on their sides. This plain of bunkers stretched for some quarter of a mile, the half-submerged hulks, bombed out onto the surface in some earlier test, like the abandoned wombs that had given birth to this herd of megaliths.

The Blocks (III)

To grasp something of the vast number and oppressive size of the blocks, and their impact upon Traven, one must try to visualize sitting in the shade of one of these concrete monsters, or walking about in the center of this enormous labyrinth that extended across the central table of the island. There were some two thousand of them, each a perfect cube 15 feet in height, regularly spaced at ten-yard intervals. They were arranged in a series of tracts, each composed of two hundred blocks, inclined to one another and to the direction of the blast. They had weathered only slightly in the years since they were first built, and their gaunt profiles were like the cutting faces of some gigantic die-plate, devised to stamp out rectilinear volumes of air the size of a house. Three of the sides were smooth and unbroken, but the fourth, facing away from the blast, contained a narrow inspection door.

It was this feature of the blocks that Traven found particularly disturbing. Despite the considerable number of doors, by some freak of perspective only those in a single aisle were visible at any point within the maze. As he walked from the perimeter line into the center of the massif, line upon line of the small metal doors appeared and receded, a world of closed exits concealed behind endless corners.

Approximately twenty of the blocks, those immediately below ground zero, were solid; the walls of the remainder were of varying thickness. From the outside, however, they appeared to be of uniform solidity.

As he entered the first of the long aisles, Traven felt the sense of fatigue that had dogged him begin to lift. His steps lightened. With their geometric regularity and finish, the

blocks seemed to occupy more than their own volumes of
space, imposing on him their calm and order. He walked on
into the center of the maze, eager to shut out the rest of the
island. After a few random turns to left and right, he found
himself alone, the vistas to the sea, lagoon and island
closed.

Here he sat down with his back to one of the blocks, the
quest for his wife and son forgotten. The sense of dissocia-
tion set off by the derelict landscape of the island began to
recede.

One development he did not expect. With dusk, and the
need to leave the blocks and find food, he realized that he
had lost himself. However, he retraced his steps, struck out
left or right at an oblique course, oriented himself around
the setting sun and pressed on resolutely north or south,
and found himself back again at his starting point. Only
when darkness came did he manage to make his escape.

Abandoning his former home near the aircraft dump,
Traven collected together what canned food he could find
in the waist turret and cockpit lockers of the Superfortresses. He pulled them across the atoll on a crude
sledge. Fifty yards from the perimeter of the blocks he took
over a tilting bunker, and pinned the fading photograph of
the blonde-haired child to the wall beside the door. The
page was falling to pieces, like the fragmenting image of
himself. Since the discovery of the blocks he had become
a creature of reflexes, kindled from levels above those of his
existing nervous system (if the automatic system was
dominated by the past, Traven sensed, the cerebro-spinal
reached towards the future). Each evening when he awoke,
he would eat without appetite and then wander away among
the blocks. Sometimes he took a canteen of water with him
and remained there for two or three days on end.

The Submarine Pens

This precarious existence continued for the following
weeks. As he walked out to the blocks one evening, he
again saw his wife and son, standing among the dunes below a camera tower, their faces watching him expression-
lessly. He realized that they had followed him across the
island from their former haunt among the dried-up lakes.
At about this time he once again saw the distant light

beckoning, and decided to continue his exploration of the island.

Half a mile farther along the atoll, he found a group of four submarine pens, built over an inlet, now drained, which wound through the dunes from the sea. The pens still contained several feet of water, filled with small luminescent fish and algae. The morning light winked at intervals from the apex of a metal scaffold. The remains of a substantial camp, only recently vacated, stood on the pier outside. Greedily, Traven heaped his sledge with the provisions inside one of the metal shacks.

With this change of diet, the beri-beri receded, and during the next days he returned often to the camp. Evidently it was the site of a biological expedition. In the field office he came across a series of large charts of mutated chromosomes. He rolled them up and took them back to his bunker. The abstract patterns were meaningless, but during his recovery he amused himself by devising suitable titles for them (later, passing the aircraft dump on one of his forays, he found the half-buried jukebox, and tore the list of records from the selection panel. Thus embroidered, the charts took on many layers of cryptic associations).

Traven: In Parenthesis
  Elements in a quantal world:
    The terminal beach
    The terminal bunker
    the blocks

                    *   *   *

The landscape is coded.

Entry points into the future = Levels in a spinal landscape = zones of significant time.

August 5. Found the man Traven. A strange derelict figure, hiding in a bunker in the deserted interior of the island. He is suffering from severe exposure and malnutrition, but is unaware of this or, for that matter, of any other events in the world around him. . . .

He maintains that he came to the island to carry out some scientific project—unstated—but I suspect that he understands his real motives and the unique role of the island. . . . In some way its landscape seems to be

involved with certain unconscious notions of time, and
in particular with those that may be a repressed premonition of our own deaths. The attractions and dan-
gers of such an architecture, as the past has shown,
need no stressing. . . .
August 6. He has the eyes of the possessed. I would
guess that he is neither the first, nor the last, to visit
the island.

—from Dr. C. Osborne, *Eniwetok Diary*.

Traven lost within the Blocks

With the exhaustion of his supplies, Traven remained
within the perimeter of the blocks almost continuously,
conserving what strength remained to him to walk slowly
down their empty corridors. The infection in his right foot
made it difficult for him to replenish his supplies from the
stores left by the biologists, and as his strength ebbed he
found less incentive to make his way out of the blocks. The
system of megaliths now provided a complete substitute for
those functions of his mind which gave to it its sense of the
sustained rational order of time and space. Without them,
Traven felt his awareness of reality shrinking to little more
than the few square inches of sand beneath his feet.

On one of his last ventures into the maze, he spent all
night and much of the following morning in a futile attempt
to escape. Dragging himself from one rectangle of shadow
to another, his leg as heavy as a club and apparently in-
flamed to the knee, he realized that he must soon find an
equivalent for the blocks or he would end his life within
them, trapped inside this self-constructed mausoleum as
surely as the retinue of Pharaoh.

He was sitting helplessly somewhere in the center of the
system, the faceless lines of tomb-booths receding from
him, when the sky was slowly divided by the drone of a
light aircraft. This passed overhead, and then, five minutes
later, returned. Seizing his opportunity, Traven struggled
to his feet and made his exit from the blocks, his head
raised to follow the faintly glistening beacon of the exhaust
trail.

As he lay in the bunker he dimly heard the aircraft
return and carry out an inspection of the site.

A Belated Rescue

"Who are you?" A small sandy-haired man peered down at him, an expression of sharp disapproval on his face. He packed a syringe away in his valise. "Do you realize you're on your last legs?"

"Traven . . . I've had some sort of accident. I'm glad you flew over."

"I'm sure you are. But why didn't you use our radio-telephone? Anyway, we'll call the Navy and have you picked up."

"No . . ." Traven sat up on one elbow and felt weakly in his hip pocket. "I have a pass somewhere. I'm carrying out research."

"Into what?" The question assumed a complete under-standing of Traven's motives. He lay in the shade under the lee of the bunker, and drank weakly from a canteen as Dr. Osborne dressed his foot. "You've also been stealing our stores."

Traven shook his head. Fifty yards away the blue and white Cessna stood on the concrete apron like a brilliant dragonfly. "I didn't realize you were coming back."

"You must be in a trance."

The young woman sitting at the controls of the aircraft climbed out and walked over to them. She glanced at the grey bunkers and towers, and seemed unaware or unin-terested in the decrepit figure of Traven. Osborne spoke to her and after a downward glance at Traven she went back to the aircraft. As she turned Traven rose involuntarily, recognizing the child in the photograph he had pinned to the the wall of the bunker. Then he remembered that the magazine could not have been more than four or five years old. Nevertheless, the conviction—indeed, almost a last desperate hope—that the child and the young woman were the same person remained.

The engine of the aircraft started. As Traven watched, it turned on to one of the roadways and took off into the wind.

Later that afternoon she drove over by jeep to the blocks and unloaded a small camp bed for Traven and a canvas awning. During the intervening hours Traven had slept.

He woke refreshed when Osborne returned from his scrutiny of the surrounding dunes.

"What are you doing here?" the young woman asked as she secured the grey ropes to the roof of the bunker.

Traven watched her move about. "I'm . . . searching for my wife and son."

"They're on this island?" Surprised, but taking the reply at face value, she looked around her.

"In a manner of speaking."

After inspecting the bunker, Osborne joined them. "The child in the photograph—is she your daughter?"

Traven hesitated. "Yes—or rather, she's adopted me."

Unable to make any sense of his replies, but accepting his assurances that he would leave the island, Osborne and the young woman drove back to their camp. Each day Osborne returned to change the dressing, driven by the young woman, who seemed now to understand the role cast for her by Traven and his private island mythology. Osborne, when he learned of Traven's previous career as a military pilot, appeared to suspect that he might be a latter-day martyr left high and dry by the moratorium on thermonuclear tests.

"A guilt complex isn't an indiscriminate supply of moral sanctions. I think you may be overstretching yours." When he mentioned the name Eatherly, Traven shook his head.

Undeterred, Osborne pressed: "Are you sure you're not making similar use of the image of Eniwetok—waiting for your Pentecostal wind?"

"Believe me, Doctor, no," Traven replied firmly. "For me the Hydrogen Bomb was a symbol of absolute freedom. Unlike Eatherly, I feel it's given me the right—the obligation, even—to do anything I choose."

"That seems strange logic," Osborne commented. "Aren't we at least responsible for our physical selves, if for nothing else?"

"Not now, I think," Traven replied. "In effect, aren't we men raised from the dead?"

Often, however, he thought of Eatherly.

* * *

Eatherly: the prototypal Pre-Third Man—dating the Pre-

Third from August 6, 1945—carrying a full load of cosmic guilt.

* * *

Shortly after Traven was strong enough to walk he had to be rescued from the blocks for a second time. Osborne became less conciliatory.

"Our work is almost complete," he said warningly. "You'll die here, Traven. What *are* you looking for among those blocks?"

To himself, Traven murmured: The tomb of the unknown civilian, *Homo hydrogenensis,* Eniwetok Man. "Doctor," he said thoughtfully, "your laboratory is at the wrong end of this island."

Tartly, Osborne replied: "I'm aware of that, Traven. There are rarer fish swimming in your head than in any submarine pen."

On the day before they left, the young woman drove Traven over to the lakes where he had first arrived. As a final present, an ironic gesture unexpected from the elderly biologist, she had brought from Osborne the correct list of legends for the chromosome charts. They stopped by the derelict jukebox and she pasted them on the selection panel.

They wandered among the supine wrecks of the Superfortresses. Traven lost sight of her, and for the next ten minutes searched in and out of the dunes. He found her standing in a small amphitheatre formed by the sloping mirrors of a solar energy device built by one of the visiting expeditions. She smiled to Traven as he stepped through the scaffolding, waiting for him motionlessly with her bland eyes. But the dozen fragmented images of themselves reflected in the broken panes—in some she was *sans* head, in others a dozen multiples of her arms circled about her like the serpent limbs of a Hindu goddess—filled Traven with a sense of exhaustion. Turning swiftly, he walked back to the jeep.

As they drove away he recovered himself. He described his glimpses of his wife and son. "Their faces are always calm," he said. "My son's particularly, though he was never really like that. I remember him always laughing. The only time his face wore a grave expression was when he was being born—then he seemed millions of years old."

The young woman nodded. "I hope you find them." As an afterthought she added: "Dr. Osborne is going to tell the Navy that you're here. Hide somewhere."

Traven thanked her.

From the center of the blocks he waved to her the following day when she flew away for the last time.

The Naval Party

When the search party came for him, Traven hid in the only logical place. Fortunately the search was perfunctory, and was called off after a few hours. The sailors had brought a supply of beer with them and the search soon turned into a drunken excursion.

On the walls of the recording towers Traven later found balloons of obscene dialogue chalked into the mouths of the shadow figures, giving their postures the priapic gaiety of the dancers in cave drawings.

The climax of the party was the ignition of a store of gasoline in an underground tank near the airstrip. As he listened, first to the megaphones shouting his name, the echoes receding among the dunes like the forlorn calls of dying birds, then to the boom of the explosion and the laughter as the landing craft left, Traven felt a premonition that these were the last sounds he would hear.

He had hidden in one of the target basins, lying among the broken bodies of the plastic models. In the hot sunlight the dozens of deformed faces gaped at him sightlessly from the tangle of limbs, their blurred smiles like those of the laughing dead.

Their faces filled his mind as he climbed over the bodies and returned to his bunker. As he walked toward the blocks he saw the figures of his wife and son standing in his path. They were less than ten yards from him, their white faces watching him with a look of almost overwhelming expectancy. Never had Traven seen them so close to the blocks. His wife's pale features seemed illuminated from within, her lips parted as if in greeting, one hand raised to take his own. His son's grave face, with its curiously fixed expression, regarded him with the same enigmatic smile of the child in the photograph.

"Judith! David!" Startled, Traven ran towards them. Then, in a sudden movement of the light, their clothes turned into shrouds, and he saw the wounds that disfigured their necks and chests. Appalled, he cried out. As they vanished he fled into the safety of the blocks.

The Catechism of Goodbye

This time he found himself, as Osborne had predicted, unable to leave the blocks.

Somewhere in the center of the maze, he sat with his back against one of the concrete flanks, his eyes raised to the sun. Around him the lines of cubes formed the horizons of his world. At times they would appear to advance towards him, looming over him like cliffs, the intervals between them narrowing so that they were little more than an arm's breadth apart, a labyrinth of corridors running between them. Then they would recede from him, separating from each other like points in an expanding universe, until the nearest line formed an intermittent palisade along the horizon.

Time had become quantal. For hours it would be noon, the shadows contained within the blocks, the heat reverberating off the concrete floor. Abruptly, he would find that it was early afternoon, or midmorning, everywhere the pointing fingers of the shadows. Only the declining gradient of his own exhaustion gave him any indication of the days that passed. Sometimes he would make a futile attempt to escape from the labyrinth, and wander among the corridors, finally taking up his seat against one of the blocks, uncertain whether this was a new one or that which he had left.

"Goodbye, Eniwetok," he murmured.

Somewhere there was a flicker of light, as if one of the blocks, like a counter on an abacus, had been plucked away.

Goodbye, Los Alamos. Again, a block seemed to vanish. The corridors around him remained intact, but somewhere in his mind had appeared a small neutral interval.

Goodbye, Hiroshima
Goodbye, Alamagordo
Goodbye, Moscow
Goodbye, London

Goodbye, Paris
Goodbye, New York
Shuttles flickered, a ripple of lost integers.
Goodbye,—
He stopped, realizing the futility of his megathlon fare-
well. Such a leave-taking required him to inscribe his sig-
nature upon every one of the particles in the universe.

Total Noon: Eniwetok

The blocks now occupied positions on an endlessly
revolving circus wheel. Around and around they moved,
carrying him upwards to heights from which he could see
the whole island and the sea, and then down again through
the disc of the concrete floor. From here he looked up at
the under-surface of this concrete cap, and inverted landscape of rectilinear hollows, the dome-shaped mounds of
the lake system, the thousands of empty cubic pits of the
blocks.

"Goodbye, Traven"

Near the end, he found to his disappointment that this
ultimate rejection gained him nothing.

In an interval of lucidity, he looked down at his emaciated
arms and legs, decorated with a lace-work of ulcers,
propped loosely in front of him, the brittle wrists and hands
like parcels of bones. To his right was a trail of disturbed
dust, the wavering trail of slack heels.

To his left lay a long corridor between the blocks, join-
ing an oblique series a hundred yards away. Among these,
where a narrow interval revealed the open space beyond,
was a crescent-shaped shadow, poised in the air above the
ground.

During the next half an hour it moved slowly, turning as
the sun swung, the profile of a dune.

The Crevice

Seizing on this cipher, which hung before him like a
symbol on a shield, Traven pushed himself through the
dust. He climbed precariously to his feet, and shielded his
eyes from all sight of the blocks. He moved forward a few
paces at a time, following the scimitar of shadow as it
came nearer.

Ten minutes later he emerged from the western perimeter of the blocks, like some tottering mendicant leaving behind a silent desert city. The dune whose shadow had guided him lay fifty yards from him. Beyond it, bearing its shadow like a screen, was a ridge of limestone that ran among the hillocks of a wasteland beyond this point of the atoll. The remains of an old bulldozer, bales of barbed wire and fifty-gallon drums lay half-buried in the sand. Traven aproached the dune, reluctant now to leave this anonymous swell of sand. He shuffled around its edges, and sat down in the mouth of a shallow crevice below the brow of the ridge.

After dusting his clothes, he gazed out patiently at the great circle of blocks.

Ten minutes later he noticed that someone was watching him.

The Marooned Japanese

This corpse, whose eyes stared up at Traven, lay to his left at the bottom of the crevice. That of a man of middle age and strong build, it rested on its back with its head on a pillow of stone, hands outstretched at its sides, as if surveying the window of the sky. The fabric of the clothes had rotted to a bleached grey vestment, but in the absence of any small animal predators on the island the skin and musculature of the corpse had been preserved. Here and there, at the angle of knee or wrist, a bony point glinted through the leathery integument of the yellow skin, but the facial mask was still intact, and revealed a male Japanese of the professional classes. Looking down at the strong nose, high forehead and broad mouth and chin, Traven guessed that the Japanese had been a doctor or lawyer.

Puzzled as to how the corpse had found itself here, Traven slid a few feet down the slope. There were no radiation burns on the skin, which indicated that the Japanese had been there for five years or less. Nor did he appear to be wearing a uniform, so had not been some unfortunate member of a military or scientific party—besides, the slope of the crevice was little more than a few degrees from the horizontal.

To the left of the corpse, within reach of his hand, was a frayed leather case, the remains of a map wallet. To the right was the bleached husk of a haversack, open to reveal a canteen of water and a small mess-tin.

Greedily, the reflex of starvation making him for the moment ignore this discovery that the Japanese had deliberately chosen to die in the crevice, Traven slid down the slope until his feet touched the splitting soles of the corpse's shoes. He reached out and seized the canteen, then prized off the lid. A cupful of flat water swilled weakly around the rusting bottom. Traven gulped down the water, the dissolved metal salts cloaking his tongue with a bitter film. The mess-tin was empty but for a tacky coating of condensed syrup. Traven scraped at this with the lid. He chewed at the tarry flakes, letting them dissolve in his mouth with a dark intoxicating sweetness. After a few moments he felt light-headed, and sat back beside the corpse in a delirium of exhaustion.

Its sightless eyes regarded him with unmoving compassion.

The Fly

(*A small fly, which Traven presumes has followed him into the fissure, now buzzes about the corpse's face. Guiltily, Traven leans forward to kill it, then reflects that perhaps this minuscule sentry has been the corpse's faithful companion, in return fed on the rich liqueurs and distillations of its pores. Carefully, to avoid injuring the fly, he encourages it to alight on his wrist*).

DR. YASUDA: Thank you, Traven. (*The voice is rough, as if unused to conversation*). In my position, you understand . . .

TRAVEN: Of course, Doctor. I'm sorry I tried to kill it—these ingrained habits, you know, they're not easy to shrug off. Your sister's children in Osaka in '44, the exigencies of war, I hate to plead them, most known motives are so despicable, one searches the unknown in the hope that . . .

YASUDA: Please, Traven, do not be embarrassed. The fly is lucky to retain its identity for so long. The son you mourn, not to mention my own two nieces and nephew, did they not die for us each day? Every parent in the world grieves for the lost sons and daughters of their earlier childhoods.

TRAVEN: You're very tolerant, Doctor. I wouldn't dare—

YASUDA: Not at all, Traven. I make no apologies for you. After all, each of us is little more than the residue of the infinite unrealized possibilities of our lives. But your son, and my nephew, are now fixed in our minds forever, their identities as certain as the stars.

TRAVEN: (*not entirely convinced*) That may be so, Doctor, but it leads to a dangerous conclusion in the case of this island. For instance, the blocks.

YASUDA: They are precisely to what I refer, Traven. Here among the blocks you at last find an image of yourself free of the doubtful attractions of time and space. This ... island is an ontological Garden of Eden, why seek to expel yourself into a world of quantal flux?

TRAVEN: Excuse me. (*The fly has flown back to the corpse's face and sits in one of the dried-up orbits, giving the good doctor an expression of quizzical beadiness. Reaching forward, Traven entices it on to his palm. He examines it carefully*). Well, yes, these bunkers of course are ontological objects, but whether this is the ontological fly seems doubtful. It's true that on this island it's the *only* fly, which is the next best thing ...

YASUDA: You can't accept the plurality of the universe—ask yourself *why*. Why should this obsess you? It seems to me, Traven, that you are hunting for the white leviathan, zero. The beach is a dangerous zone. Avoid it. Have a proper humility, pursue a philosophy of acceptance.

TRAVEN: Then may I ask why you came here, Doctor?

YASUDA: To feed this fly. "What greater love—?"

TRAVEN: (*still puzzling*) It doesn't really solve my problem. The blocks, you see ...

YASUDA: Very well, if you must have it that way ...

TRAVEN: But, Doctor—

YASUDA: (*peremptorily*) Kill that fly.

TRAVEN: That's not an end, or a beginning.

(*Hopelessly, he kills the fly. Exhausted, he falls asleep beside the corpse*).

The Terminal Beach

Searching for a piece of rope in the refuse dump behind

the dunes, Traven found a bale of rusty wire. After unwinding this, he secured a harness around the corpse's chest and dragged it from the crevice. The lid of a wooden crate served as a sledge. Traven fastened the corpse to it in a sitting position, and set off along the perimeter of the blocks. Around him the island remained silent. The lines of palms hung in the sunlight, only his own motion varying the shifting ciphers of their criss-crossing trunks. The square turrets of the camera towers jutted from the dunes like forgotten obelisks.

An hour later, when Traven reached the awning by his bunker, he untied the wire cord he had fastened around his waist. He took the chair left for him by Dr. Osborne and carried it to a point midway between the bunker and the blocks. Then he tied the body of the Japanese to the chair, arranging the hands so that they rested on the wooden arms. This gave the moribund figure a posture of calm repose.

This done to his satisfaction, Traven returned to the bunker and squatted under the awning.

As the next days passed into weeks, the dignified figure of the Japanese sat in his chair fifty yards from him, guarding Traven from the blocks. Their magic still filled Traven's reveries, but he now had sufficient strength to rouse himself at intervals and forage for food. In the hot sunlight the skin of the Japanese became more and more bleached, and sometimes Traven would wake at night and find the white figure sitting there, arms resting at its sides, in the shadows that crossed the concrete floor. At these moments he would see his wife and son watching him from the dunes. As time passed they came closer, and he would sometimes find them only a few yards behind him.

Patiently Traven waited for them to speak to him, thinking of the great blocks whose entrance was guarded by the seated figure of the dead archangel, as the waves broke on the distant shore and the burning bombers fell through his dreams. ■

"Eliot stayed contritely sober for two days after that, then disappeared for a week. Among other things, he crashed a convention of science-fiction writers in a motel in Milford, Pennsylvania. . . .

"'I love you sons of bitches,' Eliot said in Milford. 'You're

all I read any more. You're the only ones who'll talk all about
the really terrific changes going on, the only ones crazy enough
to know that life is a space voyage, and not a short one, either,
but one that'll last for billions of years. You're the only ones
with guts enough to really care about the future, who really
notice what machines do to us, what wars do to us, what cities
do to us, what big, simple ideas do to us, what tremendous mis-
understandings, mistakes, accidents and catastrophes do to us.
You're the only ones zany enough to agonize over time and distances without limit, over mysteries that will never die, over
the fact that we are right now determining whether the space
voyage for the next billion years or so is going to be Heaven
or Hell.'

"Eliot admitted later on that science-fiction writers couldn't
write for sour apples, but he declared that it didn't matter. He
said they were poets just the same, since they were more sensitive to important changes than anybody who was writing well.
'The hell with the talented sparrowfarts who write delicately of
one small piece of one small lifetime, when the issues are
galaxies, eons, and trillions of souls yet to be born.' "

from God Bless You, Mr. Rosewater by Kurt Vonnegut, Jr.
(Holt, Rinehart and Winston, 1965)

PROBLEM CHILD
Arthur Porges
from *Analog*

If relief from pain can be
found in absorbing mental work, then the mathematician is
among the most fortunate of men. In every direction, beyond the well-cultivated plains of basic analysis, lie the un-
scaled peaks of the great problems, attacked, some of them
for generations, and always without success. And surrounding them, or lying over the horizon, out of sight, whole new
empires awaiting their inevitable conquerors.

Professor Kadar was like a man within sight of Paradise,
but unable to find a path through the impassable terrain
that blocked his way. He had patiently tried hundreds, all

promising, only to be confronted, at the last moment, by the same yawning chasm that indicated No Highway.

Now it had checked him again. He dropped the pen, sighed, and put his head in his hands. There was a small, sucking sound, and the professor looked up. Briefly, he had forgot; that was one virtue of the thorny analysis that sprawled over a ream of yellow second sheets.

How long had the child been there? He came and went so silently these days. Perched on the tall chrome bar stool, so incongruous a seat for a three-year-old, he slumped like a Buddha across from his father. And always with that same inward look. The wizened face, still wearing that aged-in-the-womb expression of the newborn infant, seemed vaguely Oriental to Kadar today. Not a Mongolian idiot, definitely, the clinical psychologist had assured him. Just retarded.

The professor's eyes, deep-socketed and melancholy, met Paul's, which had, he felt, an unmistakable slant. He was conscious, more strongly than ever, of his son's sweetness and placidity. Odd that they should be so characteristic of the mentally retarded child. As if nature desired to compensate the cheated parents. Not that it was ever compensation enough. And in this case, when he remembered—could he really forget, even for a moment, even when that path to Paradise seemed open?—that Eleanor had died to birth this little vegetable, it was no comfort at all.

The slanting eyes, small and dark, turned inward again. Oriental or gypsy? Many Hungarians had Romany blood. Or was the doctor—all those experts he had consulted—wrong, and Paul Mongoloid?

Names, Kadar reflected bitterly. What did they mean? In mathematics, you called something a ring, a cycle, an ideal. What you named it was unimportant; all that mattered was its place in the structure—never things, but the relations among them; those were what counted. What was Paul's relation to the world, now and in the future?

For the present, he was only a baby; in many ways, less than a baby. Mrs. Merrit was a kind, motherly woman; not intelligent; not educated; but warm. Paul obviously liked her, if he responded to anybody, which was doubtful. His normal expression, in an adult, often suggested profound boredom.

The professor thought about the tests—the endless, expensive tests. Colored doodads, blocks, strings, geometric forms to be matched—and the brisk, young men and women who presided over the rituals. Paul had confounded all of them; Kadar felt a perverse glow of satisfaction at the thought. The boy didn't make mistakes; instead, he simply refused to cooperate. Of course, it was nothing to rejoice over. Apathy meant even more severe brain damage, the doctors seemed to think. And Paul's electroencephalographs certainly were abnormal, suggesting those of an advanced epileptic.

The child nibbled at his lips again, making that tiny murmur in his throat. The eyes turned outward briefly, met Kadar's somber gaze, then Paul slipped clumsily from the high stool and padded from the room, moving with the rather unbalanced gait of a sedentary elder.

Off for some lunch, Kadar thought. Why didn't Mrs. Merrit call the boy, instead of letting him set his own schedule? My fault, he told himself immediately. I'm letting her raise him, while I try to forget Eleanor—yes, and him, too—in my work. On the other hand, why impose disciplines on a child who never rebels? The sweet placidity of Paul was reflected in his childish routines. He ate whatever was given him—but only if hungry. He never cried; always lay quietly in bed when put there; and seldom got out until Mrs. Merrit came for him in the morning, although she mentioned occasionally, with some wonder, that he often was awake, stretched out under smooth bedclothes, with his eyes wide open.

Aside from that, his only quirk was the tall stool. At the age of two, he had already shown his preference for the flashy thing, climbing it to overlook Mrs. Merrit at her chores in kitchen and dining room.

Then, after the professor, acting on impulse, put the stool in his study, across from the big desk where he worked, Paul had come to prefer that location. Every day, for at least three hours, while Kadar scribbled away, the child sat there, sometimes apparently fascinated by the motion and hiss of the pen on paper, but more commonly with his eyes blank and unfocused.

Mrs. Merrit, naturally, thought this scandalous and unhealthy. For many weeks she tried to interest the child in a variety of toys, but without success. What the trained psychologists had been unable to accomplish, Kadar thought wryly, was not for a woman like his housekeeper to bring about between cooking and floor-mopping.

Even retarded children may be good artists. But when given crayons and big sheets of paper, Paul had made a few tentative dabs, very awkwardly, and lost interest.

The boy must at least get some exercise, Mrs. Merrit insisted, so the professor bought a jungle gym, and, to his surprise, Paul condescended to scramble about in the thing for half an hour now and then. But Kadar suspected it was that same urge to attain purely physical elevation—did the child seek a height equivalent to that of the adults around him? Was that the only break in his apathy?

Paul came back to the study, and approached the stool.

"Come here, son," the professor said, moved to try establishing a relationship that always eluded him.

Meekly, in silence, Paul padded over. Kadar looked into the slanted eyes, searching for some kind of warmth. There were undoubtedly little lights inside, but they conveyed nothing to his understanding. He put one hand on the boy's silky hair, ruffling it, and Paul stepped back—not alarmed, but somehow rejecting the act. The professor felt a sudden urge to hug him, but quelled it, he couldn't have said just why. Paul went back to the stool, scrambled up in his queerly uncoordinated way, and sat there, lumpishly, his eyes again turned inward.

It came to Kadar, then, that Eleanor had sometimes worn such a look: an expression of deep self-communion. And yet—and yet—Uncle Janos had also looked that way often—Crazy Janos, who bungled everything he tried. Come to think of it, didn't Janos have an Oriental cast of features, too? It was all so far back, and in Hungary; Kadar couldn't remember. Besides, Janos died while his nephew was still a child.

The professor reached for a fresh sheet of paper, and began again, searching for the high road to Paradise. Fifty pages of the most advanced research—a new field of mathematics; a place beside Gauss, Abel, and Galois—

hung on his finding that path. If a certain sequence converged to an irrational number, the key theorem and all that it implied was valid. And still the proof eluded him. Enough; enough; no more today; his head was on fire. Return with a fresh mind, like Poincaré and the Fuchsian Functions; that was the only hope, now. But he knew it wouldn't solve anything. Only a fresh approach, something revolutionary, could smash through the iron wall.

Swaying a little, almost like Paul in his gait, Kadar left the room. He mixed a stiff Martini, drank it slowly, and felt some of the tension go out of his muscles. Mrs. Merrit hastily made him a hot snack; she was resigned to his behavior, and knew better than to try changing it.

"Tell me," he asked her, "has Paul ever tried to say anything yet? Anything at all?"

"No," she said, her eyes full of sympathy. "Just little noises in his throat. But he understands; I'm sure he understands. You know how good he is about doing what we tell him."

"I know," Kadar said darkly. "That's hardly normal, either. No mischief; no rebellion; nothing. A vegetable—sweet, insipid; like a spoiled melon."

And he thought of Eleanor—vital, alert, bubbling: beauty without slickness or affectation; warmth without sentimentality. This was the child not of Eleanor and himself, but Crazy Janos: that was a typical joke of heredity—genes and DNA and Janos ending in Paul Kadar, whose father had five paragraphs in "American Men of Science."

He left most of the lunch untouched, and went back to the study. I won't work, he told himself; but maybe just glance over the equations again. Let my mind refresh itself; no use to keep prodding it. Deep inside his brain a tiny alarm bell was ringing. What if the theorem is false? What then? Fifty pages of meaningless squiggles: a magnificent structure with no foundation.

He entered the study, and walked to the desk. The top sheet lay there, mocking him—but what was this? The last equation was crossed out, and above it there was a long line of pencil marks. Almost like mathematical symbols, but not—by God, upside down!

Bewildered, he reversed the sheet. For a moment the writing still seemed without content, then Kadar felt his heart contract like a clenched fist. A new integral transform—powerful, elegant, and startlingly original. It would crack the tough kernel of the problem as lightning shatters an oak.

He looked up, wild-eyed. Paul met his gaze squarely. The slender throat was working; the lips moved.

"Like that . . . it has to be like that. Other way . . . the pattern is ugly," the boy mumbled, his voice a queer, high-pitched stammer, as if he had to claw the words out of a diaphragm never before used.

Kadar, still uncomprehending, stared at the writing again. Upside down—because that's the way Paul, on his high perch, always saw the symbols. Their validity didn't depend on how they were written, of course.

An illiterate might conceivably, while listing words, write a simple declarative sentence. With luck, he might even hit upon a compound one, perfectly grammatical. But what were the odds against his writing immortal poetry, like: "Rough winds do shake the darling buds of May"?

Kadar looked at Paul again. The boy didn't need blocks or crayons because his mind saw every concept with perfect and immediate clarity. Just sitting on the high stool, he had absorbed a complete mathematical education from Kadar's work. Before that, he had overlooked Mrs. Merrit, but found nothing to stir his intellect. As for speaking, no doubt that, like his gait, was a matter of physique, and relatively unimportant to such a mind.

The professor felt a great surge of joy; yet, in a moment, it was tempered with sorrow. Paul was a monster, but a superior one. He was probably above—or beyond—love in the human sense. But their minds could commune, and maybe that was the best communion of all.   ■

A short time ago, I attended a dinner meeting of the literary society, PEN, at which the subject of the evening was "The Two Cultures." Arthur Clarke, as one of the speakers, delivered an eloquent argument to the (mostly) editors and publishers assembled, on the status of science fiction as a bridge across the gap.

I think this is largely true. But listening, that evening and since, to scientists and science writers, and to literary-academic people, I have come to feel even more strongly, with Max Beerbohm, that, "There are not two cultures, only half-cultured individuals." Happily, I have also seen an increasing number of individuals reaching out from their culture-halves to complete themselves. I think I should prefer to say that SF is an area where such people often meet—and more and more often, contrive to communicate.

Arthur Porges and Donald Hall, juxtaposed here, come from opposite ends of the academic range. Porges is a retired college teacher of mathematics; in literature, an admirer of Kipling, London, Mundy, Edgar Wallace, T. H. Huxley. Hall is a member of the faculty of the Department of English Language and Literature at the University of Michigan, and a former editor of the Paris Review.

What they both have to say, each one says very differently.

THE WONDERFUL DOG SUIT
Donald Hall
from *The Carleton Miscellany*

Lester was terribly intelligent and only nine years old. He was especially good at mathematics. "Hey, Lester," his father would say to him, "if

$X^2 - Y (32 X) + \dfrac{x}{y} \div 14Y^3$, then $\sqrt{XY} = ?$" Lester would come back with an answer, quick as Jackie Robinson.

So when he graduated into the fifth grade at the head of his class, his Uncle Fred gave him a dog suit. It was the best dog suit you ever saw, and it fitted Lester perfectly. The minute he put it on you'd swear it wasn't Lester at all but some big fat mongrel.

Lester worked over his dog act until he was very good. He taught himself to shake hands, roll over, play dead and everything. Then he learned how to bury a bone, lift a leg against a bush and chase cars. When he was perfect, he showed his parents and they were impressed. "You are a *Wunderkind,* Lester," said his father.

"Bow wow," said Lester.

Now when his parents had company, they asked Lester to get into his dog suit and fool everybody. He imitated a dog's nyeh-nyeh-nyeh-nyeh-nyeh so that grown-up ladies would clap their hands and exclaim, "Oh, listen! He's trying to talk." He frisked and romped and they rubbed his ears. Then he would unzip his dog suit and step out of it, and everyone would be very surprised.

He liked his dog suit so much that he no longer studied all the time. "Lester is more of a normal boy now," said his mother sadly. He took to putting on his dog suit after school and going out to play with the kids in the park. He chased balls or sticks for them. Sometimes he played tag or ran around the bases or wrestled. It was a lot of fun for Lester, who had never belonged to a group before. The kids thought he was a smart dog and petted him all the time.

One day in the park Lester heard some kids talking about him.

"Hey, this mutt doesn't belong to nobody," said one.

"What do you want, a reward?" his companion answered.

"Nah, I'm going to take him home."

Lester thought it would be great fun to surprise the kid and his family when they took him home, so he went along. He played all the way, pretending he saw cats and things, and when he got to the kid's slum-clearance project, it was someplace he had never seen before. He was lost.

The kid took him upstairs and into a kitchen. "Hey, Ma," he said. "I brought home a mutt."

"You get that frigging mutt out of here before I cut you open," said the kid's mother absentmindedly. Lester slunk off into another room with his tail between his legs. In the other room there was a man drinking out of a bottle who kicked Lester in the side.

Lester went out into the hall. He decided he didn't like it here and that he ought to get out of his dog suit.

But the zipper was stuck!

He tried and tried, but he couldn't make it budge. What could he do? Maybe if he went home his Uncle Fred could take him back to the factory. Anyway his mother could always call the fire department. But he didn't know how to get home. He would have to ask the kid and his mother for directions.

He padded back to the kitchen. He laughed to himself as he thought how surprised they would be to hear him talk! As he came into the room he heard the mother say, "Okay, okay, okay. But he's got to eat garbage and nothing but garbage."

He said, "I realize this will come as a shock to you, but I am not a dog at all. I am a boy named Lester and I live at 2331 Hummingbird Crescent and I am entering the fifth grade next autumn. Uncle Fred gave me this dog suit but the zipper is unfortunately stuck. May I inquire directions to my house? I want to see my mother and father again. $X^2 - \sqrt{4Y}\left(\dfrac{3Y}{x}\right) = 7$."

The mother clapped her hands together and said, "Listen, he's trying to talk!" ■

Mr. Kagan will say no more about himself than that he is a graduate student of mathematics. I can add only that, in his first year of publication, two of his stories were selected for annual "Best" collections.

What follows is what I did persuade him to say something about. If your math, like mine, extends only to a vague familiarity with words like vector, tensor, set, and Riemann space, Mr. K's glossary should help you determine where the mathematical facts leave off, and the fun-and-fantasy begins.

Metamathematics: Study of the underlying structure of math.
Nonosecond = one billioneth of a second.
Gogol: 10^{100} ($\overset{\underset{100,000,000}{1}}{10}$ with a hundred zero's.)
Googolplex: $(10^{100})^{100}$
Degenerate: (in math) a trivial or simple case—a point is a degenerate circle.
Isomorph(ism): A correspondence between two math systems which preserves structure.
Hausdorf Space: A "mathematical space" where any two points can be separated ("housed-off").

Communitivity: The mathematical condition: $a \times b = b \times a$

Set: A collection or bunch

Class: A set

Group: A mathematical structure: e.g., the integers with addition as the operation.

Ring: A group with multiplication defined as a second operation.

Field: A group under addition and under multiplication, too.

Composing: Doing in a row: e.g., doing one operation, then a second, then a third.

Transformation: mapping a math structure from one place to another.

Orthogonal Transform: A transform that preserves lengths.

Inner Product Transform: A transform that preserves "inner-product."

Degenerate Transform: A transform that doesn't preserve anything in particular.

Well-Ordering Principle: Any collection of sets of a set can be ordered (but in a sequence).

Axiom of Zemelo: Assuming the well ordering principle.

Bolzano Weirstrauss Points: "Limit Points" of sequences—the values certain sequences of numbers approach infinitely closely.

THE MATHENAUTS
Norman Kagan

from *If*

It happened on my fifth trip into the spaces, and the first ever made under the private-enterprise acts. It took a long time to get the P.E.A. through Congress for mathenautics, but the precedents went all the way back to the Telstar satellite a hundred years ago, and most of the concepts are in books anyone can buy, though not so readily understand. Besides, it didn't matter if BC-flight was made public or not. All mathenauts are crazy. Everybody knows that.

Take our crew. Johnny Pearl took a pin along whenever he went baby-sitting for the grad students at Berkeley, and three months later the mothers invariably found out they were pregnant again. And Pearl was our physicist.

Then there was Goldwasser. Ed Goldwasser always sits

in those pan-on-a-post cigarette holders when we're in New York, and if you ask him, he grumbles; "Well, its an ash tray, ain't it?" A punster and a pataphysicist. I would never have chosen him to go, except that he and I got the idea together.

Ted Anderson was our metamathematician. He's about half a nonosecond behind Ephraim Cohen (the co-inventor of BC-flight) and has about six nervous breakdowns a month trying to pass him. But he's got the best practical knowledge of the BC-drive outside Princeton—if practical knowledge means anything with respect to a pure mathematical abstraction.

And me—topologist. A topologist is a man who can't tell a doughnut from a cup of coffee. (I'll explain that some other time.) Seriously, I specialize in some of the more abstruse properties of geometric structures. "Did Galois discover that theorem before or after he died?" is a sample of my conversation.

Sure, mathenauts are mathenuts. But as we found out, not quite mathenutty enough.

The ship, the *Albrecht Dold,* was a twelve-googol scout that Ed Goldwasser and I'd picked up cheap from the N.Y.U. Courant Institute. She wasn't the Princeton I.A.S. *Von-Neumann,* with googolplex coils and a chapter of the D.A.R., and she wasn't one of those new toys you've been seeing for a rich man and his grandmother. Her coils were DNA molecules, and the psychosomatics were straight from the Brill Institute at Harvard. A sweet ship. For psychic ecology we'd gotten a bunch of kids from the Bronx College of the New York City University, commonsense types—business majors, engineers, pre-meds. But kids.

I was looking over Ephraim Cohen's latest paper, *Nymphomaniac Nested Complexes with Rossian Irrevelancies* (old Ice Cream Cohen loves sexy titles), when the trouble started. We'd abstracted, and Goldwasser and Pearl had signaled me from the lab that they were ready for the first tests. I made the *Dold* invariant, and shoved off through one of the passages that linked the isomorphomechanism and the lab. (We kept the ship in free fall for convenience.) I was about halfway along the tube when the immy failed and the walls began to close in.

I spread my legs and braked against the walls of the

tube, believing with all my might. On second thought I let
the walls sink in and braked with my palms. It would've
been no trick to hold the walls for awhile. Without the
immy my own imagination would hold them, this far from
the B.C.N.Y. kids. But that might've brought more trouble
—I'd probably made some silly mistake, and the kids, who
might not notice a simple contraction or shear, would
crack up under some weirdomorphism. And if we lost the
kids . . .

So anyway I just dug my feet in against the mirage and
tried to slow up, on a surface that no one'd bothered to
think any friction into. Of course, if you've read some of
the popular accounts of math-sailing, you'd think I'd just
duck back through a hole in the fiftieth dimension to the
immy. But it doesn't work out that way. A ship in BC-
flight is a very precarious structure in a philosophical sense.
That's why we carry a psychic ecology, and that's why
Brill conditioning takes six years, plus, with a PhD. in pure
math, to absorb. Anyway, a mathenaut should never forget
his postulates, or he'll find himself floating in 27-space,
with nary a notion to be named.

Then the walls really did vanish—NO!—and I found
myself at the junction of two passages. The other had a
grabline. I caught it and rebounded, then swarmed back
along the tube. After ten seconds I was climbing down into
a funnel. I caught my breath, swallowed some Dramamine,
and burst into the control room.

The heart of the ship was pulsing and throbbing. For a
moment I thought I was back in Hawaii with my aqualung,
an invader in a shifting, shimmering world of sea fronds
and barracuda. But it was no immy, no immy—a rubber
room without the notion of distance that we take for
granted (technically, a room with topological properties
but no metric ones). Instrument racks and chairs and
books shrank and ballooned and twisted, and floor and
ceiling vibrated with my breath.

It was horrible.

Ted Anderson was hanging in front of the immy, the
isomorphomechanism, but he was in no shape to do anything. In fact, he was in no shape at all. His body was
pulsing and shaking, so his hands were too big or too small

to manipulate the controls, or his eyes shrank or blossomed. Poor Ted's nerves had gone again.

I shoved against the wall and bulleted toward him, a fish in a weaving, shifting undersea landscape, concentrating desperately on my body and the old structure of the room. (This is why physical training is so important.) For an instant I was choking and screaming in a hairy blackness, a nightmare inside-out total inversion; then I was back in the control room, and had shoved Ted away from the instruments, cursing when nothing happened, then bracing against the wall panels and shoving again. He drifted away.

The immy was all right. The twiddles circuits between the B.C.N.Y. kids and the rest of the *Dold* had been cut out. I set up an orthonormal system and punched the immy.

Across the shuddering, shifting room Ted tried to speak, but found it too difficult. Great Gauss, he was lucky his aorta hadn't contracted to a straw and given him a coronary! I clamped down on my own circulatory system viciously, while he struggled to speak. Finally he kicked off and came tumbling toward me, mouthing and flailing his notebook.

I hit the circuit. The room shifted about and for an instant Ted Anderson hung, ghostly, amid the isomorpho-mechanism's one-to-ones. Then he disappeared.

The invention of BC-flight was the culmination of a century of work in algebraic topology and experimental psychology. For thousands of years men had speculated as to the nature of the world. For the past five hundred, physics and the physical sciences had held sway. Then Thomas Brill and Ephraim Cohen peeled away another layer of the reality union, and the space-sciences came into being.

If you insist on an analogy—well, a scientist touches and probes the real universe, and abstracts an idealization into his head. Mathenautics allows him to grab himself by the scruff of the neck and pull himself up into the idealization. See—I *told* you.

Okay, we'll try it slowly. Science assumes the universe to be ordered, and investigates the nature of the ordering. In the "hard" sciences, mathematics is the basis of the ordering the scientist puts on nature. By the twentieth century, a large portion of the physical processes and materials in the universe were found to submit to such an ordering (e.g.: analytic mechanics and the motions of the planets). Some scientists were even applying mathematical structures to aggregates of living things, and to living processes.

Cohen and Brill asked (in ways far apart), "If order and organization seem to be a natural part of the universe, why can't we remove these qualities from coarse matter and space, and study them separately?" The answer was BC-flight.

Through certain purely mathematical "mechanisms" and special psychological training, selected scientists (the term "mathenaut" came later, slang from the faddy "astronautics") could be shifted into the abstract.

The first mathenautical ships were crewed with young scientists and mathematicians who'd received Tom Brill's treatments and Ephraim Cohen's skullcracking sessions on the BC-field. The ships went into BC-flight and vanished.

By the theory, the ships didn't *go* anywhere. But the effect was somehow real. Just as a materialist might *see* organic machines instead of people, so the mathenauts saw the raw mathematical structure of space—Riemann space, Hausdorf space, vector space—without matter. A crowd of people existed as an immensely complicated *something* in vector space. The study of these *somethings* was yielding immense amounts of knowledge. Pataphysics, patasociology, patapsychology were wild, baffling new fields of knowledge.

But the math universes were strange, alien. How could you learn to live in Flatland? The wildcat minds of the first crews were too creative. They became disoriented. Hence the immies and their power supplies—SayCows, Daught-AmRevs, the B.C.N.Y. kids—fatheads, stuffed shirts, personality types that clung to common sense where there was none, and preserved (locally) a ship's psychic ecology. Inside the BC-field, normalcy. Outside, raw imagination.

Johnny, Ted, Goldy and I had chosen vector spaces with certain topological properties to test Goldy's commercial concept. Outside the BC-field there was dimension but no distance, structure but no shape. Inside—

"By Riemann's tensors!" Pearl cried.

He was at the iris of one of the tubes. A moment later

Ed Goldwasser joined him. "What happened to Ted?"

"I—I don't know. No—yes, I do!"

I released the controls I had on my body, and stopped thinking about the room. The immy was working again. "He was doing something with the controls when the twiddles circuit failed. When I got them working again and the room snapped back into shape, he happened to be where the immy had been. The commonsense circuits rejected him."

"So where did he go?" asked Pearl.

"I don't know."

I was sweating. I was thinking of all the things that could've happened when we lost the isomorphomechanism. Some subconscious twitch and you're rotated half a dozen dimensions out of phase, so you're floating in the raw stuff of thought, with maybe a hair-thin line around you to tell you where the ship has been. Or the ship takes the notion to shrink pea-size, so you're squeezed through all the tubes and compartments and smashed to jelly when we orthonormalize. Galois! We'd been lucky.

The last thought gave me a notion. "Could we have shrunk so we're inside his body? Or he grown so we're floating in his liver?"

"No," said Goldy. "Topology is preserved. But I don't —or, hell—I really don't know. If he grew so big he was outside the psychic ecology, he might just have faded away." The big pataphysicist wrinkled up his face inside his beard. "*Alice* should be required reading for mathenauts," he muttered. "The real trouble is no one has ever been outside and been back to tell about it. The animal experiments and the *Norbert Wiener* and Wilbur on the *Paul R. Halmos*. They just disappeared." "You know," I said, "You can map the volume of a sphere into the whole universe using the ratio: IR: R equals R:OR, where IR and OR are the inside and outside distances for the points. Maybe that's what happened to Ted. Maybe he's just outside the ship, filling all space with his metamath and his acne?"

"Down boy," said Goldwasser. "I've got a simpler suggestion. Let's check over the ship, compartment by compartment. Maybe he's in it somewhere, unconscious."

But he wasn't on the ship.

We went over it twice, every tube, every compartment. (In reality, a mathenautic ship looks like a radio, ripped out of its case and flying through the air.) We ended up in the ecology section, a big Broadway-line subway car that roared and rattled in the middle of darkness in the middle of nothing. The B.C.N.Y. kids were all there—Freddi Urbont clucking happily away to her boy friend, chubby and smily and an education major; Byron and Burbitt, electronics engineers, ecstatic over the latest copy of *C-Quantum;* Stephen Seidmann, a number-theory major, quietly proving that since Harvard is the best school in the world, and B.C.N.Y. is better than Harvard, that B.C.N.Y. is the best school in the world; two citizens with nose jobs and names I'd forgotten, engaged in a filthy discussion of glands and organs and meat. The walls were firm, the straw seats scratchy and uncomfortable. The projectors showed we were just entering the 72nd Street stop. How real, how comforting! I slid the door open to rejoin Johnny and Ed. The subway riders saw me slip into freefall, and glimpsed the emptiness of vector space.

Hell broke loose!

The far side of the car bulged inward, the glass smashing and the metal groaning. The CUNYs had no compensation training!

Freddi Urbont burst into tears. Byron and Burbitt yelled as a bubble in the floor swallowed them. The wall next to the nose jobs sprouted a dozen phallic symbols, while the seat bubbled with breasts. The walls began to melt. Seidmann began to yell about the special status of N. Y. City University Honors Program students.

Pearl acted with a speed and a surety I'd never have imagined. He shoved me out of the way and launched himself furiously at the other end of the car, now in free fall. There he pivoted, smiled horribly and at the top of his lungs began singing "The Purple and the Black."

Goldy and I had enough presence of mind to join him. Concentrating desperately on the shape and form of the car, we blasted the air with our devotion to Sheppard Hall, our love of Convent Avenue and our eternal devotion to Lewisohn Stadium. Somehow it saved us. The room rumbled and twisted and reformed, and soon the eight of us were back in the tired old subway car that brought its daily catch of Beavers to 139th Street.

The equilibrium was still precarious. I heard Goldwasser telling the nose jobs his terrible monologue about the "Volvo I want to buy. I can be the first to break the door membranes, and when I get my hands on that big, fat steering wheel, ohh!, it'll be a week before I climb out of it!"

Pearl was cooing to Urbont how wonderful she was as the valedictorian at her junior high, how great the teaching profession was, and how useful, and how interesting.

As for me; "Well, I guess you're right, Steve. I should have gone to B.C.N.Y. instead of Berkeley."

"That's right, Jimmy. After all, B.C.N.Y. has some of the best number-theory people in the world. And some of the greatest educators, too. Like Dean Cashew who started the Privileged Student Program. It sure is wonderful."

"I guess you're right, Steve."

"I'm right, all right. At schools like Berkeley, you're just another student, but at B.C.N.Y. you can be a P.S., and get all the good professors and small classes and high grades."

"You're right, Steve."

"I'm right, all right. Listen, we have people that've quit Cornell and Harvard and M.I.T. Of course, they don't do much but run home after school and sit in their houses, but their parents all say how much happier they are—like back in high school . . ."

When the scrap paper and the gum wrappers were up to our knees and there were four false panhandlers in the car, Johnny called a halt. The little psychist smiled and nodded as he walked the three of us carefully out the door.

"Standard technique," he murmured to no one in particular. "Doing *something* immediately rather than the best thing a while later. Their morale was shot, so I—" He trailed off.

"Are they really that sensitive?" Goldwasser asked. "I thought their training was better than that."

"You act like they were components in an electronics rig," said Pearl jerkily. "You know that Premedial Sensory Perception, the ability to perceive the dull routine that normal people ignore, is a very delicate talent!"

Pearl was well launched. "In the dark ages such people were called dullards and subnormals. Only now, in our enlightened age, do we realize their true ability to know things outside the ordinary senses—a talent vital for BC-flight."

The tedium and meaninglessness of life which we rationalize away—

"A ship is more mind than matter, and if you upset that mind—"

He paled suddenly. "I, I think I'd better stay with them," he said. He flung open the door and went back into the coach. Goldwasser and I looked at each other. Pearl was a trained mathenaut, but his specialty was people, not paramath.

"Let's check the lab," I muttered.

Neither of us spoke as we moved toward the lab—slap a wall, pull yourself forward, twist round some instrumentation—the "reaction swim" of a man in free fall. The walls began to quiver again, and I could see Goldy clamp down on his body and memories of this part of the ship. We were nearing the limits of the BC-field. The lab itself, and the experimental apparatus, stuck out into vector space.

"Let's make our tests and go home," I told Goldy.

Neither of us mentioned Ted as we entered the lab.

Remember this was a commercial project. We weren't patasociologists studying abstract groups, or super-purists looking for the first point. We wanted money.

Goldy thought he had a moneymaking scheme for us, but Goldy hasn't been normal since he took Polykarp Kusch's "Kusch of Death" at Columbia, "Electrodimensions and Magnespace." He was going to build four-dimensional molecules.

Go back to Flatland. Imagine a hollow paper pyramid on the surface of that two-dimensional world. To a Flatlander, it is a triangle. Flop down the sides—four triangles. Now put a molecule in each face—one molecule, four molecules. And recall that you have infinite dimensions available. Think of the storage possibilities alone. All the books of the world in a viewer, all the food in the world in your pack. A television the size of a piece of paper; circuits looped through dim-19. Loop an entire industrial plant through hyperspace, and get one the size and shape of a billboard. Shove raw materials in one side—pull finished products out the other!

But how do you make 4-dim molecules? Goldy thought he had a way, and Ted Anderson had checked over the math and pronounced it workable. The notion rested in the middle of the lab: a queer, half-understood machine of mind and matter called a Grahm-Schmidt generator.

"Jeez, Ed! This lab looks like your old room back in Diego Borough."

"Yeah," said Goldwasser. "Johnny said it would be a good idea. Orientation against *that*."

That was the outside of the lab, raw topological space, without energy or matter or time. It was the shape and color of what you see in the back of your head.

I looked away.

Goldwasser's room was a duplicate of his old home—the metal desk, the electronics rigs, the immense bookshelves, half-filled with physics and half with religious works. I picked up a copy of Stace's *Time and Eternity* and thumbed through it, then put it down, embarrassed.

"Good reading for a place like this." Goldwasser smiled.

He sat down at the desk and began to check out his "instruments" from the locked drawer where he'd kept them. Once he reached across the desk and turned on a tape of Gene Gerard's *Excelsior!* The flat midwestern voice murmured in the background.

"First, I need some hands," said Ed.

Out in the nothingness two pairs of lines met at right angles. For an instant, all space was filled with them, jammed together every which way. Then it just settled down to two.

The lab was in darkness. Goldwasser's big form crouched over the controls. He wore his engineer's boots and his hair long, and a beard as well. He might have been some medieval monk, or primitive witchdoctor. He touched a knob and set a widget, and checked in his copy of *Birkhoff and MacLane*.

"Now," he said, and played with his instruments. Two new vectors rose out of the intersections. "Cross-products. Now I've a right- and a left-handed system."

All the while Gene Gerard was mumbling in the background: " 'Ah, now, my pretty,' snarled the Count. 'Come to my bedchamber, or I'll leave you to Igor's mercies.' The misshapen dwarf cackled and rubbed his paws. 'Decide, decide!' cried the Count. His voice was a scream. 'Decide, my dear. SEX—ELSE, IGOR!' "

"Augh," said Goldwasser, and shut it off. "Now," he said, "I've got some plasma in the next compartment."

"Holy Halmos," I whispered.

Ted Anderson stood beside the generator. He smiled, and went into topological convulsions. I looked away, and presently he came back in to shape. "Hard getting used to real space again," he whispered. He looked thinner and paler than ever.

"I haven't got long," he said, "so here it is. You know I was working on Ephraim's theories, looking for a flaw. There isn't any flaw."

"Ted, you're rotating," I cautioned.

He steadied, and continued. "There's no flaw. But the theory is wrong. It's backwards. *This is the real universe*," he said, and gestured. Beyond the lab topological space remained as always, a blank, the color of the back of your head through your own eyes.

"Now listen to me, Goldy and Johnny and Kidder." I saw that Pearl was standing in the iris of the tube. "What is the nature of intelligence? I guess it's the power to abstract, to conceptualize. I don't know what to say beyond that—I don't know what it is. But I know where it came from! Here! In the math spaces—they're alive with thought, flashing with mind!

"When the twiddles circuits failed, I cracked. I fell apart, lost faith in it all. For I had just found what I thought was a basic error in theory. I died, I vanished . . .

"But I didn't. I'm a metamathematician. An operational philosopher, you might say. I may have gone mad—but I think I passed a threshold of knowledge. I understand . . .

"They're out there. The things we thought we'd invented ourselves. The concepts and the notions and the pure structures—if you could see them . . ."

He looked around the room, desperately. Pearl was rigid against the iris of the tube. Goldy looked at Ted for a moment, then his head darted from side to side. His hands whitened on the controls.

"Jimmy," Ted said.

I didn't know. I moved toward him, across the lab to the edge of topological space, and beyond the psychic ecology. No time, no space, no matter. But how can I say it? How many people can stay awake over a book of modern algebra, and how many of those can understand?

—I saw a set bubbling and whirling, then take purpose and structure to itself and become a group, generate a second-unity element, mount itself and become a group, generate a second unity element, mount itself and become a field, ringed by rings. Near it, a mature field, shot through with ideals, threw off a splitting field in a passion of growth, and became complex.

—I saw the life of the matrices; the young ones sporting, adding and multiplying by a constant, the mature ones mating by composition: male and female make male, female and male make female—sex through anticommutivity! I saw them grow old, meeting false identities and loosing rows and columns into nullity.

—I saw a race of vectors, losing their universe to a newer race of tensors that conquered and humbled them.

—I watched the tyranny of the Well Ordering Principle, as a free set was lashed and whipped into structure. I saw a partially ordered set, free and happy broken before the Axiom of Zemelo.

—I saw the point sets, with their cliques and clubs, infinite numbers of sycophants clustering round a Bolzano-Weirstrauss aristocrat—the great compact medieval coverings of infinity with denumerable shires—the conflicts as closed sets created open ones, and the other way round.

—I saw the rigid castes of a society of transformations, orthogonal royalty, inner product gentry, degenerates—where intercomposition set the caste of the lower on the product.

—I saw the proud old cyclic groups, father and son and grandson, generating the generations, rebel and blacksheep and hero, following each other endlessly. Close by were the permutation groups, frolicking in a way that seemed like the way you sometimes repeat a sentence endlessly, stressing a different word each time.

There was much I saw that I did not understand, for mathematics is a deep, and even a mathenaut must choose his wedge of specialty. But that world of abstractions flamed with a beauty and meaning that chilled the works and worlds of men, so I wept in futility.

Presently we found ourselves back in the lab. I sat beside Ted Anderson and leaned on him, and I did not speak for fear my voice would break.

Anderson talked to Johnny and Ed.

"There was a—a race, here, that grew prideful. It knew the Riemann space, and the vector space, the algebras and the topologies, and yet it was unfulfilled. In some way— oddly like this craft," he murmured, gesturing—"they wove the worlds together, creating the real universe you knew in your youth.

"Yet still it was unsatisfied. Somehow the race yearned so for newness that it surpassed itself, conceiving matter and energy and entropy and creating them.

"And there were laws and properties for these: inertia, speed, potential, quantumization. Perhaps life was an accident. It was not noticed for a long time, and proceeded apace. For the proud race had come to know itself, and saw that the new concepts were . . . flawed." Anderson smiled faintly, and turned to Ed.

"Goldy, remember when we had Berkowitz for algebra," he asked. "Remember what he said the first day?"

Goldwasser smiled. "Any math majors?

"Hmm, that's good.

"Any physics majors?

"Physics majors! You guys are just super engineers!

"Any chemistry majors?

"Chemistry major! You'd be better off as a cook!"

Ted finished, "And so on, down to the, ahem, baloney majors."

"He was number happy," said Ed, smiling.

"No. He was right, in a way." Ted continued. "The race had found its new notions were crudities, simple copies of algebras and geometries past. What it thought was vigor was really sloth and decay.

"It knew how to add and multiply, but it had forgotten what a field was, and what commutivity was. If entropy and time wreaked harm on matter, they did worse by this race. It wasn't interested in expeditions though the fiber bundles; rather it wanted to count apples.

"There was conflict and argument, but it was too late to turn back. The race had already degenerated too far to turn back. Then life was discovered.

"The majority of the race took matter for a bride. Its esthetic and creative powers ruined, it wallowed in passion and pain. Only remnants of reason remained.

"For the rest, return to abstraction was impossible. Time, entropy, had robbed them of their knowledge, their heritage. Yet they still hoped and expended themselves to leave, well, call it a 'seed' of sorts."

"Mathematics?" cried Pearl.

"It explains some things," mused Goldwasser softly. "Why abstract mathematics, developed in the mind, turns out fifty years or a century later to accurately describe the physical universe. Tensor calculus and relativity, for example. If you look at it this way, the math were there first."

"Yes, yes, yes. Mathematicians talked about their subject as an art form. One system is more 'elegant' than another if its logical structure is more austere. But Occam's Razor, the law of simplest hypothesis, isn't logical.

"Many of the great mathematicians did their greatest work as children and youths before they were dissipated by the sensual world. In a trivial sense, scientists and mathematicians most of all are described as 'unworldly' . . ."

Anderson bobbled his head in the old familiar way. "You have almost returned," he said quietly. "This ship is really a heuristic device, an aid to perception. You are on the threshold. You have come all the way back."

The metamathematician took his notebook, and seemed to set all his will upon it. "See Ephraim gets this," he murmured. "He, you, I . . . the oneness—"

Abruptly he disappeared. The notebook fell to the floor.

I took it up. Neither Ed nor Johnny Pearl met my eyes. We may have sat and stood there for several hours, numbed, silent. Presently the two began setting up the isomorpho-mechanism for realization. I joined them.

The National Mathenautics and Hyperspace Administration had jurisdiction over civilian flights then, even as it does today. Ted was pretty important, it seemed. Our preliminary debriefing won us a maximum-security session with their research chief.

Perhaps, as I'd thought passionately for an instant, I'd

have done better to smash the immy, rupture the psychic ecology, let the eggshell be shattered at last. But that's not the way of it. For all of our progress, some rules of scientific investigation don't change. Our first duty was to report back. Better heads than ours would decide what to do next.

They did. Ephraim Cohen didn't say anything after he heard us out and looked at Ted's notebook. Old Ice Cream sat there, a big teddy-bear-shaped genius with thick black hair and a dumb smile, and grinned at us. It was in Institute code.

The B.C.N.Y. kids hadn't seen anything, of course. So nobody talked.

Johnny Pearl married a girl named Judy Shatz and they had fifteen kids. I guess that showed Johnny's views on the matter of matter.

Ed Goldwasser got religion. Zen-Judaism is pretty orthodox these days, yet somehow he found it suited him. But he didn't forget what had happened back out in space. His book, *The Cosmic Mind*, came out last month, and it's a good summation of Ted's ideas, with a minimum of spiritual overtones.

Myself. Well, a mathematician, especially a topologist, is useless after thirty, the way progress is going along these days. But *Dim-Dustries* is a commercial enterprise, and I guess I'm good for twenty years more as a businessman.

Goldwasser's Grahm-Schmidt generator worked, but that was just the beginning. Dimensional extension's made Earth a paradise, with housing hidden in the probabilities and automated industries tucked away in the dimensions.

The biggest boon was something no one anticipated. A space of infinite dimensions solves all the basic problems of modern computer-circuit design. Now all components can be linked with short electron paths, no matter how big and complex the device.

There have been any number of other benefits. The space hospitals, for example, where topological surgery can cure the most terrible wounds—and topological psychiatry the most baffling syndromes. (Four years of math is required for pre-meds these days.) Patapsychology and patasociology finally made some progress, so that political and economic woes have declined—thanks, too, to the spaces,

which have drained off a good deal of poor Earth's overpopulation. There are even spaces resorts, or so I'm told
—I don't get away much.

I've struck it lucky. Fantastically so.

The Private Enterprise Acts had just been passed, you'll
recall, and I had decided I didn't want to go spacing again.
With the training required for the subject, I guess I was
the only qualified man who had a peddler's pack, too.
Jaffee, one of my friends down at Securities and Exchange,
went so far as to say that *Dim-Dustries* was a hyper-
spherical trust (math is required for pre-laws too). But I
placated him and I got some of my mathemateers to re-
align the Street on a moebius strip, so he had to side with
me.

Me, I'll stick to the Earth. The "real" planet is a garden
spot now, and the girls are very lovely.

Ted Anderson was recorded lost in topological space.
He wasn't the first, and he was far from the last. Twiddles
circuits have burned out, DaughtAmsRevs have gone
mad, and no doubt there have been some believers who
have sought out the Great Race.   ∎

If you have not yet heard of Alfred Jarry, you were just about to.

I came across the name first in a small, brilliant-red, extremely outspoken Moroccan magazine, Gnaoua, in which one
item was not only printable (by U.S. standards) but eminently
reprintable—Jarry's "The Other Alcestis."

Turned out it was not only -able, but very much -ed. Jarry
lived in France at the turn of the century—and wrote in a vein
startlingly similar to the newest surreal-science-fantasy. He is
currently having a revival among the avant-garde, with an off-
Broadway production of his play, **Ubu Roi,** and new editions of
his work from New Directions. He is also the founder (prophet?
inventor? perpetrator? saint?) of the Science of 'Pataphysics.

Actually the Jarry renaissance began in 1961 with a special
issue of Evergreen Review, edited by Roger Shattuck (Provedi-
teur-General Propagator for the Islands and the Americas, in
the College of 'Pataphysics).

Space limitations prevent me from attempting here what Shattuck (pessimistically) set out to perform in 192 pages complete
with magnificent maps, charts, photographs and footnotes,
describing the history, scope, and organization of the illustrious

College: i.e., "the self-contradictory task of defining 'Pataphysics in nonpataphysical terms." I can offer only some gleanings. 'Pataphysics (according to Shattuck) is—

—the science of the realm beyond metaphysics (as far beyond metaphysics as metaphysics is beyond physics—in one direction or another).

—the science of imaginary solutions.

—the science of the particular, of laws governing exceptions (a "pure science, lawless, and therefore impossible to outlaw").

—imperturbable in aspect. ("The pataphysician does not burst out laughing or curse when asked to fill in quadruplicate a questionaire on his political affiliations or sexual habits: on the contrary, he details a different and equally valid activity on each of the four sheets.")

'Pataphysics "can be seen as a method, a discipline, a faith, a cult, a point of view, a hoax. It is all of these and none of them." And conclusively, "All things are pataphysical, yet few men practice 'Pataphysics consciously."

I trust this brief introduction will serve as additional explication of Mr. Kagan's story—and perhaps bring some readers to a further study of this remarkable science. (It should also be readily observable that "Family Portrait," the first published story of a young California electronics technician, is as fine an example of unconscious pataphysical writing as one might readily find: it appears to satisfy virtually every one of the precepts set forth above.)

FAMILY PORTRAIT
Morgan Kent
from *Fantastic*

She put down her sewing.

"You haven't listened to a word I've said all evening," she said.

"The last thing you said," he replied from behind his newspaper, "Was, 'so . . . that Morrison woman said to me . . .'"

"She's putting on weight, too."

"Oh? I hadn't noticed."

He read a few more paragraphs, but his attention was diverted.

"Well? Come on, what did Mattie Morrison say? I'm all agog," he said patiently.

"You look all agog."

"Oh, for heaven's sake. Look at me. Agog, agog, agog." She picked up her sewing, and peered at it.

"I don't think I'll ever be able to make a hem-line as well as she can. I'll say that for her, anyway." She made a face and began picking out the stitches. "In any case, that woman had the nerve to tell me DON'T WRITE ON THE WALL!"

He jumped.

"That's a heck of a thing to say, . . ." he began.

"Not me," she said, her voice rising. She pointed, and said, "HIM!"

He turned, and looked over his shoulder, and then roared, "Mr. Christian, come here!"

Mr. Christian, age two years and six months, scrambled to his feet, and stood carefully in front of the scribbles on the wall. He smiled engagingly.

"Well, Sir? Explain yourself."

The boy recognized the tone that meant, "I'll fix it later, Brat, but right now you better show your mother that you're sorry!" and he launched himself into a complicated explanation in which only about one word in three was decipherable. The general drift appeared to be that it wasn't really his fault, it was two other little boys that did it, and anyway, he was sorry, and was he gonna get a s'ankin'?

"Don't tempt me," his father growled. "Isn't it time for him to go to bed?"

"Past time."

"I thought so. All right, Microwatt. Go to bed. Go directly to bed. Do not pass Go. Do not collect Two Hundred Dollars."

"No!" said Mr. Christian.

His father put down his paper.

"I no s'eepy!" said Mr. Christian, and he retreated a step.

His father stood up.

"I hungee!" wailed Mr. Christian, his voice rising, and he trotted to the hallway.

His father glowered at him, and took a step in his direction.

The boy howled miserably, and tried the ultimate delaying tactic.

"I gotta go potty!"

"No you don't," his mother said positively. "You go right to bed."

Mr. Christian's bright little face vanished from the hall doorway like a blown-out candle. They heard him giggle as he shuffled his sleeper slippers down the hall.

"Really, darling. You've got to be firm with that little stinker. He plays you like his wind-up teddy bear."

"I am firm. You saw the way he took off for bed?"

"After I yelled at him."

"He was going anyway," the father said, as he settled down and picked up his paper. "Now, *please* tell me what The Morrison said."

Then little Chris, elaborately casual, trotted back into the living room. His father's eyebrows rose as he watched the boy sit down by his toys, obviously prepared for a long, happy stay.

He cleared his throat, and with exaggerated patience, asked, "And, uh, what, pray tell, are *you* doing back in here?"

"I no s'eep."

"That's true," his father mused.

"An' no light my room."

"Ah."

"An' a mon'ser my bed, Daddy."

"A monster in your bed? Oh, dear me."

Christian nodded absently. He was busy with his toys.

"All right, Private. On your feet. Let's go. Hup! Two, three, four! Move! I'll go fight off your monster, and turn on the nightlight. Come on, O pestiferous One."

The boy got up dutifully, kissed his mother good-night and followed his father down the hall into his room.

"See, Daddy? Dark!"

"So it is, ol' buddy. I'll just turn on the lamp, like this, and then you'll see that there ain't no Mon . . . YIKE!"

"See, Daddy? Mon'ser!"

And a monster there was. A reeking, wobbling, flaccid horror that grinned, toothily, and gibbering like a mad-woman, eased itself from under the bolster, and scrabbled awkwardly across the bed toward him.

Christian's mother looked up from her sewing as her husband stepped stiffly back into the living room.

"The brat in bed?" she asked.

He nodded, jerkily.

"There *was* a monster in his bed."

"What?"

"A great, ugly, black thing."

"Now really, darling. You're as bad as that boy."

"No, dammit! It was there!"

She tapped her teeth with a fingernail, and looked reflective.

"I guess he could be starting now. I was three when I started. A great big, soft-nosed pony, Mother said. I guess he could be starting early for his age. Remember, he walked early, too."

"Horrible damn thing. What has that kid been watching on TV anyway?"

"Just his regular kiddie programs in the morning," she said.

"I wish I would have taken my camera in there," he said thoughtfully. "Old Houseman, and his five-year-old. He claims she can fly now. Wait 'till he hears about this."

"And he always was a fast child. He was on table food a lot earlier than the other little ones on the block." She carried on, with her thought uninterrupted. "And your mother, on her last visitation, said something about you starting early, too. Hung a huge fireball in the living room when your father's boss came to call."

"Scorched his mustache, too," he replied. He stepped to the wall, and inspected the scribbles his son had made. "Does dots, a long squiggle, and four curved lines have any particular significance to you?"

"That child will never be a Michelangelo," she sighed heavily. "Is he asleep now?"

"Yeah. I put his 'mon'ser' away, and he was almost asleep when I left the room," he answered, and frowned at the marks on the wall. They slowly faded.

"You left a little bit, down there, in the corner," his wife said. ■

Communication—its importance, its modes, its failures, its variety of meanings—has been a major theme throughout this volume. Except for a literal handful of stories, every selection here is vitally concerned either with a problem resulting from inadequate communication—a puzzle involving some means of communication—the result of an experiment with communication—or the uses and usages of those areas of modern living which we call "Communications."

The last two selections have focused on the potentialities of man for immediate, direct contact with (and influence over) the physical environment. "The Red Egg" reverses the field, and examines the capacity for perception and (in a slightly different sense) communication by the (biological, this time) environment.

José María Gironella is a Spanish author best known for his trilogy about the Spanish Civil War, **The Cypresses Believe in God.** This story is from a collection of short works, subtitled **Journeys to the Improbable,** in which the author recorded a period of what he called "psychic experience"—hallucinations, weird images and insights, obsessive imaginings, which haunted him for two years.

THE RED EGG
José Maria Gironella

Translated from the Spanish
by Terry Broch Fontseré

from *Phantoms and Fugitives*
(Sheed and Ward, 1964)

                    The malignant tumor, cancer, flew over the rooftops of the city. It had the shape of an egg. Its flight was slow and solemn. The birds noticed something strange in its proximity and moved away from it, coasting in silence. It was a young cancer, red in color, with bluish bands. It was three years old. It had been born in an experimental laboratory, in the skin of a mouse, near a pit-coal mine. Its destiny—to die with the mouse—had seemed a small glory and it had decided to escape. This it did, breaking away and flying off through a window. Scarcely free, it soaked up the mine's atmosphere and then allowed itself to be touched by the ultraviolet rays of sunlight. It noticed itself becoming more robust, thriving. It went on molding itself with art, changing position in relation to those rays, until it attained an oval form. Its highest aspiration was to be like an egg, since this would guarantee its fecundity. Once it reached its objective, it gave itself over to the whims of the wind, up and down, seeing land-scapes it would never have known in the laboratory. Until it came upon the industrial city.

The Red Egg, three years old, gifted with one large and sensitive eye, understood that the city held in its breast all that appealed to him—paraffin, smoke, etc.—and he breathed with satisfaction. At each inhalation, a band of quills or antennae erupted around his belly, which then contracted when he exhaled. He looked at the cathedral clock: two minutes before noon. Vaguely he remembered that, in the laboratory where he was captive, every morning on the stroke of twelve a bell rang, and first a nurse entered, bringing them food, and immediately afterward came men dressed in white, protected by lead aprons.

Midday in the city was even more spectacular. The sirens of all the factories shrilled, and instantly the streets were crowded. Men and women headed for their respective homes, where there were quick kisses all around and where the babies were lifted into the air like flags. The Red Egg smiled. In the laboratory he'd fled from, he had never heard speak of love.

The passing parade of the city's inhabitants permitted the cancer to take a look at the bodies, especially those that had passed the age of thirty-five. He immediately observed that his brothers, the tumors, had carried out an intensive labor. In fact, there were already a considerable number of people who carried cancer incrusted in some part of their organism, in the stomach, in the bladder, in the larynx, etc. Some of these people already moved without vigor, coughed repeatedly and had sharpened noses. Others were com-pletely ignorant of the presence of the intruder and seated themselves at the table, unfolding their napkins with good humor. The magnitude of this labor, which had even reached children, and in one case a fetus!, did not surprise the Red Egg, since it was evident that in that city there were abundant accomplices, gestators or transmitters of cancer, such as tobacco tars, anthracite. . . . The Red Egg recognized accomplices of its malignancy even in the jars of beauty products and in the analines that colored certain foods.

The Red Egg, three years old, understood that that city combined in its breast all that was appetizing to him. He could nourish himself indefinitely with the gas tank alone and he could add to that the extreme temperatures of the iron works, alcohol and neon tubes.

Unhurriedly, he roved over the rooftops, asking himself, "Whom shall I attack?" Oh, yes, he must select a victim! The situation was a routine one for his race, but not for him. He breathed voluptuously. Which organism, he asked, would he choose from among so many thousands? Of course, it had to be a human organism, a man or a woman. He could not understand why many of his brothers preferred to adhere to trees, to mushrooms, to fish or to butterflies. And which part would he abide in? The skin and mouth were imprudent. With radio therapy or with a scalpel they could attack him in any surgery. The lungs offered more security and so did the digestive apparatus, whose remote cloisters, yet unknown, constituted a guarantee of impunity. And he must not forget the brain! The Red Egg philosophized in his fashion on the subject. Curious, yes, curious and flattering to be gnawing at the mind, at the faculty to speak and coordinate, to be eating metaphysics, to assassinate the noble potentialities of the being, little by little.

Unexpectedly—the municipal clock pointed to one— something occurred that stunned the Red Egg: as though obedient to an imaginary baton, all the bells of the city began to ring, undoubtedly announcing a forthcoming festivity. The impact of the sound waves hit the cancer point blank, especially those of the cathedral bells that rolled at his side. The fact that these waves were gay and basically contrary to death gave him indescribable anguish. The circle of quills and antennae sprang out round his belly with fulminating aggressiveness but it did not cure him of the nausea he felt. Irritated, he leapt away with decision, toward the west, where it was clear, where there were no steeples. There he recovered. He saw two women hanging out clothes on a roof top. One of them had a carcinoma on one knee! In spite of which she laughed and gestured as though she were eternal. Suddenly, on the outskirts of the city, beyond the ball field, an immense sea of crosses and tombs surged before his green eye. This sight brought

back his self-confidence, confidence in his power. A cemetery! It was the first time he had had direct contact with
one. In his three years of life he had only seen two cadavers,
both of them white mice. It was obvious that many drops in
that sea of crosses were due to the action of his brothers.
The graveyard constituted, then, a victorious summary, a
living testimony of the power and inheritance of his stock.

Certain people in the city discovered that strange presence
over their roofs. So strange was it that "a slow oval
object" should be seen floating on its own between the
steeples, that terror overtook each of these observers, although for the moment none of them dared communicate
the news to anyone else. They tried to ascertain if the phenomenon was real, provable. The binoculars sealed their
doubts! A red and oval object, gliding smoothly, like certain
birds. Occasionally turning upon itself.

The first warning came from the Air Base. Nothing registered on the radar, but the observer on watch, a veteran
of the war, discovered the Red Egg. At the same instant
that he was focusing his fieldglasses to make sure it was
not an hallucination, an old paralytic at the other end of
the city, who spent his semi-death close to a balcony, looked
up on high and exclaimed to himself, "What's that?"
Whereupon he insisted on binoculars, and a granddaughter
obtained them from a nearby store. "A red and oval egg,
with something in the middle, resembling an eye!" The
paralytic alerted his kin. A group was formed that would
go on growing. And the same occurred with the watchman
of a factory, installed in his high wooden sentry-box. And
with a talkative storyteller, who went up to the roof to feed
his pigeons, as usual.

The band of musicians that was to gather in the square
to announce with clash and clatter the following day's fes-
tivities, disintegrated. Within an hour the news had run
from mouth to mouth. Like a lever, it made heads lean
back to scan the skies. And there was a diversity of opinions.
There were many who attempted, without success, to spot
the cancer. "It must have been a piece of paper!" they
exclaimed, incredulous. "It must have been a witch!" But,
suddenly, someone would shout, "There it is!" And many
forefingers became arrows. There was the greatest number

of eyewitnesses at a few minutes past one, that is, when the cancer became dizzy and went off through space toward the west, crossing through various clean and clear areas.

At two o'clock sharp, all the observation posts were taken, and the diagnosis was positive and unanimous. The Red Egg, the mysterious presence, was a fact. When a photographer appeared with a plate on which the silhouette of the tumor could be seen clearly contrasted over the gas tank, the news was considered official, and a superstitious panic completely took hold of the populace.

The authorities met in the hurry of hysteria, but they could not prevent the tumultuous mobilization of the population's reflexes, they could not prevent the men who used blowers at their work from looking at these instruments with the same fearful and impatient perplexity with which firemen look at their long metal stepladders. All the conjectures agreed on one point: there was something about the Red Egg, in its appearance, that was repugnant to the depths of a human being, and it was evident that, in spite of its smallness and its being called "a ball" or "a top" by the children, it represented a threat of unpredictable magnitude. Of course, no one thought of an object from another planet, and only a pair of cloistered nuns alluded to the devil; it was generally believed to be a complex robot, with electric and fulminating bowels, or a beast. An unknown animal, freed from some remote sleep. The bad thing was that its manner of moving about was reminiscent of beings endowed with free will.

The tumor soon noticed that the city had spotted him. But he didn't care. Man was so limited, the sun had only to hide to blind him. And since the bells had been silenced, what stillness their muteness created! Almost insolently, he turned several cartwheels in the air, coming to rest at last by the lightning rod of an official building.

At that moment, two chemists in a canning factory who had been examining some photographic plates, insinuated a diagnosis: there was a possibility that the Red Egg was fleshy, that it contained flesh matter. Upon hearing this suggestion, made with great timidity, an illustrious neighbor of the city, the gravedigger, had a sudden illumination. While the authorities continued their meeting without daring to take any measures, the gravedigger looked up and clenching his fists shouted, "It's a cancer!" With the help of binoculars he looked up again and repeated, more firmly this time, "It's a cancer!"

The impressive word ran through the streets and crossed bridges with as many feet as it had letters, or like an escaping stream of blood. "It's a cancer!" Ah, no one knew those "quills" or "antennae" like the gravedigger! His own wife had been a victim of those quills and now lay in the cemetery, converted into one of those drops in that sea of crosses, fifty yards away from where her bedroom had once been. "The doctors!" demanded the gravedigger. "The doctors should act!"

The first reaction was a collective paralysis. Immobility. After that, fantastic ideas crossed men's minds: to bury oneself in stone and mortar or, even better, to flee. But a cancer must run faster than an idea and must filter through walls without effort. And guns? And airplanes? And fumigating machines?

The authorities, in fact, did appeal to the doctors. Various internes advised keeping calm, realizing that the action of cancer in the organism is slow. On the other hand, others opined that the cellular degeneration was produced instantaneously, so that it was imperative to prevent the tumor from diving and penetrating a body. As for the specialists, they surprised everyone. They wanted to apprehend the tumor *alive,* not to destroy it. "This would at last enable us to discover its secret."

The doctors reviewed the means at their disposal for attacking the growth. The Red Egg sharpened his antennae and smiled to hear them speak of washings of blood, of mustard gas, of mistletoe, celandine, hydrastis, creosote. . . . Actually, he feared only radio therapy and the surgeon's knife, and neither of these two could hurt him at a distance. "Therefore, I'll wait in peace. . . ."

"I'll wait. . . ." From his lightning rod, the cancer had returned to his philosophizing, now master of himself and without nausea. The fear imprinted in the eyes of the populace produced an excited euphoria in him. The city was already familiar to him, he knew its shadows and its most hidden corners. He observed that the human traffic seemed to increase around the churches, around the hospitals and the Air Base. The pious against him? The army against him? Pooh!

The cancer decided to wait until nightfall to throw himself into the attack, by sliding down any chimney hole. In the meantime, he would choose his victim. Who? Ah, this was his limitation: he could attack but one single creature.

He thought first of the old paralytic, the one in semideath, who informed on his presence. He had degenerated intestinal flora and the task would be easy. Then he thought of the photographer who had taken the most revealing plate; there was a syphilitic inheritance in him, and the task would be even simpler. Then he thought of the priests, who spend their lives speaking of death, of the mayor, of the gravedigger! A pretty combination!

None of these victims was to his liking. The Red Egg pondered, while the sky clouded, permitting him to go undetected.

In midafternoon, the Red Egg felt hungry. He looked about him and saw nothing that would do. The factories had not reopened, and in consequence were not expelling smoke. The gas tank was out of the way, as were the gasoline stations. Finally he discovered that the weather vane on which he'd settled was covered with rust and mold, and by rubbing against it he absorbed it, immediately swelling out like a great beer drinker.

Sundown increased the general nervousness. Normally healthy people who had spent these hours saying the rosary began to notice alarming symptoms and even had fits of coughing and vomiting. "I have pains here!" "I feel this or that!" They feared that they had been attacked by the tumor. Their eyes interrogated each other and they avoided mirrors.

At seven sharp the hopeless ones, the people already afflicted by cancer, showed their faces. They went to the authorities, saying, "Tell us if we can help!"

The example of these sick was decisive. Decisive thanks, once again, to the gravedigger. The gravedigger thought of his dead wife and he flew out into the street ready to face up to the cancer. He was counting on the firemen's ladders and on helicopters, but even more on his own instinct. He defied the Red Egg and his outcry caught on. Men who had lost their wives and women who had lost their husbands began opening their doors and coming out into the street. At the start, it was a timid gathering. But there were so many cancer-mutilated families! A throng grew in the main square. Heads looked up from various vantage points. Someone spat upward. A boy screamed out, "Try to come down! We're waiting for you!" The cancer victims who had been operated on successfully were outstanding: with their crippled bodies, their withered lungs, their plastic rectums. Those whose larynxes had been affected emitted grunts through a hole opened in their chests. They could not shout, "Try to come down! We're waiting for you!" They could only think it. They could grunt it. And they did. And there were those who breathed asthmatically through rubber tubes.

The tumor did not appear. Concealed among the clouds, he was a spectator to that unfolding of events. Men suffered! Their aspect was similar to the mice in the laboratory and also to the young tumors attacked by the Cyclotron.

Then, a modest figure came forward, asserting that she had seen the cancer cry. It was a school teacher, from a school in the suburbs. In the school there was a small telescope, and with this apparatus she had seen the cancer weeping. "It's true," confirmed a bell ringer. "I too have seen him cry." The gravedigger became angry, but the doctors admitted it was possible. "All living organisms can weep."

The teacher was a disheveled young woman who believed in invisible things. She proposed they gather together all the children of the city so that the cancer should feel compassion. "After all, we're here to defend the children, aren't we?"

The teacher tossed her hair a little more until she won out with her idea. Several hundred children were brought together in the cathedral square, in correct formation, looking upwards. "Why are we doing this?" The children still thought that the Red Egg was a "little ball" or "a top." Until the schoolteacher told them they were mistaken, and that it was death.

The children, upon hearing this word, burst out crying: they were living organisms. They huddled inside their coats. Some tried to run away. The lyrical project of the teacher, which consisted of loosening childish comets and multicolored balloons inscribed with "PITY" in the direction of the cancer, came tumbling down. No one shared her sensibility, and there was a general disbanding of children.

Shadows began sniffing here and there, touching buildings and faces with the evening mystery. The cancer prepared for action. He was nervous because of the cats, camping on the roofs and the walls. He was nervous because he had been born in a mouse. Besides, he discovered a soldier hidden under an eave, with his rifle poised to shoot. There were the firemen, with the ladders ready, the rumble of the helicopters could be heard nearby, and from the Air Base beams of light scanning the sky. No, he could not underestimate the inhabitants' will to defend themselves.

The Red Egg felt besieged. There was a certain disproportion between his size and the scandalous forces organized to combat him. But his size was precisely his guarantee of immunity. At this, he pulled himself together. He again absorbed a dose of rust and mold, he nourished himself by inhaling emanations from the gas tank, and he mobilized his self-esteem with a glance at the cemetery, which was his guarantee of effectiveness.

At nine sharp, at the instant in which the Red Egg definitely selected his victim, a scream echoed in the cathedral square, piercing the belly of the tumor. "All right, then—kill me!" a man about forty years old, a chimney sweep by trade, had flung out. He was alone in the world and he understood that his work put him in constant mourning. "Why such hesitation?" repeated the man, looking upward. "Kill me!" He loosened the front of his shirt. Powerful hands covered his mouth and made him shut up. It was necessary that suicides should not disrupt the sequence of events.

The cancer was not to be deflected. He went bounding up the chimney which, as a matter of fact, crowned the hospital building. Once there, he stood at the opening and bid farewell to the moon, to the cats and to the rooftops, "Au revoir," he said. And he leaned into the chimney with his belly of quills.

He started down the blackened tube which on several

occasions had been cleaned by the chimney sweep. Once down, he dragged himself through an aseptic corridor, with white doors on either side. He knew the plan of the building from memory. But his presence there was provocative. At the moment, no one passed by; but he would have to choose between the shadowed halls or the risk of being discovered and dying.

On either side there were cancer patients. He greeted their tumors; the sick experienced an unusual twitch. In a large ward he discovered a man immunized against the tumor. He was a cultivator of bees. Each time they stung him, the bees injected formic acid, which apparently acted as a neutralizer.

Finally he arrived without incident at the recently inaugurated Surgery Number Three. The victim was inside! It was the surgeon. The most distinguished man in the city, and the most vigorous. Everyone called him "the Doctor." His scalpel was the most competent in the land. His fingers were long, agile, elegant. Expert fingers. So much so that according to the data in the hospital file, they were directly responsible for the death of almost a thousand tumors in one year, two years, three. . . . He was the most anxious and determined enemy of cancer. Neither the internes nor the radio therapists could compare with him. The internes felt impotent and the radio therapists often injured healthy tissues or induced sterility.

The Doctor was there, while at home his wife and children waited, oppressed. With hands gloved, raised, he prepared to intervene. His assistants, encased in green robes, trembled and would have preferred to watch the door rather than the table where the patient lay. The patient, stretched out on the table, anesthetized, had a cancer, an umbilical cancer. The Red Egg immediately recognized the malignancy, but he could do nothing to prevent its uprooting. He had not been given the power to strike like lightning or with the speed of a heart attack.

The Doctor ordered, "Scissors!" In that moment the Red Egg, sliding surreptitiously, reached the Doctor's right shoe and rubbed himself in its wax, which also nourished him. He remained there for a few minutes, while the Doctor tore up the sublingual tumor by the roots, completely, assassinating it, frustrating its intent to found a small deadly colony in the patient's throat.

The Doctor made a gesture of victory and turned. In that instant, the Red Egg climbed up the conic hole of his trouser. He penetrated the body in the region of the liver and murmured, "There! Let's see you operate on yourself, now!"

The Doctor noticed only a slight tremor. As for the cancer, he adhered rigorously to the tissues and settled himself to rest a full twenty-four hours. It had been a hard day. Now there was nothing to do but wait, since neither the Roentgen rays, nor the cyclotron could reach him there. Now there was nothing else to do but grow, to grow little by little until the Doctor, the superman, the only one in the city who had not interrupted his daily work, became pale, felt himself failing, until he would hear, from the mouth of a colleague the irrevocable verdict. ■

Of course, a true-bred science-fiction writer would have done it differently; the cancer cell's consciousness would have been based on the latest RNA-DNA "cell-imprinting" theories, and there wouldn't have been any flying over rooftops: perhaps an adventurous infiltration of the circulatory system instead.

The point is that the near-incredible breakthroughs in medicine and biochemistry this past decade have once again opened the whole area to unlimited speculation. Who is to say, with any certainty, that individual cells ("normal" or otherwise) do not possess "consciousness," if they have—as they seem to—a structure for "memory"? How do we determine the "good" or "bad" nature of "drugs", when the same products are adduced as cures for mental disorders and as causes of psychotic breakdowns? What tests can determine accurately whether the disease or the cure (or both or neither) are psychogenic, when solid evidence is produced for apparent "faith healings"? Whose testimony is more valid in the case of a drug like Krebiozen: the positive claims of those who have used it, without scientific tests or control? Or the laboratory-pure negative report of the Food and Drug Administration—negative in two senses, since it says in effect only what was not found in the product?

The FDA has become supercautious: DMSO—dimethyl sulfoxide —is still not released for any but experimental use. Many ordinary citizens have become wildly experimental ("Here, try my pills!"). The laws governing narcotics are hopelessly confused, and apparently as hopeless to enforce.

Once upon a time, common sense could distinguish between cures and quackery; but then, we used to think charlatans and miracle-makers were identical in the twentieth century.

THE POWER OF POSITIVE THINKING
M. E. White
from *New Directions 18* (New Directions, 1964)

It was Saturday. When I got up I found my cousins (I was raised by an uncle, an aunt, and two older cousins) packing away a lot of men's clothing that hung in the closet in Uncle Joe's bedroom. I said, "Good morning."

They both smiled and said, "Go call the Goodwill Industries, darling."

I said that I would be very happy to phone the Goodwill. First, however, I made a routine check of the house—for Uncle Joe. I didn't find him, and so, naturally, I assumed that he was no longer with us and that we were giving his clothes away, that's the way it was with Aunt Maude. We gave all her clothes to the Salvation Army. I called the Goodwill.

Then I just sat there in the hall for a while and thought about calling a practitioner to pray for me. I have been thinking wrong all week and am still menstruating as a result. Interestingly enough, I think wrong on the average of once a month, but I hate to call the practitioner this often; so, instead, I just thought that I would work on it myself. I have had an extremely religious upbringing, but this religion is no fly-by-Sunday affair, and one has to work constantly at becoming better and better. That is what finally happened to Uncle Joe, you see, he just became so good that he finally divested himself of all mortal error. Right there at the end, though, I thought he'd lost his faith

—moaning like he did. That is probably one reason that I am menstruating today because I thought wrong of Uncle Joe.

I went back into the bedroom and relayed the phone message. "They'll come this afternoon," I said. My cousins were still busy emptying drawers of socks and ties. A large number of boxes were piled in the hallway, and I began to drag these out to the service porch.

What bothered me about Uncle Joe's disappearance was the necessity of speaking to Miss Collins about it. Miss Collins is one of the headshrinkers at our school, which is quite progressive, and, since I don't take Health and Hygiene, because of a religious conflict, I spend an hour every day talking to her. Last week she got quite upset when she found that Aunt Maude was no longer with us either. She said, "How is your aunt? I haven't seen her for quite some time," and I had to admit that I didn't know because I hadn't seen her for almost a year myself.

After all the clothes had been bundled and lugged out to the service porch, I drove my cousins down to the hairdresser's. They always have their hair done on Saturdays. Then I came back to wait for the Goodwill truck to come. The truck and three men came about the middle of the afternoon.

"Lots of clothes," the driver observed.

"Yeah," I said, dragging out boxes.

"You folks moving out or something?"

I said, "No," and smiled, trying in a friendly manner to discourage conversation.

All three of the Goodwill men were dressed, or tattooed, similarly: battleships, anchors, hearts, large MOTHERS, pin-up girls designated, from the left: Ida, May, and Rosalie. The driver of the truck also had a large number of butterflies tattooed around his navel, and his Levi's were pulled low enough to make me wonder where the butterflies stopped, but I've learned to keep my curiosity to myself.

"That it, girlie?"

I nodded, and they drove away.

Then I went down to the Farmer's Market to get the bread. We get three loaves every two weeks and freeze them. At the Market I ran into a couple of girls from school. They said, "Hi, diphtheria," referring to a disease that I don't believe in and a shot that I did not take with the rest of my classmates. Instead, I had spent the time with Miss Collins, who said that, even though the shots conflicted with my religious beliefs, I should take them in respect to those who believe differently and might, therefore, catch diphtheria from me. If I don't get the disease, I can't see how anyone is going to catch it from me. I did not upset Miss Collins with this simple explanation, however, and told her that I would think seriously over the matter of contagious diseases.

After I got the bread, I picked up my cousins at Ivan's. At dinner that night there was another empty place and an extra potato. We all sat at one end of the dining-room table.

Clarice said, "Have another potato," at regular intervals. Unfortunately, I wasn't very hungry.

Finally, Alice ate the potato, which was a relief. I mean it was nice to get rid of the potato. "Did the Goodwill take everything?" she asked.

I said, yes, that they had come about two.

"That's nice. I hope it didn't keep you from doing anything you wanted to do this afternoon."

I said that it didn't. It didn't.

After dinner I went right to bed. At first, I couldn't get to sleep, and, then, when I did, I had a dream. People started crawling over me like ants. The room squirmed with them, big, dark, on the walls, the ceiling, the dresser, and me. Then, suddenly, they began to disappear, the ones at the back first and then the ones nearer to me. Pretty soon I was all alone. I went outside—nobody. I drove down Wilshire to Figueroa without meeting another driver although there were a few empty cars parked at random in the street and at stop signs. Olympic was strangely lifeless, too. Finally, I stopped at a gas station to use the pay phone; no one I knew answered, so I phoned some people I didn't know in the A's. They didn't answer either.

In the morning Clarice shook me and said, "Get up, darling." I was certainly surprised to see her. "You won't have time for breakfast if you don't get up," she said. I just stared at her.

"Get up," Clarice repeated. She combed a high forehead wave of bluish gray hair into place and smiled at me in the dresser mirror.

I got up and brushed my teeth. After I had dressed and stuffed down two biscuits, we left for church.

The lesson was "Probation after Death," and the church was filled when we arrived, which struck me funny. Dreams can seem very real, and I wasn't quite awake. The first reader got up and said, "Depart from evil, and do good; and dwell for evermore."

Then everyone stood up to recite the responsive reading:

"Know ye not, that so many of us as we were baptized into Jesus Christ were baptized into his death?

"Therefore we are buried with him by baptism into death: that like as Christ was raised up from the dead by the glory of the Father, even so we also should walk in the newness of life.

"For if we have been planted together in the likeness of death, we shall be also in the likeness of his resurrection."

At this point my mind began to wander. I pictured myself pushing the rock away from the sepulchre and staring down at the nail holes in my hands. Then I sat down on the ground and began examining the holes in my feet. A lot of other people followed me out of the cave and began doing the same thing:

"No one will believe it when I tell them."

"Where are my gloves? Looking at these holes makes me feel like puking."

"By God, I can stick two fingers through each hand."

"Now ain't that lucky. I can damn near get my whole fist through mine."

"I'm scarred for life."

"You're lucky to be here at all. I've been suffocating in that cave for three days. Bats, and I don't know what all, probably in there."

As more people began to pour out of the cave, I saw Uncle Joe. He came over to me and said, "It's getting so you stand in line for everything these days. Can't do a damn thing but what there are a million other people with the same idea."

Uncle Joe was just about to experiment sticking his umbrella through his left foot when I focused again on the reader, who was just closing with the benediction: "Mind is immortal truth; matter is mortal error."

That afternoon I went to the beach. I took the Bible with

me and marked next week's lesson. There were a lot of Muscle Beach recruits at Playa del Rey since Muscle Beach had been closed. They were all tattooed. I think tattoos are interesting because they are essentially attempts to retain permanent error. I had to laugh, but I tried not to be critical.

I had the same dream that night that I had had the night before. I phoned the L.A. *Times,* Madison 5-4321, to ask them where everyone was, but the phone just rang and rang and rang, and no one answered. I thought that, perhaps, everyone was in Russia making friends or maybe in Bombay sterilizing the Indians. Although this idea was somewhat consoling, I was still a little disappointed that no one had told me they were going. Just when I was really beginning to feel relieved with my solution, however, I saw the entire population of L.A. nailed up, yowling with pain, heads to the left, one cross after another. When someone finally lighted the fire under them, I began to toss and turn until I woke myself up. I was much happier to be awake.

I ate two eggs for breakfast this morning. I didn't really want two, but I was still harboring an "extra-potato" idea of our food supply, and I didn't want anything to go to waste. I also had some orange juice, fresh—we have an orange tree in the back yard—some biscuits, and some mashed-ant jam, black raspberry, I believe. Then I washed everything down with Postum, which is made from vegetables and doesn't contain any caffein. We don't drink coffee or any other stimulants because, if one were to heighten his imaginative powers in any way, a number of mortal errors might occur. "The Creator of ideas is not the creator of illusions." I stacked my breakfast dishes in the sink, put on a jacket, and then walked to school.

At school the first thing I did was stop by Miss Collins's office, which was a very busy place, as usual, and I had to wait. Now and then nearly everyone is sent down to see one of the headshrinkers for one reason or another, a fact that the school joyfully interprets to mean that the students need help, a need that they, forward-looking and progressive as they are, have satisfied sufficiently by hiring four headshrinkers. The school administration likes to face the facts. While I appreciate this positive approach, I still feel very uncomfortable about seeing Miss Collins, which I have the slight suspicion is in the same category as seeing a doctor. The mind is, after all, the cure, not the disease.

The bell rang, and everyone else left—probably for Health and Hygiene, which is a required course except by special dispensation. I said, "Hello," to Miss Collins and smiled. I might say that I am almost always nice and pleasant—and patient, thinking right as I do. The greeting was somehow the easiest; I slowed down considerably after that and didn't say anything for a few minutes while I tried to think of a suitable explanation for Uncle Joe, one that Miss Collins would understand and yet wouldn't disturb my own beliefs. I finally came up with, "My uncle's gone." That seemed to me to be a reasonable assertion, but it visibly upset Miss Collins probably because it came just the week after the news about Aunt Maude. Under the circumstances, I tried to be more cheerful.

"Where did he go?" she asked suspiciously.

Well, I didn't really know exactly, I admitted, but we had sent all his clothes to the Goodwill, and he hadn't been to dinner for a couple of nights; so he wasn't there all right.

"You mean he died?" Miss Collins asked, emphasizing the last word sharply.

I said, "No."

"Suppose you explain in your own words what did happen to him."

"Well," I said, "his mind just joined the Universal Mind, and, when it did, it forgot its material imperfections such as the body, which is, after all, only formed of mortal error and illusion." Clearly, this explanation didn't satisfy Miss Collins, and, since three days hadn't elapsed yet, I didn't find it altogether satisfactory myself; because, for all I knew, Uncle Joe was still waiting to be resurrected somewhere in the vicinity of Golgotha, a thought that led me to conclude that sterilization wasn't going to help the overpopulation problem in the Middle East much.

"When your aunt died," Miss Collins asked very slowly, although she enunciated quite clearly anyway, "where did they bury the body?"

"They gave her clothes to the Salvation Army," I said,

in as near an approximation to an answer as I could arrive at.

Miss Collins withdrew a file of papers on which she had previously noted my views in a cramped, pinched handwriting. She wrote down a few words that I attempted to read upside down but couldn't. I rather suspected that they said, "Total lack of perspective," as that seemed to be one of her favorite commentaries, one that I had read backwards on several other occasions. Then she started in about my parents. Miss Collins shows an ever increasing interest in my parents.

In a somewhat condescending manner, she asked again if both my parents were . . . "gone."

I said that I supposed so. I was just being agreeable really; I didn't have to answer at all because we have discussed this very same thing any number of times. Still, Miss Collins always acted as though it were news.

She asked if I remembered my parents at all.

I said, "No."

Then she asked if I had ever seen any pictures of them.

I said, "No," again, and then I happened to think of a newspaper picture I'd seen and qualified my answer by saying that I had once seen a blurred picture of my mother in an old newspaper. The paper, I believe, was wrapped around some dill pickles in the garage, but I'm not absolutely sure about that.

This revelation made Miss Collins begin to write again. She said, "You did," as though she had just come to a conclusion.

I said, yes, that there was a long article about her and how she had jumped off a building.

Miss Collins lost some of her previous enthusiasm. "And how do you feel about that?" she asked.

Well, I admitted that, at the time, I had thought it fairly amusing, but it had just slipped my mind. I think newspapers sensationalize everything and don't usually read them; I think one should only read worthwhile, uplifting material that portrays the good in man, not degrading pulp.

Then Miss Collins asked if I still had the article, and I said that I'd thrown it away, which seemed to disappoint her.

I explained that I didn't think that sort of nonsense was

worth saving, and Miss Collins, I could tell, was very impressed with my reasoning because she copied that statement down word for word. It is always interesting to me what some people will pick out as important.

"What did they do with the body?"

"What body?" Then I decided that she must have meant, "What did the newspapers do with the body?" and I said, "Oh they had it splattered all over Fifth and Flower, right downtown."

She said that she was referring to my uncle's body now. "Everyone is free to have whatever religious or nonreligious view of death that he may please. When you say that you don't believe in death, what you really mean is that you believe in a spiritual afterlife, but, nevertheless, the fact remains that the body has to be disposed of." Miss Collins can be very tolerant when she gets things worded around to her satisfaction.

I said that I not only didn't believe in his death but that I didn't believe in his body either. I said this mainly for dramatic effect as I suspect that Miss Collins is a materialist, and, although I never show any prejudices and am as friendly as possible to those with different opinions, I always maintain my own beliefs whether it does them any good or not.

"One has to make some concessions to the views of others. Society and . . . et cetera."

Often, at times like this, I play a game called "logical positivist" where one makes minute inquiry into other people's grammar and sentential constructions, confuses their vocabulary in every possible manner, and pays no attention to the standard procedures of communication. Although I feel that this is a sensible approach to Miss Collins's foray of jargon, it does make one appear unfortunately naïve so I don't play the game much.

Next, Miss Collins began a long harangue about normal responses to one's uncle's "passing" into which I interjected several polite replies. Health and Hygiene was almost over, and I kept glancing at the clock. I also noticed that Miss Collins had taken a good page and a half of notes although I seriously doubt that a direct quotation would have resulted in that much. Miss Collins is, I believe, somewhat imaginative.

When the bell rang, I left and went to my classes. In art I made several charcoal drawings. I think that all art should be as uplifting and serene as possible, and so, usually, I just take some blue charcoal, blue is my favorite color, and then I cover a piece of drawing paper with it. One can, if they hurry, make several such drawings in one period. Today, I made three; I have done more. They are all quite good—nice and blue, all of them.

Next, I went to history, American history—meaning the Civil War, as usual. There is another history class at this same time called the Civil War Period, a title that seems to me to be a lot more honest and straightforward. Now and then, however, I work up some enthusiasm for American history's progression as I am well aware that the world didn't end in 1865. I have not, of course, expressed to my teacher my general disinclination to be excited by the study of the Civil War, year after year.

After a rousing list of famous dates, I went to math. We looked at obtuse triangles. From there I went to lunch and then to Latin and French classes. It was generally a nice day; I wouldn't want to complain.

The sun was shining, and I walked down Pico to Beverly Drive and then home. When I got to the house, my cousins weren't there. Usually, they get home from work before I get home from school, but today they didn't; in fact, they weren't there for dinner either; so I just had a sandwich.

Finally, these two policemen came to the door. I don't know why I went with them except that I didn't have anything else to do and they seemed very nice—they wanted to know about my cousins. I didn't know that my cousins knew any policemen, but I just assumed that maybe they did after all, and I was very pleasant because any friends of my cousins are also friends of mine. After a while, however, it became apparent that they didn't know my cousins after all because they wanted me to describe them in great detail. I don't mean to seem critical, but I tend to find the police mentality somewhat delinquent. I had to repeat myself over and over again. I didn't complain, of course, and don't now. I suppose that some people just have a greater memory span than others, a peculiar and interesting fact, but I know that in God's mind it doesn't really matter and that it shouldn't bother me, one of God's creatures, either. ■

I have been conscious for some years of the gradual merging of SF with the "mainstream." The trend is dramatically noticeable this year; but my own big discovery in the work on this Annual was the extent to which SF and the avant-garde had already merged, and begun to overlap.

For some time, Reginald Bretnor and David Bunch had been murmuring about the reviews and quarterlies and "little magazines"; they still seemed unlikely sources to me, until Carol Emshwiller called my attention to the Redgrove story in Paris Review last year.

About the same time, James Ballard wrote me the first of several angry letters of praise for William Burroughs. During the year, I had occasion to review Burroughs' strange, brilliant surreal-science-fantastic **Nova Express**, and found myself impressed and fascinated by a book whose confusing (and perhaps pretentious) style might otherwise have prevented me from reading it at all. Meanwhile, Short Story International had begun demonstrating, with reprints, that the magazines I had thought of as "anti-story" were not necessarily to be so considered.

There were the letters from Redgrove, and more from Ballard and Bunch. And somewhere in there, I met Seymour Krim, then editor of Nugget (and of **The Beats**, an anthology of same), who set about undercutting my preconceptions mercilessly.

My sincere thanks to all these people. The fruits of the explorations I was led to are just beginning to show in this Annual; meanwhile, it is most hopeful to have become aware of the extent to which the experimentalists in style and the explorers in ideas have begun to identify with each other.

Robert Wallace is neither SF-er, avant-garde-ist, foreign-born, student, teacher, nor—exactly—newsman. He is a staff writer for Life magazine, which I feel completes the spectrum almost unbelievably well.

A LIVING DOLL
Robert Wallace
from *Harper's*

You must excuse the rambling quality of this letter, irksome as it may be to your legal mind. But you are my attorney; I may be in some kind of trouble. I would like to know exactly what sort of trouble it is, and what can be done about it.

Doubtless you recall my daughter. A few years ago, when you were in my apartment on 55th Street going over the details of my will, she bit you on the wrist. I will always recall your graceful attitude—it must have been a painful bite because she had already cut her twelve-year molars, but you merely whimpered. Today, at sixteen, she still has the distressing habit. Or at least I believe she has. As you will note from the postmark, I am out of the country and have not seen her for several weeks.

Early in December I went shopping for her Christmas presents. She wanted a book on voodoo and a large doll, as lifelike as possible. She also wanted a packet of needles and pins and a primitive drum from some Caribbean country, Haiti I believe, but in consideration of the neighbors I decided not to buy her one.

I had no difficulty in locating the needles and pins, and was much pleased with them. Today they make needles and pins exactly as they did when I was a boy. It is satisfying to find an old-fashioned product still manufactured in the old-fashioned way, containing no plastic. As you know, I detest technological advance. The sight of Park Avenue, lined with those hideous steel and glass buildings, brings tears to my eyes. Indeed, prior to my departure I had formed a small committee with the object of changing the name of Park Avenue to Fourth Avenue North. But that is another matter.

You may not be familiar with the technological advances that have been made in dolls. I certainly was not. It had been a good many years since I had taken a close look at a doll, and when I went into the toy store I expected to find dolls of the classic clothespin type with china heads and glass eyes. I knew that some of these dolls could, when properly manipulated, open and close their eyes and say "Mama." However, I was totally unprepared for what I saw. When I located the doll counter I was shocked; more than shocked. It looked like the municipal morgue.

Many of the dolls were very large. I did not at that time pick one up and stand it upright, although I judged that in spiked heels it would have stood as high as my shoulder. The larger dolls were enclosed in clear plastic cases, to which were attached labels listing their abilities. Do you realize that many dolls can walk considerable distances, eat, and talk? By "talk" I do not mean "Mama." I mean that they can make speeches of some length. Furthermore, they are no longer made of rubber or china, but of a fleshlike plastic that is positively indecent to touch. And some, as perhaps you have heard, have mechanical heartbeats.

As a lawyer, you may be interested in a printed notice which is attached to the cases of the most advanced dolls. It says, "Pending a ruling by the Supreme Court, the manufacturer is of the opinion that the sale and ownership of this doll in no way violates the 13th Amendment." Another legal question which you may find intriguing concerns the disposal of these dolls when they are worn out. Must they be buried?

I hesitated for some time before making my selection, but finally chose one which—or who—looked like a senior at Bryn Mawr. I chose her only partially because of her appearance; what clinched the selection was that I could clearly see her lips, through the soundproof plastic case, form the word, "Help!"

The doll was delivered to my apartment late on December twenty-fourth and I immediately hid her in a closet. After trimming the tree, sending my daughter to bed, and bandaging my wrist, I opened the plastic case. The doll stepped out, shook hands politely, and asked if she might have a glass of water and an aspirin. As I was fetching the aspirin, however, she followed me to the medicine cabinet and said that she had changed her mind; she would like a martini.

I was, again, shocked. But the doll explained that she did not often drink martinis; disapproved of the habit in young ladies; but felt the need of a drink because of her long confinement and the buffeting she had received in the delivery truck. I understood, and directed her to the liquor cabinet, where she mixed two cocktails, one for me. I have never in my life tasted a better martini.

After she had finished her drink, I tried as diplomatically as I could to broach the matter of getting her back into the plastic case so that I could wrap her up. It was extremely embarrassing, the more so because of the interesting and adult conversation she carried on. One can scarcely interrupt a young lady and wrap her up in the midst of a discussion of the murals of Orozco and Rivera—she is fond of Mexican art and knows a good deal about it. Therefore I waited, hoping that she would grow tired and fall asleep, so that I could take the necessary action.

But she continued to talk brilliantly. Her opinions coincided with mine on many points, and when she commenced to discuss her hopes, her dreams, and her difficult lot in life, I was genuinely moved. We talked, as I recall, for several hours. Once or twice I felt obliged to tiptoe into my daughter's room to see whether we had awakened her—but there she lay, sound asleep, her face in its customary mask of surly confusion.

Christmas morning was somewhat of a disappointment to my daughter. I gave her only the needles and pins, plus a large, empty plastic container. I explained that I had bought it as a joke and as a test of skill. If my daughter could fit herself into the plastic case, I would give her $100, with which she could do her own Christmas shopping. One of the conditions of the game was that before entering the case she must wash her face, comb her hair out of her eyes, put on a clean dress, and make herself as presentable as possible. This she did, and then popped herself into the case, which seemed to have been designed expressly to fit her. She was quite indignant when I would not let her out of it, or so I gathered from her facial expressions. She shouted, but no sound emerged.

On the day after Christmas I returned the case to the

toy store. The place was full of parents and children making exchanges. One doll was being returned because she could not, as advertised, speak French; only a rather vulgar Italian. Another had been sold with the guarantee that she could make a good sauce *béarnaise*, but evidently it was an inferior one. In the clamor and confusion I had no difficulty in placing my own case on the counter, and walked away unnoticed. I vividly recall the expression on my daughter's face at that moment and often, since then, I have tried to imagine what has happened to her. Someone, doubtless, purchased her and took her home. And doubtless the purchaser soon returned her to the store—who would want a doll who is obviously insane and keeps telling outrageous lies about some imaginary ogre?

The doll and I are now in Mexico City, where I have enrolled her in the Lycée. She is an endearing child, eager to learn; one whom any father would be delighted to have as a daughter. She fetches me my pipe and slippers, kisses my furrowed forehead when I am weary, and is the very model of filial affection.

As my lawyer, will you please inform me whether there are any legal difficulties to straighten out? If there are, will you attend to them? Thanks. ■

"Living Doll" was written, according to my information, when a doll in a New York toy store spoke to the author, and bit his finger. "Actually, it was not a bite but a nibble, although it so startled him that he promptly went home and wrote this letter." David Bunch lives in St. Louis, and works as an airforce cartographer. He is also one of my chief suppliers of roadmaps to the "little magazine" world. I knew him to be widely published there, and wrote a letter full of questions when I began to realize it was territory I had to explore. I got back not only answers, but a package full of publications to start me off on the tour.

TRAINING TALK
David R. Bunch
from *Fantastic*

It was one of those days when cheer came out of a rubbery sky in great splotches and globs of half-snow and eased down the windowpanes like breakups of little glaciers. I decided it was as good a time as any to talk to them about Geryl.

Little Sister was doing cutout angels on the floor, her thin mouth a red hyphen of do-or-die centered in the squiggly yellow parenthesis of her long, raggedy hair. And Little Brother, muscled like a sweaty boxer, with his shirt off near the fire, was hammering at a train track that had got twisted. She was four. He was five.

"Little Sister," I called, "Little Brother. Could you leave off the toys long enough to discuss sense, maybe? You're both growing up, growing up. No doubt about that, no doubt about that." I had turned moody there that winter day, in the soft chair with my pipe lit and my shoes off and my feet stretched tautly toward the electric logs in the mock fireplace that glowed off-fire red. They came and stood before me, trembling slightly in the attention attitude that I insisted on out of respect for me. "Little Brother!" I snapped, "you're not dressed for a conference. Little Sister! your hair's all raggedy." He ran to put his shirt on; she ran to comb her hair.

They were back. "Kids," I said, growing reflective, "do you, either of you, have any idea what really happened to Aunt Geryl?" "She's in heaven!" Little Sister said, and her face glowed with a memory and the beautiful-story-line of cutouts she had been doing. "She's dead," Little Brother said forthrightly, "and either in heaven or hell. It's not my place to say. But probably hell." He'd never liked Aunt Geryl. She was always after him about his toys on the floor, especially the train tracks that seemed to curve everywhere. She and Little Sister had been favorites with each other.

"Where's Mother?"

"Chicago!"

"Los Angeles!"

Well, you can stop guessing," I said. "It's Kansas City. But who cares? And that wasn't what I called you over about anyway. If it were just Mother, you could go on beating your train tracks all afternoon and cut out those silly angels till supper. I wouldn't care. I'd just sit here and let this north-pole stuff slam down on the windowpanes and run down to the ground and form a gray ice blanket from here to the graveyard. Which is what it's doing, in case you hadn't looked.—But I think we all liked Geryl. At any rate, she helped us out . . . at a tragic tragic time . . . when your mother—But enough of that! And anyway I think it only fair that we not go into any nonsense about what's happened and where Geryl's gone.—You kids will probably learn as you grow older that I'm a little different from some people. What I mean is, I believe in calling a thing a thing. That is, I don't believe in dressing it up. Especially about my friends. I don't think they should be lied about. People I don't like, people I don't know—all right, dress it up. Say they went to the moon, or Mars, or heaven, or hell, or star XYZ. I don't care. Why should I?"

"No reason, Pop," Little Brother said.

"You shouldn't care, Daddy," Little Sister said.

"All right! How hungry are you going to be tomorrow? And which do you like best, chicken or baloney? Tomorrow's Sunday, you know."

"CHICKEN!" they both squealed.

"All right! Go get me the baloney then, one of you, out of the cold box. I don't care which one goes. We'll keep the chicken."

Little Brother beat Little Sister in getting started for the baloney. "All right, Little Sister, instead of just standing there, you can get me the best two of your angels." She went and, after a long time, selected her prizes.

When they got back, I told them, "All right, we're going to take a little time and do something with this sausage. We're going to carve out a Geryl for each of you, taking our time and making them as nice as we can. Oh, we'll doll them all up! with crepe paper and ribbons and bows and string, and maybe even a little hair from that real-hair doll we've been meaning to send to the hospital! We'll probably need both the butcher's knife and the paring knife to do the job right."

They got the knives, and I plunged into the baloney skin with the butcher's knife and maneuvered around in there until I had two cylinders of sausage cut out, each about six inches long and an inch or more in diameter. I proceeded to sculpt them to look like Geryl as nearly as I could, long sausage nose, long dish-pan-hands face, and little short shaggy-bob hair fixed on. Little Sister and Little Brother watched all the time with interest, exchanging nervous glances with each other now and again and trembling violently once in awhile. My training talks with them were always a little tense, and I could tell they lost weight at such times, but I couldn't help that. A lone parent has the whole load of the training obligation toward his children on his hands.

When the Geryls were ready, as near as I could get them, I said, "All right, you know those two cigar boxes we've been saving, that I said might come in handy for a training talk. Get them. We'll line them with shiny paper." When we had the cigar boxes ready, all glinty and coffin-looking, we put the baloney figures in and the gold angels and sealed the lids down with red sealing wax. "Now we have a baloney stick, carved, and a gold angel in each box," I said. "So before the ground starts to freeze,"—the rain-snow had taken a turn toward pellety sleet by now—"you chaps just hustle right out and get this stuff under the soil." They bundled into their winter heavies, took tiny shovels from sand pails and strode into the slingshot sleet. I watched from the window and saw Little Brother do his burial quickly by a young plum tree. Little Sister, taking more time, did hers in the open and marked it with a stone white with ice.

Little Brother waited patiently for her to finish.

When they came in stamping and wheezing and all fired up with the cold, I told them simply, from my usual iceberg distance of dignity, "You may each go back to your own kettle tendings and pot watchings now—whatever you were doing before, I mean. In about six months we'll try to get together on this thing again, dig into these burials and finish up this training talk about Aunt Geryl.

We'll reach a conclusion about what really happened to her, where she's gone, the efficacy of heaven and hell, the Promise and all that. Or we'll certainly try to."

Little Sister went listlessly back to her angels, and Little Brother seemed old—old, going for his train tracks. . . .

When six months had gone by on the baloney sticks and the angels and it was May, green May, we went to open the caskets. "WHERE'S MOTHER?" I yelled to the children suddenly and without warning as we strolled above the green grave sites of our serious grim keen experiments before we started to dig. "New Orleans!" Little Sister cried, and Little Brother guessed, "Boston!" "WHO CARES?" I raved back. "It's neither of those hell places, and I wouldn't have asked you, except I glanced and saw a black heavy heart up there on those two tiny limbs in that elm tree, and I spoke without volition. And never mind that big word 'volition.' Just say that I spoke without meaning to. Just say that the spring sometimes bemuses one until he is unguardful; all brainwashed to giddiness and standing caught with his words down—he knows not—

"LET'S DIG!" We fell to delving then where Little Sister had buried her Geryl and, after about five seconds of spading fast and tossing, my spade all at once fell on a hollow thuddy noise. I sprang forward to claw with my hands, and soon I lifted the box forth. Then I dropped it.

There was a rattling sound! There was a slithery and slathery sound, there was a rasping, like rope being pulled through crushed paper. The box lived! It lived?? Out of one carved baloney stick and a little girl's gold angel something had hatched! ! Something had hatched? ? ? WHAT had hatched! ! ! ?

For a moment I stood in awe while sunlight flooded the falsely pleasant world of May and that queer dry sound of slithering continued in the cigar box that was our training-talk casket. Then, recovering my sure knowledge of the world and casting awe to the ground, I cautiously shattered the wax that sealed our casket lid shut and, using the spade for my safety, I pried open the box.

"Kill it, Father, kill it! Don't let it get away!" Little Brother shrieked, and he jigged, and he held his nose from the sausage that was now well over six months of age.

"My cutout! He's done a nest in my cutout!" Little Sister cried and jumped, and then she clutched her nose and her chest and went still and white-faced as cathedral statuary.

But I stood brave with heavy hands, as stones, while we looked at each other, measured each other steadily. It had two sharp cold eyes in a head shaped like the forward end of a spear. It hoisted a calm slick-stick part of itself upon three circles of chill, and it weaved the spearhead there in the sunny air of May, a wedge that I could not stop regarding. Then noiselessly it left, not even rattling the angel, deftly unslung from its orbs and, feeding the straightening circles over the side of the box, slipped itself to the ground.

"We'll all come back tomorrow!" I yelled. "This is all for today!" I cried. "We'll try to draw some conclusions. Later. We'll dig—we'll spade—we'll bring up Little Brother's casket! We'll assess." And suddenly, my legs going to jelly-mush and water, I sat hurriedly down to the freshly dug ground. I handwaved the children from me, told them to go do some kind of games, while I watched a thing that I thought was going deeper into the safety and gloom of the cold and dark-turned soil. Then, quite unexpectedly at the edge of an especially large clod I had turned in the early digging, it brought up its head, and it looked at me for a cold instant from its camouflage, almost the color of wet soil. Then, breaking for open ground, it glided into the emerald grass of May and completely disappeared from my straining eyes, leaving me to my fears and my fresh confusions. But it was scared! I clung to that thought. It knew it had met a master.

Idly, weakly, I reached for the training-talk casket, my thoughts struck numb with wonderment. I had problems. Yes, real problems now. What miracle? What dark miracle? How into the box, the carefully sealed box? What's to know? And what's ever to know after this? And then my eyes fell upon it. Oh, the saving of all the cold judgments. What joy! At a corner of the box there was a place of warping—the glue had given way, the short nails had been bested—caused, no doubt, by dampness in the soil. A hole gaped there, quite small, but big! big as the world. . . .

But my joy was short-lived and my extreme relief cut down to its death almost before its real borning. In my mind that night, thinking and thinking, I knew, yes, KNEW! that such a snake, if it was a snake—such a creature—had never been seen in that part of the country before. I could hardly wait for next day. YES! What strange sign might we not find to help us in the very next training-talk casket. . . .   ■

> The RNA of a worm
> Instructs it which way to turn,
> But the RNA of his teachers
> Might transmit noncurricular features
> The student's not intended to learn.
>   Dr. John Aeschlimann
>   (from "The Worm Re-Turns")

The theme is still mortality: but instead of attempting to teach it, the hero of this doctor story (or if we must categorize, I suppose it should be a doctor-doctor-doctor story, for two authors and one protagonist), finds himself in a position to operate it.

   The doctor-authors here are, respectively, from New York and California, a first-timer and an old-timer in SF. Dr. Smith is an ear, nose, and throat surgeon, whose previous publications have been in "very little magazines" and a college humor magazine. Dr. Nourse is "on extended leave of absence from practice to catch up on writing obligations," and his list of caught-up-with-and-published writing, in and out of SF, is too long to recite here.

A MIRACLE TOO MANY
Philip H. Smith and
Alan E. Nourse
from *Fantasy and Science Fiction*

                      When it first began, Dr. Stephen Olie's curious gift appeared in the manner of most true miracles, insidiously and without fanfare. At first Dr. Olie wasn't certain that *anything* out of the ordinary had happened. Later, when it became obvious that something more than his own native skill as a physician was at work, he refused to accept the idea of a miracle and resisted for weeks the temptation to analyze his gift scientifically. In those rare cases when medical miracles do happen (as indeed they do), few doctors are foolish enough to inquire into them too closely, and fewer still expect them to occur again. But in Dr. Olie's case, things were disturbingly different.

It happened the first time with the one patient of all his patients that Dr. Olie most dreaded to see. Mary Castle was a small, pale six-year-old whose weekly visit to his office was an ordeal for her mother and her doctor alike. Childhood leukemia is always a fearful illness; in Mary Castle's case the progress of the disease had been swift and inexorable since diagnosis had been made a few weeks before. In the face of expert consultation, the newest drugs, transfusions and supportive care the little girl had become steadily sicker, until the doctor found himself shrinking from each weekly visit.

Now, as the child and her mother were escorted into his examining room, Dr. Olie reviewed the chart hopelessly. Last week her white blood count had begun climbing again, her hemoglobin level sagging dangerously. He knew that today he would again find the enlarging lymph nodes and distended spleen, the hemorrhagic blotches on the child's legs, the shortness of breath— all the dreadful stigmata of a cruel and relentless killer. And he knew, bitterly, that he had nothing to offer the child but a word of encouragement and a smile as false as the smile of death itself.

As the office nurse poked her neat head through the door, Dr. Olie closed the chart. A wave of anger and frustration swept through his mind. *If only there were something I could do,* he thought. *If only there could be some magic in my fingers*—. Shaking his head, he walked into the examining room and smiled warmly at the child. "Well, Mary, how are you today?"

The little girl tried to return the smile. "All right, I guess."

"Fine, we'll just see how things are going." Gently the doctor examined her skin, checked her throat, then asked her to lie down as he went through the ritual of examination. From the corner the child's mother watched him, silently and hopelessly. For a moment he studied the listless child on the table and then gently probed with his fingers, feeling the tense spleen almost filling her abdomen. The child looked worse than the week before, her skin grey, her breathing labored.

"Doctor, you've got to tell me," the mother suddenly blurted. "Nothing seems to be helping; how much longer is it going to be?"

Dr. Olie caught the mother's eye, shook his head in warning. "Why, we're doing fine!" he said. "Right, Mary? Before long your tummy will be feeling better and your breathing will be better and everything. Of course, we may have to go back to the hospital for another transfusion this week, but that won't be so bad. After all, if it's going to make you well—"

His voice trailed off and a chill went up his back as he stared at the girl. While he talked, his hand had been gently probing, and now, suddenly, something had changed. The child's skin looked more pink and the enlarged spleen, like a deflating balloon, seemed to be shrinking under his fingertips. Even as he watched, a new luster was appearing in the little girl's eyes and, incredibly, she giggled. "You're tickling me!"

Dazed, the doctor felt for the swollen lymph nodes and failed to find them. He stared in amazement as the hemorrhages seemed to fade from the child's skin. Thirty minutes later Mary Castle was a pink and glowing little girl, playing happily in the examining room as they waited for the emergency blood-count report. It was impossible, and Dr. Olie knew it, but the blood count had returned to normal. Two days later the child was exuberantly healthy, eating vast quantities of food and demanding to go back to school.

And nobody understood why, least of all Dr. Olie.

In the busy weeks that followed, Dr. Olie did not forget the strange case of Mary Castle's miraculous recovery. He simply discredited it. Spontaneous remission of leukemia *had* been recorded before in medical history (though never so swiftly or dramatically); since Dr. Olie's scientific mind did not admit of miracles, he just refused to think about the case at all. Instead, he buried himself in the busy routine of his general medical practice with office hours, home calls, deliveries and hospital rounds. He was so busy trying not to think about Mary Castle that he hardly noticed the extreme rapidity with which his everyday office cases seemed to be recovering from their illnesses— the ulcer patients who seemed to be feeling better before they walked out of his office, the pneumonia patients whose fevers broke even while he was listening to their chests, the patients whose abcesses stopped hurting the moment he touched them and were healed completely in 24 hours. There were always the possibilities of coincidence and the well-known vagaries of human illness to call to account for such speedy recoveries—but as time went on, coincidence piled upon coincidence until a case occurred that Dr. Olie simply could not ignore.

The patient was a middle-aged man complaining of progressive weakness and fever. "I'm getting scared, Doc," he said. "I've lost 20 pounds in the last two months, and last night I coughed up some blood."

"Bright red blood?" the doctor asked.

"Yes. Is that bad?"

"We'll see. Let's have a look at a film."

There was no question of the diagnosis as Dr. Olie studied the wet X ray. Advanced tuberculosis is hard to miss on a chest film. But when he began to examine the patient's chest, the characteristic sounds of the infection which had been present at first ceased abruptly. The fever and cough the nurse had noted on his chart suddenly were gone, and the man seemed to be breathing more deeply and freely.

"That's funny," the man said. "I'd have sworn I felt lousy when I came in here, and now I'm feeling great. In fact, I feel like going out and having a steak."

Dr. Olie's hand was shaking as he put down the stethoscope. "Let me see another chest film first," he said. "And don't worry about the cost—this one's on the house."

The second film, taken 20 minutes after the first, revealed nothing but normal, healthy-looking chest.

After the office closed that night, Dr. Olie sat for a long time staring at the two films side by side on his view box. There was no way it could have happened—no way at all —but there it was. This he could not ignore—and now that the dam had broken, he thought back to the succession of curious coincidences that had been tripping over each other in the past few weeks. Individually, just coincidences. Taken together, a pattern. The touch of his hand, a few words, and the patient was cured. Minor things perhaps could be dismissed as "normal remissions"—but not a case like this one. And not the case of Mary Castle.

He knew there had to be an answer, but no answer made sense. This was not scientific medicine that he was dealing with. This was miracle-working. And then he thought of the day he had leafed through Mary Castle's chart so hopelessly, grasping for straws in desperation. *If only there could be some magic in my fingers—*

Dr. Olie shivered as a hint of panic rose in his mind.

There is a time-honored tradition that the doctor may bury his mistakes without recrimination, but must never advertise his successes.

In Dr. Stephen Olie's case, advertisement was hardly necessary. Little by little, word of the doctor's incredible feats of healing began to spread, first through the town and then farther afield. At first the stories were received with skepticism. Everyone knew that doctors could not cure by magic—but it was hard to argue with a living, breathing neighbor who swore he had been cured by just such curious handiwork. One by one the most skeptical themselves began slinking quietly to Dr. Olie's office and coming back cured of everything from carbuncles to cancer. Soon the office nurse was having trouble scheduling appointments; the doctor's tiny waiting room was crowded to overflowing as the lame, the halt and the blind trouped in and the doctor's fingertips continued their miracles. The office opened a little earlier each morning and closed a little later. The doctor began hurrying from examining room to examining room, racing faster and faster to keep up with the deluge of patients.

Home calls went by the board. There simply were not hours enough in the day to make them, and the doctor's hospital admissions dropped sharply as fewer and fewer of his patients seemed to require hospitalization. Soon Dr. Olie began hearing remarks and complaints from his once-friendly medical colleagues as the traffic jams outside his office increased in frequency.

In the middle of an especially busy day, three grim-faced

gentlemen appeared in his office and were hurried into his consultation room in spite of the standing-room-only crowd outside. "They're from the County Medical Society," his nurse whispered as they stalked up the hall. "Some kind of a delegation. They insisted upon seeing you at once."

The leader of the delegation was a highly successful society surgeon named Bronson. He did not waste time with pleasantries. "Doctor, there have been a number of very strange reports about you at the Society recently."

Dr. Olie sighed and sank wearily back in his swivel chair. "You mean patients have been complaining?"

Dr. Bronson looked momentarily embarrassed. "Not *patients,* exactly," he said. "But some of your colleagues have become concerned about certain—ah—questionable practices going on here. You realize that it is the obligation of the Medical Society to uphold the ethics of the profession—"

"You mean that it's unethical for me to cure my patients?" Dr. Olie asked quietly.

Dr. Bronson glanced uneasily at his colleagues. "No one would say *that,* of course," he said quickly. "But we have to question a man who seems to cure so many so quickly."

Dr. Olie looked relieved. "I see! It's ethical to cure them, but unethical to cure them quickly, eh? I should drag it out a bit more?"

The surgeon flushed angrily. "Doctor, you know quite well what I'm trying to say. No one is questioning the *fact* of your—ah—success in practice, if it is a fact. It's your methods that are under scrutiny."

"I'm simply practicing medicine the best way I know how," Dr. Olie replied.

"You mean by faith healing?"

Dr. Olie pulled X rays from his file. "Would you consider this faith healing?" he asked quietly.

"I would consider this outright fraud!" Dr. Bronson sputtered. "What's going on in this office? What have you been doing? The Society insists on an answer."

"Then tell them that I've been curing impossible cases. And that I haven't the faintest idea how."

Dr. Bronson shook his head angrily. "Doctor, we are

representing the Medical Society officially. There have always been renegades in medicine who have preyed upon helpless neurotics. It is our duty to protect the public against charlatans—"

"But there's nothing neurotic about cancer of the lung." Dr. Olie said. "Nor osteomyelitis. Nor septicemia."

"Then if you have some miraculous drug, it's your ethical duty to study it scientifically, document its actions, run 'double blind' studies to evaluate it—"

"And, of course, share it with my colleagues." Dr. Olie rose abruptly. "I'm sorry, Doctor. There is no miracle drug. I think you are wasting your time, and I'm quite certain that you're wasting mine. Now, if you will excuse me, I have patients to see."

"Then this is your final word?" Dr. Bronson said ominously, rising with his delegation.

"There's nothing more I can say."

"Very well." The surgeon drew himself up. "You realize that the Society will not be satisfied with my report. No doubt you will be hearing further."

Dr. Olie did hear further—but not quite in the manner he expected. The Medical Society delegation had hardly left when the phone was ringing with an emergency call for Dr. Bronson. "Yes, he was here—but he's gone now. I don't know where you could reach him."

The voice on the wire was frantic. "But I *have* to reach him. When he saw my husband this morning, everything seemed fine, but now John can hardly breathe. It's a cancer case, Doctor. If you can't reach Dr. Bronson, could you possibly come yourself?"

Dr. Olie hurried, and it was well that he did. The patient's name was John Stevenson, and he was in great pain, obviously in the terminal stages of a wasting disease. He was choking for breath, his heart rate frantic and irregular. A brief history clarified the picture: an unsuccessful operation to arrest a carcinoma of the lung, followed by supportive care as the tumor spread and fluid filled the chest cavity. Dr. Bronson's treatment had been expert, meticulous and thoroughly scientific.

Two minutes after Dr. Olie's hand touched John Stevenson's wrist, the man's breathing became more free and the grey color left his face. His heart rate slowed to normal.

Administering a sedative, Dr. Olie reassured the family (privately hoping that the man would survive until Dr. Bronson could be contacted). Having done all he could, he hurried back to the office, and had all but forgotten the incident by the time his last patient was seen, sometime after midnight. Then, dismissing the office nurse for the night and locking the doors, the doctor settled back in his chair to drink in the blessed silence and solitude for a few moments and settle his own quivering nerves.

The silence was shattered by a pounding on the office door, and a white-faced and furious Dr. Bronson burst in upon him.

"What devil's work did you do on John Stevenson?" Bronson shouted, glaring at him through bloodshot eyes.

Dr. Olie blinked. "Devil's work? I merely answered a call after you had left here this afternoon. I thought at first that he was terminal, but he seemed to quiet down a bit after I'd seen him."

"Quiet down!" Dr. Bronson stared at him. "Do you know what that man was doing when his family reached me? He was digging into a five-pound steak, that's what! I saw him with my own eyes—breathing freely, good color, hungry! I tell you, he was riddled with carcinoma. He was ready to die at any moment, and now he looks better than he did the first day I saw him. It's impossible!"

Dr. Olie nodded wearily. "I know. But it's true. Tomorrow he'll be even better. In 48 hours you won't find a trace of tumor in his chest. Believe me, I don't know *how* it's true, but that's what you'll find."

Shaking, Dr. Bronson sank down in a chair. "All right," he said. "I believe you. But you did something, didn't you? You *must* have done something. Will you just tell me what you did?"

Dr. Olie told him. He told him in detail, from the very beginning, and then as the surgeon's temper and incredulity subsided the two doctors sat and talked on into the small hours of the morning. Faced with the impossible, they sought an explanation and got nowhere. When they finally parted, the sunrise was no redder than their bleary eyes.

A few days later Dr. Bronson called him up. "You won't get anything in writing from us," he said. "But we are all convinced that you're on the up-and-up. We don't like to admit that such a thing as 'healing hands' exist— and for good reason, as you damned well know. We don't dare to, because it would open the door to charlatanry, quackery, and all kinds of abuse—

"But it *does* exist! Not often, of course . . . and it baffles explanation. All I can say for now, on behalf of my colleagues and myself, is: thank Heaven you are a regular and respectable member of the medical profession! There *is* no scientific way to explain what you are doing. But you'll have no further complaints from us, I assure you."

During the next few weeks, the crush of Dr. Olie's office practice increased in geometric progression. The miracle of his fingertips did not wear off; on the contrary, he seemed able to cure any and every case that came under his care. His waiting room filled to overflowing, and three policemen were assigned to keep order outside. The doctor could neither sleep nor eat. Bit by bit he approached the brink of exhaustion, but still drove himself, if only to avoid thinking about the enigma that lay in the touch of his hand.

The crusher came when John Stevenson, who happened to be the publisher of the local newspaper, featured the story of his miraculous cure in a full-page Sunday editorial. The wire services picked up the story, complete with half-tone cuts of before-and-after X rays, and certified pathology reports. From then on practice became impossible. Dr. Olie was deluged with telephone calls, telegrams and personal pleadings for help. When his office nurse found him one morning asleep in his swivel chair in the same position she had left him the night before, she firmly closed up the office, led him stumbling out to her car and drove him upstate to a friend's farm for sanctuary.

After three solid days' sleep and a week of good food and daily tranquilizers, the doctor's tremors began to subside and he felt almost human again. He continued to rest. Time had no meaning here; he might have recuperated for two weeks or two years, but one day he felt well enough to walk down to the lake shore and take an old rowboat out to fish for awhile. Clouds played tag with the sun; when the doctor beached the boat again, he found himself whistling.

Walking up the hill from the lake, he was suddenly aware of the world about him again, and once again he gave thought to grappling with the terrible power he seemed to have acquired.

Two tall men in grey topcoats were waiting for him as he reached the house. "Dr. Olie?"

"Yes."

One of them extended FBI identification. "I'm sorry, but you'll have to come with us. We need you."

"How did you find me?"

"Your trail was easy to follow. Now, if you will just come with us—"

"But why?" Dr. Olie protested. "You can't just come and cart off a private citizen—"

"I'm sorry. We have orders. You see, there has been a disaster—an assassination attempt on the President. He is failing rapidly, and the White House physician has sent for you, against considerable protest."

The trip to Washington was swift, first in a large black car and then by helicopter. Before he knew what had happened, Dr. Olie was being rushed along carpeted corridors, through a maze of rooms and into a sickroom where a small grey man lay in coma with a bullet lodged in his brain. Swiftly the doctor examined his patient. Moments later the President was sitting up in bed, shaking his head in confusion and asking to be carried to a chair. A day later the President's recovery was so complete that careful X ray examination failed even to locate the bullet.

An attempt was made to keep the episode secret, but there was a leak to the Press from somewhere high in the Administration. Overnight Dr. Stephen Olie was famous. Congress paused in their deliberations to declare him a National Resource while the United Nations claimed him for humanity. Leading clergymen the world over debated the moral issue of whom he should save first, since it was obviously impossible for him to go to the aid of every desperately ill patient. On one occasion, in the cause of peace, he was whisked into a bulky foreign aircraft and flown nonstop to the Kremlin to cure a certain high-ranking official of his cirrhosis. The newspapers debated the morality of that, also.

A committee was set up, composed of two physicians,

two Senators and Adlai Stevenson, to determine who
should have priority on Dr. Olie's services. The committee
could not agree. Meanwhile, Dr. Olie was kept busy 20
hours a day treating long lines of patients on a first-come,
first-serve basis. On the second day a riot broke out; the
doctor was saved from the lethally grateful embrace of the
mob only with the greatest difficulty. He was taken to a
master bedroom in Blair House and put to bed, given
vitamin injections and subjected to electrocardiograms.
Double shifts of special nurses babied him. Presently he
forced them to let him sit up in a chair and was left alone
to stare out the window at the grey buildings of the city
(except for the Secret Service men who were assigned to
insure his personal protection).

For three days he sat, hardly moving, barely eating,
searching to find a solution to the dilemma as frustration,
rage and desperation arose in his mind.

For another three days he sat staring at his hands. Once,
he had wished for a miracle—an idle, hopeless, vagrant
thought—and the miracle somehow had come about. And
now, hour by hour, as committees, newspapers, television
programs, governments, clergymen, doctors and lawyers
all clamored for his services he was hating that vagrant
thought, wishing desperately to retract it. *If only he had
never wished it. If only the magic could be gone—*

His brooding was interrupted by a representative from
the White House. He was most regretful to interrupt the
doctor's rest, but a famous Senator had developed laryngitis
on the eve of a critical filibuster and the President re-
quested that Dr. Olie see him.

Dr. Olie declined.

The representative blinked. "But sir, it's an important
part of the Administration's program. The President personally asks—"

"I said no," the doctor replied.

"But I'm afraid the President insists—"

Dr. Stephen Olie rose slowly from his chair, feeling a
chill going through his body. Then something seemed to
break in his mind; in a moment of blind, screaming rage he
fought them off, smashing his fists against the wall, throwing chairs through windows, tearing his clothes and cursing,
as the Secret Service men—doubtless afraid of damaging

the holder of the Great Gift—fell back and looked at him, fearfully.

He felt filled with rage and hate. He had not asked that the gift be given to him; he had not even realized it when it at first was. Every trace of love or even compassion for humanity seemed to leave him, now—a mob, greedy and grasping for life, avid for it, having together no thoughts or hopes except for themselves—not caring if their incessant demands and ceaseless pressure to be healed drained the healer dry and left him dead of fatigue; just so long as they themselves were made whole.

Save me! was the relentless cry. Save *me!* And not one, not a single damned one of them, paused to say (with even a trace of concern): *Physician, heal thyself* . . .

And as the rage and hatred mounted up in him he felt— suddenly—a great change. This time it was unmistakable, though the *why* of it was as unanswerable as the *why* of the other, earlier change. Or the *how*. And with the change descended a great calm. Strangely, he now felt better. Different, certainly, but better.

"Forgive me," he said. "I'll see the senator now. I am much better. . . ."

"Laryngitis, hmm?" he said, happily, as the senator croaked at him. "Well, let's just see what we can do."

Smiling, feeling the power surge in him, he felt the senatorial pulse and touched the senatorial throat. The senator took a horrible gasp, turned blue and dropped dead at his feet.

The Secret Service men stared at Dr. Olie, moved toward him, moved—except for one—away from him. The exception clasped him grimly on the shoulder. And at once fell, choking, to the floor. In a second he was still. Dr. Olie shrugged.

"It's really very simple," he said, answering the unvoiced question. "You've all heard of the power of life and death." Those in the room shrank back still farther from him. He got up from his chair, stretched. "Now," he said, "it's complete, you see. Now it's complete. . . ."

No one tried to stop him as he walked out. The word had spread rapidly. He went to his hotel room and there, humming tunelessly, he cut his common carotid artery with a razor blade. ∎

Somewhere along the way, in the work on each of these Annuals, the shape begins to appear.

It is in the nature of speculation that it cannot dwell continuously on one subject: there is just so much that one man's knowledge and imagination can do with a theme; then he needs either fresh information or a fresh topic. Perhaps because writers inside the field stimulate each other, perhaps under the impact of outside events, the same kind of topical drift seems to occur in SF as a whole. Each Annual, at least, has proved to have some distinct emphasis of its own; each one is different from the others.

To some degree, these pattern shifts are predictable—or at least recognizably expectable, when they occur. I have mentioned the new writers entering the field, and the closing gaps between "culture camps." These changes, I believe, are part of a much wider and more important phenomenon.

I think there is a desperate and determined—if often intuitive and unconscious—effort on behalf of thinking, imaginative people, from all backgrounds, in all intellectual and social microcosms, to place themselves in a "whole culture," to "despecialize," while there is still time; to widen, by whatever efforts they can make, the intellectual environment that limits our evolution toward sapience and sanity.

Certainly, the direction of the broad SF field these past ten years has been continuously and (one cannot but feel) meaningfully toward areas most likely to attract just these newcomers: the examination of human behavior, both individually and in groups; an investigation into the nature of interpersonal communication; an attempt to formulate a relationship between man and the technological environment he has created, and is continuing to create, for himself; and the study of man in his most immediate natural environment—that is to say, the mind-body relationship.

It is in, or out of, this last trend that the big qualitative change occurred this year. I expected to find a large number of automation stories, learning-process stories, political-sociological-anthropological stories—perhaps a few psychiatry and/or religion stories. I was not prepared for a broad-spectrum probing of the essential nature of life and death; the meaning and mechanics of mortality; the significance of procreation and of child-rearing; the metaphysics, and biophysics of death.

THE LAST LONELY MAN
John Brunner
from *New Worlds SF*

"Don't see you in here much any more, Mr. Hale," Geraghty said as he set my glass in front of me.

"Must be eighteen months," I said. "But my wife's out of town and I thought I'd drop by for old time's sake." I looked down the long bar and round at the booths against the opposite wall, and added, "It looks as though you don't see anybody much any more. I never saw the place so empty at this time of evening. Will you have one?"

"Sparkling soda, if you please, Mr. Hale, and thank you very much." Geraghty got down a bottle and poured for himself. I never knew him to drink anything stronger than a beer, and that rarely.

"Things have changed," he went on after a pause. "You know what caused it, of course."

I shook my head.

"Contact, naturally. Like it's changed everything else."

I stared at him for a moment, and then I had to chuckle. I said, "Well, I knew it had hit a lot of things—like the churches in particular. But I wouldn't have thought it would affect you."

"Oh, yes." He hoisted himself on a stool behind the bar; that was new since I used to come here regularly. Eighteen months ago he wouldn't have the chance to sit down all evening long; he'd be dead on his feet when the bar closed. "I figure it this way. Contact has made people more careful in some ways, and less in others. But it's cut out a lot of reasons for going to bars and for drinking. You know how it used to be. A bartender was a sort of professional open ear, the guy to spill your troubles to. That didn't last long after Contact came in. I knew a tenderhearted bartender who went on being like that for a while after Contact. He got himself loaded to *here* with lonely guys—and gals too." Geraghty laid his palm on the top of his head.

"Occupational risk!" I said.

"Not for long, though. It hit him one day what it would be like if they all came home to roost, so he went and had them all expunged and started over with people he chose himself, the way anyone else does. And round about then it all dried up. People don't come and spill their troubles any more. The need has mostly gone. And the other big reason for going to bars—chance company—that's faded out too. Now that people know they don't have to be scared of the biggest loneliness of all, it makes them calm and mainly self-reliant. Me, I'm looking round for another trade. Bars are closing down all over."

"You'd make a good Contact consultant," I suggested, not more than half-joking. He didn't take it as a joke, either.

"I've considered it," he said seriously. "I might just do that. I might just."

I looked around again. Now Geraghty had spelled it out for me, I could see how it must have happened. My own case, even if I hadn't realized it till now, was an illustration. I'd spilled troubles to bartenders in my time, gone to bars to escape loneliness. Contact had come in about three years ago, about two years ago it took fire and everyone but everyone lined up for the treatment, and a few months after that I quit coming here, where I'd formerly been as much of a fixture as the furniture. I'd thought nothing of it— put it down to being married and planning a family and spending money other ways.

But it wasn't for that. It was that the need had gone.

In the old style, there was a mirror mounted on the wall behind the bar, and in that mirror I could see some of the booths reflected. All were empty except one, and in that one was a couple. The man was nothing out of the ordinary, but the girl—no, woman—took my eye. She wasn't so young; she could be forty or so, but she had a certain something. A good figure helped, but most of it was in the face. She was thin, with a lively mouth and laughter wrinkles round the eyes, and she was clearly enjoying whatever she was talking about. It was pleasant to watch her enjoying it. I kept my eyes on her while Geraghty held forth.

"Like I say, it makes people more careful, and less care-

345

ful. More careful about the way they treat others, because
if they don't behave, their own Contacts are liable to
expunge them, and then where will they be? Less careful
about the way they treat themselves, because they aren't
scared much of dying any more. They know that if it
happens quick, without pain, it'll just be a blur and then
confusion and then picking up again and then melting into
someone else. No sharp break, no stopping. Have you
picked anyone up, Mr. Hale?"

"Matter of fact, I have," I said. "I picked up my father
just about a year ago."

"And was it okay?"

"Oh, smooth as oil. Disconcerting for a while—like
having an itch I couldn't scratch—but that passed in about
two or three months and then he just blended in and there
it was."

I thought about it for a moment. In particular, I thought
about the peculiar sensation of being able to remember how
I looked in my cradle, from outside, and things like that.
But it was comforting as well as peculiar, and anyway there
was never any doubt about whose memory it was. All the
memories that came over when a Contact was completed
had indefinable auras that labeled them and helped keep
the receiver's mind straight.

"And you?" I said.

Geraghty nodded. "Guy I know in the Army. Just a
few weeks back he had a car smash. Poor guy lived for
ten days with a busted back, going through hell. He was in
bad shape when he came over. Pain—it was terrible!"

"Ought to write your Congressman," I said. "Get this
new bill through. Hear about it?"

"Which one?"

"Legalize mercy killing provided the guy has a valid
Contact. Everyone has nowadays, so why not?"

Geraghty looked thoughtful. "Yes, I did hear about it.
I wasn't happy about it. But since I picked up my buddy
and got his memory of what happened—well I guess I'm
changing my mind. I'll do like you say."

We were quiet for a bit then, thinking about what Contact
had done for the world. Geraghty had said he wasn't happy
at first about this euthanasia bill—well, I and a lot of other
people weren't sure about Contact at first, either. Then we

saw what it could do, and had a chance to think the matter out, and now I felt I didn't understand how I'd gone through so much of my life without it. I just couldn't think myself back to a world where when you died you had to stop. It was horrible!

With Contact, that problem was solved. Dying became like a change of vehicle. You blurred, maybe blacked out, knowing you would come to, as it were, looking out of somebody's eyes that you had Contact with. You wouldn't be in control any more, but he or she would have your memories, and for two or three months you'd ease around, fitting yourself to your new partner and then bit by bit there'd be a shift of viewpoint, and finally a melting together, and *click*. No interruption; just a smooth painless process taking you on into another instalment of life as someone who was neither you nor someone else, but a product of the two.

For the receiver, as I knew from experience, it was at worst uncomfortable, but for someone you were fond of you could take far more than discomfort.

Thinking of what life had been like before Contact, I found myself shuddering. I ordered another drink—a double this time. I hadn't been out drinking for a long while.

I'd been telling Geraghty the news for maybe an hour, and I was on my third or fourth drink, when the door of the bar opened and a guy came in. He was medium-sized, rather ordinary, fairly well-dressed, and I wouldn't have looked at him twice except for the expression on his face. He looked so angry and miserable I couldn't believe my eyes.

He went up to his booth where the couple were sitting— the one where the woman was that I'd been watching—and planted his feet on the ground facing them. All the attractive light went out of the woman's face, and the man with her got half to his feet as if in alarm.

"You know," Geraghty said softly, "that looks like trouble. I haven't had a row in this bar for more than a year, but I remember what one looks like when it's brewing."

He got up off his stool watchfully, and moved down the

bar so he could go through the gap in the counter if he had to.

I swiveled on my stool and caught some of the conversation. As far as I could hear, it was going like this.

"You expunged me, Mary!" the guy with the miserable face was saying. *"Did* you?"

"Now look here!" the other man cut in. "It's up to her whether she does or doesn't."

"You shut up," the newcomer said. "Well, Mary? *Did* you?"

"Yes, Mack, I did," she said. "Sam had nothing to do with it. It was entirely my idea—and your fault."

I couldn't see Mack's face, but his body sort of tightened up, shaking, and he put his arms out as though he was going to haul Mary out of her seat. Sam—I presumed Sam was the man in the booth—seized his arm, yelling at him.

That was where Geraghty came in, ordering them to quit where they were. They didn't like it, but they did, and Mary and Sam finished their drinks and went out of the bar, and Mack, after glaring after them, came up and took a stool next but one to mine.

"Rye," he said. "Gimme the bottle—I'll need it."

His voice was rasping and bitter, a tone I realized I hadn't heard in maybe months. I suppose I looked curious; anyway, he glanced at me and saw I was looking at him, and spoke to me.

"Know what that was all about?"

I shrugged. "Lost your girl?" I suggested.

"Much worse than that—and she isn't so much a lost girl as a heartless she-devil." He tossed down the first of the rye that Geraghty had brought for him. I noticed that Geraghty had moved to the other end of the counter and was washing glasses. If he was out of the habit of listening to people's troubles, I wouldn't blame him, I thought.

"She didn't look that way," I said at random.

"No, she doesn't." He took another drink and then sat for a while with the empty glass between his hands, staring at it.

"I suppose you have Contacts?" he said at last. It was a pretty odd question, and I answered it automatically out of sheer surprise.

"Well—yes of course I have!"

"I haven't," he said. "Not now. Not any more. *Damn* that woman!"

I felt the nape of my neck prickle. If he was telling the truth—well, he was a kind of living ghost! Everyone I knew had at least one Contact; I had three. My wife and I had a mutual, of course, like all married couples, and as insurance against our being killed together in a car wreck or by some similar accident I had an extra one with my kid brother Joe and a third with a guy I'd known in college. At least, I was fairly sure I did; I hadn't heard from him in some months and he might perhaps have expunged me. I made a mental note to look him up and keep the friendship moving.

I studied this lonely guy. His name was Mack—I'd heard him called that. He was probably ten years older than I was, which made him in his middle forties—plenty old enough to have dozens of potential Contacts. There was nothing visibly wrong with him except this look of unspeakable misery he wore—and if he really had no Contacts at all, then I was surprised the look was of mere misery, not of terror.

"Did—uh—did Mary know that she was your only Contact?" I said.

"Oh, she knew. Of course. That's why she did it without telling me." Mack refilled his glass and held the bottle toward me. I was going to refuse, but if someone didn't keep the poor devil company, he'd probably empty the bottle himself, and then maybe walk out staggering drunk and fall under a car and be done for. I really felt sorry for him. Anyone would have.

"How did you find out?"

"She—well, she went out tonight and I called at her place and someone said she'd gone out with Sam, and Sam generally brings her here. And there she was, and when I put it to her she confessed. I guess it was as well the bartender stepped in, or I'd have lost control and maybe done something really serious to her."

I said, "Well—how come she's the only one? Have you no friends or anything?"

That opened the floodgates.

The poor guy—his full name was Mack Wilson—was an orphan brought up in a foundling home which he hated;

he ran away in his teens and was committed to reform school for some petty theft or other, and hated that too, and by the time he got old enough to earn his living, he was sour on the world, but he'd done his best to set himself straight, only to find that he'd missed learning how. Somewhere along the line he'd failed to get the knack of making friends.

When he'd told me the whole story, I felt he was truly pitiable. When I contrasted his loneliness with my comfortable condition, I felt almost ashamed. Maybe the rye had a lot to do with it, but it didn't feel that way. I wanted to cry, and I hardly even felt foolish for wanting.

Round about ten or ten-thirty, when most of the bottle had gone, he slapped the counter and started to get down from his stool. He wobbled frighteningly. I caught hold of him, but he brushed me aside.

"Home, I guess," he said hopelessly. "If I can make it. If I don't get run down by some lucky so-and-so who's careless what he hits because he's all right, he has Contacts aplenty."

He was darned right—that was the trouble. I said, "Look, don't you think you should sober up first?"

"How in hell do you think I'll get to sleep if I'm not pickled?" he retorted. And he was probably right there, too. He went on, "You wouldn't know, I guess: what it's like to lie in bed, staring into the dark, without a Contact anywhere. It makes the whole world seem hateful and dark and hostile. . . ."

"Jesus!" I said, because that really hit me.

A sudden glimmer of hope came into his eyes. He said, "I don't suppose—no, it's not fair. You're a total stranger. Forget it."

I pressed him, because it was good to see any trace of hope on *that* face. After a bit of hesitation, he came out with it.

"You wouldn't make a Contact with me, would you? Just to tide me over till I talk one of my friends round? I know guys at work I could maybe persuade. Just a few days, that's all."

"At this time of night?" I said. I wasn't sure I liked the idea; still, I'd have him on my conscience if I didn't fall in.

"They have all-night Contact service at LaGuardia

Airport," he said. "For people who want to make an extra
one as insurance before going on a long flight. We could
go there."

"It'll have to be a one-way, not a mutual," I said. "I don't
have twenty-five bucks to spare."

"You'll do it?" He looked as though he couldn't believe
his ears. Then he grabbed my hand and pumped it up and
down, and settled his check and hustled me to the door and
found a cab and we were on the way to the airport before I
really knew what was happening.

The consultant at the airport tried to talk me into having
a mutual; Mack had offered to pay for it. But I stood firm
on that. I don't believe in people adding Contacts to their list
when the others are real friends. If something were to
happen to me, I felt, and somebody other than my wife, or
my brother, or my long-time friend from college, were to
pick me up, I was certain they'd all three be very much hurt
by it. So since there were quite a few customers waiting
to make an extra Contact before flying to Europe, the
consultant didn't try too hard.

It had always been a source of wonder to me that Contact was such a simple process. Three minutes' fiddling
with the equipment; a minute or two to put the helmets
properly on our heads; mere seconds for the scan to go to
completion during which the brain buzzed with fragments
of memory dredged up from nowhere and presented like
single movie frames to consciousness . . . and finished.

The consultant gave us the standard certificates and the
warranty form—valid five years, recommended reinforce-
ment, owing to personality development, temporal-geo-
graphical factor, in the event of death instantaneous transfer, adjustment lapse, in the event of more than one
Contact being extant some possibility of choice, and so on.
And there it was.

I never had been able to make sense of the principle on
which Contact worked. I knew it wasn't possible before the
advent of printed-molecule electronics, which pushed the
information capacity of computers up to the level of the
human brain and beyond. I knew vaguely that in the first
place they had been trying to achieve mechanical telepathy,
and that they succeeded in finding means to scan the entire

content of a brain and transfer it to an electronic store. I knew also that telepathy didn't come, but immortality did.

What it amounted to, in lay terms, was this: only the advent of death was enough of a shock to the personality to make it want to get up and go. Then it wanted but *desperately*. If at some recent time the personality had been, as it were, shown to someone else's mind, there was a place ready for it to go to.

At that point I lost touch with the explanations. So did practically everybody. Resonance came into it, and maybe the receiver's mind vibrated in sympathy with the mind of the person about to die; that was a fair picture, and the process worked, so what more could anyone ask?

I was later in coming out from under than he was; this was a one-way, and he was being scanned which is quick, while I was being printed which is slightly slower. When I came out he was trying to get something straight with the consultant, who wasn't interested, but he wouldn't be just pushed aside—he had to have his answer. He got it as I was emerging from under the helmet.

"No, there's no known effect. Sober or drunk, the process goes through!"

The point had never occurred to me before—whether liquor would foul up the accuracy of the Contact.

Thinking of the liquor reminded me that I'd drunk a great deal of rye and it was the first time I'd had more than a couple of beers in many months. For a little while I had a warm glow, partly from the alcohol partly from the knowledge that, thanks to me, this last lonely man wasn't lonely any more.

Then I began to lose touch. I think it was because Mack had brought the last of the bottle along and insisted on our toasting our new friendship—or words like that. Anyway, I remembered that he got the cab and told the hackie my address and then it was the next morning and he was sleeping on the couch in the rumpus room and the doorbell was going like an electric alarm.

I pieced these facts together a little afterwards. When I opened the door, it was Mary standing there, the woman who had expunged Mack the day before.

She came in quite politely, but with a determined expression which I couldn't resist in my morning-after state, and told me to sit down and took a chair herself.

She said, "Was it true what Mack told me on the phone?"

I looked vacant. I *felt* vacant.

Impatiently, she said, "About him making a Contact with you. He called me up at two A.M. and told me the whole story. I wanted to throw the phone out the window, but I hung on and got your name out of him, and some of your address, and the rest from the phone book. Because I wouldn't want anybody to have Mack wished on him. Not anybody."

By this time I was starting to connect. But I didn't have much to say. I let her get on with it.

"I once read a story," she said. "I don't remember who by. Perhaps you've read it too. About a man who saved another man from drowning. And the guy was grateful, gave him presents, tried to do him favors, said he was his only friend in all the world, dogged his footsteps, moved into his home—and finally the guy who'd saved him couldn't stand it any longer and took him and pushed him back in the river. That's Mack Wilson. That's why Mack Wilson has been expunged by everybody he's conned into making Contact with him in the past two mortal years. I stood it for going on three months, and that's about the record, as I understand it."

There was a click, a door opening, and there was Mack in shirt and pants, roused from his sleep in the rumpus room by the sound of Mary's voice. She got in first. She said, "You see? He's started already."

"You!" Mack said. "Haven't you done enough?" And he turned to me. "She isn't satisfied with expunging me and leaving me without a Contact in the world. She has to come here and try to talk you into doing the same! Can you imagine anybody hating me like that?"

On the last word his voice broke, and I saw that there were real tears in his eyes.

I put my muddled mind together and found something to say.

"Look," I said. "All I did this for was just that I don't think anyone should have to go without a Contact nowadays. All I did it for was to tide Mack over." I was mainly talking to Mary. "I drank too much last night and he brought me home and that was why he's here this morning.

I don't care who he is or what he's done—I have Contacts myself, I don't know what I'd do if I didn't, and until Mack fixes up something, maybe with somebody where he works, I'll go bail for him. That's all."

"That's the way it started with me," Mary said. "Then he moved into my apartment. Then he started following me on the street to make sure nothing happened to me. He said."

"Where would I have been if something had?" Mack protested.

Just then I caught sight of the clock on the wall, and saw it was noon. I jumped up.

"Jesus!" I said. "My wife and kids get back at four, and I promised to clear the apartment up while they were away."

"I'll give you a hand," Mack said. "I owe you that, at least."

Mary got to her feet. She was looking at me with a hopeless expression. "Don't say you weren't warned," she said.

So she was right. So Mack was very helpful. He was better around the house than a lot of women I've known, and, though it took right up until my wife got home with the children, the job was perfect. Even my wife was impressed. So since it was getting on toward the evening, she insisted on Mack staying for supper with us, and he went and got some beer, and over it he told my wife the spot that he'd been put in, and then, at around nine or half past, he said he wanted an early night because of work tomorrow, and went home.

Which seemed great under the circumstances. I dismissed what Mary had said as the bitterness of a disappointed woman, and felt sorry for her. She hadn't looked the type to be so bitter when I first saw her the evening before.

It was about three or four days later that I began to catch on. There was this new craze for going to see pre-Contact movies, and though I didn't feel that I would get a bang out of watching soldiers and gunmen kill each other without Contact to look forward to, my wife had been told by all her friends that she oughtn't to miss out on this eerie thrill.

Only there was the problem of the kids. We couldn't take eleven-month twins along, very well. And we'd lost our regular sitter, and when we checked up there just didn't seem to be anyone on hand.

I tried to talk her into going alone, but she didn't like the idea. I'd noticed that she'd given up watching pre-Contact programs on TV, so that was of a piece.

So we'd decided to scrap the idea, though I knew she was disappointed, until Mack called, heard the problem, and at once offered to sit in.

Great, we thought. He seemed willing, competent, and ever eager to do us the favor, and we had no worries about going out. The kids were fast asleep before we left.

We parked the car and started to walk around to the movie house. It was getting dark, and it was chilly, so we hurried along although we had plenty of time before the start of the second feature.

Suddenly my wife glanced back and stopped dead in her tracks. A man and a boy following close behind bumped into her, and I had to apologize and when they'd gone on asked what on earth was the trouble.

"I thought I saw Mack following us," she said. "Funny . . ."

"Very funny," I agreed. "Where?" I looked along the sidewalk, but there were a lot of people, including several who were dressed and built similarly to Mack. I pointed this out, and she agreed that she'd probably been mistaken. I couldn't get her to go beyond *probably*.

The rest of our walk to the movie was a kind of sidelong hobble, because she kept staring behind her. It got embarrassing after a while, and suddenly I thought I understood why she was doing it.

I said, "You're not really looking forward to this, are you?"

"What do you mean?" she said, injured. "I've been looking forward to it all week."

"You can't really be," I argued. "Your subconscious is playing tricks on you—making you think you see Mack, so that you'll have an excuse to go back home instead of seeing the movies. If you're only here because of your *kaffeeklatsch* friends who've talked you into the idea, and you don't actually think you'll enjoy it, let's go."

I saw from her expression I was at least half right. But she shook her head. "Don't be silly," she said. "Mack would think it was awfully funny, wouldn't he, if we came right home? He might think we didn't trust him, or something."

So we went in, and we sat through the second feature and were duly reminded of what life was like—and worse, what death was like—in those distant days a few years ago when Contact didn't exist. When the lights went up briefly between the two pictures, I turned to my wife.

"I must say—" I began and broke off short, staring.

He *was* there, right across the aisle from us. I knew it was Mack, not just someone who looked like Mack, because of the way he was trying to duck down into his collar and prevent me from recognizing him. I pointed, and my wife's face went absolutely chalk-white.

We started to get to our feet. He saw us, and ran.

I caught him halfway down the block, grabbing his arm and spinning him round, and I said, "What in hell is this all about? This is just about the dirtiest trick that anyone ever played on me!"

If anything happened to those kids, of course, that was the end. You couldn't make a Contact for a child till past the age of reading, at the earliest.

And he had the gall to try and argue with me. To make excuses for himself. He said something like, "I'm sorry, but I got so worried I couldn't stand it any longer. I made sure everything was all right, and I only meant to be out for a little while, and—"

My wife had caught up by now, and she turned it on. I never suspected before that she knew so many dirty words, but she did, and she used them, and she finished up by slapping him across the face with her purse before leading me into a dash for the car. All the way home she was telling me what an idiot I'd been to get tangled up with Mack, and I was saying what was perfectly true—that I did the guy a favor because I didn't think anyone should have to be lonely and without a Contact any more—but true or not it sounded hollow.

The most terrifying sound I ever heard was the noise of those two kids squalling as we came in. But nothing was wrong with either of them except they were lonely and

miserable, and we comforted them and made a fuss of them
till they quietened down.

The outside door opened while we were breathing sighs
of relief and there he was again. Of course, we'd left him a
key to the door while we were out, in case he had to step
round the corner or anything. Well, a few minutes is one
thing—but tracking us to the movie house and then sitting
through the show was another altogether.

I was practically speechless when I saw who it was. I let
him get the first few words in because of that. He said,
"Please, you must understand! All I wanted was to make
sure nothing happened to you! Suppose you'd had a
crash on the way to the movie, and I didn't know—where
would I be then? I sat there and worried about it till I just
couldn't stand any more, and all I meant to do was make
sure you were safe, but when I got down to the movie house
I got worried about your coming home safe and—"

I still hadn't found any words because I was so blind
angry. So, since I couldn't take any more, I wound up and
let him have it on the chin. He went halfway backwards
through the open door behind him, catching at the jamb
to stop himself falling, and his face screwed up like a
mommy's darling who's got in a game too rough for him
and he started to snivel.

"Don't drive me away!" he moaned. "You're the only
friend I have in the world! Don't drive me away!"

"Friend!" I said. "After what you did this evening I
wouldn't call you my friend if you were the last guy on
Earth! I did you a favor and you've paid it back exactly
the way Mary said you would. Get the hell *out* of here and
don't try to come back, and first thing in the morning I'm
going to stop by at a Contact agency and have you expunged!"

"No!" he shrieked. I never thought a man could scream
like that— as though red-hot irons had been put against his
face. "No! You can't do that! It's inhuman! It's—"

I grabbed hold of him and twisted the key out of his
fingers, and for all he tried to cling to me and went on
blubbering I pushed him out of the door and slammed it in
his face.

That night I couldn't sleep. I lay tossing and turning,

staring up into the darkness. After half an hour of this, I
heard my wife sit up in the other bed.

"What's the trouble, honey?" she said.

"I don't know," I said. "I guess maybe I feel ashamed of
myself for kicking Mack out the way I did."

"Nonsense!" she said sharply. "You're too soft-hearted.
You couldn't have done anything else. Lonely, or not
lonely, he played a disgusting, wicked trick on us—leaving
the twins alone like that after he'd promised! You didn't
promise him anything. You said you were doing him a
favor. You couldn't know what sort of a person he'd turn
out to be. Now you relax and go to sleep. I'm going to
wake you early and make sure of getting you to a Contact
agency before you go in to work."

At that precise moment, as though he'd been listening, I
picked him up.

I could never describe—not if I tried for twenty life-
times—the slimy, underhand, snivelly triumph that was in
his mind when it happened. I couldn't convey the sensation
of "Yah, tricked you again!" Or the undertone of "You
treated me badly, see how badly I can treat you."

I think I screamed a few times when I realized what had
happened. Of course. He'd conned me into making a
Contact with him, just as he'd done to a lot of other people
before—only they'd seen through him in good time and
expunged without telling him, so that when he found out,
it was too late to cheat on the deal the way he'd cheated
me.

I'd told him I was going to expunge him in the morning
—that's a unilateral decision, as they call it, and there wasn't
a thing he could do to stop me. Something in my voice
must have shown that I really meant it. Because, though
he couldn't stop me, he could forestall me, and he'd done
exactly that.

He'd shot himself in the heart.

I went on hoping for a little while. I fought the nastiness
that had come into my mind—sent my wife and kids off to
her parents again over the weekend—and tried to sweat it
out by myself. I didn't make it. I was preoccupied for a
while finding out exactly how many lies Mack had told me
—about his reform school, his time in jail, his undiscovered

thefts and shabby tricks played on people he called friends
like the one he'd played on me—but then it snapped, and
I had to go and call up my father-in-law and find out if my
wife had arrived yet, and she hadn't, and I chewed my nails
to the knuckle and called up my old friend Hank, who said
hullo, yes of course I still have your Contact you old so-
and-so and how are you and say I may be flying up to New
York next weekend—

I was *horrified*. I couldn't help it. I guess he thought I
was crazy or at any rate idiotically rude, when I tried to
talk him out of flying up, and we had a first-rate argument
which practically finished with him saying he'd expunge the
Contact if that was the way I was going to talk to an old
pal.

Then I panicked and had to call my kid brother Joe, and
he wasn't home—gone somewhere for the weekend, *my*
part of my mind told me, and nothing to worry about.
But Mack's part of my mind said he was probably dead and
my old friend was going to desert me and pretty soon I
wouldn't have a Contact at all and then I'd be permanently
dead and how about that movie last night with people being
killed and having no Contacts at all?

So I called my father-in-law again and yes my wife and
the twins were there now and they were going on the lake in
a boat belonging to a friend and I was appalled and tried
to say that it was too dangerous and don't let them and
I'd come up myself and hold them back if I had to and—

It hasn't stopped. It's been quite a time blending Mack
in with the rest of me; I hoped and hoped that when the
click came things would be better. But they're worse.

Worse?

Well—I can't be sure about that. I mean, it's true that
until now I was taking the most appalling risks. Like going
out to work all day and leaving my wife at home alone—
why, anything might have happened to her! And not seeing
Hank for months on end. And not checking with Joe every
chance I got, so that if he was killed I could have time to
fix up another Contact to take his place.

It's safer now, though. Now I have this gun, and I don't
go out to work, and I don't let my wife out of my sight at
all, and we're going to drive very carefully down to Joe's
place, and stop him doing foolish things too, and when I've

got him lined up, we'll go to Hank's and prevent him from making that insanely risky flight to New York and then maybe things will be okay.

The thing that worries me, though, is that I'll have to go to sleep some time, and—what if something happens to them all when I'm asleep? ◼

> Come, let us sit upon the ground
> And tell sad stories of the death of kings. . . .

In a year of much violence and tension, many displays of courage both wise and foolhardy—and a large number of shocking public deaths—too many by violence—the most profound shock and loss, to me, was the peaceful passing of Richard McKenna, who died in his sleep at the age of fifty-one of no known cause. Mac had published only a handful of short stories; I had the honor of reprinting the first one, "Casey Agonistes," in an earlier Annual. He had written one fairy-tale-successful book, **The Sand Pebbles**, which he himself regarded as his "apprentice novel." He did not live long enough to finish the second. What follows is from a speech he delivered at the University of North Carolina, in December, 1962:

"Any human life from birth to death can be understood as a gestalt in time. The linear sequence of any man's experience and behavior forms a meaningful pattern, just as do the sequential notes of a musical composition. They form a mosaic distributed in time rather than in space. The arrangement is governed by the same principles as a spatial gestalt and closure can come only with death. A human life is an integrated whole which is more than the sum of its parts. But the wholeness is not achieved, nor is the final degree of integration achieved, until death. Therefore any experience, no matter how far back it seems to lie along the time-track, is not complete either. It will not be complete until the gestalt is closed and each experience making it up is given its final significance by virtue of its place in, and contribution to, the whole.

"The individual human past is not immutable. Everything in it is still happening and will not cease to happen until the gestalt is closed. Every past experience is subject to change, as the configuration of the forming whole is changed. Each

man of us is living his own personal work of art, cannot avoid
doing so, cannot evade artistic responsibility for his product,
because that is one of the fundamental consequences of being
human.

"When I first met that thought, I found it a very huge one.
I have since improved my grip upon it by alternate approaches
through existential philosophy, but it is still the scientific
formulation of it which for me affords the most conviction. It
is not a new thought. . . . It is contained in the proverb,
"While there's life, there's hope."

I think that can be stated inversely. Most religions, probably
all revolutions, have based their philosophy on the postulate:
While there is hope, there is life. If the hope outlasts the
individual's life-span (as it may well do, in religion, in revolution, in any life of dedication to creativity), perhaps the final
configuration of the life itself remains open to change, when
the body is already in decay.

THE MAN WHO FOUND
PROTEUS
Robert Rohrer
from *Fantastic*

Jake came running out of the
mine like all hell and stopped just outside and looked back
inside and stood panting into the mouth of the cave for a
good while. Jake's eyes were wide open and his face was
white under the dirt, just like he was scared. As a matter of
fact, he was scared.

Jake stood there looking into the mine with his shirt
front going up and down and the hair on his neck going
mostly up, and the mine was dark so Jake could not see a
damned thing, which was fine with him. He'd seen enough
ee-nough.

Finally, when it looked like nothing was going to come
out of the mine and get him, Jake stopped panting and
started thinking. This was a bad move, especially for Jake,
and the situation got pretty unhealthy. Jake started thinking

that maybe he was crazy. He was getting old, and he'd been living out there on the edge of the desert for a long time with this mine that didn't look like it was going to be any great shakes, and he started thinking, "Well, maybe I'm goin' crazy." After all, you don't see a chunk of rock get up and walk away just every day. You don't see anything like that at all, unless you're sort of off, so Jake started thinking, "Maybe I'm goin'—crazy."

Jake was standing there thinking and his old mule was standing there thinking, too, Jake had one of those old mules just like every dried-up prospector has, and Jake said to the mule, "Mule, I think mebbe I'm goin' crazy."

Mule said, "Mebbe y'are, Jake."

Jake said, "Gawd!" and he ran pretty quick into his shack. When he'd closed the door he sat down on that half-rotten cot he had and he began to think some more, and things got unhealthy again. Jake started pulling his hair out and hitting himself on the head; he was tolerably upset.

Finally Jake got up enough grit to look out the window of his shack and see if Mule was still out there. There was Mule, standing out on the dead orange ground, chewing on something that Jake couldn't imagine what it was because all the food was in the back of the shack.

Mule looked up at Jake with two solid black eyes and hollered, "Hey Jake, where's muh food, I'm *hongry*."

Jake yelled out the window, "You ain't gonna get no food from *me*, you dam' mule!"

"Aw-w-w," said Mule, and turned into a trickle of water and went splish-splash into the mine.

Jake said, "Gawd!" and was about ready to stand on his head when he thought, "Hold on there, Jake, get a-holt of yourself," which was the first healthy thought he'd had in a good time. "There's gotta be one o' them logical explanations for this, asides that I'm loco, which mebbe I am," he thought, and he sat down on the dirt floor and concentrated, hard.

After a while he started a headache from all that hard thinking, and he still couldn't figure out a logical explanation for a rock getting up and walking off, or a mule talking and then turning into water. Jake muttered, "That ain't no way for a ol' mule to act," and he kept on thinking, *that*

*ain't no way for a ol' mule to act, that ain't no way for a ol'
mule to act;* and then he got a pretty good-sized idea for his
type brain. Maybe that mule he saw out there *wasn't* a
mule.

Jake jumped up and went around back of the shack
where he kept Mule hitched up, and sure enough, Mule's
bridle was there all hitched to the hitching post and dangling in the air, and there were some white mule-bones lying
on the hard baked earth.

Jake got a nasty look on his face and said, "Somebody
et my mule." He and Mule had been pretty good friends.
Mule was the only one left from the old days before the
others had died, and now Mule was gone and old Jake was
all alone. Jake was pretty mad, and he stomped around past
the three crosses to the front of the shack again because
he wanted to get his old shotgun.

He stopped cold before he went inside because somebody had written in big red-crayon letters across the face
of the shack, "I'M HUNGRY." This made Jake pretty
sure that there was some no-good lout out there who was
running around eating mules and who ought to have his
head blown off, so Jake walked into the shack and loaded
up his shotgun and put the box of shells in his pocket.

Just when he was about to go outside again, there were a
couple of knocks on the door, and Jake shot his gun
straight at the door. That pretty well tore the door to hell,
and Jake didn't hear anybody yelling so he cussed because
he figured he'd missed and ruined the door for nothing.

He loaded up again and pushed open what was left of
that door. Right away his mouth fell open, because out
there on the ground in big red clear block-type letters was
"I'M HUNGRY!" There were even a block-type exclamation point and a block-type underline.

Jake said, "Wha-a-a-t the hell?" Right while he watched,
those letters changed around until they said "I'LL EAT
ANYTHING!"

Jake said, "Rg-l-s-p-ch?" which was a pretty complicated
word for Jake.

The letters sat there for a while and finally they changed
and said, "WELL?"

By that time Jake had gotten a little bit of control over

himself, and he said, "Who the Bill Hill Blazes are you, anyhow?"

"The letters wriggled around and said, "I AM PRO-TEUS." They wriggled around again and said, "I HAVE COME A LONG WAY." They wriggled around again and said, "I DO NOT KNOW WHERE THE HELL I AM." They wriggled around again and said, "I AM LOST. I AM STARVING." They wriggled around again and said, "GIVE ME FOOD, CHOP-CHOP."

"You already et muh mule," said Jake, since he'd figured out that this Proteus must have eaten Mule.

"YOUR MULE WAS FULL OF LICE./I NEED SOMETHING WITH VITAMINS AND/MINERALS TO GET ME OUT OF THIS/HOLE."

"Well, you ain't gettin' nothin' from me," said Jake, and he let those letters have it right in the vowels with his shotgun. The letters got together in one heap and hopped back into the mine.

Jake walked right up to the mine and squinted into it and shined his flashlight into it. He was so scared by that time that he didn't know he was scared any more. And he was angry about Mule, too.

Jake said, "Hey! You in there?"

Nobody said anything in the mine, so Jake took his shotgun and shot it into the mine a couple of times.

Almost right away something went *bam! bam!* in the mine, and Jake's old felt hat got pulled right off his head and he felt a breeze across his left cheek. He yelled, "Hey! Hey!" He turned around to get the hat but there wasn't much left of it so he loaded up and charged straight into the mine. If he'd looked back, he'd have seen the little shot pellets that had torn his hat and almost his cheek bouncing along right behind him. They finally passed him, but he didn't see them because it was too dark.

Jake got in to about the place where that rock had gotten up and he saw something he sure hadn't seen before. There was a big crack in the floor—it wasn't really *big*, but it was pretty wide and it looked like it went down a long, long way. Jake shined his flashlight down into it and he couldn't see anything like a bottom anywhere. There was a kind of green slime all the way down the side of the crack.

All this sort of made Jake shiver, because he wasn't a

fissure man, and so he walked on into the cave, waving his flashlight all over the place before he took a step.

All of a sudden a "STOP" sign jumped up in front of Jake. Jake let the sign have it with both barrels, but all the little pieces hopped back together and turned into a rattlesnake.

Jake swung his shotgun down holding the barrels and he missed the snake and that took care of the shotgun. He started stomping around after the snake—he had on high leather boots, so he didn't have to worry—and when he finally got his foot right smack on the snake it wasn't a snake anymore, it was a two-inch nail, and Jake cussed like the devil and jumped up and down with one leg.

The nail turned into a rubber ball and bounced away. Jake hobbled after the ball as fast as he could. Finally he caught the ball and he went *wham* right down on the ground, because it wasn't a rubber ball any more, it was a portable hi-fi-stereo combination radio-TV set with built-in jacks for earphones and a war movie going on.

Jake lay there with his hand stuck underneath the TV-radio. Then the war movie cut off and an announcer came on and said, "We now have a special announcement. Everybody needs vitamins. You need vitamins, I need vitamins. I need vitamins more than you do, because I've had to do without them for three thousand years. I've been crawling around under the ground everyday, day in and day out. It's hot, sweaty work, and I get tired and dragged out. Won't you contribute your vitamins to the Vitamins for Half-Dead Greek Gods Association/5763 Red Lane/Rum-Tum-Tummy, Nebraska? Thank you." A Messerschmitt went *wham!* into a tree.

Jake got red in the face and said, "No! No! No! I ain't gonna give you any of my grub! I'm gonna get my gasoline and burn you up, *that's* what I'm gonna do!" He jerked his hand from under the TV set and stood up.

Right away he had to duck again, because the TV set turned into a locomotive and went pounding out of the mine at full throttle. Jake heard a lot of crashing outside, and he guessed what it was. He showed his teeth and limped out into the open heat of the sun.

The back of his shack was flying up into the air board by board. By the time Jake got back there, all the tins were either open and hollowed out, or gone. There were the big letters on the floor: "AND I'M STILL HUNGRY, TOO! !" The letters turned into an MG and va-*voomed* back into the mine.

Jake didn't stop to think about what the thing's still being hungry might mean. His foot hurt, and his hand hurt, and he was mad as hell. He waded into what was left of his cellar and started searching for the gasoline cans.

By the time he found the cans, the sun was almost down and the light was dim. Jake's eyes weren't any too good anyway, and he walked toward a big black spot he thought was the mine and when he got to it it wasn't there any more, it was a little more to his left. Jake shook his head and flicked on his flashlight and went inside, muttering "I'm gonna burn you *up*" all the time.

At first he didn't notice, but the farther and farther that Jake got into the mine, the less and less it looked like a mine to him. There was something funny about the walls, and maybe about the ground. All of a sudden old Jake got a pretty scary idea, and his chest got all knotted up inside, and he turned around to scram out of there.

Just then the mine started shaking, and the ground sort of pushed up, and Jake fell down. He didn't even have a chance to get close to the mouth of that cave before CHOMP!

■ Rugged.

The last two selections for this year are both concerned with the sort of Immortality that gets capitalized—that of the gods, the demigods, the saints and angels.

There are virtually no other similarities, between stories or authors.

Robert Rohrer is a nineteen-year-old student at Emory University in Atlanta, Georgia—another of the Wunderkinder, who reports that he wrote his first salable story at thirteen, and sold it two years later. "I like music; I play the piano, and write more than I study. . . . My father is a physics professor and can't understand why I'm not a scientist."

Isaac Bashevis Singer was born in Radzymin, Poland, in 1904. He came to the United States in 1935, and has worked since then as writer and book reviewer for the Jewish Daily Forward in New York. He has received awards and grants in several

countries for his work, and his stories have been appearing,
over the last two or three years, in most of the "quality"
magazines in this country.

YACHID AND YECHIDA*
Isaac Bashevis Singer

Translated from the Yiddish
by the Author and Elizabeth Pollet.

from *Short Friday*,
(Farrar Straus and Giroux, 1964)

                            In a prison where souls
bound for Sheol—Earth they call it there—await destruc-
tion, there hovered the female soul Yechida. Souls forgot
their origin. Purah, the Angel of Forgetfulness, he who
dissipates God's light and conceals His face, holds dominion
everywhere beyond the Godhead. Yechida, unmindful of
her descent from the Throne of Glory, had sinned. Her
jealousy had caused much trouble in the world where she
dwelled. She had suspected all female angels of having
affairs with her lover Yachid, had not only blasphemed
God but even denied him. Souls, she said, were not created
but had evolved out of nothing: they had neither mission
nor purpose. Although the authorities were extremely patient and forgiving, Yechida was finally sentenced to death.
The judge fixed the moment of her descent to that cemetery
called Earth.

The attorney for Yechida appealed to the Superior
Court of Heaven, even presented a petition to Metatron,
the Lord of the Face. But Yechida was so filled with sin
and so impenitent that no power could save her. The attendants seized her, tore her from Yachid, clipped her
wings, cut her hair, and clothed her in a long white
shroud. She was no longer allowed to hear the music of
the spheres, to smell the perfumes of Paradise and to

   * "Jachid and Jachidah," in its original publication: the trans-
literation is changed here to conform more closely with the
Yiddish pronunciation: Yah-chid and Y'chee-duh—the "ch" as
in the German ach, or the Hebrew lechayim.

meditate on the secrets of the Torah, which sustained the soul. She could no longer bathe in the wells of balsam oil. In the prison cell, the darkness of the nether world already surrounded her. But her greatest torment was her longing for Yachid. She could no longer reach him telepathically. Nor could she send a message to him, all of her servants having been taken away. Only the fear of death was left to Yechida.

Death was no rare occurrence where Yechida lived but it befell only vulgar, exhausted spirits. Exactly what happened to the dead, Yechida did not know. She was convinced that when a soul descended to Earth it was to extinction, even though the pious maintained that a spark of life remained. A dead soul immediately began to rot and was soon covered with a slimy stuff called "semen." Then a grave digger put it into a womb where it turned into some sort of fungus and was henceforth known as a "child." Later on, began the tortures of Gehenna: birth, growth, toil. For according to the morality books, death was not the final stage. Purified, the soul returned to its source. But what evidence was there for such beliefs? So far as Yechida knew, no one had ever returned from Earth. The enlightened Yechida believed that the soul rots for a short time and then disintegrates into a darkness of no return.

Now the moment had come when Yechida must die, must sink to Earth. Soon, the Angel of Death would appear with his fiery sword and thousand eyes.

At first Yechida had wept incessantly, but then her tears had ceased. Awake or asleep she never stopped thinking of Yachid. Where was he? What was he doing? Whom was he with? Yechida was well aware he would not mourn for her for ever. He was surrounded by beautiful females, sacred beasts, angels, seraphim, cherubs, ayralim, each one with powers of seduction. How long could someone like Yachid curb his desires? He, as she, was an unbeliever. It was he who had taught her that spirits were not created, but were products of evolution. Yachid did not acknowledge free will, nor believe in ultimate good and evil. What would restrain him? Most certainly he already lay in the lap of some other divinity, telling those stories about himself he had already told Yechida.

But what could she do? In this dungeon all contact with the mansions ceased. All doors were closed: neither mercy, nor beauty entered here. The one way from this prison led down to Earth, and to the horrors called flesh, blood, marrow, nerves, and breath. The God-fearing angels promised resurrection. They preached that the soul did not linger forever on Earth, but that after it had endured its punishment, it returned to the Higher Sphere. But Yechida, being a modernist, regarded all of this as superstition. How would a soul free itself from the corruption of the body? It was scientifically impossible. Resurrection was a dream, a silly comfort of primitive and frightened souls.

2

One night as Yechida lay in a corner brooding about Yachid and the pleasures she had received from him, his kisses, his caresses, the secrets whispered in her ear, the many positions and games into which she had been initiated, Dumah, the thousand-eyed Angel of Death, looking just as the Sacred Books described him, entered bearing a fiery sword.

"Your time has come, little sister," he said.

"No further appeal is possible?"

"Those who are in this wing always go to Earth."

Yechida shuddered. "Well, I am ready."

"Yechida, repentance helps even now. Recite your confession."

"How can it help? My only regret is that I did not transgress more," said Yechida rebelliously.

Both were silent. Finally Dumah said, "Yechida, I know you are angry with me. But is it my fault, sister? Did I want to be the Angel of Death? I too am a sinner, exiled from a higher realm, my punishment to be the executioner of souls. Yechida, I have not willed your death, but be comforted. Death is not as dreadful as you imagine. True, the first moments are not easy. But once you have been planted in the womb, the nine months that follow are not painful. You will forget all that you have learned here. Coming out of the womb will be a shock; but childhood is often pleasant. You will begin to study the lore of death, clothed in a fresh, pliant body, and soon will dread the end of your exile."

Yechida interrupted him. "Kill me if you must, Dumah, but spare me your lies."

"I am telling you the truth, Yechida. You will be absent no more than a hundred years, for even the wickedest do not suffer longer than that. Death is only the preparation for a new existence."

"Dumah, please. I don't want to listen."

"But it is important for you to know that good and evil exist there, too, and that the will remains free."

"What will? Why do you talk such nonsense?"

"Yechida, listen carefully. Even among the dead there are laws and regulations. The way you act in death will determine what happens to you next. Death is a laboratory for the rehabilitation of souls."

"Make an end of me, I beseech you."

"Be patient, you still have a few more minutes to live and must receive your instructions. Know, then, that one may act well or evilly on Earth and that the most pernicious sin of all is to return a soul to life."

This idea was so ridiculous that Yechida laughed despite her anguish.

"How can one corpse give life to another?"

"It's not as difficult as you think. The body is composed of such weak material that a mere blow can make it disintegrate. Death is no stronger than a cobweb; a breeze blows and it disappears. But it is a great offense to destroy either another's death or one's own. Not only that, but you must not act or speak or even think in such a way as to threaten death. Here one's object is to preserve life, but there it is death that is succored."

"Nursery tales. The fantasies of an executioner."

"It is the truth, Yechida. The Torah that applies to Earth is based on a single principle: Another man's death must be as dear to one as one's own. Remember my words. When you descend to Sheol, they will be of value to you."

"No, no, I won't listen to any more lies." And Yechida covered her ears.

3

Years passed. Everyone in the higher realm had forgotten Yechida except her mother, who still continued to light memorial candles for her daughter. On Earth Yechida had a new mother as well as a father, several brothers and sisters, all dead. After attending a high school, she had begun to take courses at the university. She lived in a large necropolis where corpses are prepared for all kinds of mortuary functions.

It was spring, and Earth's corruption grew leprous with blossoms. From the graves with their memorial trees and cleansing waters arose a dreadful stench. Millions of creatures, forced to descend into the domains of death, were becoming flies, butterflies, worms, toads, frogs. They buzzed, croaked, screeched, rattled, already involved in the death struggle. But since Yechida was totally inured to the habits of Earth, all this seemed to her part of life. She sat on a park bench staring up at the moon, which from the darkness of the nether world is sometimes recognized as a memorial candle set in a skull. Like all female corpses, Yechida yearned to perpetuate death, to have her womb became a grave for the newly dead. But she couldn't do that without the help of a male with whom she would have to copulate in the hatred which corpses call "love."

As Yechida sat staring into the sockets of the skull above her, a white-shrouded corpse came and sat beside her. For a while the two corpses gazed at each other, thinking they could see, although all corpses are actually blind. Finally the male corpse spoke:

"Pardon, Miss, could you tell me what time it is?"

Since deep within themselves all corpses long for the termination of their punishment, they are perpetually concerned with time.

"The time?" Yechida answered. "Just a second." Strapped to her wrist was an instrument to measure time but the divisions were so minute and the symbols so tiny that she could not easily read the dial. The male corpse moved nearer to her.

"May I take a look? I have good eyes."

"If you wish."

Corpses never act straightforwardly but are always sly and devious. The male corpse took Yechida's hand and bent his head toward the instrument. This was not the first time a male corpse had touched Yechida but contact with this one made her limbs tremble. He stared intently but could not decide immediately. Then he said: "I think it's ten minutes after ten."

"Is it really so late?"

"Permit me to introduce myself. My name is Yachid."

"Yachid? Mine is Yechida."

"What an odd coincidence."

Both hearing death race in their blood were silent for a long while. Then Yachid said: "How beautiful the night is!"

"Yes, beautiful!"

There's something about spring that cannot be expressed in words."

"Words can express nothing," answered Yechida.

As she made this remark, both knew they were destined to lie together and to prepare a grave for a new corpse. The fact is, no matter how dead the dead are, there remains some life in them, a trace of contact with that knowledge which fills the universe. Death only masks the truth. The sages speak of it as a soap bubble that bursts at the touch of a straw. The dead, ashamed of death, try to conceal their condition through cunning. The more moribund a corpse, the more voluble it is.

"May I ask where you live?" asked Yachid.

Where have I seen him before? How is it his voice sounds so familiar to me? Yechida wondered. *And how does it happen that he's called Yachid? Such a rare name.*

"Not far from here," she answered.

"Would you object to my walking you home?"

"Thank you. You don't have to. But if you want . . . It is still too early to go to bed."

When Yachid rose, Yechida did, too. Is this the one I have been searching for? Yechida asked herself, the one destined for me? But what do I mean by "destiny"? According to my professor, only atoms and motion exist. A carriage approached them and Yechida heard Yachid say:

"Would you like to take a ride?"

"Where to?"

"Oh, just around the park."

Instead of reproving him as she intended to, Yechida said: "It would be nice. But I don't think you should spend the money."

"What's money? You only live once."

The carriage stopped and they both got in. Yechida

knew that no self-respecting girl would go riding with a strange young man. What did Yachid think of her? Did he believe she would go riding with anyone who asked her? She wanted to explain that she was shy by nature, but she knew she could not wipe out the impression she had already made. She sat in silence, astonished at her behavior. She felt nearer to this stranger than she ever had to anyone. She could almost read his mind. She wished the night would continue for ever. Was this love? Could one really fall in love so quickly? And am I happy? she asked herself. But no answer came from within her. For the dead are always melancholy, even in the midst of gaiety. After a while Yechida said: "I have a strange feeling I have experienced all this before."

"*Déjà vu*—that's what psychology calls it."

"But maybe there's some truth to it. . . ."

"What do you mean?"

"Maybe we've known each other in some other world."

Yachid burst out laughing. "In what world? There is only one, ours, the earth."

"But maybe souls do exist."

"Impossible. What you call the 'soul' is nothing but vibrations of matter, the product of the nervous system. I should know, I'm a medical student." Suddenly he put his arm around her waist. And although Yechida had never permitted any male to take such liberties before, she did not reprove him. She sat there perplexed by her acquiescence, fearful of the regrets that would be hers tomorrow. I'm completely without character, she chided herself. But he is right about one thing. If there is no soul and life is nothing but a short episode in an eternity of death, then why shouldn't one enjoy oneself without restraint? If there is no soul, there is no God, free will is meaningless. Morality, as my professor says, is nothing but a part of the ideological superstructure.

Yechida closed her eyes and leaned back against the upholstery. The horse trotted slowly. In the dark all the corpses, men and beasts, lamented their death—howling, laughing, buzzing, chirping, sighing. Some of the corpses staggered, having drunk to forget for a while the tortures of hell. Yechida had retreated into herself. She dozed off, then awoke again with a start. When the dead sleep, they once more connect themselves with the source of life. The illusion of time and space, cause and effect, number and relation ceases. In her dream Yechida had ascended again into the world of her origin. There she saw her real mother, her friends, her teachers. Yachid was there, too. The two greeted each other, embraced, laughed and wept with joy. At that moment, they both recognized the truth, that death on Earth is temporary and illusory, a trial and a means of purification. They traveled together past heavenly mansions, gardens, oases for convalescent souls, forests for divine beasts, islands for heavenly birds. No, our meeting was not an accident, Yechida murmured to herself. There is a God. There is a purpose in creation. Copulation, free will, fate—all are part of His plan. Yachid and Yechida passed by a prison and gazed into its window. They saw a soul condemned to sink down to Earth. Yechida knew that this soul would become her daughter. Just before she woke up, Yechida heard a voice:

"The grave and the gravedigger have met. The burial will take place tonight." ∎

SUMMATION
Judith Merril

"There have been more changes in the past 65 years than in all other centuries put together. No longer do most people believe in the orderly progression of cause and effect; no longer do they believe in the natural goodness of man and the inevitability of progress. Stability is gone. This is an era of quibble, doubt, and qualm. Science, technology, art, architecture, music, literature have all acquired new values, and revolutionary conflicts rage."

Call that one #1. (Here's your chance to see if you can tell the writers from the scientists, or the mainstream from SF.)

#2: "I am going to make one big hypothesis—a religious hypothesis —that the emergence of intelligent life is not a meaningless accident. But I am not going to follow orthodox religions by presuming that I know what the meaning is. . . . Let us see how much of the plan we can discover."

#3: "The next great breakthrough in science—the breakthrough that will have the kind of impact on us all that the Hiroshima bomb had —will be in the area of psychophysiology: mind and brain. And the man who will bring it about walks the earth today."

(#4, "Today, science stands fair to join Religion, Motherhood, and the Flag as a domain so sacrosanct and so sanctimonious, that leg-pulling isn't allowed, levity is forbidden, and smiling is scowled at."

(Three of these nine quotes are by tried-and-true science-fiction writers; three are by scientists; three by serious writers.)

#5: "At any given time recording devices fix the nature of absolute need and dictate the use of total weapons—like this: Take two opposed pressure groups. Record the most violent and threatening statements of group one with regard to group two. Record the answer and take it back to group one—back and forth between opposed pressure groups. This process is known as feed back. You can see it operating in any barroom quarrel—in any quarrel for that matter. Manipulated on a global scale feeds back nuclear war . . ."

#6: "Each of us wants what Ponce de León wanted, and unless the road maps are all wrong, we are well on our way to finding it. . . . It is, in fact, a good betting probability that some of us, and perhaps a great many of us, may never have to die at all."

(Well, perhaps I made it sound a little less complex than it is; at least one of these authors spreads over all three categories, and three of those in the "scientist" and "serious" groups have written some science fiction.)

#7: "I believe it is realistic to say that the manned lunar program will be carried to a successful conclusion in spite of the wasted time and cost; but let's be clear. This isn't science. It's adventure and propaganda."

(For purposes of the Concept Guessing Game, I am considering Arthur C. Clarke a science-fiction writer, along with Frederik Pohl and Theodore Sturgeon.)

#8: "We need very urgently to know that we are not strangers and aliens in the physical universe. . . . We did not arrive like birds on barren branches; we grew out of this world, like leaves and fruit. Our universe "humans" just as a rosebush "flowers." We are living in a world where men all over the planet are linked by an immense network of communications, and where science has made us theoretically aware of our interdependence with the entire domain of organic and inorganic nature."

(The three scientists: Philip Abelson, editor of Science; Fred Hoyle, cosmologist; James V. McConnell, comparative psychologist.)

#9: "The most controversial, and widely criticized of all space experiments took place in mid-Pacific on July 8, 1963, when . . . the AEC and the Department of Defense detonated a megaton bomb 200 miles above Johnston Island. (Sociological note: In the press releases, it's always a "nuclear device." I say it's a bomb, but I say the hell with it.)"

(And seriously three more: William S. Burroughs, of **Naked Lunch**, etc.; John Gunther, **Inside** author; Alan Watts, Zen philosopher-theologian.)

The answers are here; you'll get to them. But if you make an honest try at matching them up first for yourself, you may get my point better. SF has become more sophisticated, as well as more literate. We can no longer rely on flashing-panel gadgets or mad scientists, any more than on poor prose or flamboyant illustrations, to set it apart from other literature. Nor can we determine the nature from the source: there are comparatively few specialty magazines, and any publication is likely to carry some SF. Presumably, the distinctive quality is in the concepts; and if the SF writer's ideas are different from other people's, it ought to show up in such vigorous statements as those above.

(Burroughs, Hoyle, and McConnell are the three who have written some SF; does that help?)

Throughout this volume, I have been pointing out the meeting places on the literary scene where the once-sequestered science-fictionist now mingles freely with the journalist, the experimentalist, the poet and philosopher, and an occasional visitor from the academic or international world of letters. I have mentioned the journalists, and the newsmen in particular, who have made their way onto the SF scene—as well as the students and avant-gardistes. But there is another change in the author statistics that is more significant.

Most of the people included in this Tenth Annual are mostly-writers: that is, writing is the occupation by which they earn their living, and with which they would have to fill in tax returns and credit applications. Fully half of them this year are full-time free-lancers—and half of the balance have writing jobs.

Ten years ago, when I began editing this series, the number of people writing SF who did not have other jobs was very small (and the number of full-time SF-writers smaller yet, by far). The average contributor was either a spare-time science-fictionist—a scientist, technician, teacher, doctor, what-have-you?—who regarded his writing as a second profession, and probably wrote only SF, or a would-be freelancer who took his writing seriously enough, but still had to have an outside job to eat on.

Nine of the authors in this book have nonwriting jobs (and "nonwriting" includes the PR men and English professor).

Let me hasten to make clear that the change has not occurred because science-fiction writing has become a lucrative business. It is quite as miserably underpaid as it used to be. The difference is, simply, and once again, that the distinction between the specialty writer and the writer-in-general has almost vanished. For instance—

The Big Names of SF—the names everybody knows—Sturgeon, Heinlein, Asimov, Bradbury, Clarke—how many of them are actually "SF writers" today? Only Heinlein still writes primarily in the genre.

Conversely, the best new names in the field, this last decade, are almost all either young writers of serious literary intentions, who regard SF as one of their preferred modes of expression (Aandahl, Aldiss, Davidson, Ellison, Sheckley, Wilhelm, to name a few who do not happen to be represented this year); or already established writers just discovering the uses of the speculative and imaginative techniques (George P. Elliott, "Cordwainer Smith," John Hersey, Charles Einstein, Graham Greene, for instance).

(All right, you can start eliminating. Numbers 1, 2, and 3 are, respectively, John Gunther, in Look magazine's special "Inside the Twentieth Century" issue, January 12, 1965; Fred Hoyle, in Of Men and Galaxies, University of Washington Press, 1964; Theodore Sturgeon, in IF magazine, March, 1964. Try again on the other six.)

Or look at the new books.

Unfortunately, Anthony Boucher is no longer reviewing SF regularly enough to continue his annual surveys for these anthologies. I did not seek to replace him (as how could one, in any case?) this year, because at the time I received his regrets, I had just started, myself, to do reviews for Fantasy and Science Fiction—the same column Boucher had brightened with his unique style and erudition for the first ten years of the magazine's history. I cannot speak comprehensively of the 1964 books: I started too late for that. But there are some comments I can make on the basis of the past six months, and one of them is about the books that are sent to a magazine with a name like Fantasy and Science Fiction.

Of course, everything on the various publishers' "science-fiction category" lists comes in (including re-re-re-reprints of Edgar Rice

Burroughs). Almost any other fiction has to be asked for specifically: for instance, Simon & Schuster publishes John Christopher, but not on their "science-fiction list," for some reason; we had to ask for a copy of **Sweeney's Island**, just as we did for Hersey's **White Lotus** (Knopf, 1965) and Burroughs' **Nova Express** (Grove, 1965)—and was glad I had asked, with Christopher and Burroughs. Hersey was sadly disappointing, after **The Child Buyer** the year before.

(**Nova Express** is the source for Quote #5; and I must admit I cheated slightly on this one, and changed Burroughs' unmistakable punctuation to a more conventional system, to make it less obvious.)

We got Singer's **Short Friday** (Farrar, 1964) and McConnell's **The Worm Re-Turns** (Prentice-Hall, 1965), but not Gironella's **Phantoms and Fugitives** (Sheed and Ward, 1964), or Gary's **Hissing Tales**, although Harper & Row did send Fred Hoyle and John Elliot's **Andromeda Breakthrough**.

(#4, by the way, is from McConnell's "Compulsory Preface" in **The Worm Re-Turns.**)

Holt sent Kurt Vonnegut's **God Bless You, Mr. Rosewater** (a non-SF novel, full of references to science fiction, by an author associated with the genre—and God bless Holt for publishing it!) but New Directions did not send their enlarged 1965 reissue of Jorge Luis Borges' remarkable **Labyrinths,** nor did Viking send R. K. Narayan's fine collection of Indian lengends, **Gods, Demons, and Others** (1964).

Snobbishness or confusion? It is hard to say; but easy enough to see that someone, somewhere, needs to take a long, fresh look at this mixed-up business of literary "categories."

In some ways, the nonfiction submissions are even more curious: we got Sullivan's superb **We Are Not Alone** (McGraw-Hill, 1964), and Bonestell-Ley's **Beyond the Solar System** (Viking, 1964), but not Arthur C. Clarke's **Man in Space** (Life Library, 1964); we were sent Rosalind Heywood's **ESP: A Personal Memoir** (Dutton, 1964)—one of the most sensible, as well as best-written, books on the subject I've ever seen—but not David Solomon's fascinating anthology of articles, **LSD, The Consciousness-Expanding Drug** (Putnam, 1964).

(Alan Watts' selection in **LSD** was the source for #8.)

If I seem to be saying that the situation is just as confused one place as another—why, it's only because that is what I mean to say.

With the final criterion of authorship slipping out from under them, publishers, general reviewers, and the poor book salesmen have no way to tell their friends from SF.

(And how much better did you do? The last three mix-matches: #6 is by Frederik Pohl, from "Intimations of Immortality," in Playboy, June, 1964. #7 is by Philip Abelson, quoted in an article, "$30,000,-000,000 Trip to the Moon," in Cosmopolitan, October, 1964. #9 is from Arthur C. Clarke's "The Meddlers," in Playboy, March, 1964.)

There is, however, still some small area of solid ground, and within its limits, some items of interest to mention; for instance—

SF Horizons, a new British periodical devoted to criticism, edited by Harry Harrison and Brian Aldiss. The first issue contained a particularly interesting taped discussion between C. S. Lewis, Kingsley Amis, and Aldiss.

Extrapolation, a science-fiction newsletter published by the Conference on Science-Fiction of the Modern Language Association—a fine, scholarly critical journal.

And Double : Bill. Those of you who saw the Ninth Annual will recall my discussion at some length of the survey conducted for this fan publication by Lloyd Biggle. I based my comments, and the list of participants, on two installments of the survey—and discovered too late that there was a third I had not yet received. There is little to add to the conclusions, but I should like to include now the names of the remainder of participating authors: Charles Beaumont, James Blish, Anthony Boucher, Leigh Brackett, Marion Zimmer Bradley, Reginald Bretnor, Terry Carr, Arthur C. Clarke, Hal Clement, Avram Davidson, Lester Del Rey, August Derleth, Horace Gold, Edmond Hamilton, Joe Hensley, Robert W. Lowndes, Richard Lupoff, Mack Reynolds, Eric Frank Russell, James H. Schmitz, Robert Silverberg, E. E. "Doc" Smith, George O. Smith, William Temple, Theodore Thomas, Ted White, Kate Wilhelm, Jack Williamson and Robert F. Young.

Finally, I should like to express my thanks to some of the many people whose interest and assistance is necessary to make a volume of this sort at all possible. For suggestions of inclusions, and assistance in obtaining material, much thanks to Barbara Norville, Eva McKenna, Margaret Scoggins, Francesca van der Ling, Anthony Boucher, Ed Ferman, Dick Wilson, and the infinitely patient librarians at the Port Jervis, N.Y., Public Library. For clerical help, messenger service, and an assortment of literary bottle-washing jobs, my sincere gratitude to Karen Emden, Ann Pohl, Rick Raphael, and John Walter. For critical reactions, my thanks to Virginia Kidd Blish, Seymour Krim, Fritz Leiber, and the panel of Teen-Age Book Reviewers introduced to me by Miss Scoggins, who heads the Young Adult Services at the New York Public Library. And my most earnest appreciation to Bob Silverstein, for some of all the foregoing, but even more for a rare and admirable editorial restraint.

Judith Merril
April, 1965

HONORABLE MENTIONS

Amz: Amazing Stories
Anal: Analog Science Fact & Fiction
Fant: Fantastic
F&SF: Fantasy and Science Fiction
Gal: Galaxy
Gam: Gamma
Harp: Harper's Magazine
If: If
KR: Kenyon Review
Knt: Knight
MQV: Michigan's Quarterly Voices
NW: New Worlds (British)
Nug: Nugget
Plby: Playboy
Rog: Rogue
SMM: Saint Mystery Magazine
SEP: Saturday Evening Post
SciF: Science Fantasy (British)
Sm: Smith
WoT: Worlds of Tomorrow
"BF&SF:14": *Best from Fantasy and Science Fiction,* ed. Avram Davidson (Doubleday, 1964)
DSE: The Dark Side of the Earth, Alfred Bester (Signet, 1964)
HT: Hissing Tales, Romain Gary (Harper and Row, 1964)
MoJ: The Machineries of Joy, Ray Bradbury (Simon and Schuster, 1964)
SiO: Sturgeon in Orbit, Theodore Sturgeon (Pyramid, 1964)
WBSF:65: World's Best Science Fiction: 1965, ed. Donald A. Wollheim and Terry Carr (Ace, 1965)
BRIAN W. ALDISS: "The Dark Light-Years," *WoT,* Apr.
 "Pink Plastic Gods," *SciF,* June-July.
POUL ANDERSON: "Mustn't Touch," *Anal,* June.
 "The Master Key," *Anal,* July.

ANONYMOUS: "Blast Off," *SciF*, June-July.

CHRISTOPHER ANVIL: "Hunger," *Anal*, May.

J. G. BALLARD: "The Illuminated Man," *BF&SF:14*

RAYMOND E. BANKS: "The Seawater Papers," *Anal*, July.

JANE BEAUCLERK: "We Serve the Star of Freedom," *F&SF*, July.

ALFRED BESTER: "Out of this World," *DSE*

JEROME BIXBY: "Natural History of the Kley," *WoT*, Nov.

WILBUR G. BIGGS: "Daughter of the Clan," *Fant*, Nov.

BEN BOVA AND MYRNA R. LEWIS: "Men of Good Will," *Gal*, June; and *WBSF:65*

LEIGH BRACKETT: "Purple Priestess of the Mad Moon," *F&SF*, Oct.

RAY BRADBURY: "Almost the End of the World," *MoJ*

R. BRETNOR: "Demigod," *Amz*, Oct.

NEAL BROOKS: "Abraham Awoke," *Rog*, Mar.

ROSEL GEORGE BROWN: "The Artist," *Amz*, May.

JOHN BRUNNER: "See What I Mean!" *Anal*, Jan.

DAVID R. BUNCH: "Keeping It Simple," *Sm#3*

TERRY CARR: "Touchstone," *BF&SF:14*

CURT CLARK: "Nackles," *F&SF*, Jan.

JAMES COLVIN: "The Deep Fix," *SciF*, Apr.

MIRIAM ALLEN DEFORD: "The Apprentice God," *WoT*, Apr.

LESTER DEL REY: "To Avenge Man," *Gal*, Dec.

PHILIP K. DICK: "Little Black Box," *WoT*, Aug.
"Precious Artifact," *Gal*, Oct.
"What the Dead Men Say," *WoT*, June.

GORDON R. DICKSON: "The Man from Earth," *Gal*, June.

THOMAS M. DISCH: "A Thesis on Social Forms and Social Controls in the U.S.A.," *Font*, Jan.
"Nada," *BF&SF:14*
"Now is Forever," (ps: Dobbin Thorpe) *Amz;* and *WBSF:65*

S. DORMAN: "The Deepest Blue in the World," *F&SF*, Sept.

DAPHNE DU MAURIER: "The Blue Lenses," *SSI*, Sept.

SHERI S. EBERHART: "Ballad of the Interstellar Merchants," *WoT*, Feb.

HARLAN ELLISON: "Lonely Ache," *Knight*, July.

R. C. FITZPATRICK: "On the House," *F&SF*, Nov.

DANIEL F. GALOUYE: "Centipedes of Space," *Fant*, Apr.

RANDALL GARRETT: "Tin Lizzie," *Amz*, June.

ROMAIN GARY: "The New Frontier," *HT*

PHYLLIS GOTTLIEB: "Valedictory," *Amz*, Aug.

RON GOULART: "Society for the Prevention," *Gam #3*

JOSEPH GREEN: "Single Combat," *NW*, Jul.-Aug.

ROBERT M. GREEN, JR.: "No Place Like Where," *F&SF*, May.

WALT GROVE: "John Green's Little Angel," *Plby*, July.
WYMAN GUIN: "A Man of the Renaissance," *Gal*, Dec.
ED HAMILTON: "The Pro," *F&SF*, Oct.
HARRY HARRISON: "Portrait of the Artist," *F&SF*, Nov.
         "Rescue Operation," *Anal*, Dec.
FRANK HERBERT: "The Mary Celeste Move," *Anal*, Oct.
PATRICIA HIGHSMITH: "The Snail Watchers," *Gam* #3.
EDWARD D. HOCHS: "The Wolfram Hunters," *SMM*, Mar.
HAYDEN HOWARD: "Gremmie's Reef," *If*, Oct.
BEN IRWIN: "The Day the Weapons Worked," *Nug*, Sept.
EDWARD JESBY: "Sea Wrack," *F&SF*, May; and *WBSF:65*
S. S. JOHNSON: "The House by the Crab Apple Tree," *BF&SF:14*
LANGDON JONES: "I Remember, Anita," *NW*, Sept.
RAYMOND F. JONES: "Rider in the Impossible," *F&SF*, Sept; and
         WBSF:65
NORMAN KAGAN: "Four Brands of Impossible," *F&SF*, Sept;
         and *WBSF:65*
THOM KEYES: "Period of Gestation," *SciF*, Sept.-Oct.
R. A. LAFFERTY: "The Man with the Speckled Eyes," *F&SF*, Dec.
ALLEN KIM LANG: "Thaw and Serve," *BF&SF:14*
KEITH LAUMER: "Placement Test," *Amz*, July.
URSULA K. LEGUIN: "The Rule of Names," *Fant*, Apr.
FRITZ LEIBER: "When the Change Winds Blow," *F&SF*, Aug;
         and *WBSF:65*
CLARICE LISPECTOR (trans: Elisabeth Bishop): "The Smallest
         Woman in the World," *KR*, Sum.
ROBERT LORY: "Appointment at Ten O'clock," *F&SF*, Jan.
ERNST MASON: "Earth Eighteen," *Gal*, Apr.
J. T. MCINTOSH: "Planet of Change," *Fant*, Sept.
DEAN MCLAUGHLIN: "The Permanent Implosion," *Anal*, Feb.
L. W. MICHAELSON: "The Burning Bush," *SSI*, July.
BARRY P. MILLER: "The Mermaid and the Archer," *Fant*, Nov.
MICHAEL MOORCOCK: "The Time Dweller," *NW*, Feb.
DICK MOORE: "After Everything, What?" *F&SF*, Nov.
HUGH NISSENSON: "The Mission," *Plby*, Dec.
ALAN E. NOURSE: "The Compleat Consumators," *BF&SF:14*
EDGAR PANGBORN: "Maxwell's Monkey," *Gal*, Oct.
HERBERT PEMBROKE: "Situation Unbearable," *Anal*, Oct.
FREDERIK POHL: "The Children of Night," *Gal*, Oct.
         "The Fiend," *Plby*, Mar.
TOM PURDOM: "Greenplace," *F&SF*, Nov; and *WBSF:65*
FLORENCE ENGEL RANDALL: "The Boundary Beyond," *Fant*, July.
RICK RAPHAEL: "Once a Cop," *Anal*, May.
KIT REED: "On the Orphan's Colony," *F&SF*, July.
MACK REYNOLDS: "Genus Traitor," *Anal*, Aug.

WALT AND LEIGH RICHMOND: "Shortsite," *Anal*, Apr.
                        "Gallagher's Glacier," *Anal*, Nov.
KEITH ROBERTS: "Anita," *SciF*, Sept.-Oct.
ERIC ST. CLAIR: "Olsen and the Gull," *BF&SF:14*
WINSTON P. SANDERS: "Sunjammer," *Anal*, Apr.
ROBIN SCOTT: "Third Alternative," *Anal*, Mar.
ARTHUR SELLINGS: "The Well Trained Heroes," *Gal*, June.
ROBERT SILVERBERG: "Neighbor," *Gal*, Aug.
HENRY SLESAR: "Prisoner in Orbit," *Amz*, Apr.
CORDWAINER SMITH: "The Boy Who Bought Old Earth," *Gal*,
                  Apr.
                  "The Dead Lady of Clown Town," *Gal*,
                  Aug.
GEORGE O. SMITH: "Counter-Foil," *Anal*, Apr.
LARRY D. SPENCE: "The General," *MQV*, Spring.
NORMAN SPINRAD: "Subjectivity," *Anal*, Jan.
THEODORE STURGEON: "Extrapolation," *SiO*
ALBERT TEICHNER: "Body of Thought," *Fant*, June.
WILLIAM F. TEMPLE: "A Niche in Time," *Anal,* May; and
                   WBSF:65
THEODORE L. THOMAS: "The Soft Woman," *Fant*, Feb.
B. TRAVEN: "Sun Creation," *F&SF*, Apr.
R. UNDERWOOD: "The Crazy Mathematicians," *F&SF*, Apr.
GORDON WALTERS: "Last Order," *Fant*, Jan.
WILLIAM WOOD: "One of the Dead," *SEP*, Oct. 31.
GARY WRIGHT: "The Ultimate Racer," *If*, Nov.
ROBERT F. YOUNG: "The Second Philadelphia Experiment,"
                 F&SF, July.
ROGER ZELAZNY: "Lucifer," *WoT*, June.